D0992990

PREFACE

The present version of M. Zola's novel 'L'Argent' supplies one of the missing links in the English translations of the Rougon-Macquart series which the author initiated some five and twenty years ago, and brought to a close last summer by the publication of 'Doctor Pascal.' Judged by the standard of popularity, 'L'Argent' may be said to rank among M. Zola's notable achievements, for not only has it had an extremely large sale in the original French, but the translations of it into various Continental languages have proved remarkably successful. This is not surprising, as the book deals with a subject of great interest to every civilized community. And with regard to this English version, it may, I think, be safely said that its publication is well timed, for the rottenness of our financial world has become such a crying scandal, and the inefficiency of our company laws has been so fully demonstrated, that the absolute urgency of reform can no longer be denied.

A work, therefore, which exposes the evils of 'speculation,' which shows the company promoter on the war-path, and the 'guinea-pig' basking at his ease, which demonstrates how the public is fooled and ruined by the brigands of Finance, is evidently a work for the times, even though it deal with the Paris Bourse instead of with the London market. For the ways of the speculator, the promoter, the wrecker, the defaulter, the reptile journalist, and the victim, are much the same all the world over; and it matters little whence the example may be drawn, the warning will apply with as much force in England as in France.

The time for prating of the purity of our public life, and for thanking the Divinity that in financial as in other matters we are not as other men, has gone by. When disasters like that of the Liberator group are possible, when examples of financial unsoundness are matters of every-day occurrence, when the very name of 'trust company' opens up visions of incapacity, deceit, and fraud, it is quite certain that things are ripe for stringent inquiry and reform.

Of course the cleansing of the Augean stable of finance in this country will prove a Herculean labour; but although callous Governments and legislators may postpone and shirk it, the task remains before them, ever threatening, ever calling for attention, and each day's delay in dealing with it only adds to the evil. We are overrun with rotten limited liability companies, flooded with swindling 'bucket-shops,' crashes and collapses rain upon us, and the 'promoter' and the 'guinea-pig' still and ever enjoy impunity. It is becoming more and more impossible to burke the issue. It stares us in the face. Even if the various measures of political and social reform, about which we have heard so much of recent years, should yield all that their partisans declare they will, it is doubtful whether there would be much national improvement. For the rottenness of our social system must still remain the same; the fabric must still repose upon as unsound a basis as it does now if the brigands of Finance remain free to plunder the community and to pave their way to ephemeral wealth and splendour with the bodies of the thrifty and the credulous.

One may well ask why this freedom should be allowed them. The man in the street who wishes to lay odds against the favourite for the Derby is promptly mulcted in pocket or consigned to limbo, but the promoter of the swindling company, and the keeper of the swindling 'bucket-shop,' who deliberately defraud other people of their money, are at liberty to ply their nefarious callings with no worse fate before them

3

than a short suspension of their discharge should they choose to close their books with the aid of the Bankruptcy Court. There cannot be two moralities, although a distinguished Frenchman, the late M. Nisard, once tried to demonstrate that there were, and was laughed to scorn for his pains. We know that there is but one true morality—the same for the rich as for the poor, the same for the legislator as for the elector, the same for the defaulter who dabbles in millions as for the welsher who sneaks half-crowns. And it should be borne in mind that the harm done to the community at large by the thousands of bookmakers disseminated throughout the United Kingdom is as nothing beside that which is done by the half thousand financial brigands who infest the one city of London. It may, I think, be safely said that more people were absolutely ruined by the crash of the Liberator group than by all the betting on English racecourses over a period of many years.

There have been, I believe, over 2,200 applicants for relief to the fund which has been raised for the benefit of the sufferers of so-called Philanthropic Finance, and among the number it appears there are nearly 1,400 single women and widows. Some of the victims have committed suicide, others have gone mad. Thousands, moreover, who are too proud to beg, find themselves either starving or in sadly straitened circumstances, with nothing but a pittance left them of their former little comforts. This is a specimen of the work done by the brigand of Finance.

Of course there are reforms urgently needed in the very organisation of the Stock Exchange; and reforms needed with regard to the conditions under which public companies may be launched. Why should men be allowed to ask the public to subscribe millions of money for the purchase of properties which are literally valueless? Why, moreover, should directors be allowed to proceed to 'allotment,' when but a tithe of the shares placed on the market have been taken up? And surely the time has come for the proper auditing of accounts under Government supervision. The neglectful auditor and the fraudulent promoter are as much in need of abolition as the ornamental 'guinea-pig.' And such abolition, and the enforcement of many reforms, might be secured by a self-supporting Ministry of Commercial Finance. Some institution of the kind will doubtless be founded in time to come; and, meanwhile, if all that is told us of the purity of our public life be true, I fail to see why a series of measures directed against the brigands of Finance should not promptly receive the assent of both Houses of Parliament and become law. Surely no member of the Lords or the Commons would dare to stand up and plead the cause of the negligent director who imperils the safety of other people's money? Surely not one of our legislators would dare to take the fraudulent promoter and the rogue of the 'bucket-shop' under his protecting wing? And, as such measures must of necessity be non-contentious, why do not some of our social reformers initiate them, instead of for ever and ever harping upon 'Bills' which are not likely to be included in the Statute-book for another score of years?

I am not against public companies. Let us have them; let us have as many good ones as we can get, but let them be honestly founded and honestly administered. It is through the multiplicity of public companies that we may eventually attain to Collectivism, which so many great thinkers of the age deem to be the future towards which the world is slowly but surely marching. And when that comes, perhaps, as Sigismond Busch, one of M. Zola's characters, foreshadows in the following pages, we shall have some other means of exchange than money—the metallic money of the present day. Sigismond Busch is a Karl Marxite, a believer in the universal fraternity

4

Émile Zola Classics
Money

Émile Zola
Translated by Ernest Alfred Vizetelly

Copyright © Émile Zola & Ernest Alfred Vizetelly
All rights reserved.
ISBN-13:9798568518808

Published in London
1900

of humanity, a fraternity which he regretfully admits is still far away from us. Of a very different stamp to him is M. Zola's hero—if hero he can be called—Saccard, the scheming financier, the sanguine promoter and manager of the Universal Bank, the poet of money, the apostle of gambling, ever intent on gigantic enterprises, believing that the passion for gain should be fostered rather than discouraged, and that in order to set society on a proper basis it is necessary to destroy the financial power of the Jews.

Saccard is one of M. Zola's favourite creations. After figuring in the 'Fortune des Rougon,' he played a prominent part in 'La Curée;' and he is further alluded to in 'Doctor Pascal,' Clotilde, the heroine of that work, being his daughter. Certainly Saccard, the worshipper of Mammon, the man to whom money is everything in life, is a true type of our *fin-de-siècle* society. It has often occurred to me that in sketching this daring and unscrupulous financier M. Zola must have bethought himself of Mirès, whose name is so closely linked to the history of Second Empire finance. Mirès, however, was a Jew, whereas Saccard is a Jew-hater, and outwardly, at all events, a zealous Roman Catholic. In this respect he reminds one of Bontoux, of Union Générale notoriety, just as Hamelin the engineer reminds one of Feder, Bontoux's associate. Indeed, the history of M. Zola's Universal Bank is much the history of the Union Générale. The latter was solemnly blessed by the Pope, and in a like way M. Zola shows us the Universal receiving the Papal benediction. Moreover, the secret object of the Union Générale was to undermine the financial power of the Jews, and in the novel we find a similar purpose ascribed to Saccard's Bank. The Union, we know, was eventually crushed by the great Israelite financiers, and this again is the fate which overtakes the institution whose meteor-like career is traced in the pages of 'L'Argent.'

There is a strong Jewish element in this story, and here and there some very unpleasant things are said of the chosen people. It should be remembered, however, that these remarks are the remarks of M. Zola's characters and not of M. Zola himself. He had to portray certain Jew-haters, and has simply put into their mouths the words which they are constantly using. This statement is not unnecessary, for M. Zola counts many friends and admirers among writers and readers of the Jewish persuasion, and some of them might conceive the language in which their race is spoken of to be expressive of the author's personal opinions. But such is not the case. M. Zola is remarkably free from racial and religious prejudices. And, after all, I do not think that any Hebrew reader can take exception to the portrait of Gundermann, the great Jew financier, the King of the Money Market, who in a calm methodical way brings about the ruin of Saccard and Hamelin. Gundermann, moreover, really existed and may be readily identified.

In Daigremont, another financier, but a Catholic, we have a combination of Achille Fould and Isaac Pereire. Daigremont's house is undoubtedly Fould's, and so is his gallery of paintings. And there are other characters in the story who might in a measure be identified. For instance, readers acquainted with the social history of France during the last half century will doubtless trace a resemblance between the Princess d'Orviedo and a certain foreign Duchess. Then the Viscount de Robin-Chagot is strangely suggestive of a Rohan-Chabot, whose financial transactions brought him before a court of law during the latter period of the Second Empire. Various personalities are merged in the character of the courtly Marquis de Bohain, that perfect type of the aristocratic rogue; but Rougon is undoubtedly Eugène Rouher *tout*

5

craché, whatever M. Zola may pretend to the contrary. M. Zola himself will be found in the book, for surely Paul Jordan, the impecunious journalist with 'an idea for a novel,' is the author of the Rougon-Macquart series in the far-away days when he lived on the topmost floor of a modest house on the Boulevard de Clichy.

In Huret we are presented with a specimen of the corrupt Deputy, and in this connection it may be pointed out that the venal French legislator by no means dates from the Panama scandals. In fact, there were undoubtedly more corrupt members in the Corps Législatif of the Second Empire than there have ever been in the Parliament of the Third Republic. Only, in those glorious Imperial times, anything approaching a scandal was promptly hushed up, and more than once the Emperor himself personally intervened to shield his peccant supporters. M. Schneider, who presided over the Corps Législatif in its later days, was undoubtedly a very honest man; but it would be impossible to say the same of his predecessors—Walewski, who claimed descent from the great Napoleon, and Morny, who was the little Napoleon's illegitimate half-brother. It is notorious that Morny made millions of money by trickery and fraud; and that the Emperor himself was well aware of it was proved conclusively by the papers found in his *cabinet* at the Tuileries after the Revolution of 1870. Roguery being thus freely practised in high places, a considerable number of Deputies undoubtedly opined that there was no occasion for them to remain honest.

'L'Argent,' however, is no mere story of swindling and corruption. Whilst proving that money is the root of much evil, it also shows that it is the source of much good. It does not merely depict the world of finance; it gives us glimpses of the charitable rich, the decayed *noblesse* striving to keep up appearances, the thrifty and the struggling poor. Further, it appears to me to be a less contemplative work than many of M. Zola's novels. It possesses in no small degree that quality of 'action' in which, according to some critics, the great *naturaliste's* writings are generally deficient. The plot, too, is a sound one, and from beginning to end the interest never flags.

In preparing the present version for the press I have followed the same course as I pursued with regard to 'Dr. Pascal.' Certain passages have been condensed, and others omitted; and in order to reconnect the narrative brief interpolations have here and there been necessary. Nobody can regret these changes more than I do myself, but before reviewers proceed to censure me (as some of them did in the case of 'Dr. Pascal'), I would ask them to consider the responsibility which rests upon my shoulders. If they desire to have verbatim translations of M. Zola's works, let them help to establish literary freedom.

And now, by way of conclusion, I have a request to make. After perusing the story of Saccard's work of ruin, the reader will, perhaps, have a keener perception of all the misery wrought by that Liberator crash to which I have previously alluded. I would point out, however, that whereas Saccard's bank was essentially a speculative enterprise, the Liberator and its allied companies claimed that they never embarked in any speculative dealings whatever. Their shareholders had no desire to gamble; they only expected to obtain a fair return from the investment of their hard-earned savings. Their position therefore deserving of all commiseration. Unfortunately, the fund raised for their benefit still falls far short of the amount required; and so I would ask all who read 'Money,' and who have money to spare, to send some little of their store to the Rev. J. Stockwell Watt at the office of the Fund, 16 Farringdon Street, E.C. In complying with this suggestion they will be doing a good action. And I may say that nothing would afford greater pleasure either to M. Zola or myself than to learn that this book had in some degree a contributed alleviate so much undeserved misery and hardship.

E. A

6

E. A. V.

Table of Contents

MONEY

CHAPTER I
THE TEMPLE OF MAMMON

Eleven o'clock had just struck at the Bourse when, making his way into Champeaux' restaurant, Saccard entered the public room, all white and gold and with two high windows facing the Place. At a glance he surveyed the rows of little tables, at which the busy eaters sat closely together, elbow to elbow; and he seemed surprised not to see the face he sought.

As a waiter passed, laden with dishes, amid the scramble of the service, he turned to him and asked: 'I say, hasn't Monsieur Huret come?'

'No, monsieur, not yet.'

Thereupon, making up his mind, Saccard sat down at a table, which a customer was leaving, in the embrasure of one of the windows. He thought that he was late; and whilst a fresh cover was being laid he directed his looks outside, scrutinising the persons passing on the footway. Indeed, even when the table had been freshly laid, he did not at once give his orders, but remained for a moment with his eyes fixed on the Place, which looked quite gay on that bright morning of an early day in May. At that hour, when everybody was at lunch, it was almost empty: the benches under the chestnut trees of a fresh and tender green remained unoccupied; a line of cabs stretched from one to the other end of the railing, and the omnibus going to the Bastille stopped at the office at the corner of the garden, without dropping or taking up a single passenger. The sun's rays fell vertically, lighting up the whole monumental pile of the Bourse, with its colonnade, its pair of statues, and its broad steps, at the top of which there was as yet only an army of chairs ranged in good order.

Having turned, however, Saccard recognised Mazaud, a stock-broker, sitting at the table next to his own. He held out his hand. 'Dear me, you are here? Good morning,' said he.

'Good morning,' answered Mazaud, shaking hands in an absent-minded fashion.

Short, dark, a very brisk, good-looking man, Mazaud, at the age of two and thirty, had just inherited the business of one of his uncles. He seemed to be altogether taken up with the person opposite him, a stout gentleman with a red and shaven face, the celebrated Amadieu, whom the Bourse revered since his famous deal in Selsis mining stock. When the Selsis shares had fallen to fifteen francs, and anyone who bought them was looked upon as a madman, he had put his whole fortune, two hundred thousand francs, into the affair at a venture, without calculation or instinct—indeed, through mere obstinate confidence in his own brutish luck. Now that the discovery of real and important veins had sent the price of the shares up above a thousand francs, he had made fifteen millions; and his imbecile operation, which ought to have led to his being shut up in an asylum, had raised him to the level of men of great financial intellect. He was saluted and, above all things, consulted. Moreover, he placed no more orders, but seemed to be satisfied, enthroned as it were upon his unique and legendary stroke of genius.

Mazaud must have been dreaming of securing his patronage.

Saccard, having failed to obtain even a smile from Amadieu, bowed to the table opposite, where three speculators of his acquaintance, Pillerault, Moser, and Salmon, were gathered together.

'Good day. Quite well?' he asked.

8

'Yes, thanks—Good morning.'

Among these men also he divined coldness, in fact almost hostility. Pillerault, however, very tall, very thin, with spasmodic gestures, and a nose like a sabre-blade set in the bony face of a knight-errant, habitually displayed the familiarity of a gambler—the gambler who makes recklessness a principle, for he declared that he plunged head over heels into catastrophes whenever he paused to reflect. He had the exuberant nature of a 'bull,' ever turned towards victory; whereas Moser, on the contrary, short of stature, yellow-skinned, and afflicted moreover by a liver complaint, was continually lamenting, in incessant dread of some approaching cataclysm. As for Salmon, a very fine-looking man struggling against old age, and displaying a superb beard of inky blackness, he passed for a fellow of extraordinary acumen. Never did he speak; he answered only by smiles; folks could never tell in what he was speculating, or whether he was speculating at all; and his way of listening so impressed Moser, that the latter, after making him his confidant, was frequently so disconcerted by his silence that he ran off to countermand an order.

Amid the indifference exhibited towards him, Saccard, with feverish and provoking glances, went on finishing his survey of the room, and he exchanged no other nod except with a tall young man sitting three tables away, the handsome Sabatani, a Levantine with a long dark face, illumined by magnificent black eyes, but spoiled by an evil, disquieting mouth. This fellow's amiability put the finishing touch to his irritation. A defaulter on some foreign Stock Exchange, one of those mysterious scamps whom women love, Sabatani had tumbled into the market during the previous autumn. Saccard had already seen him at work as figure-head in a banking disaster, and now he was little by little gaining the confidence of both the *corbeille*[1] and the *coulisse*[2] by scrupulous correctness of behaviour and an unremitting graciousness even towards the most disreputable.

A waiter, however, was standing before Saccard. 'What are Monsieur's orders?'

'Oh, anything you like—a cutlet, some asparagus.' Then calling the waiter back, he added: 'You are sure that Monsieur Huret did not come in before me and go away again?'

'Oh! absolutely sure.'

So there he was, after the crash which in October had once more forced him to wind up his affairs, to sell his mansion in the Parc Monceau, and rent a suite of rooms. The Sabatani set alone saluted him; his entrance into a restaurant where he had once reigned no longer caused all heads to turn, all hands to be stretched forth. He was a good gambler; he harboured no rancour with regard to that last scandalous and disastrous speculation in land, from which he had scarcely saved more than his skin. But a fever of revenge was kindling within him; and the absence of Huret, who had formally promised to be there at eleven o'clock to acquaint him with the result of an application which he had undertaken to make to his—Saccard's—brother, Rougon, the then triumphant minister, exasperated him especially against the latter. Huret, a docile deputy, and one of the great man's creatures, was after all merely a messenger. But Rougon, he who could do anything, was it possible that he had abandoned him in this fashion? Never had he shown himself a good brother. That he should have been angry after the catastrophe, and have broken with him in order not to be compromised himself, was natural enough; but ought he not to have come secretly to his assistance during the last six months? And now would he have the heart to refuse him the final lift which he solicited through a third party, not daring indeed to see him in person, for fear lest he might be carried away by some fit of passion? Rougon had only to say a word to put him on his feet again, with all huge, cowardly Paris beneath his heels.

'What wine will Monsieur drink?' asked the waiter.

'Your ordinary Bordeaux.'

Saccard, who, with his absent-mindedness and lack of appetite, was letting his cutlet grow cold, raised his eyes as he saw a shadow pass over the table-cloth. It was the shadow of Massias, a stout, red-faced *remisier*,[3] whom he had known in want, and who glided between the tables with his list of quotations in his hand. Saccard was exasperated at seeing him march past him, without stopping, in order to hand the list to Pillerault and Moser. With their thoughts elsewhere, engaged in a discussion together, these two barely gave it a glance; no, they had no order, they would give one some other time. Massias, not daring to approach the celebrated Amadieu, who was leaning over a lobster salad and conversing in a low tone with Mazaud, thereupon came back to Salmon, who took the list, studied it for some time, and then returned it without a word. The room was growing animated. The door swung every moment as other *remisiers* entered. Loud words were being exchanged at a distance, and all the passion for business rose as the hour advanced. Saccard, whose eyes continually turned to the window, saw also that the Place was now gradually filling, that vehicles and pedestrians were flocking in; whilst on the steps of the Bourse, of dazzling whiteness in the sunlight, men were already appearing one by one, like black spots.

'Again I tell you,' said Moser, in his disconsolate voice, 'that those complementary elections of March 20[4] are a most disturbing symptom. In fact, all Paris is nowadays on the side of the Opposition.'

Pillerault shrugged his shoulders, however. What difference could it make that Carnot[5] and Garnier-Pagès should be added to the ranks of the Left?

'It is like the question of the Duchies,'[6] resumed Moser; 'it is fraught with complications. It is indeed; you needn't laugh. I don't say that we were bound to make war on Prussia to prevent her from laying hands on Denmark; but there were other means of action. Yes, yes, when the big begin to eat the little, one never knows where it will all end, and, as for Mexico——'

Pillerault, who was in one of his fits of satisfaction with everything, interrupted with a shout of laughter: 'Oh, no, my dear fellow, don't weary us any more with your terrors about Mexico. Mexico will be the glorious page of the reign. Where the deuce did you get the idea that the Empire is ailing? Wasn't the loan of three hundred millions covered more than fifteen times over last January? An overwhelming success! Well, I'll give you *rendez-vous* for '67, yes, in three years from now, when the Universal Exhibition which the Emperor has just decided upon will open.'

'I tell you that things are very bad,' declared Moser in despair.

'Oh, leave us in peace; everything is all right.'

Salmon looked at them in turn, smiling in his profound way. And Saccard, who had been listening, connected the difficulties of his personal situation with the crisis upon which the Empire seemed to be entering. He was once more down; and now was this Empire, which had made him, about to tumble over like himself, suddenly falling from the highest to the most miserable destiny? Ah! for twelve years past, how he had loved and defended that *régime*, in which he had felt himself live, grow, and imbibe sap, like some tree whose roots plunge into fitting soil. But if his brother were determined to tear him from it, if he were to be cut off from those who were exhausting that fertile soil of enjoyment, then might all be swept away in the great final smash-up!

He now sat waiting for his asparagus, his thoughts wandering away from the room, where the hubbub kept on increasing, his mind invaded by memories of the past. He had just caught sight of his face in a large mirror opposite, and it had surprised him. Age had made no impression upon his short slight figure; his fifty years seemed to have been scarcely more than eight and thirty. He still had the slender build and vivacious manners of a young man. His dark, sunken marionette's face, with its sharp nose and small glittering eyes, had, with the march of years, adapted itself to his supple, active youthfulness, so long abiding that as yet his still bushy hair was without a single white thread. And irresistibly he recalled his arrival in Paris on the morrow of the *coup d'état*, that winter evening when he had alighted on the pavement, penniless, hungry, with a perfect rage of appetite to satisfy. Ah! that first trip through the streets, when, even before unpacking his trunk, he had felt the need of rushing through the city to conquer it in his greasy overcoat and his boots trodden down at heel! Since that night he had often risen very high; a river of millions had flowed through his fingers, yet he had never been able to make a slave of fortune, something of his own that he could dispose of, and keep under lock and key, alive and real. Falsehood and fiction had always dwelt in his safes, the gold in which had always slipped out through unknown holes. And now he again found himself upon the pavement, as in the far-off days of the beginning, as young and as hungry as then, still unsatisfied, tortured by the same need of enjoyment and conquest. He had tasted of everything, but was not satiated, having lacked both opportunity and time, he thought, to bite deeply enough into persons and things. At this present hour he felt less wretched at finding himself on the pavement than a beginner would have felt, and this although the latter would probably have been sustained by illusion and hope. He was seized with a feverish desire to begin all over again, to regain everything, to rise higher than he had ever risen before, to place his foot at last full upon the conquered city. No longer the lying finery of the façade, but the solid edifice of fortune, the true royalty of gold enthroned upon real money bags full to overflowing—that was what he wanted.

Moser's voice, which again rose sharp and shrill, aroused him for a moment from his reflections. 'The Mexican expedition costs fourteen million francs a month; Thiers has proved it, and one must really be blind not to see that the majority in the Chamber is shaken. The Left now counts thirty odd members. The Emperor himself clearly sees that absolute power is becoming impossible, for he himself is coming forward as a promoter of liberty.'

Pillerault vouchsafed no further answer, but contented himself with a contemptuous sneer.

'Yes, I know the market seems firm to you,' continued Moser; 'as yet business prospers. But wait till the end. There has been far too much pulling down and rebuilding in Paris, you see. The great public works have exhausted everybody's savings. As for the powerful financial houses, which seem to you so prosperous, wait till one of them goes down, and then you will see all the others tumble in a row—to say nothing of the fact that the lower orders are getting restless. That International Association of the working classes, which has just been founded to improve the position of those who labour, inspires me with great fear. There is a revolutionary movement in France, which is becoming more pronounced every day—yes, I tell you that the worm is in the fruit. There will be a general burst up at last!'

Thereupon came a noisy protest. That confounded Moser had one of his liver attacks decidedly. He himself, however, while talking on, did not take his eyes off the neighbouring table, where, amid all the noise, Mazaud and Amadieu continued conversing in low tones. Little by little the entire room began to feel uneasy over that prolonged confidential chat. What could they have to say to each other that they should be whispering in that way? Undoubtedly Amadieu was placing some orders, preparing some deal or other. For three days past, unfavourable rumours had been circulating respecting the works at Suez. Moser winked, and lowered his voice: 'You know,' said he, 'that the English wish to prevent them from working there. We may very likely have war.'

This time Pillerault was shaken by the very enormity of the news. It was incredible, yet the report at once flew from table to table, acquiring the force of certainty. England had sent an ultimatum, demanding an immediate cessation of work. Clearly enough, Amadieu was talking of it with Mazaud, and giving him orders to sell all his Suez shares. A buzz of panic arose in the odour-laden atmosphere, amid the increasing clatter of the crockery. And at that moment the general emotion was brought to a climax by the sudden entry of Mazaud's clerk, little Flory, a fellow with a flabby face, overgrown with a thick chestnut beard. He rushed in with a number of *fiches*[7] in his hand, and gave them to his employer, saying something in his ear.

'All right,' answered Mazaud quietly, as he classified the *fiches* in his pocket-book; then taking out his watch, he added: 'Already noon! Tell Berthier to wait for me. And be there yourself; go up after the telegrams.'

When Flory had gone, he resumed his talk with Amadieu, taking some other *fiches* from his pocket, and placing them on the table-cloth beside his plate. Every minute or so some customer passing him on his way out leaned over him and said a word or two, which he rapidly noted down on one of the bits of paper between a couple of mouthfuls. The false news which had originated no one knew where, which had been born of nothing, was growing and swelling like a storm-cloud.

'You mean to sell, don't you?' asked Moser of Salmon.

However, the latter's silent smile had something so sharp and knowing about it, that he was left in anxiety, suddenly doubting the existence of this ultimatum from England, which he did not even remember had been invented by himself.

'For my part, I shall buy as long as anyone will sell,' concluded Pillerault, with the boastful temerity of a gambler without a system.

Meantime Saccard—his temples heated by the fever of speculation, which was stimulated by all the noise attending the close of the luncheon hour in that narrow room—had at last made up his mind to eat his asparagus, again full of irritation against Huret, whom he had now given up. He, as a rule so prompt in coming to a decision, had for weeks past been hesitating, a prey to conflicting doubts. He realised the imperative necessity of slipping into a new skin, and had at first dreamed of an entirely new life, in the upper circles of the Civil Service, or else in political spheres. Why should not a seat in the Legislature land him in the Cabinet, like his brother? He was discontented with speculation on account of its continual instability, huge sums being as quickly lost as won. Never had he slept on a real million, owing nothing to anyone. And now that he was subjecting his conscience to examination, he said to himself that perhaps he was of too passionate a nature for financial warfare, which required so much coolness. That must be the reason why, after such an extraordinary life of mingled luxury and need, he had come out of the fray empty-handed, badly scorched by ten years' formidable trafficking in the soil of new Paris—trafficking in which many others, not nearly as sharp as himself, had amassed colossal fortunes. Yes, perhaps he had mistaken his real vocation. With his activity and ardent faith perhaps he would triumph at one bound in the hubbub of politics. Everything depended, however, on his brother's answer. If Rougon should repulse him, throw him back into the gulf of speculation, well, it would undoubtedly be so much the worse for him and everyone else; he would then risk the grand stroke which he had not as yet spoken of to anyone, the huge affair which he had been dreaming of for weeks past, and which frightened even himself, so vast it was, so calculated to shake the world whether it succeeded or collapsed.

Pillerault had raised his voice again. 'I say, Mazaud,' he asked, 'is everything settled about Schlosser?'

'Yes,' answered the broker, 'he will be posted to-day. What would you have? It is annoying, of course, but I had received the most alarming reports, and was the first to move in the matter. It is necessary to make a sweep from time to time, you know.'

'I have been told,' said Moser, 'that your colleagues, Jacoby and Delarocque, lost large sums by him.'

The broker made a vague gesture. 'Bah! we always have to make an allowance for losses. That fellow Schlosser must belong to a gang; he will now be free to go and play the wrecker on the Bourse of Berlin or Vienna.'

Saccard's eyes had fallen upon Sabatani, whose secret association with Schlosser had been revealed to him by chance some time previously. Both had been playing a well-known game, the one 'bulling' and the other 'bearing' the same stock, he who lost being free to share the other's profit and then disappear. However, the young Levantine was quietly settling his score for the dainty repast which he had just made; after which, with the caressing grace of a semi-Oriental, semi-Italian, he came forward to shake hands with Mazaud, whose customer he was. Leaning over, he gave an order to the broker, which the latter inscribed upon a *fiche*.

'He is selling his Suez,' murmured Moser, and thereupon, distracted with doubt, he added aloud: 'I say, what do you think of Suez?'

Silence fell amid all the hubbub of voices; every head at the neighbouring tables turned. The question summed up the growing anxiety. However, Amadieu, who had simply asked Mazaud to lunch, in order to recommend one of his nephews to him, remained impenetrable, having indeed nothing to say; while the broker, who was becoming astonished at the number of orders to sell which he was receiving, contented himself with shaking his head, in accordance with his professional habit of discretion.

'Suez, why, it's capital,' declared Sabatani in his sing-song voice, as before going out he stepped aside to shake hands gallantly with Saccard.

For a moment afterwards it seemed to Saccard that he could still feel the pressure of the Levantine's soft, supple, almost feminine hand. In his uncertainty as to the course he should take to begin his life anew, he looked upon all who were there as sharpers. Ah! if they forced him to it, how he would hunt them down, how he would shear them, those trembling Mosers, those boastful Pilleraults, those Salmons, hollower than gourds, and those Amadieus whose chance success had transformed them into geniuses! The clatter of plates and glasses had begun again; voices were growing hoarse; and the doors swung faster than ever in the hasty eagerness that consumed them all to be across the way, at the game, if there was to be a crash in Suez. And in the middle of the Place, now crowded with pedestrians and crossed by cabs in all directions, Saccard, looking out of the window, saw that the shining steps of the Bourse were sprinkled with human insects—insects ever climbing—men correctly

13

dressed in black, who gradually filled the colonnade, while behind the railings there vaguely appeared a few women, prowling about under the chestnut trees.

Suddenly, while he was cutting some cheese which he had just ordered, a gruff voice made him raise his head.

'I beg your pardon, my dear fellow, but it was impossible for me to come sooner.'

So here at last was Huret, a Norman of Calvados, with the thick broad face of a shrewd peasant who affected the air of a simple man. He straightway told the waiter to bring him whatever he pleased, the dish of the day, with some vegetables.

'Well?' drily asked Saccard, containing himself.

The other, however, evinced no hurry, but watched him like a sly, prudent man. Then, beginning to eat, bringing his face forward and lowering his voice, he said: 'Well, I saw the great man. Yes, at his house this morning. Oh, he spoke very kindly of you, yes, very kindly.'

He paused, drank a large glass of wine, and put a potato in his mouth.

'And what else?' asked Saccard.

'What else, my dear fellow, why this: He is very willing to do what he can for you; he will find you a very comfortable berth, but not in France. Say, for instance, the governorship of one of our colonies, one of the good ones. You would be the master there, a real little prince.'

Saccard had turned very pale. 'I say,' he exclaimed, 'you must be having a joke with me, mocking at me, surely. Why not penal servitude at once? Ah! so he wants to get rid of me. Let him look out, or I shall end by embarrassing him in earnest.'

Huret, with his mouth full, remained conciliatory. 'Come, come,' said he, 'we only wish your own welfare; leave us to act.'

'Leave myself to be suppressed, eh? Why, only just now they were saying here that there soon won't be a single mistake left for the Empire to make. Yes, the Italian war, Mexico, the attitude of the Government towards Prussia! Upon my word, it is the truth! You will be up to such stupidity and folly, that all France will rise up to pitch you out.'

On hearing this, Huret, deputy, faithful creature of the minister as he was, at once became anxious, turned pale, and looked about him. 'Ah, come, come, I cannot follow you. Rougon is an honest man; there is no danger as long as he is at the helm. No, not another word—you misunderstand him, I must really say so——'

Clenching his teeth so as to deaden his voice, Saccard furiously interrupted him. 'Very well, love him—keep house together. Yes or no, will he give me his patronage here, in Paris?'

'In Paris, never!'

Without adding a word, Saccard rose and called the waiter in order to pay his score, whilst Huret, who knew his temper, calmly continued swallowing huge mouthfuls of bread, and let him go, through fear of a scene. Just then, however, quite a sensation was caused in the room.

Gundermann[8] had just entered it—Gundermann the banker-king, the master of the Bourse and of the world, a man of sixty, whose huge bald head, thick nose and round goggle-eyes betokened immense obstinacy and weariness. Never did he go to the Bourse; in fact he even pretended that he sent no official representative thither; neither did he ever breakfast in a public place. Only from time to time he happened, as on this occasion, to show himself at Champeaux' restaurant, where he would seat himself at one of the tables that he might simply drink a glassful of Vichy water. For

14

twenty years he had suffered from a gastric affection, and nourished himself exclusively with milk.

All the waiters were at once on the move to bring him his glass of water, and all who were lunching suddenly became very humble. Moser sat like one overwhelmed, contemplating this man who knew all secrets and who made stock rise or fall at will, just as the Divinity makes the thunder growl. Even Pillerault saluted him, like one whose only faith is in the irresistible force of the milliard. It was half-past twelve, and Mazaud, who was hurriedly leaving Amadieu, stepped back and bent low before the banker, from whom he sometimes had the honour to receive an order. Many *boursiers*, similarly on the point of departing, remained standing around the demigod, forming about him a very deferential court, amid the disarray of the soiled tablecloths; and it was with veneration that they watched him take the glass of water in his trembling hand and carry it to his pale lips.

Formerly, during his speculations in the lands of the Monceau Plain, Saccard had had sundry discussions and even a quarrel with Gundermann. They could not get on together—the one passionate and fond of the pleasures of life, the other sober and coldly logical. Accordingly the former, his fit of passion increased by this triumphal entrance, was going away, when the other called him.

'I say, my good friend, is it true that you are giving up business? Really, you act wisely; it is the best course.'

This, to Saccard, was like a lash across his face. He straightened his little figure, and in a clear voice, as sharp as a sword, replied: 'I am about to establish a banking house with a capital of twenty-five millions, and I expect to call upon you soon.'

And thereupon he went out, leaving behind him the fiery hubbub of the room, where all were now jostling one another, eager not to miss the opening of the Bourse. Ah! to succeed at last, to set his heel once more upon these people, who turned their backs upon him, and to struggle for power with that king of wealth, and some day perhaps beat him! He had not really decided to launch his great enterprise, and was surprised at the phrase which the necessity of answering had wrung from him. But could he tempt fortune elsewhere, now that his brother abandoned him, and that men and things were galling him back into the struggle, even as the bleeding bull is galled back into the arena?

For a moment he stood quivering on the edge of the footway. It was that active hour when all the life of Paris seems to flow into that central square between the Rue Montmartre and the Rue Richelieu, those two teeming arteries that carry the crowd along. From the four crossways at the four corners of the Place, streams of vehicles poured in uninterruptedly, whisking across the pavement amid an eddying mob of foot passengers. The two rows of cabs at the stand, beside the railings, were continually breaking and reforming; while along the Rue Vivienne the victorias of the *remisiers* stretched away in a compact line, above which towered the drivers, reins in hand and ready to whip up at the first signal. The steps and peristyle of the Bourse were quite black with swarming frock-coats; and from among the *coulissiers*, already installed under the clock and hard at work, there arose the clamour of bull and bear, the flood-tide roar of speculation dominating all the rumbling hubbub of the city. Passers-by turned their heads, curious and fearful as to what might be going on there— all those mysterious financial operations which few French brains can penetrate, all that sudden ruin and fortune brought about—how, none could understand—amid gesticulation and savage cries. And Saccard, standing on the kerb of the footway,

15

deafened by the distant voices, elbowed by the jostling, hurrying crowd, dreamed once more of becoming the Gold King, the sovereign of that fever-infested district, in the centre of which the Bourse, from one till three o'clock, beats as it were like some enormous heart.

Since his fall, however, he had not dared to re-enter the edifice; and on this day also a feeling of suffering vanity, a conviction that he would be received as a beaten man, prevented him from ascending the steps. Yet, like the lovers driven from the presence of a mistress whom they still desire, even while thinking that they hate her, he ever and ever returned to the spot, making the tour of the colonnade under various pretexts, entering the garden and strolling along in the shade of the chestnut-trees. Perambulating this dusty square, grassless and flowerless, where shady speculators and bareheaded women of the neighbourhood nursing their babies mingled together on the benches near the newspaper stalls, he affected a disinterested saunter, raised his eyes, and watched, absorbed by the exciting thought that he was besieging the monumental pile, drawing his lines more and more closely around it, in order that he might some day re-enter it in triumph.

Having made his way into the garden at the right-hand corner, under the trees facing the Rue de la Banque, he at once fell upon the Little Bourse, where discredited stock is negotiated, a Bourse of hawker-brokers—the 'Wet Feet' as others have nicknamed them with ironical contempt—men who quote in the open air, and in the mud on rainy days, the shares and debentures of defunct companies. There, an unclean Jewry was gathered in a tumultuous group—fat, shining faces, withered profiles like those of voracious birds, an extraordinary assemblage of typical noses, all drawn together as by a prey, all eagerly, angrily disputing, with guttural shouts, and seemingly ready to devour one another. He was passing on, when, a little apart, he noticed a stout man looking in the sunlight at a ruby, which he held up delicately between his huge dirty fingers.

'What! is it you, Busch? You remind me that I intended to call at your place,' said Saccard.

Busch, who kept an agency in the Rue Feydeau at the corner of the Rue Vivienne, had on several occasions been very useful to him in moments of difficulty. He was standing there in a state of ecstasy, examining the water of the jewel, with his broad flat face upturned and the glow of his heavy grey eyes extinguished, as it were, by the bright light. The white tie which he always wore was twisted round his neck like a bit of rope; while his second-hand frock coat, a superb garment once upon a time, but now wonderfully threadbare and covered with grease spots, reached up to the light hair falling in scanty rebellious locks from his head, which on the top was quite bald. Nobody could tell the age of his hat, browned by the sun and washed by countless showers. At last he decided to descend to earth again. 'Ah! Monsieur Saccard, so you are taking a little walk this way?' said he.

'Yes, I have a letter in the Russian language—a letter from a Russian banker in business at Constantinople. It occurred to me that your brother could translate it for me.'

Busch, who with a gentle movement was still unconsciously rolling the ruby between the fingers of his right hand, held out the left, saying that the translation would be forwarded that very evening. But Saccard explained that it was only a matter of ten lines. 'I will go up,' said he; 'your brother will read it to me at once.'

He was, however, at that moment interrupted by the arrival of a woman of colossal proportions, a certain Madame Méchain, well known to the frequenters of the Bourse as one of those fierce, wretched female speculators whose fat hands dabble in all sorts of suspicious jobs. Her red, puffy, full-moon face, with little blue eyes, a little hidden nose, and a little mouth whence came a child-like piping voice, protruded from an old mauve bonnet, tied askew with garnet ribbons; and her gigantic bosom and dropsical body strained almost to bursting point her mud-stained poplin gown, once green but now turning yellow. She carried on her arm an immense old black leather bag, as deep as a valise, which never left her. That afternoon the bag, so full that it seemed likely to burst, drew her down on the right side, like a tree that has grown slantwise.

'Here you are, then?' said Busch, who had evidently been waiting for her.

'Yes, and I have received the Vendôme papers; I have brought them,' she replied.

'Good! Let us be off to my place, then. There's nothing to be done here to-day.'

Saccard had darted a wavering glance at the vast leather bag. He knew that into it inevitably fell all sorts of discredited stock, the shares of bankrupt companies, in which the 'Wet Feet' still speculate—shares issued at five hundred francs, but which they dispute for at twenty or even ten sous apiece, either in the vague hope of an improbable rise or, more practically, as merchandise which they can sell at a profit to fraudulent bankrupts who are desirous of having something to show by way of explaining their pretended losses. In the deadly battles of speculation, La Méchain was the raven that followed the armies on the march; not a company, not a large financial establishment was founded, but she appeared with her bag, sniffing the air, awaiting the corpses, even in the prosperous hours of triumphant issues. For she well knew that ruin was inevitable, that the day of massacre would come, when there would be dead to eat, shares to pick up for nothing, from amid the mire and the blood. And Saccard, who even then was revolving a grand banking project in his mind, gave a slight shudder, and felt a presentiment at sight of that bag, that charnel-house, as it were, of depreciated stock, into which passed all the dirty paper swept away from the Bourse.

Busch was on the point of taking the old woman off, when Saccard stopped him, saying: 'Then I can go up? I am certain of finding your brother, eh?'

The Jew's eyes softened with an expression of anxious surprise. 'My brother! Why, certainly. Where do you expect him to be?'

'Very well, then; I will go up directly.'

Allowing them to move away, Saccard thereupon resumed his slow walk under the trees, towards the Rue Notre-Dame-des-Victoires. This is one of the most frequented sides of the Place, overlooked by houses occupied by commercial firms and petty manufacturers, whose gilt signboards were flaming in the sunlight. Blinds, too, were flapping at the balconies; and a whole family of provincials stood gaping at the window of a hotel. Saccard mechanically raised his head, and looked at these people, whose amazement made him smile, comforting him with the thought that plenty of investors would always be found in the provinces. Behind him, the clamour of the Bourse, the distant flood-tide roar, was still resounding, haunting him, following him like a threat of doom which would presently overtake him.

Another meeting, however, made him pause.

'What, Jordan, you at the Bourse?' he exclaimed, shaking hands with a tall, dark young man, with a small moustache and a determined, wilful air.

For ten years past, Jordan, whose father, a Marseilles banker, had committed suicide in consequence of some disastrous speculations, had been tramping the pavements of Paris with the fever of literature within him, in a gallant struggle against black misery. One of his cousins, residing at Plassans, where he knew the Rougon family, had formerly recommended him to Saccard, at the time when the latter was receiving all Paris at his mansion of the Parc Monceau.

'Oh! at the Bourse, never!' answered the young man, with a violent gesture, as if he were driving away the tragic memory of his father. Then, beginning to smile, he added: 'You know that I have got married—yes, to a little friend of my childhood's days. We were betrothed at the time when I was rich, and she has persisted in taking me—poor devil though I now am.'

'Quite so; I received the notification,' said Saccard. 'And do you know that I used to be in business relations with your father-in-law, Monsieur Maugendre, when he had his awning factory at La Villette? He must have made a pretty fortune there.'

The conversation was taking place near a bench; and at this point Jordan interrupted it to introduce a short, stout gentleman, of military bearing, who was sitting there, and with whom he had been talking when Saccard came up. 'Captain Chave, an uncle of my wife's,' said he. 'Madame Maugendre, my mother-in-law, is a Chave, of Marseilles.'

The captain had risen, and Saccard bowed. He was by sight acquainted with the owner of that apoplectic face, set on a neck stiffened by long wearing a military choker—that type of the petty cash gambler, whom one is certain to find somewhere about the Bourse every day from one to three o'clock. The game that men of this class play is one of small winnings, an almost certain profit of from fifteen to twenty francs, which must be realised before the day's operations are over.

Jordan, with his good-natured laugh, now added, by way of explaining his presence: 'My uncle is a ferocious speculator, with whom I sometimes stop to shake hands as I pass by.'

'Why,' said the captain, simply. 'I'm obliged to speculate, since the Government, with its beggarly pension, leaves me to die of hunger.'

Saccard, whom the young man interested by reason of his courageous battle for existence, next asked him how things were going in the domain of literature, and Jordan, again becoming merry, thereupon described in what a sorry fashion he had started housekeeping on the fifth storey of a house in the Avenue de Clichy; for the Maugendres, who distrusted a poet, and thought they had gone very far indeed in consenting to the marriage, had given their daughter nothing by way of portion, under the pretext that she would have their fortune intact, increased by their savings, when they were dead and gone. No, said Jordan, literature did not feed its man; he had an idea of a novel, but could not find time to write it, and had been obliged to embrace journalism, knocking off anything that his position called for, from leading articles to law reports and even news 'pars.'

'Well,' said Saccard, 'if I start my great enterprise, I shall perhaps need you. So come and see me.'

After bowing he turned away, and found himself behind the Bourse. There the distant clamour, the howling of the gamesters at last ceased, subsided into a vague hum, lost amid the rumbling of the street traffic. The steps on this side, like those in front, were, it is true, invaded by people; but the brokers' room, whose red hangings could be seen at the high windows, here intervened between the hubbub of the main hall and the colonnade, where sundry fastidious and richer speculators, some alone and others in little groups, were sitting comfortably in the shade, transforming the

18

vast open peristyle into a sort of club. The rear of the building was, moreover, something like the rear of a theatre—the stage entrance, as it were, reached by that equivocal and comparatively quiet street, the Rue Notre-Dame-des-Victoires, which was lined with wine-shops, cafés, beer-houses, and taverns, all swarming with a special class of customers strangely mingled. The signboards also betokened an evil growth that had sprung up at the very brink of the great cloaca: a growth of disreputable insurance companies, blackmailing financial journals, syndicates, banks, agencies, counting-houses, an entire series of cut-throat places on a petty scale, installed in dingy shops or on first floors no bigger than one's pocket-handkerchief. On the footways and in the middle of the street, everywhere in fact, men were prowling, waiting, as on the outskirts of a wood.

Saccard had stopped inside the Bourse railings, raising his eyes to the door leading to the brokers' room, with the piercing glance of the commander of an army who is examining from every side the fortress which he proposes to storm—when a tall fellow, coming out of a tavern, crossed the street and approached him with a very low bow.

'Ah! Monsieur Saccard, have you nothing for me? I have altogether left the Crédit Mobilier, and am looking for a situation.'

Jantrou was an ex-professor, who had left Bordeaux for Paris in consequence of some shady affair. Obliged to quit the University, without caste or position, but a handsome fellow with his black fan-shaped beard, and his tendency to early baldness, and lettered, intelligent, and amiable withal, he had, at the age of twenty-eight, landed at the Bourse, where for ten years he had dragged out an unclean life as a *remisier*, earning scarcely more money than was necessary for the gratification of his vices. And now, quite bald and as disconsolate as a hussy whose wrinkles threaten her with a loss of livelihood, he was still awaiting the opportunity which should start him on the road to success and fortune.

Saccard, on seeing him so humble, bitterly recalled the salutations of Sabatani at Champeaux' restaurant. The disreputable and the unsuccessful alone remained friendly to him. However, he was not without esteem for this man's keen intelligence, and he well knew that the desperate make the bravest troops, those ready to dare everything, having nothing to lose and everything to gain. So he received him fairly cordially. 'A situation?' he repeated. 'Well, perhaps that can be found. Come and see me.'

'It's Rue Saint-Lazare now, isn't it?'

'Yes, Rue Saint-Lazare; in the morning.'

They chatted. Jantrou spoke very excitedly about the Bourse, repeating, with the rancour of a man who has not been lucky in his knavery, that none but a knave could be successful there. For his part, said he, it was all over; he wanted to try something else; it seemed to him that, thanks to his University culture, and his knowledge of the world, he might conquer a fine position in discharging administrative duties. Saccard nodded approval. And, as they were now outside the railings, walking along the footway in the direction of the Rue Brongniart, they both became interested in a dark brougham, a very correct equipage, which had stopped in that street, with the horse turned towards the Rue Montmartre. The back of the high-perched coachman was as motionless as a rock, but they had twice noticed a woman's head appear at the carriage door, and then quickly disappear. All at once this head was again thrust out, and this time it lingered at the window, giving a long, backward, impatient look in the direction of the Bourse.

'The Baroness Sandorff,' muttered Saccard.

It was a very strange brown head, with burning black eyes beneath dark lids; a passionate face, with blood-red lips, and only marred by rather a long nose. Altogether its possessor seemed very pretty and precociously mature for her five-and-twenty years, having the look of a Bacchante garmented by the foremost dressmakers of the reign.

'Yes, the Baroness,' repeated Jantrou. 'I knew her when she was a young girl, at her father's, Count de Ladricourt. Oh! a mad speculator he was, and revoltingly brutal. I went to take his orders every morning; one day he came near giving me a beating. I shed no tears when he died in an apoplectic fit, ruined after a series of lamentable "settlements." The little one then had to make up her mind to marry Baron Sandorff, Counsellor to the Austrian Embassy, who was thirty-five years older than herself, and whom she had positively driven mad with her fiery glances.'

'I know,' said Saccard, simply.

The Baroness's head had again dived back into the brougham, but it almost immediately reappeared, more ardent than ever, and turned so as to command a better view of the Place.

'She speculates, doesn't she?'

'Oh, like a crazy woman! Whenever there is a crisis, she is to be seen there in her carriage, following the quotations, feverishly taking notes in her memorandum book, giving orders—and see! it was Massias whom she was waiting for: here he comes to join her.'

In fact, Massias, his quotations in his hand, was running up as fast as his short legs would carry him, and they saw him rest his elbows on the carriage door, and pop his head through the open window, in order to confer with the Baroness. Then Saccard and Jantrou stepped away a little, so that they might not be caught spying on the pair, and as the *remisier* came back, still on the run, they called him. He at first gave a glance back, to make sure that he was hidden by the street corner, and then he stopped short, out of breath, his florid face quite purple, but still gay, with big blue eyes as limpid as those of a child.

'But what is the matter with them all?' he cried. 'There's Suez all going to rack and ruin. There are rumours of a war with England, a piece of news that revolutionises them all, and that comes no one knows whence. War, indeed! who can have invented such a cram? Or did it invent itself all alone? At all events, there's a nice to-do!'

'Does the lady still bite?' asked Jantrou with a wink.

'Oh, madly! I am carrying her orders to Nathansohn.'

Saccard, who was listening, remarked: 'Ah, yes, so it's true, then; I had heard that Nathansohn had joined the *coulisse*.'

'A very nice fellow is Nathansohn,' repeated Jantrou, 'and one who deserves to succeed. We were at the Crédit Mobilier together. But he'll succeed, he will, for he is a Jew. His father, an Austrian, is in business at Besançon, as a watchmaker, I believe. The fever took him one day at the Crédit, you know, when he saw how things were managed. He said to himself that it wasn't such a trick, after all; that it was only necessary to get a room, put a wire grating across it, and open a wicket; and he has opened a wicket. And you, Massias, are you satisfied?'

'Oh, satisfied! You've been in the mill; you are right in saying that it is necessary to be a Jew; otherwise it is useless to try to understand. There's no such thing as a look in, nothing but cursed bad luck. What a filthy trade! But when a man is in it, he stays. And, besides, I have good legs still, and keep on hoping all the same.'

Thereupon he started off, running and laughing. He was said to be the son of a Lyons magistrate, removed from his post for unworthiness, and had stranded at the Bourse, after the disappearance of his father, not caring to continue his law studies.

With short, slow steps, Saccard and Jantrou retraced their way towards the Rue Brongniart, and there they again found the Baroness's brougham; but the windows were now raised, and the mysterious carriage appeared to be empty, while the coachman seemed more motionless than ever, still waiting—as he often had to do, until the very last quotations.

'She is devilishly provoking,' resumed Saccard, brutally. 'I understand the old Baron.'

A singular smile came over Jantrou's face. 'I fancy that he has had enough long ago. And he is very stingy, they say. And do you know who now pays her bills, speculation never sufficing?'

'No.'

'Delcambre!'

'Delcambre, the Public Prosecutor! that tall, dry man, so stiff and yellow! a future minister! Is it possible?'

Thereupon, in great good-humour, altogether enlivened, the pair separated with a vigorous handshake, after the one had reminded the other that he should take the liberty of calling on him shortly.

As soon as he found himself alone again, Saccard once more heard the loud voice of the Bourse, persistently swelling like that of the rising tide. He had turned the corner, and was making his way towards the Rue Vivienne, by this side of the Place, which through the complete absence of cafés has a more solemn aspect than any other. He passed the Chamber of Commerce, the Post Office, and the great advertising agencies, becoming more and more deafened, growing more and more feverish, as he drew nearer to the principal façade. And when by an oblique glance he could again command a view of the peristyle, he paused afresh as if reluctant to finish his circuit of the colonnade, to complete his investment of it. Here, where the footway broadened, life spread, burst forth upon him; torrents of customers invaded the cafés, the pastrycook's shop never emptied, and pedestrians were ever pausing, fascinated by the display in the shop windows, especially in those of a silversmith's establishment, which were all ablaze with large pieces of plate. And at the four cross-ways, at the four corners of the Place, the flood of cabs and wayfarers seemed to be increasing in inextricable entanglement; whilst the traffic at the omnibus station added to the block, and the carriages of the *remisiers*, ranged in a line, prevented access to the footway almost from one end of the railing to the other. Saccard's eyes, however, were fixed on the high steps, where frock-coats clustered in the sunlight. Then they were lifted towards the columns, towards the compact mass of speculators—the dense swarm, the blackness of which was scarcely relieved by the pale faces in the crowd. All were standing, no chairs could be seen; the curve formed by the *coulisse* under the clock could only be divined by the prevalent ebullition, the fury of gestures and words which made the very atmosphere quiver.

More calmness prevailed on the left, among a group of bankers, who were engaged either in arbitrage operations, in fixing the foreign exchange rates, or in negotiating English cheques, and whose ranks were continually being traversed by people on their way to the telegraph office. Speculators overflowed even from the side galleries, crowding and crushing together; and, leaning on the balustrades between the columns, there were some who presented belly or back, as if they were at home, or at a theatre, lolling against the velvet-upholstered front of a private box. The quivering and rumbling, like that of a steam-engine at work, was ever increasing, agitating the entire Bourse—subsiding only for a second to burst forth yet louder, in the same way as a flame may flicker and then flare high again. And gazing on it all, Saccard suddenly recognised the *remisier* Massias, who descended the steps at full speed and leaped into his carriage, the driver of which forthwith lashed his horse into a gallop.

Then Saccard felt his fists clench, and, violently tearing himself away, turned into the Rue Vivienne, which he crossed in order to reach the corner of the Rue Feydeau, where Busch's office was situated. He had just remembered the Russian letter which he had to get translated. As he was entering the house, however, a young man, standing in front of the stationer's shop on the ground floor, bowed to him, and he recognised Gustave Sédille, son of a silk manufacturer in the Rue des Jeûneurs, whom his father had placed with Mazaud, to study the mechanism of finance. Saccard smiled paternally upon this tall, elegant young fellow, strongly suspecting why he was mounting guard there. Conin's stationery shop had been supplying note-books to the entire Bourse since little Madame Conin had begun to help her husband—fat Conin, as he was called—who never left his back shop, there attending to the manufacturing part of his business, whilst she continually came and went, serving at the counter and doing errands outside. She was plump, blonde, and pink, a real curly-haired little sheep, with light silky hair, a pleasing, coaxing manner, and imperturbable gaiety. She was very fond of her husband, it was said, but this certainly did not prevent her from flirting with the gentlemen of the Bourse. As he passed, Saccard saw her smiling at Gustave through the window. What a pretty little sheep she was! The sight gave him a delightful sensation, akin to that of a caress. Then he at last went upstairs.

For twenty years Busch had occupied a small *logement*, comprising two chambers and a kitchen, high up, on the fifth floor. Born at Nancy, of German parents, he had come here from his native town, and had gradually extended the circle of his business, which was wonderfully complicated, without feeling the need of a larger office. Relinquishing the room overlooking the street to his brother Sigismond, he contented himself with a little chamber on this side of the courtyard of the house—a little chamber in which old papers, batches of documents, packages of all kinds were so piled up, that there was no room left except for a single chair beside the desk. One of his principal lines of business was a traffic in depreciated shares and debentures, thousands of which he collected together, serving as an intermediary between the Little Bourse of the 'Wet Feet' and the bankrupts embarrassed to account for their real or imaginary losses. He accordingly followed the market, at times buying direct, but more frequently supplied with batches of stock that were brought to him. In addition also to usury and a secret traffic in jewels and precious stones, he particularly occupied himself with the purchase of 'bad debts.' This it was that filled his office with old paper to overflowing, this it was that sent him forth to the four corners of Paris, sniffing and watching, with connections in all circles of society. As soon as he heard of a failure, he hurried off, prowled around the liquidator, and ended by buying up everything which could not immediately be realised. He kept a watch on the notaries' offices, looked out for inheritances difficult of settlement, and attended the sales of hopeless claims. He himself published advertisements, in this wise attracting impatient creditors who preferred to get a few coppers down rather than run the risk of prosecuting their debtors. And from all these manifold sources this *chiffonnier* of bad debts derived supply upon supply of paper, huge basketfuls, an ever-increasing pile of unpaid notes of hand, unfulfilled agreements, unredeemed acknowledgments of liability, unkept engagements of every kind. Then a sorting-out became necessary, a fork had to be thrust into this mess of broken victuals, a special and very delicate scent being required in the operation. To avoid waste of effort, it was necessary to make a choice in this ocean of debtors, who were either insolvent or had disappeared. In principle, Busch asserted that every claim, even the most seemingly hopeless, may some day become valuable again; and he had a series of portfolios, admirably classified, to which corresponded an index of names, which he read over from time to time to refresh his memory. However, naturally enough, among the insolvent ones, he more closely followed those who seemed to him to have near chances of fortune. Prosecuting his inquiries, he stripped people bare, discovered what means they possessed, penetrated family secrets, took note of all rich relatives, and especially of such newly-acquired situations as allowed of an attachment of salary. He thus often allowed a man to ripen for years, in order to strangle him at his first success. As for the debtors who disappeared, these stimulated him to yet greater energy, threw him into a fever of continual search, with his eyes on every signboard as he scoured the streets, and on every name printed in the newspapers. He hunted for addresses as a dog hunts for game, and as soon as he held the vanished and insolvent ones in his clutches, he became ferocious, clearing their pockets with bills of costs, sucking them dry, getting a hundred francs for what had cost him ten sous, brutally explaining the while what risks he ran as a speculator, forced to extort from those whom he caught all that he pretended to lose by those who slipped like smoke through his fingers.

In hunting for debtors, La Méchain was one of the helpers whom Busch was fondest of employing; for although he was obliged to have a little band of 'game-beaters' in his service, he lived in distrust of these disreputable, famishing assistants; whereas La Méchain had property of her own—an entire *cité* behind the Butte Montmartre, the Cité de Naples, as it was called, a vast tract of land covered with tumble-down shanties, which she let out by the month, a nook of frightful poverty, where starvelings were heaped together in filth, a crowd of pigsties which the wretched fought for, and whence she pitilessly swept away her tenants and their dung-heaps as soon as ever they ceased to pay her. However, her unfortunate passion for speculation consumed her, ate up all the profits of her *cité*. And she had also a taste for financial losses, ruins, and fires, amid which melted jewels can be stolen. When Busch charged her with obtaining some information, or ferreting out a debtor, she would sometimes even spend money out of her own pocket in view of furthering her researches, such was the pleasure she took in them. She called herself a widow, but no one had ever known her husband. She came, too, no one knew whence, and seemed always to have been about fifty years old, and monstrously fat, with the piping voice of a little girl.

On this occasion, as soon as La Méchain had taken her seat on the single chair in Busch's office, the room became full, blocked up by her mass of flesh. Busch stood like a prisoner at his desk, buried, as it were, with only his square head showing above the ocean of papers. 'Here,' said she, removing from her old bag the huge pile of papers that distended it, 'here is what Fayeux has sent me from Vendôme. He bought everything for you at that sale in connection with the Charpier failure, which you told me to call to his attention—one hundred and ten francs.'

Fayeux, whom she called her cousin, had just established an office down there as a collector of dividends. His ostensible business was to cash the *coupons* of the petty bondholders of the district; and, as the depositary of these *coupons* and the cash they yielded, he speculated in the most frenzied manner.

'The country isn't worth much,' muttered Busch, 'but there are discoveries to be made there all the same.'

He sniffed the papers, and began sorting them out with an expert hand, roughly classifying them in accordance with a first appraisement, in which he seemed to be guided by their mere smell. As he proceeded, his flat face grew dark, and he paused at last with an expression of disappointment.

'Humph! there is no fat here, nothing to bite. Fortunately it did not cost much. Here are some notes, and here some more. If they are signed by young people, who have come to Paris, we shall perhaps catch them.' Then, with a slight exclamation of surprise, he added: 'Hallo, what's this?'

At the bottom of a sheet of stamped paper he had just found the signature of the Count de Beauvilliers, and the sheet contained only three lines of large handwriting, evidently traced by an old man: 'I promise to pay the sum of ten thousand francs to Mademoiselle Léonie Cron on the day she attains her majority.

'The Count de Beauvilliers,' he slowly continued, thinking aloud; 'yes, he had several farms, quite a large estate, in the vicinity of Vendôme. He died of a hunting accident, leaving a wife and two children in straitened circumstances. I held some of his notes formerly, which with difficulty I got them to pay—he was a wild droll, not good for much——'

Suddenly he burst into a loud laugh, reconstructing in his mind the story attaching to the note.

'Ah! the old sharper, he played the little one a nice trick with this bit of paper, which is legally valueless. Then he died. Let me see, this is dated 1854, ten years ago. The girl must be of age now. But how could this acknowledgment have got into Charpier's hands? He was a grain merchant, who lent money by the week. No doubt the girl left this on deposit with him in order to get a few crowns, or perhaps he had undertaken to collect it.'

'But this is very good,' interrupted La Méchain—'a real stroke of luck.'

Busch shrugged his shoulders disdainfully. 'Oh no, I tell you that it is legally worth nothing. If I should present it to the heirs, they may send me about my business, for it would be necessary to prove that the money is really due. Only, if we find the girl, I may induce them to be reasonable, and come to an understanding with us, in order to avoid a disagreeable scandal. You understand? Look for this Léonie Cron; write to Fayeux, and tell him to hunt her up down there. That done, we may perhaps have a laugh.'

He had made two piles of the papers, with the intention of thoroughly examining them when he should be alone, and now sat motionless, with his hands open, one resting on each pile.

A spell of silence followed; then La Méchain resumed: 'I have been attending to the Jordan notes. I really thought that I had found our man again. He has been employed somewhere, and now he is writing for the newspapers. But they receive you so badly at the newspaper offices; they refuse to give you addresses. And besides, I think that he does not sign his articles with his real name.'

Without a word, Busch had stretched out his arm to take the Jordan portfolio from its place. It contained six notes of hand of fifty francs each, dated five years back and maturing monthly—a total sum of three hundred francs—which the young man had undertaken to pay to a tailor in days of poverty. Unpaid on presentation, however, the capital sum had been swollen by enormous costs, and the portfolio fairly overflowed with formidable legal documents. At the present time the debt had increased to the sum of seven hundred and thirty francs and fifteen centimes. 'If he has a future before him,' muttered Busch, 'we shall catch him one of these days.' Then, some sequence of ideas undoubtedly forming in his mind, he exclaimed: 'And that Sicardot affair, are we going to abandon it?'

La Méchain lifted her fat arms to heaven with a gesture of anguish. A ripple of despair seemed to course through her monstrous person. 'Oh, Lord!' she wailed, with her piping voice, 'it will cost me my very skin.'

This Sicardot affair was a very romantic story which she delighted to tell. A cousin of hers, Rosalie Chavaille, a daughter of her father's sister, living with her mother in a small lodging on the sixth floor of a house in the Rue de la Harpe, had fallen a victim to a married man, who occupied with his wife a room sublet to him on the second floor. There were some abominable circumstances in connection with the affair, but the girl's mother, consenting to silence, had merely required that the evil-doer should pay her the sum of six hundred francs, divided into twelve notes of fifty francs each, payable monthly. Before the first month was at an end, however, the man—an individual of gentlemanly appearance—had disappeared, and all trace of him was lost, whilst misfortunes continued falling thick as hail. Rosalie gave birth to a boy, lost her mother, and fell into a life of vice and abject poverty. Stranded in the Cité de Naples, her cousin's property, she had dragged about the streets till the age of twenty-six; but at last, during the previous year, she had been lucky enough to die, leaving behind her her son Victor, whom La Méchain had to keep; and of the whole adventure there only remained the twelve unpaid notes of hand. They had never been able to learn more of the individual who had signed them than that he called himself Sicardot.

With a fresh gesture, Busch took down the Sicardot papers, contained in a thin grey paper wrapper. No costs had accumulated, so there were merely the twelve notes.

'If Victor were only a nice child!' explained the old woman in a sorrowful voice. 'But he's dreadful! Ah! it is hard to be encumbered with such inheritances—an urchin who will end on the scaffold, and those bits of paper which will never bring me anything!'

Busch kept his big pale eyes obstinately fixed upon the notes. How many times already had he thus studied them, hoping that some hitherto unnoticed detail, something in the form of the letters, or in the grain of the stamped paper, would supply him with a clue! He asserted at times that that fine, pointed handwriting was not altogether unknown to him. 'It is curious,' he repeated once more, 'I am certain that I have somewhere already seen such *a*'s and *o*'s as these, so elongated that they resemble *i*'s.'

Just then there came a knock; and he asked La Méchain to stretch out her hand to open the door, for the room communicated direct with the staircase. You had to cross it in order to reach the second chamber, the one that overlooked the street. As for the kitchen, this was a stifling hole on the other side of the landing.

'Come in, monsieur,' said La Méchain, and Saccard entered. He was smiling, inwardly amused by the copper plate screwed upon the door, and bearing in large letters the words: 'Disputed Claims.'

'Oh yes, Monsieur Saccard, you have come for that translation—my brother is there in the other room. Come in, pray come in.'

La Méchain, however, absolutely barred the passage, and scrutinised the new-comer with an air of increasing surprise. No end of manœuvring was necessary for Saccard to effect an entrance; he had to retreat to the stairs again whilst she stepped out, and drew back on the landing, so that he might pass in and finally reach the adjoining room, into which he disappeared. During these complicated movements, La Méchain had not once taken her eyes off him.

'Oh!' she faintly gasped, like one sorely oppressed, 'this Monsieur Saccard, I never had so near a view of him before. Victor is the perfect image of him.'

Busch looked at her, at first failing to understand; then a sudden light dawned upon his mind, and in a stifled voice he swore: 'Thunder! that's it; I knew very well that I had seen that handwriting somewhere.'

And this time he rose, rummaged among his batches of papers, and at last found a letter that Saccard had written him during the previous year to ask him for an extension of time in favour of an insolvent lady. He quickly compared the handwriting of the notes with that of this letter. The a's and the o's were clearly the same, though they had grown yet more pointed with the lapse of time; and there was also a marked similarity between the capital letters.

'It is he, it is he,' he repeated. 'Only, let me see, why Sicardot? Why not Saccard?'

In his mind, however, there awoke a confused recollection of some story of Saccard's past—a story which an agent, named Larsonneau, now a millionaire, had once told him: Saccard tumbling into Paris on the day after the *coup d'état*, coming there to exploit the rising power of his brother Rougon; then, first of all, his poverty in the dingy streets of the old Latin Quarter; next, his rapidly acquired fortune, under cover of a disreputable marriage, when he had been lucky enough to lose his first wife. It was at the time of those difficult beginnings that he had changed his name from Rougon to Saccard, by simply transforming his first wife's name, which was Sicardot.

'Yes, yes, Sicardot; I remember perfectly,' muttered Busch. 'He had the effrontery to sign notes with his wife's name. No doubt the family assumed that name when they came to the Rue de la Harpe. And then the rascal took all sorts of precautions, ready to move at the slightest alarm. Ah! so he was not only hunting for money; well, well, one of these days his doings will cost him dear.'

'Hush! hush!' resumed La Méchain. 'We have him now, and well may one say that there is indeed a Providence. At last, then, I am to be rewarded for all that I have done for that poor little Victor, whom I dearly love all the same, in spite of the fact that there is nothing to be done with him.'

She was radiant; her little eyes sparkled amid all the melting, puffy flesh of her face.

Busch, however, after the momentary fever attending this long-sought-for solution, brought to him by chance, grew cold again as he reflected, and shook his head. Undoubtedly. Saccard, although ruined for the moment, was still good to shear. One might have fallen upon a less desirable father. Only he would not allow himself to be annoyed; he had terrible teeth. And besides, he was certainly unaware that he had an illegitimate son; he might deny it, in spite of the extraordinary resemblance that

26

had so astounded La Méchain. Moreover, he was now for the second time a widower, free, under no obligation to account for his past to anyone, so that, even if he should acknowledge the child, there was no threat that could be utilised against him. As for merely realising the six hundred francs which the notes represented, that would be really too paltry a stroke; the miraculous help which chance had brought must be turned to better account than that. He must reflect, nurse the affair, find a way of cutting the crop at harvest time, and not before. 'We mustn't be in a hurry,' he concluded. 'Besides, he is down; let us give him time to get up again.'

And, before dismissing La Méchain, he finished dealing with the little matters with which she was charged—a young woman who had pawned her jewels for her lover; a son-in-law whose debt would be paid by his mother-in-law, if they could find a way to work it; in short, some of the most delicate varieties of the complex and difficult business of collecting bad debts.

Saccard, on entering the adjoining room, had stood for a second dazzled by the bright light that streamed in through the sunny window panes, unhindered by any curtain. This room, with its walls covered with paper bearing a design of blue flowrets on a light background, was almost bare; there was merely a little iron bedstead in one corner, a deal table in the middle, and two straw-bottomed chairs. Along the partition on the left, some planks, scarcely planed, served as a bookcase, loaded with volumes, pamphlets, journals, and papers of all sorts. But the broad sunlight at this height imparted to all the bareness a sort of youthful gaiety, a smile of artless freshness. And Busch's brother, Sigismond, a beardless fellow of five and thirty, with long, scanty, chestnut hair, was sitting at the table, his broad, bumpy forehead buried in his thin hand, so absorbed in his perusal of a manuscript that he did not turn his head, not having heard the door open.

He was an intelligent man was this Sigismond, educated in the German universities, and speaking not only French, his mother tongue, but German, English, and Russian. He had made the acquaintance of Karl Marx at Cologne in 1849, and had become the most highly prized of the contributors to the 'New Rhenish Gazette.' From that moment his religion had been fixed; he professed Socialism with an ardent faith, giving his entire being to the idea of an approaching social renovation, which would assure the happiness of the poor and humble. Since his master, banished from Germany, and forced to leave Paris after the days of June, had been living in London, writing and trying to organise the party, Sigismond, on his side, had vegetated in his dreams, so careless as to his material life that he would surely have perished of hunger had his brother not taken him to live with him in the Rue Feydeau, near the Bourse, with the idea that he might utilise his knowledge of languages as a professional translator. This elder brother adored his junior with a maternal passion. Ferocious wolf though he was towards debtors, quite capable of wading through blood that he might steal half a franc, he was straightway moved to tears and evinced all the passionate, minute tenderness of a woman whenever this tall, absent-minded fellow, who had remained a child, was in question. He had given him the fine room overlooking the street, he served him as a domestic, and took entire charge of their strange household, sweeping the floors, making the beds, and ordering the food which a little restaurant in the neighbourhood sent up twice a day. Moreover, he so active, with his head full of a thousand business matters, not merely suffered his brother to remain idle—for, thwarted by private writing, very few translations were made—but he even forbade him to work, anxious as he was concerning an ominous little cough.

27

And in spite of his stern love of money, his murderous greed, which converted money-making into the sole motive of life, he smiled indulgently at the theories of this revolutionist, relinquishing capital to him like a toy to a child, at the risk of seeing him break it.

On his side, Sigismond did not even know what his brother did in the next room. He was utterly ignorant of all that frightful traffic in depreciated stock, and of the purchase of bad debts; he lived in a loftier region, in a sovereign dream of justice. The idea of charity wounded his feelings, made him angry: charity was alms, inequality consecrated by kindness, and he admitted nought but justice, the rights of each individual man regained and adopted as the unchangeable principles of the new social organisation. And thus, following the example of Karl Marx, with whom he was in constant correspondence, he spent his days in studying this organisation, incessantly modifying and improving upon paper the society of to-morrow, covering immense pages with figures, building up on the basis of science the whole complicated scaffolding of universal happiness. He took capital from some, to distribute it among all the others; he moved billions, displaced the wealth of the world with a stroke of his pen; and this he did in that bare room, without any other passion than his dream, without any desire of enjoyment to satisfy, so frugal that his brother had to get angry in order to make him drink wine and eat meat. He desired that the labour of every man, measured according to his strength, should assure the satisfaction of his appetites; but, for his own part, he was killing himself with work, and living upon nothing—a real sage, exalted in his studious occupations, disengaged from material life, very gentle and very pure. Since the previous autumn, however, he had been coughing more and more; consumption was seizing hold of him, but he did not even condescend to notice it and nurse himself.

Saccard having made a movement, Sigismond at last raised his large vague eyes, and was astonished, although he knew the visitor.

'I have come to get a letter translated.'

The young man's surprise increased, for he had done all he could to discourage his customers, the bankers, speculators, and brokers, all that circle of the Bourse who receive, especially from England and Germany, so many communications on financial matters, company prospectuses and statutes, circulars, and so forth.

'Yes, a letter in Russian. Oh! only ten lines long.'

Thereupon Sigismond stretched out his hand, Russian having remained his speciality, he alone translating it rapidly among all the other translators of the neighbourhood, who mainly lived by German and English. The rarity of Russian documents in the Paris market explained his long periods of idleness.

He read the letter aloud in French. It was, in three sentences, a favourable reply from a Constantinople banker, a simple yes as to a matter of business.

'Ah! thank you,' exclaimed Saccard, who seemed delighted; and he asked Sigismond to write the few lines of translation on the back of the letter. But Sigismond was seized with a terrible fit of coughing, which he stifled in his handkerchief, in order not to disturb his brother, who always ran in whenever he heard him cough in that way. Then, the attack over, he rose and went to open the window wide, for he was stifling, and wished to breathe the air. Saccard, who had followed him, gave a glance outside, and raised a slight exclamation: 'Oh! so you see the Bourse? How queer it looks from here!'

28

Never in fact had he seen it under such a singular aspect, in a bird's-eye view, with the four vast zinc slopes of its roof extraordinarily developed and bristling with a forest of pipes. The lightning-rods rose erect like gigantic lances threatening the sky. And the edifice itself was nothing but a cube of stone, streaked with columns at regular intervals, a bare, ugly cube of a dirty gray hue, surmounted by a ragged flag. But, above all else, the steps and the peristyle astonished him, covered with black ants, a swarm of ants in revolution, all agog, in a state of wonderful commotion, which was not to be explained from such a height, and prompted a feeling of pity.

'How small they all look!' continued Saccard; 'it seems as if one could take the whole of them in the hand, with one grip.' Then, knowing his companion's ideas, he added with a laugh: 'When are you going to sweep all that away with a kick?'

Sigismond shrugged his shoulders. 'What is the use? You are demolishing yourselves fast enough.'

Then, little by little, he became animated, overflowing with the subject he was full of. A proselytising spirit launched him, at the slightest word, into an exposition of his system. 'Yes, yes, you are working for us without suspecting it,' said he. 'You are a few usurpers, who expropriate the mass of the people, and when you have gorged yourselves we shall only have to expropriate you in our turn. Every monopoly, every phase of centralisation, leads to collectivism. You are setting us a practical example, in the same way as the large estates absorbing the small patches of land, the large producers devouring the petty home industries, the great financial establishments and great stores killing all competition, and battening on the ruin of the little banks and the little shops, are slowly but surely leading towards the new social state. We are waiting for everything to crack, for the existing method of production to end in the intolerable disorder which will be its ultimate consequence. Then the *bourgeois* and the peasants themselves will aid us.'

Saccard, feeling interested, looked at him with a vague anxiety, although he took him for a madman. 'But come, explain to me, what is this collectivism of yours?'

'Collectivism is the transformation of private capital, living by the struggle of competition, into a unitary social capital, exploited by the labour of all. Imagine a society in which the instruments of production will be the property of all, in which everybody will work according to his intelligence and strength, and in which the products of this social co-operation will be distributed to each in proportion to his effort! There can be nothing more simple, eh? Common production in the factories, yards, and workshops of the nation! Then an exchange, a payment in kind! If there should be over-production, the surplus will be lodged in public warehouses, from which it will be taken to fill up any deficits that may arise. One will have to strike a balance. And this, like one blow of an axe, will fell the rotten tree. No more competition, no more private capital, and, therefore, no more "business" of any kind—neither commerce, nor markets, nor Bourses. The idea of profit will thenceforth have no meaning. The sources of speculation, of incomes acquired without work, will be dried up.'

'Oh! oh!' interrupted Saccard, 'that would change many people's habits, and no mistake! But what would you do with those who have incomes to-day? Gundermann, for instance, would you take away his milliard?'

'Not at all; we are not robbers. We should redeem his milliard, all his shares, debentures, and State bonds, with certificates of enjoyment, divided into annuities. And just imagine this immense capital thus replaced by an overwhelming wealth of

29

articles of consumption: in less than a century your Gundermann's descendants would, like other citizens, be reduced to personal labour; for the annuities would finally become exhausted, and they would not have been able to capitalise their forced economies, the overplus of their overwhelming supply of articles of consumption, even admitting that the right of inheritance should be left untouched. I tell you that this would at one stroke sweep away, not only individual enterprises, companies, syndicates, and so forth, but also all the indirect sources of income, all systems of credit, loans, rentals, and so on. Nothing but labour would be left as a measure of value. Wages would naturally be suppressed, for in the present capitalistic system they are never equivalent to the exact product of labour; but at the utmost represent no more than is strictly necessary for the labourer's daily maintenance.[9] And it must be admitted that the existing system alone is guilty in the matter, that the most honest employer is clearly forced to follow the stern law of competition, to exploit his workmen, if he himself wishes to live. We have to destroy our entire social system. Ah! just think of it, Gundermann stifling under the burden of his certificates of enjoyment, his heirs unable to consume everything, obliged to give to others, and to take up the pick or the chisel, like other comrades!'

Thereupon Sigismond burst into a good-natured laugh, like a child at play, still standing by the window, with his eyes fixed on the Bourse, where swarmed the black ant-hill of speculation. A burning flush was rising to his cheeks; he had no other amusement than to picture in this wise the comical ironies of to-morrow's justice.

Saccard's uneasiness had increased. Suppose this wide-awake dreamer were after all speaking the truth. Suppose he had divined the future. He explained things that seemed very clear and sensible. 'Bah!' muttered Saccard, as though to reassure himself, 'all that won't happen next year.'

'Certainly not,' rejoined the young man, again becoming serious and weary. 'We are in the transition period, the period of agitation. There will perhaps be revolutionary violences; they are often inevitable. But the exaggerations and outbursts are temporary. Oh! I do not conceal the great immediate difficulties. All this future that I dream of seems impossible. It is difficult to give people a reasonable idea of this future society, the society of just labour, whose morals will be so different to ours. It is like another world in another planet. And then, it must be confessed, the scheme of reorganisation is not ready; we are still hunting for it. I, who now scarcely sleep at all, exhaust my nights in searching. For instance, it is certain that our adversaries can say to us: "If things are as they are, it is because the logic of human actions has made them so." Hence, what a task to take the river back to its source, and direct it into another valley! The existing social system certainly owes its centuries of prosperity to the individualist principle, which emulation and personal interest endow with a fertility of production that is ever being renewed. Will collectivism ever attain to such fertility, and by what means are we to stimulate the productive functions of the workman when the idea of profit shall have been destroyed? There, to my mind, lies the doubt, the anguish, the weak point over which we must fight, if we wish the victory of Socialism to be some day won. But we *shall* conquer, because we are Justice. There! you see that building in front of you? You see it?'

'The Bourse?' said Saccard. 'Why, yes, of course I see it.'

'Well, it would be stupid to blow it up, because it would be rebuilt. Only I predict to you that it will go up of itself when the State shall have expropriated it, and have become the sole universal bank of the nation; and, who knows? perhaps it will then serve as a public warehouse for our surplus wealth, as one of the store-houses where our grandchildren will find the necessary supply of luxury for their days of festivity.'

Thus, with a sweeping comprehensive gesture, did Sigismond reveal this future of universal average happiness. And he had become so excited that a fresh fit of coughing shook him, and sent him back to his table, with his elbows among his papers and his head in his hands, striving to stifle the harsh rattle in his throat. But this time he did not succeed in stopping it. The door suddenly opened, and Busch, having dismissed La Méchain, ran in with a bewildered air, suffering himself at the sound of that abominable cough. He at once leaned over, and took his brother in his long arms, as one takes hold of a child to soothe its pain.

'Come, youngster,' said he, 'what is the matter with you, that you are stifling like this? You know I wish you to send for a doctor. This isn't reasonable. You surely must have talked too much.'

And thereupon he darted a side glance at Saccard, who had remained in the middle of the room, quite upset by what he had just heard from the lips of that tall fellow, so passionate and so ill, who from his window on high doubtless cast a spell over the Bourse with all his stories of sweeping everything away, in order to build up everything afresh.

'Thanks; I leave you,' said the visitor, in a hurry to get outside again. 'Send me my letter, with the ten lines of translation. I expect some others, and we will settle for them all together.'

The attack being over, however, Busch detained him a moment longer. 'By the way,' said he, 'the lady who was here just now used to know you—oh! a long time ago.'

'Ah! where was that?'

'In the Rue de la Harpe, in '52.'

Despite his usual perfect mastery over himself, Saccard turned pale. A nervous twitch distorted his mouth. Not that he, at that minute, remembered the girl whom he had wronged; he had never even known of her becoming a mother, he was ignorant of the existence of the child. But he always greatly disliked being reminded of the wretched years of his *début* in life.

'Rue de la Harpe! Oh! I only lived there a week, at the time of my arrival in Paris, just long enough to look for rooms. *Au revoir!*'

'*Au revoir!*' emphatically answered Busch, who deceived himself with the idea that Saccard's embarrassment implied confession, and who was already wondering how largely he might profit by the adventure.

On finding himself in the street, Saccard mechanically turned back towards the Place de la Bourse. He was trembling, and did not even look at little Madame Conin, whose pretty blonde face was smiling in the doorway of the stationery shop. The agitation had increased on the Place; it was with uncurbed flood-tide violence that the clamour of the speculators swept across the roadway to the footwalks swarming with people. It was the last roar, the roar which bursts forth as soon as the clock points to a quarter to three, the battle of the last quotations, the rageful longing to know who will come away with his pockets full. And, standing at the corner of the Rue de la Bourse, opposite the peristyle, Saccard fancied that, amid all the confused jostling under the columns he could recognise 'bear' Moser and 'bull' Pillerault quarrelling, and that he could hear the shrill voice of broker Mazaud coming from the depths of the great hall, but drowned occasionally by the shouts of Nathansohn, sitting under the clock in the *coulisse*. However, a vehicle, fringing the gutter as it drove up, came near spattering him with mud. Massias leaped out, even before the driver had stopped, and darted up the steps at a bound, bringing, quite out of breath, some customer's last order.

And Saccard, still motionless and erect, with his eyes fixed on the *mêlée* above him, ruminated over his life, haunted by the memory of his beginnings, which Busch's question had just awakened. He recalled the Rue de la Harpe, and then the Rue Saint-Jacques, through which he had dragged his boots, worn down at heel, on arriving in Paris to subdue it like a conquering adventurer; and a fury seized him at the thought that he had not subdued it yet, that he was again upon the pavement, still watching for fortune, still unsatisfied, tortured by such an appetite for enjoyment that never had he suffered more. That mad fellow Sigismond was right: labour cannot give one life; merely wretches and fools labour, to fatten the others. There was only gambling that was worth anything—gambling which in one afternoon can at one stroke bring comfort, luxury, life, broad and entire. Even if this old social world were fated to crumble some day, could not a man like himself still find time and room to satisfy his desires before the Downfall?

But just then a passer-by jostled him without even turning to apologise. He looked, and recognised Gundermann taking his little walk for his health, and saw him enter a confectioner's, whence this gold king sometimes brought a franc box of *bonbons* to his grand-daughters. And that elbow-thrust, at that minute, in the fit of fever that had been rising in him since he had begun the circuit of the Bourse, was like the whip-stroke, the last shove that determined him. He had completed his investment of the fortress, now he would make the assault. He swore to begin a merciless struggle; he would not leave France, he would defy his brother, he would play the final rubber, a battle of terrible audacity, which should either put Paris beneath his heels or throw him into the gutter with a broken back.

Until the moment when the Bourse closed Saccard obstinately lingered there, erect at his post of menace and observation. He watched the peristyle clearing, the steps blackening again as the whole fagged, heated crowd slowly scattered. Both on the foot and roadways around him the block continued—an endless flow of people, the eternal crowd of future victims, the investors of to-morrow, who could not pass that great lottery office of speculation without turning their heads, curious and fearful as to what might be going on there, as to all those mysterious financial operations which are the more attractive to French brains as they are penetrated by so few of them.

CHAPTER II
DREAMS AND SCHEMES

When, after his last and disastrous land speculation, Saccard had been obliged to leave his palace in the Parc Monceau, which he abandoned to his creditors in order to avoid a yet greater catastrophe, his first idea had been to take refuge with his son Maxime. The latter, since the death of his wife, now sleeping in a little cemetery in Lombardy, had been living alone in a mansion in the Avenue de l'Impératrice, where he had planned out his life with a prudent and ferocious egoism. There he spent the fortune of the deceased, methodically, without ever overstepping the bounds, like a man in feeble health whom vice had prematurely ripened; and it was in a clear voice that he refused to lodge his father in his house, wishing, he explained with his smiling, prudent air, that they might continue on good terms together.

Saccard thereupon thought of some other retreat, and was on the point of taking a little house at Passy, a retired merchant's *bourgeois* asylum, when he recollected that the first and second floors of the Orviedo mansion, in the Rue Saint-Lazare, were still unoccupied, with doors and windows closed. The Princess d'Orviedo, who had withdrawn into three rooms on the second floor since her husband's death, had not even put up any notice 'To Let' at the carriage entrance, where the weeds were growing. A low door at the other end of the façade led to the second storey by a servants' staircase. And in the course of his business relations with the Princess, during the visits that he paid her, Saccard had often been astonished at the negligence which she showed in the matter of deriving some profit from her property. But she shook her head in reply to his remarks; she had theories of her own as to money matters. However, when he applied in his own name, she consented at once, and for the ridiculous rent of ten thousand francs made over to him both the sumptuous ground and first floors, decorated in princely fashion, and worth certainly double the money.

The magnificence displayed by Prince d'Orviedo was well remembered. It was in the feverish flush of his immense financial fortune, when he had come from Spain to Paris amid a rain of millions, that he had bought and redecorated this mansion, pending the erection of the palace of marble and gold with which he dreamed of astonishing the world. The edifice dated from the last century; it had been one of those pleasure-houses built in the midst of vast gardens by noble gallants. Partially demolished, however, and re-erected in a severer style, it had of its park of former days merely retained a large court, bordered with stables and coach-houses, which the projected Rue du Cardinal-Fesch would surely sweep away. The Prince acquired the mansion from the heirs of a Mademoiselle Saint-Germain, whose property had formerly extended to the Rue des Trois-Frères, as the further end of the Rue Taitbout was once called. The entrance of the mansion was still in the Rue Saint-Lazare, adjoining a large building of the same period, the whilom Folie-Beauvilliers, which the Beauvilliers still occupied, after passing through a period of slow ruin; and they there possessed some remnants of an admirable garden, with magnificent trees, likewise condemned to disappear in the approaching transformation of the district.

In the midst of his disaster, Saccard still dragged about with him a number of servants, the *débris* of his over-numerous household, a valet, a *chef*, and his wife who had charge of the linen, another woman who had remained no one knew why, a coachman and two ostlers; and he filled up the stables and coach-houses, putting two horses and three carriages in them, and arranged a servants' dining-hall on the ground floor of the house. He had not five hundred francs in cash in his coffers, but lived at the rate of two or three hundred thousand francs a year. And with his own person he managed to fill the vast first-floor apartments, the three drawing- and five bed-rooms, not to mention the immense dining-room, where covers could be laid for fifty persons. Here a door had formerly opened upon an inner staircase, leading to another and smaller dining-room on the second floor, and the Princess, who had recently let this part of the second floor to an engineer, M. Hamelin, a bachelor, living with his sister, had contented herself with closing the door by the aid of a couple of stout screws. She herself shared the old servants' staircase with the Hamelins, while Saccard had the main stairway at his own entire disposal. He partially furnished a few rooms with some remnants from his Parc Monceau establishment, and left the others empty, succeeding, nevertheless, in restoring some life to that series of bare, gloomy walls, whence an obstinate hand seemed to have torn even the smallest shreds of hangings on the very morrow of the Prince's death. And here then he was able to indulge afresh his dream of a great fortune.

The Princess d'Orviedo was at that time one of the most curious notabilities of Paris. Fifteen years previously she had resignedly married the Prince, whom she did not love, in obedience to the formal command of her mother, the Duchess de Combeville. At that period this young girl of twenty had been famous for her beauty and exemplary conduct, being very religious, and perhaps a little too serious, although loving society passionately. She was ignorant of the singular stories current regarding the Prince, the sources of his regal fortune estimated at three hundred millions of francs—his whole life of frightful robberies, perpetrated, not on the skirts of a wood and weapon in hand, after the fashion of the noble adventurers of former days, but according to the system of the correct modern bandit, in the broad sunlight of the Bourse, where amidst death and ruin he had emptied the pockets of poor credulous folks. Over there in Spain, and here in France, the Prince for twenty years had appropriated the lion's share in every great legendary piece of rascality. Although suspecting nothing of the mire and blood in which he had just picked up so many millions, his wife at their first meeting had felt a repugnance towards him, which even her religious sentiments were powerless to overcome; and to this antipathy was soon added a secret, growing rancour at having no child by this marriage, to which she had submitted for obedience' sake. Maternity would have sufficed her, for she adored children; and thus she came to hate this man, who, after taking from her all hope of love, had even been unable to satisfy her maternal longings. It was then that the Princess was seen to precipitate herself into a life of unheard-of luxury, dazzling Paris with the brilliancy of her *fêtes*, and displaying in all things such magnificence that even the Tuileries were said to be jealous. Then suddenly, on the day after the Prince died from a stroke of apoplexy, the mansion in the Rue Saint-Lazare fell into absolute silence, complete darkness. Not a light, not a sound; doors and windows alike remained closed; and the rumour spread that the Princess, after violently stripping the lower part of the house, had withdrawn, like a recluse, into three little rooms on the second floor, with old Sophie, her mother's former maid, who had brought her up. When she reappeared in public, she wore a simple black woollen dress, with a lace *fichu* concealing her hair. Short and still plump, with her narrow forehead and her pretty round face with pearly teeth hidden by tightly-set lips, she already had a yellow complexion, with the silent countenance of a woman who has but one desire, one purpose in life, like a nun long immured in the cloister. She had just reached thirty, and lived henceforth solely for deeds of charity on a colossal scale.

The surprise of Paris was very great, and all sorts of extraordinary stories began to circulate. The Princess had inherited her husband's entire fortune, the famous three hundred millions of francs,[10] which the newspapers were always talking about. And the legend which finally sprang up was a romantic one. A man, a mysterious stranger dressed in black, it was said, had suddenly appeared one evening in the Princess's chamber just as she was going to bed, without her ever understanding by what secret door he had gained admission; and what this man had told her no one in the world knew; but he must have revealed to her the abominable origin of those three hundred millions, and perhaps have exacted from her an oath to offer reparation for so many iniquities, if she wished to avoid the most frightful catastrophes. Then the man had disappeared; and now during the five years that she had been a widow, either in obedience to an order received from the realms beyond, or through a simple revolt of honesty when the record of her fortune had fallen into her hands, she had lived in a burning fever of renunciation and reparation. All the pent-up feelings of this woman, who had not known love, and who had not succeeded in becoming a mother, and especially her unsatisfied affection for children, blossomed forth in a veritable passion for the poor, the weak, the disinherited, the suffering, from whom she believed the stolen millions to be withheld, to whom she swore to restore them royally in a rain of alms. A fixed idea took possession of her, a thought she could not get rid of had been driven into her brain; she henceforth simply looked upon herself as a banker with whom the poor had deposited those millions, in order that they might be employed for their benefit in the most advantageous way. She herself was but an accountant, a business agent, living in a realm to figures, amidst a population of notaries, architects, and workmen. She had established a vast office in town, where a score of employees worked. In her three small rooms at home she only received four or five intermediaries, her lieutenants; and there she passed her days, at a desk, like the director of some great enterprise, cloistered far away from the importunate among a growing heap of papers spread out all around her. It was a dream to relieve every misery, from that of the child who suffers from being born, to that of the old man who cannot die without suffering. During those five years, scattering gold by the handful, she had founded the St. Mary's Infant Asylum at La Villette—an asylum with white cradles for the very little and blue beds for the bigger ones—a vast, well-lighted establishment, already occupied by three hundred children; then had come the St. Joseph's Orphan Asylum at Saint Mandé, where a hundred boys and a hundred girls received such education and training as are given in *bourgeois* families; next an asylum for the aged at Châtillon, capable of accommodating fifty men and fifty women, and finally a hospital—the St. Marceau Hospital it was called—in one of the suburbs of Paris. Here the wards, containing a couple of hundred beds, had only just been opened. But her favourite foundation, that which at this moment absorbed her whole heart, was the Institute of Work,[11] a creation of her own, which was to take the place of the House of Correction, and where three hundred children, one hundred and fifty girls and one hundred and fifty boys, rescued from crime and debauchery on the pavements of Paris, were to be regenerated by good care and apprenticeship at a trade. These various foundations, with large donations to public establishments and a reckless prodigality in private charity, had in five years devoured almost a hundred millions of francs. At this rate, in a few years more she would be ruined, without having reserved even a small income to buy the bread and milk upon which she now lived. When her old servant Sophie, breaking her accustomed silence, scolded her with a harsh word, prophesying that she would die a beggar, she gave a feeble smile, now the only one that ever appeared on her colourless lips, a divine smile of hope.

It was precisely in connection with the Institute of Work that Saccard made Princess d'Orviedo's acquaintance. He was one of the owners of the land which she bought for this institution, an old garden planted with beautiful trees reaching to the Park of Neuilly, and skirting the Boulevard Bineau. He had attracted her by his brisk way of doing business; and, certain difficulties arising with her contractors, she wished to see him again. He himself had become greatly interested in what she was doing—struck, charmed by the grand plan which she had imposed upon the architect: two monumental wings, one for the boys, the other for the girls, connected with each other by a main building containing the chapel, the common departments, the offices, and various services; and each wing with its spacious yard, its workshops, its outbuildings of all sorts. But what particularly fired his enthusiasm, given his own taste for the grand and the gorgeous, was the luxury displayed, the very vastness of the edifice, the materials employed in building it—materials which would defy the centuries—the marble lavished upon all sides, the kitchen walled and floored with *faïence*, and with sufficient accommodation for the roasting of an ox, the gigantic dining-halls with rich oak panellings and ceilings, the dormitories flooded with light and enlivened with bright paintings, the linen room, the bath room, and the infirmary, where all the appointments bespoke extreme refinement; and on all sides there were broad entrances, stairways, corridors, ventilated in summer and heated in winter; and the entire house, bathed in the sunlight, had the gaiety of youth, the complete comfort which only immense wealth can procure. When the anxious architect, considering all this magnificence useless, spoke to the Princess of the expense, she stopped him with a word: she had enjoyed luxury; she wished to give it to the poor, that they might enjoy it in their turn—they who create the luxury of the rich. Her fixed idea centred in this dream; to gratify every desire of the wretched, to provide them with the same beds, the same fare, as the fortunate ones of this world.

There was to be no question of a crust of bread, or a chance pallet by way of alms; but life on a large scale within this palace, where they would be at home, taking their revenge, tasting the enjoyment of conquerors. Only, amidst all this squandering, all these enormous estimates, she was abominably robbed; a swarm of contractors lived upon her, to say nothing of the losses due to inadequate superintendence; the property of the poor was being wasted. And it was Saccard who opened her eyes to this, begging her to let him set her accounts straight. And he did this in a thoroughly disinterested way, solely for the pleasure of regulating this mad dance of millions which aroused his enthusiasm. Never before had he shown himself so scrupulously honest. In this colossal, complicated affair he proved the most active, most upright of helpers, giving his time and even his money, taking his reward simply in the delight which he felt at such large sums passing through his hands. Scarcely anyone but himself was known at the Institute of Work, whither the Princess never went, any more than she visited her other establishments, preferring to remain hidden within her three little rooms, like some invisible good fairy, whilst he was adored, blessed, overwhelmed with all the gratitude which she did not seem to desire.

It was at this time undoubtedly that Saccard began nursing the indefinite project, which, when once he was installed as a tenant in the Orviedo mansion, became transformed into a sharp, well-defined desire. Why should he not devote himself entirely to the management of the Princess's charitable enterprises? In the period of doubt in which he found himself, vanquished on the field of speculation, not knowing how to rebuild his fortune, this course appeared to him like a new incarnation, a sudden deifical ascent. To become the dispenser of that royal charity, the channel through which would roll that flood of gold that was pouring upon Paris! There were two hundred millions left; what works might still be created, what a city of miracle might be made to spring from the soil! To say nothing of the fact that he would make those millions fruitful, double, triple them, know so well how to employ them that he would make them yield a world. Then, in his passionate fever, his ideas broadened; he lived in this one intoxicating thought of scattering those millions broadcast in endless alms, of drowning all happy France with them; and he grew sentimental, for his probity was without a reproach—not a sou stuck to his fingers. In his brain—the brain of a visionary—a giant idyl took shape, the idyl of one free from all self-consciousness, an idyl in no wise due to any desire to atone for his old financial brigandage. There was the less cause for any such desire, as at the end there still lay the dream of his entire life, the conquest of Paris. To be the king of charity, the adored God of the multitude of the poor, to become unique and popular, to occupy the attention of the world—it even surpassed his ambition. What prodigies could he not realize, should he employ in goodness his business faculties, his strategy, obstinacy, and utter freedom from prejudice! And he would have the irresistible power which wins battles, money, coffers full of money, which often does so much harm, and which would do so much good as soon as it should be used to satisfy his pride and pleasure.

Then, enlarging his project still further, Saccard came to the point of asking himself why he should not marry the Princess d'Orviedo. That would determine their mutual position, and prevent all evil interpretations. For a month he manœuvred adroitly, disclosed superb plans, sought to make himself indispensable; and one day, in a tranquil voice, again becoming ingenuous, he made his proposal, developed his great project. It was a veritable partnership that he proposed; he offered himself as the liquidator of the sums stolen by the Prince; pledged himself to return them to the poor tenfold. The Princess, in her eternal black dress, with her lace fichu on her head, listened to him attentively, no emotion whatever animating her sallow face. She was very much struck with the advantages that such an association might offer, and quite indifferent to the other considerations. However, having postponed her answer till the next day, she finally refused; she had upon reflection doubtless realized that she would no longer be sole mistress of her charities, and these she meant to dispense with absolute sovereignty, even if she did so madly. However, she explained that she would be happy to retain him as a counsellor; and showed how precious she considered his collaboration by begging him to continue to attend to the Institute of Work, of which he was the real director.

For a whole week Saccard experienced violent chagrin, as one does at the loss of a cherished idea; not that he felt himself falling back into the abyss of brigandage; but, just as a sentimental song will bring tears to the eyes of the most abject drunkard, so this colossal idyl of good accomplished by dint of millions had moved his corsair soul. Once more he fell, and from a great height: it seemed to him that he was dethroned. From money he had always sought to derive, in addition to the satisfaction of his appetites, the magnificence of a princely life, and never had he sufficiently achieved it. He grew enraged as one by one his tumbles carried away his hopes. And thus, when his project was destroyed by the Princess's quiet, precise refusal, he was thrown back into a furious desire for battle. To fight, to prove the strongest in the stern war of speculation, to eat up others in order to keep them from eating him, was, after his thirst for splendour and enjoyment, the one great motive of his passion for business. Though he did not heap up treasure, he had another joy, the delight attending on the struggle between vast amounts of money pitted against one another—fortunes set in battle array, like contending army corps, the clash of conflicting millions, with defeats and victories that intoxicated him. And forthwith there returned his hatred of Gundermann, his ungovernable longing for revenge. To conquer Gundermann was the chimerical desire that haunted him, each time that he found himself prostrate, vanquished. Though he felt the childish folly attaching to such an attempt, might he not at least cut into him, make a place for himself opposite him, force him to share, like those monarchs of neighbouring countries and equal power who treat each other as cousins? Then it was that the Bourse again attracted him; his head once more became full of schemes that he might launch; conflicting projects claimed him in all directions, putting him in such a fever that he knew not what to decide until the day came when a supreme, stupendous idea evolved itself from amidst all the others, and gradually gained entire possession of him.

Since he had been living in the Orviedo mansion, Saccard had occasionally seen the sister of the engineer Hamelin, who lived in the little suite of rooms on the second floor, a woman with an admirable figure—Madame Caroline she was familiarly called. What had especially struck him, at their first meeting, was her superb white hair, a royal crown of white hair, which had a most singular effect on the brow of this woman, who was still young, scarcely thirty-six years old. At the age of five and twenty her hair had thus turned completely white. Her eyebrows, which had remained black and very thick, imparted an expression of youth, and of extreme oddity, to her ermine-girt countenance. She had never been pretty, for her nose and chin were too pronounced, and her mouth large with thick lips expressive of exquisite kindliness. But certainly that white fleece, that wavy whiteness of fine silken hair, softened her rather stern physiognomy, and added a grandmother's smiling charm to the freshness and vigour of a beautiful, passionate woman. She was tall and strongly built, with a free and very noble carriage.

Every time he met her, Saccard, shorter than she was, followed her with his eyes, in an interested way, secretly envying her tall figure, her healthy breadth of shoulders. And gradually, through the servants, he became acquainted with the whole history of the Hamelins, Caroline and George. They were the children of a Montpellier physician, a remarkable *savant*, an enthusiastic Catholic, who had died poor. At the time of their father's death the girl was eighteen and the boy nineteen; and, the latter having just entered the Polytechnic School, his sister followed him to Paris, where she secured a place as governess. It was she who slipped five-franc pieces into his hand, and kept him in pocket-money during his two years' course; later, when, having graduated with a low rank, he had to tramp the pavements, it was still she who supported him until he found employment. They adored each other, and it was their dream never to separate. Nevertheless, an unhoped-for marriage offering itself—the good grace and keen intelligence of the young girl having made the conquest of a millionaire brewer in the house where she was employed—George wished her to accept; a thing which he cruelly repented of, for, after a few years of married life, Caroline was obliged to apply for a separation in order to avoid being killed by her husband, who drank and pursued her with a knife in fits of imbecile jealousy. She was then twenty-six years old, and again found herself poor, obstinately refusing to claim any alimony from the man whom she left. But her brother had at last, after many attempts, put his hand upon a work that pleased him: he was about to start for Egypt, with the Commission appointed to prosecute the first investigations connected with the Suez Canal, and he took his sister with him. She bravely established herself at Alexandria, and again began giving lessons, while he travelled about the country. Thus they remained in Egypt until 1859, and saw the first blows of the pick struck upon the shore at Port Said by a meagre gang of barely a hundred and fifty navvies, lost amid the sands, and commanded by a handful of engineers. Then Hamelin, having been sent to Syria to ensure a constant supply of provisions, remained there, in consequence of a quarrel with his chiefs. He made Caroline come to Beyrout, where other pupils awaited her, and launched out into a big enterprise, under the patronage of a French company—

the laying out of a carriage road from Beyrout to Damascus, the first, the only route opened through the passes of the Lebanon range. And thus they lived there three years longer, until the road was finished; he visiting the mountains, absenting himself for two months to make a trip to Constantinople through the Taurus, she following him as soon as she could escape, and fully sharing the revivalist projects which he formed, whilst tramping about this old land, slumbering beneath the ashes of dead and vanished civilisations. He had a portfolio full of ideas and plans, and felt the imperative necessity of returning to France if he was to give shape to all his vast schemes, establish companies, and find the necessary capital. And so, after nine years' residence in the East, they started off, and curiosity prompted them to return by way of Egypt, where the progress made with the works of the Suez Canal filled them with enthusiasm. In four years a city had grown up on the strand at Port Said; an entire people was swarming there; the human ants were multiplying, changing the face of the earth. In Paris, however, dire ill-luck awaited Hamelin. For fifteen months he struggled on with his projects, unable to impart his faith to anyone, too modest as he was, too taciturn, stranded on that second floor of the Orviedo mansion, in a little suite of five rooms, for which he paid twelve hundred francs a year, farther from success than he had even been when roaming over the mountains and plains of Asia. Their savings rapidly decreased, and brother and sister came at last to a position of great embarrassment.

In fact, it was this that interested Saccard—the growing sadness of Madame Caroline, whose hearty gaiety was dimmed by the discouragement into which she saw her brother falling. She was to some extent the man of the household; George, who greatly resembled her physically, though of slighter build, had a rare faculty for work, but he became absorbed in his studies, and did not like to be roused from them. Never had he cared to marry, not feeling the need of doing so, his adoration of his sister sufficing him. This whilom student of the Polytechnic School, whose conceptions were so vast, whose zeal was so ardent in everything he undertook, at times evinced such simplicity that one would have deemed him rather stupid. Brought up, too, in the narrowest Romanism he had kept the religious faith of a child, careful in his observance of all rites and ceremonies like a thorough believer; whereas his sister had regained possession of herself by dint of reading and learning during the long hours when he was plunged in his technical tasks. She spoke four languages; she had read the economists and the philosophers, and had for a time been moved to enthusiasm by socialistic and evolutionary theories. Subsequently, however, she had quieted down, acquiring—notably by her travels, her long residence among far-off civilisations—a broad spirit of tolerance and well-balanced common-sense. Though she herself no longer believed, she retained great respect for her brother's faith. There had been one explanation between them, after which they had never referred to the matter again. She, with her simplicity and good-nature, was a woman of real intelligence; and, facing life with extraordinary courage, with a gay bravery which withstood the cruel blows of fate, she was in the habit of saying that a single sorrow alone remained within her—that of never having had a child.

Saccard was able to render Hamelin a service—some little work which he secured for him from some investors who needed an engineer to report upon the output of a new machine, and thus he forced an intimacy with the brother and sister, and frequently went up to spend an hour with them in their *salon*, their only large room, which they had transformed into a work room. This room remained virtually bare, for its only furniture consisted of a long designing table, a smaller table covered with papers, and half a dozen chairs. Books were heaped up on the mantel-shelf, whilst on the walls an improvised decoration enlivened the blank space—a series of plans, of bright water-colour drawings, each held in place by four tacks. The plans were those which Hamelin had gathered together in his portfolio of projects; they were the notes he had taken in Syria, the bases on which he hoped to build up all his future fortune; whereas the water-colours were the work of Madame Caroline—Eastern views, types, and costumes which she had noted while accompanying her brother about, which she had sketched with keen insight into the laws of colour, though in a very unpretending way. Two larger windows overlooking the garden of the Beauvilliers mansion admitted a bright light to illumine these straggling designs, typical of another life, of an ancient society sinking into dust, which the plans, firmly and mathematically outlined, seemed about to put upon its feet again, supported, as it were, by the solid scaffolding of modern science. And Saccard, when he had rendered himself useful, with that display of activity which made him so charming, would often linger before the plans and water-colours, seduced, and continually asking for fresh explanations. Vast schemes were already germinating in his brain.

One morning he found Madame Caroline seated alone at the little table which she used as her desk. She was dreadfully sad, her hands resting among her papers.

'What can you expect?' said she, 'things are turning out very badly. I am brave, but everything seems about to fail us at once; and what distresses me is the powerlessness to which misfortune reduces my poor brother, for he is not valiant, he has no strength except for work. I thought of getting another situation as governess, that I might at least help him. But I have sought, and found nothing. Yet I cannot go out working as a charwoman.'

Never had Saccard seen her so upset, so dejected. 'The devil! you have not come to that!' he cried.

She shook her head, and evinced great bitterness against life, which she usually accepted so jovially, even when at its worst. And Hamelin just then coming in with the news of a fresh disappointment, big tears ran slowly down her cheeks. She spoke no further, but sat there, her hands clenched on the table, her eyes wandering away into space.

'And to think,' said Hamelin, 'that there are millions awaiting us in the East, if someone would only help me to make them!'

Saccard had planted himself in front of a plan representing a view of a pavilion surrounded by vast store-houses. 'What is that?' he asked.

'Oh! something I did for my amusement,' explained the engineer. 'It's the plan of a dwelling at Beyrout for the manager of the Company which I dreamed of, you know, the United Steam Navigation Company.'

He became animated, and went into fresh particulars. During his stay in the East, he had noticed how defective were all the transport services. The various companies established at Marseilles were ruining one another by competition, and were unable to provide vessels in sufficient number or of sufficient comfort. One of his first ideas, the very basis indeed of his many enterprises, was to syndicate these services, to unite them in one vast, wealthy company, which should exploit the entire Mediterranean, and acquire the sovereign control thereof, by establishing lines to all the ports of Africa, Spain, Italy, Greece, Egypt, Asia, and even the remotest parts of the Black Sea. It was a scheme worthy at once of a shrewd organiser and a good patriot; it meant the

East conquered, given to France, to say nothing of the close relations which it would establish with Syria, where lay the vast field of his proposed operations.

'Syndicates,' murmured Saccard—'yes, nowadays the future seems to lie in that direction. It is such a powerful form of association! Three or four little enterprises, which vegetate in isolation, acquire irresistible vitality and prosperity as soon as they unite. Yes, to-morrow belongs to the association of capital, to the centralised efforts of immense masses. All industry and commerce will end in a single huge bazaar, where a man will provide himself with everything.'

He had stopped again, this time before a water-colour which represented a wild locality, an arid gorge, blocked up by a gigantic pile of rocks crowned with brambles. 'Oh! oh!' he resumed, 'here is the end of the world. There can be no danger of being jostled by passers-by in that nook.'

'A Carmel gorge,' answered Hamelin. 'My sister sketched it while I was making my studies in that neighbourhood,' and he added simply: 'See! between the cretaceous limestone and the porphyry which raised up that limestone over the entire mountain-side, there is a considerable vein of sulphuretted silver—yes, a silver mine, the working of which, according to my calculations, would yield enormous profits.'

'A silver mine?' repeated Saccard eagerly.

Madame Caroline, with her eyes still wandering far away, had overheard them amid her fit of sadness, and, as if a vision had risen before her, she said: 'Carmel, ah! what a desert, what days of solitude! It is full of myrtle and broom, which make the warm air balmy. And there are eagles continually circling aloft—and to think of all this silver, sleeping in that sepulchre, beside so much misery, where one would like to see happy multitudes, workshops, cities spring up—a whole people regenerated by toil.'

'A road could easily be opened from Carmel to Saint Jean d'Acre,' continued Hamelin. 'And I firmly believe that iron, too, would be found there, for it abounds in all the mountains in the neighbourhood. I have also studied a new system of extraction, by which large savings could be made. All is ready; it is only a matter of finding the capital.'

'The Carmel Silver Mining Company!' murmured Saccard.

But it was now the engineer who, with raised eyes, went from one plan to another, again full of this labour of his life, seized with fever, at thought of the brilliant future which was sleeping there while want was paralysing him. 'And these are only the small preliminary affairs,' he continued. 'Look at this series of plans; here is the grand stroke, a complete railway system traversing Asia Minor from end to end. The lack of convenient and rapid communication, that is the primary cause of the stagnation into which this rich country has sunk. You would not find a single carriage road there, travel and transport being invariably effected by means of mules or camels. So imagine the revolution if the iron horse could penetrate to the confines of the desert! Industry and commerce would be increased tenfold, civilisation would be victorious, Europe would at last open the gates of the East. Oh! if it interests you, we will talk of it in detail. And you shall see, you shall see!'

And such was his excitement that he could not refrain from straightway entering into explanations. It was especially during his journey to Constantinople that he had studied his projected railway system. The great, the only difficulty was presented by the Taurus mountains; but he had explored the different passes, and asserted that a direct and comparatively inexpensive line was possible. However, it was not his intention to make the system complete at one stroke. On obtaining a full grant from the Sultan, it would be prudent at the outset to merely lay down the mother line, from Broussa to Beyrout, by way of Angora and Aleppo. Later on, they might lay down branch lines from Smyrna to Angora, and from Trebizond to Angora, by way of Erzeroum and Sivas. 'And after that, and after that,' he continued; but, instead of finishing, he contented himself with a smile, not daring to tell how far he had carried the audacity of his projects.

'Ah! the plains at the foot of Taurus,' said Madame Caroline, in the slow, low voice of an awakened sleeper; 'what a delightful paradise! One has only to scratch the earth, and harvests spring up in abundance. The boughs of the fruit trees, peach, cherry, fig, and almond, break under their weight of fruit. And what fields of olive and mulberry— dense as woods! And what a natural, easy existence in that light atmosphere, under that sky for ever blue!'

Saccard began to laugh, with that shrill laugh betokening a fine appetite, which was his whenever he scented fortune. And, as Hamelin went on talking yet of more projects, notably of the establishment of a bank at Constantinople, with just an allusion to the all-powerful relations which he had left behind him, especially with the *entourage* of the Grand Vizier, he interrupted him to say gaily: 'Why, it is Tom Tiddler's land, one could sell it!' Then, very familiarly resting both hands on the shoulders of Madame Caroline, who was still sitting at the table, he added: 'Don't despair, madame. I have great sympathy for you; between us, your brother and I, we will do something that will benefit all of us. You'll see; be patient, and wait.'

During the ensuing month Saccard again procured some little jobs for the engineer; and though he talked no further of the latter's grand enterprises, he must have steadily thought of them, hesitating the while on account of their crushing magnitude.

The bond of intimacy between them was drawn tighter, however, by the wholly natural fashion in which Madame Caroline came to occupy herself with his household, the household of a single man, whose resources were diminished by useless expenses, and who was the worse served the more servants he had. He, so shrewd out of doors, famous for the vigour and cunning of his hand when any huge robbery had to be perpetrated, let everything go helter-skelter at home, careless of the frightful waste that tripled his expenses; and the absence of a woman was cruelly felt, even in the smallest matters. When Madame Caroline perceived how he was being pillaged, she at first gave him advice, and then intervened in person, with the result of effecting a saving in two or three directions, so that one day he laughingly offered her a position as his housekeeper. Why not? She had sought a place as governess, and might well accept an honourable situation, which would permit her to wait. The offer made in jest became a serious one. Would it not give her occupation, and enable her to assist her brother to the extent, at any rate, of the three hundred francs a month that Saccard was willing to give? And so she accepted. She reformed the household in a week, discharging the *chef* and his wife, and replacing them by a female cook, who, with the valet and the coachman, would suffice for Saccard's requirements. Further, she retained but one horse and one carriage, assumed authority over everything, and examined the accounts with such scrupulous care that at the end of the first fortnight she had reduced expenses by one-half. He was delighted, and jokingly told her that it was he who was now robbing her, and that she ought to have claimed a percentage on all the profits that she realised for him.

Then a very intimate life began. Saccard had the idea of removing the screws that fastened the door which supplied communication between the two suites of rooms, and they went up and down freely, from one dining-room to the other, by the inner staircase. While her brother was at work, shut up from morning till night, busy with the task of putting his Eastern designs in order, Madame Caroline, leaving her own household to the care of the one servant in her employ, came down at all hours of the day to give her orders, as though she were at home. It had become Saccard's joy to see this tall, stately woman continually appear and cross the rooms with a firm, superb step, bringing with her the ever-unexpected gaiety of her white hair flying about her young face. Again she was very gay; she had recovered her courage now that she felt she was useful once more, her time occupied, her feet ever on the move. Without any affectation of simplicity, she always wore a black dress, in the pocket of which could be heard the jingling of her bunch of keys; and it certainly amused her—she, the woman of learning, the philosopher—to be solely a good housewife, the housekeeper of a prodigal, whom she was beginning to love as one loves naughty children. He, greatly attracted for a time, calculating that after all there was but a difference of fourteen years between them, had asked himself what would happen should he some day talk to her of love. He knew, however, that a friend of her brother's, a Monsieur Beaudoin, a merchant whom they had left at Beyrout, and whose return to France was near at hand, had been much in love with her, to the point indeed of offering to wait for the death of her husband, who had just been shut up in an asylum, crazy with alcoholism.

In this connection it suddenly happened that Madame Caroline subsided into deep sorrow. One morning she came down dejected, extremely pale, and with heavy eyes. Saccard could learn nothing from her; in fact, he ceased to question her, so obstinately did she declare that there was no trouble, and that she was just as usual. Only on the following day did he understand matters on finding in the rooms upstairs the printed notification of M. Beaudoin's marriage to an English consul's daughter, who was both very young and immensely rich. The blow must have been the harder because of the arrival of the news in this way, without any preparation, without even a farewell. It was a complete collapse in the unfortunate woman's existence, the loss of the far-off hope to which she had clung in hours of disaster. And chance also proved abominably cruel, for only two days before she had learnt that her husband was dead; for forty-eight hours she had been able to believe in the approaching realisation of her dream, and then her life had fallen into ruin, leaving her as if annihilated. That same evening, when, in accordance with her habit, she entered Saccard's rooms to talk of the orders for the next day, he spoke to her of her misfortune so gently that she burst out sobbing; and then the inevitable came to pass, words of comfort were at last followed by words of love, and Madame Caroline fell.

For a fortnight afterwards she remained in a state of frightful sadness. The strength of life, that impulse which makes existence a necessity and a delight, had abandoned her. She attended to her manifold occupations, but like one whose mind was far away, without any illusion as to the ratio and interest of things. She personified the human machine still toiling on, but in despair over the annihilation of everything. And, amid this shipwreck of her bravery and gaiety, she had but one distraction, that of passing all her spare time with her brow pressed against the panes of one of the windows of the large work-room, her eyes fixed upon the garden of the neighbouring mansion, that Hôtel Beauvilliers where, since the first days of her sojourn in the neighbourhood, she had divined the presence of anguish, of one of those hidden miseries which are all the more distressing by reason of the effort made to save appearances. There, too, were beings who suffered, and her sorrow was, so to speak, steeped in their tears; at sight of which she was so overcome with melancholy as to deem herself insensible, dead, lost in the sorrow of others.

These Beauvilliers—who, to say nothing of their immense estates in Touraine and Anjou, had formerly possessed a magnificent mansion in the Rue de Grenelle—now, in Paris, only owned this old pleasure-house, built at the beginning of the last century outside the city walls, and at present shut in among the gloomy buildings of the Rue Saint-Lazare. The few beautiful trees of the garden lingered there, as at the bottom of a well; and the cracked, crumbling entrance-steps were covered with moss. The place seemed like some corner of Nature put in prison, a meek, mournful nook where dumb despair reigned, and where the sun only cast a greenish light, which chilled one's shoulders. And in this still, damp, cellar-like place, at the top of the disjoined steps, the first person noticed by Madame Caroline had been the Countess de Beauvilliers, a tall, thin woman of sixty, with perfectly white hair and a very noble old-time air. With her large straight nose, thin lips, and particularly long neck, she looked like a very old swan, meekly woeful. Then, almost immediately behind her, had come her daughter, Alice de Beauvilliers, now twenty-five years old, but with such an impoverished constitution that one would have taken her for a little girl, had it not been for the spoiled complexion and already drawn features of her face. She was her mother over again, but more puny and with less aristocratic nobility, her neck elongated to the point of ugliness, having nothing left her, indeed, but the pitiful charm that may cling to the last daughter of a great race. The two women had been living alone since the son, Ferdinand de Beauvilliers, had enlisted in the Pontifical Zouaves, after the battle of Castelfidardo, lost by Lamoricière. Every day, when it did not rain, they thus appeared, one behind the other, and, descending the steps, made the circuit of the little central grass-plot, without exchanging a word. The path was merely edged with ivy; flowers would not have grown in such a spot, or perhaps they would have cost too dear. And the slow promenade—undoubtedly a simple constitutional—made by those two pale women, under the centenarian trees which long ago had witnessed so many festivities, and which the neighbouring *bourgeois* houses were now stifling, was suggestive of a melancholy grief, as though they had been performing some mourning ceremony for old, dead things.

Her interest aroused, Madame Caroline had watched her neighbours out of tender sympathy, without evil curiosity of any kind; and gradually from her view of the garden she penetrated their life, which they hid with jealous care from the street. There was still a horse in the stable, and a carriage in the coach-house, in the care of an old domestic who was at once valet, coachman, and door-porter; just as there was a cook, who also served as a chambermaid; but if the carriage went out at the main gate, with the horse properly harnessed, to take the ladies visiting, and if there was a certain display at table in the winter, at the fortnightly dinners to which a few friends came, how long were the fasts, how sordid the economies that were hourly practised in order to secure this false semblance of fortune! In a little shed, screened from every eye, there were, in order to reduce the laundry bill, continual washings of wretched garments worn out by frequent soaping, and mended thread by thread; three or four vegetables were picked for the evening meal; bread was allowed to grow stale on a board, in order that less of it might be eaten; all sorts of avaricious, mean, and

44

touching practices were resorted to: the old coachman would sew up the holes in Mademoiselle's boots, the cook would blacken the tips of Madame's faded gloves with ink; and then the mother's dresses were passed over to the daughter after ingenious transformations; and hats and bonnets lasted for years, thanks to changes of flowers and ribbons.

When they were expecting no one, the reception rooms on the ground floor were kept carefully closed, as well as the large apartments of the first storey; for, of the whole large pile, the two women now occupied but one small room, which they used both as their dining-room and boudoir. When the window was partly open, the Countess could be seen mending her linen, like some needy little *bourgeoise*; while the young girl, between her piano and her box of water-colours, knit stockings and mittens for her mother. One very stormy day, both were seen to go down into the garden, and gather up the sand of the pathway, which the violence of the rain was sweeping away.

Madame Caroline now knew their history. The Countess de Beauvilliers had suffered much from her husband, a rake of whom she had never complained. One evening they had brought him home to her at Vendôme, with the death-rattle in his throat and a bullet-hole through his body. There was talk of a hunting accident, some shot fired by a jealous gamekeeper whose wife or daughter he had probably seduced. And the worst of it was that with him vanished that formerly colossal fortune of the Beauvilliers, consisting of immense tracts of land, regal domains, which the Revolution had already found diminished, and which his father and himself had now exhausted. Of all the vast property, a single farm remained, the Aublets, situated at a few leagues from Vendôme and yielding a rental of about fifteen thousand francs, the sole resource left for the widow and her two children. The mansion in the Rue de Grenelle had long since been sold; and that in the Rue Saint-Lazare consumed the larger part of the fifteen thousand francs derived from the farm, for it was heavily mortgaged, and would in its turn be sold if they did not pay the interest. Thus scarcely six or seven thousand francs were left for the support of four persons, of the household of a noble family still unwilling to abdicate. It was now eight years since the Countess, on becoming a widow with a son of twenty and a daughter of seventeen, had, amid the crumbling of her fortune, and with her aristocratic pride waxing within her, sworn that she would live on bread and water rather than fall. From that time she had indeed had but one thought—to hold her rank, to marry her daughter to a man of equal nobility, and to make a soldier of her son. At first Ferdinand had caused her mortal anxieties in consequence of some youthful follies, debts which it became necessary to pay; but, warned of the situation in a solemn interview with his mother, he had not repeated the offence, for he had a tender heart at bottom, albeit he was simply an idle cypher in the world, unfitted for any employment, any possible place in contemporary society. And, now that he was a soldier of the Pope, he was still a cause of secret anguish to the Countess, for he lacked health, delicate despite his proud bearing, with impoverished, feeble blood, which rendered the Roman climate dangerous for him. As for Alice's marriage, it was so slow in coming that the sad mother's eyes filled with tears when she looked at her daughter already growing old, withering whilst she waited. Despite her air of melancholy insignificance, the girl was not stupid; she had ardent aspirations for life, for a man who would love her, for happiness; but, not wishing to plunge the house into yet deeper grief, she pretended to have renounced everything; making a jest of marriage, and saying that it was her vocation to be an old maid; though at night she would weep on her pillow, almost dying of grief at the thought that she would never be mated. The Countess, however, by prodigies of avarice, had succeeded in laying aside twenty thousand francs, which constituted Alice's entire dowry. She had likewise saved from the wreck a few jewels—a bracelet, some finger-rings and ear-rings, the whole possibly worth ten thousand francs—a very meagre dowry, a wedding-gift of which she did not dare to speak, since it was scarcely enough to meet the necessary expenditure, should the awaited husband ever appear. And yet she would not despair, but struggled on in spite of everything, unwilling to abandon a single one of the privileges of her birth, still as haughty, as observant of the proprieties as ever, incapable of going out on foot, or of cutting off a single *entremets* when she was receiving guests, but ever reducing the outlay of her hidden life, condemning herself for weeks to potatoes without butter, in order that she might add another fifty francs to her daughter's ever-insufficient dowry. It was a painful, puerile daily heroism that she practised, whilst week by week the house was crumbling a little more about their heads.

So far, however, Madame Caroline had not had an opportunity of speaking to the Countess and her daughter. Although she finally came to know the most private details of their life, those which they hid from the entire world, she had as yet only exchanged glances with them, those glances that suddenly turn into a feeling of secret sympathy. The Princess d'Orviedo was destined to bring them together. She had the idea of appointing a sort of committee of superintendence for her Institute of Work—a committee composed of ten ladies, who would meet twice a month, visit the Institute in detail, and see that all the departments were properly managed. Having reserved the selection of these ladies for herself, she designated, among the very first, Madame de Beauvilliers, who had been a great friend of hers in former days, but had become simply her neighbour, now that she had retired from the world. And it had come about that the committee of superintendence, having suddenly lost its secretary, Saccard, who retained authority over the management of the establishment, had recommended Madame Caroline as a model secretary, such a one as could not be found elsewhere. The duties of the post were rather arduous; there was much clerical work, and even some material cares, that were somewhat repugnant to the ladies of the committee. From the start, however, Madame Caroline had shown herself an admirable hospitaller; for her unsatisfied longing for maternity, her hopeless love of children, kindled within her an active tenderness for all those poor creatures whom it was sought to save from the Parisian gutter. In this wise, at the last meeting of the committee, she had met the Countess de Beauvilliers; but the latter had given her rather a cold salute, striving to conceal her secret embarrassment, for she undoubtedly realised that this Madame Caroline was an eye-witness of her poverty. However, they now both bowed whenever their eyes met, since it would have been gross impoliteness to pretend they did not recognise each other.

One day, in the large workroom, while Hamelin was correcting a plan in accordance with some new calculations he had made, and Saccard, standing by, was watching his work, Madame Caroline, at the window as usual, gazed at the Countess and her daughter as they made their tour of the garden. That morning she noticed that they were wearing shoes which a rag-picker would have scorned to touch.

'Ah! the poor women!' she murmured; 'how terrible and distressing it must be, that comedy of luxury which they think themselves obliged to play!'

So saying, she drew back, hiding herself behind the window-curtain, for fear lest the mother should see her and suffer yet more intensely at being thus watched. She herself had grown calmer during the three weeks that she had been lingering every morning at that window; the great sorrow born of her abandonment was quieting down; it seemed as if the sight of the woes of others induced a more courageous acceptance of her own, that fall which she had deemed the fall of her entire life. Again, indeed, she occasionally caught herself laughing.

For a moment longer, and with an air of profound meditation, she watched the two women pace the garden, green with moss; then, quickly turning towards Saccard, she exclaimed: 'Tell me why it is that I cannot be sad. No, it never lasts, has never lasted; I cannot be sad, whatever happens to me. Is it egotism? Really, I do not think so. Egotism would be wrong; and, besides, it is in vain that I am gay; my heart seems ready to break at sight of the least sorrow. Reconcile these things; I am gay, and yet I should weep over all the unfortunates who pass if I did not restrain myself— understanding as I do that the smallest scrap of bread would serve their purpose better than my vain tears.'

So speaking, she laughed her beautiful brave laugh, like a courageous woman who prefers action to garrulous pity.

'And yet,' she continued, 'God knows that I have had occasion to despair of everything! Ah! fortune has not favoured me so far. After my marriage, falling as I did into a perfect hell, insulted, beaten, I really believed that there was nothing for me to do but to throw myself into the water. I did not throw myself into it, however, and a fortnight later, when I started with my brother for the East, I was quite lively again, full of immense hope. And at the time of our return to Paris, when almost everything else failed us, I passed abominable nights, when I pictured ourselves dying of hunger amid all our fine projects. We did not die, however, and again I began to dream of wonderful things, happy things, that sometimes made me laugh as I sat alone. And lately, when I received that frightful blow, which I still don't dare to speak of, my heart seemed torn away; yes, I positively felt it stop beating; I thought that it had ceased to be, I fancied that I myself no longer existed, annihilated as I was. But not at all! Here is existence returning; to-day I laugh, and to-morrow I shall hope; I shall be longing to live on, to live for ever. Is it not extraordinary that I cannot long be sad?'

Saccard, who was laughing also, shrugged his shoulders. 'Bah! you are like the rest of the world. Such is life,' he said.

'Do you think so?' she cried, in astonishment. 'It seems to me there are some people who are so sad that they never know a gay moment, people who render their own life intolerable, in such dark colours do they paint it. Oh! not that I entertain any illusion as to the pleasantness and beauty which it offers. In my case it has been too hard: I have seen it too closely, too freely, under all aspects. It is execrable when it is not ignoble. But what would you have? I love it all the same. Why? I do not know. In vain does everything crumble around me; on the morrow I find myself standing on the ruins, gay and confident. I have often thought that my case is, on a small scale, the case of humanity, which certainly lives in frightful wretchedness, cheered up, however, by the youth of each succeeding generation. After each crisis that throws me down, there comes something like a new youth, a spring time whose promise of sap warms me and inspirits my heart. So true is this that, after some severe affliction, if I go out into the street, into the sunshine, I straightway begin loving, hoping, feeling happy again. And age has no influence upon me; I am simple enough to grow old

47

without noticing it. You see, I have read a great deal more than a woman should; I no longer know where I myself am going, any more than this vast world knows where it is going, for that matter. Only, in spite of myself, it seems to me that I am going, indeed that we are all going, towards something very good and thoroughly gay.'

Although affected, she ended by turning the matter into jest, trying to hide the emotion born of her hope; whilst her brother, who had raised his head, looked at her with mingled adoration and gratitude.

'Oh! you,' he declared, 'you are made for catastrophes; you personify the love of life, whatever it may be.'

These daily morning conversations gradually became instinct with a kind of fever. If Madame Caroline returned to that natural inherent gaiety of hers, it was due to the courage which Saccard, with his active zeal for great enterprises, imparted. It was, indeed, now almost decided: they were going to turn the famous portfolio to account; and when the financier's shrill voice rang out everything seemed to acquire life, to assume colossal proportions. They would, in the first place, lay hands on the Mediterranean, conquer it by means of their steamship company. And, enumerating all the ports where they would establish stations, he mingled dim classical memories with his stock-exchange enthusiasm, chanting the praises of that sea, the only one which the old world had known, that blue sea around which civilisation had blossomed, and whose waves had bathed the ancient cities—Athens, Rome, Tyre, Alexandria, Carthage, Marseilles—all those seats of commerce and empire that have made Europe. Then, when they had ensured themselves possession of that vast waterway to the East, they would make a start in Syria with that little matter of the Carmel Silver Mining Company, just a few millions to gain *en passant*, but a capital thing to introduce, for the idea of a silver mine, of money found in the bowels of the earth and thrown up by the shovelful, was still attractive to the public, especially when ticketed with a prodigious, resounding name like that of Carmel. There were also coal mines there, coal just beneath the rock, which would be worth gold when the country should be covered with factories; to say nothing of other little ventures, which would serve as interludes—the establishment of banks and industrial syndicates, and the opening up and felling of the vast Lebanon forests, whose huge trees were rotting where they stood for want of roads. Finally, he came to the giant morsel, the Oriental Railway Company, and then he began to rave, for that system of railroads cast over Asia Minor from one end to the other, like a net, to him meant speculation, financial life, at one stroke seizing hold of a new prey—that old world still intact, with incalculable wealth concealed under the ignorance and grime of ages. He scented the treasure, and neighed like a war-horse at the smell of powder.

Madame Caroline, albeit possessed of sterling good sense, and not easily influenced by feverish imaginations, yielded at last to this enthusiasm, no longer detecting its extravagance. In truth, it fanned her affection for the East, her longing to again behold that wonderful country, where she had thought herself so happy; and, by a logical counter-effect, without calculation on her part, it was she who, by her glowing descriptions and wealth of information, stimulated the fever of Saccard. When she began talking of Beyrout, where she had lived for three years, she could never stop; Beyrout lying at the foot of the Lebanon range, on a tongue of land, between a stretch of red sand and piles of fallen rock; Beyrout with its houses reared in amphitheatral fashion amid vast gardens; a delightful paradise of orange, lemon, and palm trees. Then there were all the cities of the coast: on the north, Antioch, fallen from its whilom splendour; on the south, Saida, the Sidon of long ago, Saint Jean d'Acre, Jaffa, and Tyre, now Sur, which sums them all up: Tyre, whose merchants were kings, whose mariners made the circuit of Africa, and which to-day, with its sand-choked harbour, is nothing but a field of ruins, the dust of palaces, where stand only a few fishermen's wretched and scattered huts.

And Madame Caroline had accompanied her brother everywhere; she knew Aleppo, Angora, Broussa, Smyrna, and even Trebizond. She had lived a month at Jerusalem, sleeping amid the traffic of the holy places; then two months more at Damascus, the queen of the East, standing in the midst of a vast plain—a commercial, industrial city, which the Mecca and Bagdad caravans fill with swarming life. She was also acquainted with the valleys and mountains, with the villages of the Maronites and the Druses, perched upon table-lands or hidden away in gorges, and with the cultivated and the sterile fields. And from the smallest nooks, from the silent deserts as from the great cities, she had brought back the same admiration for inexhaustible, luxuriant nature, the same wrath against evil-minded humanity. How much natural wealth was disdained or wasted! She spoke of the burdens that crushed both commerce and industry, the imbecile law that prevents the investment of more than a certain amount of capital in agriculture, the routine that leaves the peasant with nothing but the old plough which was in use before the days of Christ, and the ignorance in which millions of men are steeped even to-day, like idiotic children stopped in their growth. Once upon a time the coast had proved too small; the cities had touched each other; but now life had gone away towards the West, and only an immense, abandoned cemetery seemed to remain. No schools, no roads, the worst of Governments, justice sold, execrable officials, crushing taxes, absurd laws, idleness, and fanaticism, to say nothing of the continual shocks of civil war, massacres which destroyed entire villages.

And at thought of this she became angry, and asked if it was allowable that men should thus spoil the work of nature, a land so blest, of such exquisite beauty, where all climates were to be found—the glowing plains, the temperate mountain-sides, the perpetual snows of the lofty peaks. And her love of life, her ever-buoyant hopefulness, filled her with enthusiasm at the idea of the all-powerful magic wand with which science and speculation could strike this old sleeping soil, and suddenly reawaken it.

'Look here!' cried Saccard, 'that Carmel gorge which you have sketched, where there are now only stones and mastic-trees, well! as soon as we begin to work the silver mine, there will start up first a village, then a city! And we will clear all those sand-choked harbours, and protect them with strong breakwaters. Large ships will anchor where now mere skiffs do not venture to moor. And you will behold a complete resurrection over all those depopulated plains, those deserted passes, which our railway lines will traverse—yes! fields will be cleared, roads and canals built, new cities will spring from the soil, life will return as it returns to a sick body, when we stimulate the system by injecting new blood into the exhausted veins. Yes! money will work these miracles!'

And such was the evoking power of his piercing voice that Madame Caroline really saw the predicted civilisation rise up before her. Those bare diagrams, those sketches in outline, became animated and peopled; it was the dream that she had sometimes had of an East cleansed of its filth, drawn from its ignorance, enjoying its fertile soil and charming sky, amid all the refinements of science. She had already witnessed such a miracle at Port Said, which in so few years had lately sprung up on a barren shore;

49

at first some huts to shelter the few labourers who began the operations, then a city of two thousand souls, followed by one of ten thousand, with houses, huge shops, a gigantic pier, life and comfort stubbornly created by toiling human ants. And it was just this that she saw rising again—the forward, irresistible march, the social impulse towards the greatest possible sum of happiness, the need of action, of going ahead, without knowing exactly whither, but at all events with more elbow-room and under improved circumstances; and amid it all there was the globe turned upside down by the ant-swarm rebuilding its abode, its work never ending, fresh sources of enjoyment ever being discovered, man's power increasing tenfold, the earth belonging to him more and more every day. Money, aiding science, yielded progress.

Hamelin, who was listening with a smile, then gave vent to a prudent remark: 'All this is the poetry of results, and we are not yet at the prose of starting.'

But Saccard's enthusiasm was only increased by the extravagance of Madame Caroline's conceptions, and matters even became worse when, on beginning to read some books about the East, he opened a history of Bonaparte's Egyptian expedition. The memory of the Crusades already haunted him, the memory of that return of the West to its cradle the East, that great movement which had carried extreme Europe back to the original country, still in full flower, and where there was so much to learn. But he was struck still more by the towering figure of Napoleon, going thither to wage war, with a grand and mysterious object. Though he had talked of conquering Egypt, of installing a French establishment there, and of thus placing the commerce of the Levant in the hands of France, he had certainly not told all; and in all that was vain and enigmatical about the expedition, Saccard fancied he could detect some mysterious, hugely ambitious project, an immense empire refounded, Napoleon crowned at Constantinople as Emperor of the East and the Indies, thus realising the dream of Alexander, and rising to a greater height than even Cæsar and Charlemagne. Had he not said at Saint Helena, in speaking of Sidney Smith, the general who had stopped him before Saint Jean d'Acre: 'That man ruined my fortune'? And it was this gigantic thought of conquering the East, the scheme which the Crusaders had attempted, and which Napoleon had been unable to accomplish, that inflamed Saccard; though, in his case, it was to be a rational conquest, effected by the double agency of science and money. Since civilisation had flown from the East to the West, why should it not come back towards the East, returning to the first garden of humanity, to that Eden of the Hindustan peninsula which had fallen asleep beneath the fatigue of centuries? He would endow it with fresh youth; he would galvanise the earthly paradise, make it habitable again by means of steam and electricity, replace Asia Minor in the centre of the world, as a point of intersection of the great natural highways that bind the continents together. And it was no longer a question of gaining millions, but milliards and milliards.

After that, Hamelin and he engaged in long conversations every morning. Vast as was their hope, the difficulties that presented themselves were numerous and colossal. The engineer, who had been at Beyrout in 1862, at the very time of the horrible butchery of the Maronite Christians by the Druses—a butchery which had necessitated the intervention of France—did not conceal the obstacles which would be encountered among those populations, who were ever battling together, delivered over to the tender mercies of the local authorities. However, he had powerful relations at Constantinople, where he had assured himself the support of the Grand Vizier, Fuad Pasha, a man of great merit, an avowed partisan of reforms, from whom, he flattered himself, he would obtain all necessary grants. On the other hand, whilst prophesying the inevitable bankruptcy of the Ottoman Empire, he saw a rather favourable circumstance in its unlimited need of money, in the loans which followed one upon another from year to year: for although a needy Government may offer no personal guarantee, it is usually quite ready to come to an understanding with private enterprises, if it can detect the slightest profit in them. And would it not be a practical way of solving the eternal and embarrassing Eastern question to interest the empire in great works of civilisation, and gradually lead it towards progress, that it might no longer constitute a monstrous barrier between Europe and Asia? What a fine patriotic *rôle* the French Companies would play in all this!

Then, one morning, Hamelin quietly broached the secret programme to which he sometimes alluded, and which he smilingly called the crowning of his edifice.

'When we have become the masters,' said he, 'we will restore the kingdom of Palestine, and put the Pope there. At first we might content ourselves with Jerusalem, with Jaffa as a seaport. Then Syria will be declared independent, and can be annexed. You know that the time is near when it will be impossible for the Papacy to remain at Rome under the revolting humiliations in store for it. It is for that day that we must have all in readiness.'

Saccard listened open-mouthed whilst Hamelin said these things in a thoroughly unaffected way, actuated solely by his deep Catholic faith. The financier himself did not shrink from extravagant dreams, but never would he have gone to such a point as this. This man of science, apparently so cold, quite astounded him. 'It's madness!' he cried. 'The Porte won't give up Jerusalem.'

'Oh! why not?' quietly rejoined Hamelin. 'It is always in such desperate need of money! Jerusalem is a burden to it; it would be a good riddance. The Porte, you know, often can't tell what course to take between the various sects which dispute for possession of the sanctuaries. Moreover, the Pope would have true supporters among the Syrian Maronites, for you are not unaware that he has established a college for their priests at Rome. In fact, I have thought the matter over carefully, have calculated everything, and this will be the new era, the triumphant era of Catholicism. It may be said that we should be sending the Pope too far away, that he would find himself isolated, thrust out of European affairs. But with what brilliancy and authority would he not radiate when once he was enthroned in the holy places, and spoke in the name of Christ from the very land where Christ Himself spoke! That is his patrimony, there should be his kingdom. And, rest easy, we will build this kingdom up, firm and powerful; we will put it beyond the reach of political disturbances, by basing its budget—guaranteed by the resources of the country—on a vast bank for the shares of which the Catholics of the entire world will scramble.'

Saccard, who had begun to smile, already attracted by the magnitude of the project, although not convinced, could not help christening this bank with a joyous 'Eureka! The Treasury of the Holy Sepulchre, eh? Superb! There you have it!'

But just then his eyes met those of Madame Caroline, beaming with common-sense. She was smiling also, but like one who is sceptical, even a little vexed. She felt ashamed of his enthusiasm.

'All the same, my dear Hamelin,' said he, 'it will be best for us to keep secret this crowning of the edifice, as you call it. Folks might make fun of us. And, besides, our programme is already a terribly heavy one; it is a good plan to reserve the final result, the glorious ending, for the initiated alone.'

'Undoubtedly; such has always been my intention,' declared the engineer. 'That shall be the mystery.'

And thereupon, that very day, they finally decided to turn the portfolio of schemes to account, to launch the whole huge series of projects. They would begin by founding a small financial establishment, to promote the first enterprises; then success aiding, they would, little by little, subjugate the market and conquer the world.

The next day, as Saccard went up to take some order from the Princess d'Orviedo respecting the Institute of Work, he remembered the dream that he had for a moment cherished of becoming this queen of charity's prince-consort, the mere dispenser and manager of the fortune of the poor. And he smiled, for he now thought all that a little silly. He was built to make life, not to dress the wounds that life has made. And now he was about to find himself at work again, in the thick of the battle of interests, in the midst of that race for happiness which has brought about the very progress of humanity, from century to century, towards greater joy and greater light.

That same day he found Madame Caroline alone in the work-room among the diagrams. She was standing at one of the windows, detained there by the appearance of the Countess de Beauvilliers and her daughter in the neighbouring garden at an unusual hour. The two women were reading a letter with an air of deep sadness; a letter, no doubt, from the son Ferdinand, whose position at Borne could not be a brilliant one.

'Look,' said Madame Caroline, on recognising Saccard. 'Another sorrow for those unfortunates. The poor women in the streets give me less pain.'

'Bah!' he gaily cried, 'you shall ask them to come to see me. We will enrich them also, since we are to make everybody's fortune.'

And, in his happy fever, he sought her lips, to press a kiss upon them. But she abruptly drew back, and became grave and pale.

'No, I beg of you,' said she.

'Really, would it pain you?'

'Yes, deeply.'

'But I adore you.'

'No, do not say that—you are going to be so busy. Besides, I assure you that I shall feel true friendship for you if you prove the active man I think, and do all the great things you say. Come, friendship is far better!'

He listened to her, still smiling and irresolute. 'Then, friends only?' said he.

'Yes, I will be your comrade, I will help you. Friends, great friends!' With these words she offered him her cheeks, and he, conquered, and realizing that she was right, imprinted two loud kisses upon them.

CHAPTER III
SACCARD MAKES A START

The letter from the Russian banker at Constantinople, which Sigismond had translated, was a favourable reply awaited before launching the enterprise in Paris; and on the next day but one Saccard, on waking, had an inspiration that he must act at once, and, before night, form the syndicate which he wished to make sure of, in order to secure the immediate allotment of the fifty thousand shares of his projected company. The capital of the latter was to be five and twenty millions, each share representing five hundred francs.

In jumping out of bed, he had at last just thought of a name for this company, such as he had long been seeking. The words 'Universal Bank' had suddenly flamed up before him, in letters of fire as it were, in the still dark room. 'The Universal Bank,' he kept on repeating whilst he dressed himself, 'the Universal Bank, that is both simple and grand; it takes in everything, covers the world. Yes, yes, it is excellent! the Universal Bank!'

Until half-past nine o'clock he walked up and down his spacious rooms, absorbed in doubt as to where he should begin hunting for the necessary millions in Paris. Twenty-five millions of francs—such a sum is still to be found at a turn of the street; it was rather the embarrassment of making a selection that made him reflect, for he wished to proceed with some method. He drank a glass of milk, and evinced no vexation when the coachman came up to tell him that his horse was not well, having undoubtedly caught cold, so that it would be prudent to send for the veterinary surgeon.

'All right, do so. I will take a cab,' said Saccard.

Once out of doors, however, he was surprised by the keen bitterness of the wind; it was like a sudden return of winter in this month of May, which only the night before had been so mild. It was not yet raining certainly, but dense yellow clouds were rising on the horizon. Still he did not take a cab; a walk, he thought, would warm him up; he might, first of all, go on foot to Mazaud's office, in the Rue de la Banque; for he had an idea of sounding the broker with regard to Daigremont, the well-known speculator, the lucky member of every syndicate. On reaching the Rue Vivienne, however, such a shower of hail and water fell from the sky, now overspread with livid clouds, that he took refuge under the carriage entrance of a house.

He had been standing there for a moment, watching the downpour, when, above the noise it made, there arose a jingling sound of gold, which attracted his attention. Continuous, light, and musical, this sound seemed to come from the bowels of the earth, as in some tale of the 'Arabian Nights.' He turned his head, took his bearings, and saw that he was standing in the doorway of a house occupied by a banker named Kolb, whose especial business it was to deal in gold. Buying up specie in states where it was cheap, he melted it, and sold it in ingots in the countries where it commanded higher prices; and thus, from morning till night, on casting days there arose from the basement that crystalline jingle of gold coins carried by the shovelful from cases to the melting-pot. The ears of the passers-by fairly rang with the sound from one year's end to the other. Saccard smiled with satisfaction as he heard this music, which was like the subterranean voice of the entire Bourse district. He interpreted it as a happy omen.

The rain had ceased falling, so he crossed the Place, and at once found himself at Mazaud's. Unlike the majority of his colleagues, the young broker had his private abode on the first floor of the very house in which his offices were situated. He had, in fact, simply taken over the rooms occupied by his uncle, when, on the latter's death, he had agreed with his joint heirs to purchase the business.

It was striking ten o'clock, and Saccard went straight up to the offices, at the door of which he met Gustave Sédille.

'Is Monsieur Mazaud in?'

'I do not know, monsieur; I have just come.'

The young man smiled; always a late arrival, he took things at his ease, like the mere unpaid amateur he was, quite resigned to spending a year or two in this fashion, in order to please his father, the silk manufacturer of the Rue des Jeûneurs.

Saccard passed through the outer office, saluted by both cashiers, the one who dealt with specie and the one who dealt with stock, and then entered the room set aside for the two 'authorised clerks,' where he only found Berthier, the one whose duty was to receive customers, and who accompanied his employer to the Bourse.

'Is Monsieur Mazaud in?'

'Why, I think so; I just left his private room. But no—he isn't there. He must be in the "cash" office.'

He pushed open a door near at hand, and glanced round a rather large room, in which live employees were at work, under the orders of a head clerk.

'No; that's strange. Look for yourself in the "account" office there, yonder.'

Saccard entered the account office. It was there that the head accountant, the pivot of the business as it were, aided by seven employees,[12] went through the memorandum-book, handed him by the broker every afternoon after the Bourse, and entered to the various customers the sales and purchases which had been effected according to their orders. In doing this, he referred to the numerous *fiches* in order to ascertain the customers' names, for these did not appear in the memorandum-book, which contained only brief notes of the transactions: such a stock, such an amount bought or sold, at such a rate, from such a broker.

'Have you seen Monsieur Mazaud?' inquired Saccard.

But they did not even answer him. The head accountant having gone out, three of the clerks were reading their newspapers, and two others were staring up at the ceiling; while the arrival of Gustave Sédille had just keenly interested little Flory, who in the morning made entries, and in the afternoon looked after the telegrams at the Bourse. Born at Saintes, of a father employed at the local registry office, he had started in life as a clerk to a Bordeaux banker; after which, reaching Paris towards the close of the previous autumn, he had entered Mazaud's office with no other prospect before him than the possible doubling of his salary in ten years' time. At first he had conducted himself well, performing his duties regularly and conscientiously. But during the last month, since Gustave had entered the office, he had been going astray, led away by his new comrade—a fellow of very elegant tastes, and well provided with money—who was launching out in no small degree, and had made him acquainted with women. With bearded chin and cheeks, Flory was possessed of a sensual nose, an amiable mouth, and soft eyes; and he had now reached the point of indulging in little secret, inexpensive pleasure parties, with a *figurante* of the Variétés—a slim grasshopper from the Parisian pavements, the runaway daughter of a Montmartre door-porter. She was named Mdlle. Chuchu, and was fairly amusing with her *papier-mâché* face, in which gleamed a pair of beautiful large brown eyes.

Standing behind Flory and Gustave Sédille, Saccard heard them whispering women's names. He smiled, and addressing himself to Flory, inquired: 'Haven't you seen Monsieur Mazaud?'

'Yes, monsieur, he came to give me an order, and then went down to his apartments again. I believe that his little boy is ill; he was told that the doctor had come. You had better ring at his door, for he will very likely go out without coming up again.'

Saccard thanked him, and hurried down to the floor below. Mazaud was one of the youngest of the official brokers, and an extremely lucky man to boot; for by the death of his uncle he had come into one of the largest businesses in Paris at an age when one can still learn. Though short, he was very pleasant-looking, with a small brown moustache and piercing black eyes; and he displayed great activity, and a very alert mind. He was already known in the *corbeille* for his vivacity of mind and body, such a desideratum in his calling, and one which, coupled with a keen scent and remarkable intuition, was sure to place him in the first rank; to say nothing of the fact that he possessed a shrill piercing voice, received direct information from foreign Bourses, did business with all the great bankers, and was reputed to have a second cousin employed at the Havas News Agency. His wife, whom he had married for love, and who had brought him a dowry of twelve hundred thousand francs, was a charming young woman, and had already presented him with two children, a little girl now three years and a boy some eighteen months old.

As Saccard came down he found Mazaud ushering out the doctor, who was laughingly tranquillising his paternal anxiety.

'Come in,' said the broker to Saccard. 'It's true, you know—with these little creatures you at once get anxious; the slightest ailment, and you think them lost.'

So saying, he ushered him into the drawing-room, where his wife was still seated, holding the baby on her knees, while the little girl, glad to see her mother gay, was raising herself on tip-toe to kiss her.

'You see that we were foolish,' said he.

'Ah! that makes no difference, my friend,' she answered. 'I am so glad that he has reassured us!'

In presence of all this happiness, Saccard halted, bowing. The room, luxuriously furnished, was redolent of the happy life of this household, which nothing had yet disunited. During four years of wedlock, Mazaud had been accused of nothing save a fleeting curiosity with regard to a vocalist at the Opéra Comique. He remained a faithful husband, just as he had the reputation of not yet speculating too heavily on his own account, despite all the natural impetuosity of youth. And a pleasant perfume of luck, of unclouded felicity could really be detected here, amid the discreet peacefulness of the apartment, amid the delicious odour with which a large bouquet of roses, overflowing from a china vase, had scented the entire room.

Madame Mazaud, who was slightly acquainted with Saccard, addressed him gaily: 'Is it not true, monsieur, one need only wish it to be always happy?'

'I am convinced of it, madame,' he answered. 'And besides, there are persons so beautiful and good that misfortune never dares to touch them.'

She had risen, radiant. Kissing her husband in her turn, she went out, carrying the little boy, and followed by the little girl, who had been hanging on her father's neck. The latter, wishing to hide his emotion, turned towards his visitor with the bantering remark: 'You see we don't lead a dull life here.'

Then he quickly added: 'You have something to say to me? Let us go upstairs, eh? We shall be more at our ease there.'

Up above, in the cashiers' office, Saccard recognised Sabatani, who had called for some money due to him; and he was surprised to see how cordially the broker shook hands with his customer. However, as soon as he was seated in Mazaud's private room, he explained his visit by questioning the broker as to the formalities which were necessary to secure the quotation of a new security in the official list. In a careless way he spoke of the affair which he was about to launch, the Universal Bank, with a capital of twenty-five millions. Yes, a financial establishment which would especially patronise certain great enterprises, which he just alluded to. Mazaud listened with perfect composure, and, in the most obliging way, explained the formalities that were requisite. However he was in no wise duped; Saccard had certainly not called on him merely with reference to this trifling matter, and so when his visitor at last mentioned the name of Daigremont he gave an involuntary smile. Certainly Daigremont had a colossal fortune behind him; it was said that his fidelity was not of the surest; but then who is faithful in business and in love? Nobody! For the rest, he (Mazaud) hardly cared to speak the full truth about Daigremont, for they had quarrelled, and their quarrel had been the talk of the whole Bourse. Daigremont now gave most of his orders to a Bordeaux Jew, named Jacoby, a tall man of sixty, with a broad, gay face, whose roaring voice was celebrated, but who was growing heavy and corpulent; and there was a sort of rivalry between him and Mazaud, between the young man favoured by fortune and the elder who owed his position to long service, for Jacoby had been a mere authorised clerk until—financed by sleeping partners—he had finally succeeded in purchasing his employer's business. Though of very great experience and shrewdness, he was sorely handicapped by his passion for speculation, and, in spite of considerable profits, always seemed on the eve of a catastrophe. His money melted away on settling days.

'In any case,' concluded Mazaud, yielding at last to his resentment against the man he had quarrelled with, spite of all his scruples, 'it is quite certain that Daigremont played his allies false in that Caraccas affair, and swept away the profits—I consider him a very dangerous man.' Then, after a pause, he added: 'But why don't you apply to Gundermann?'

'Never!' cried Saccard, in a fit of passion.

Just then Berthier, the authorised clerk, came in and whispered a few words in the broker's ear. The Baroness Sandorff had come to pay her losses, and was raising all sorts of quibbling objections by way of trying to reduce her account. Mazaud generally hastened to receive her in person, but, when she had lost, he avoided her like the plague, certain as he was that his gallantry would be put to too severe a test. There are no worse clients than women, for as soon as they have to pay money away they become absolutely dishonest.

'No, no; tell her that I am not in,' he answered testily. 'And don't abate a centime, you understand?'

When Berthier had gone, seeing by Saccard's smile that he had heard him, he continued: 'It is true, my dear fellow, she's very pretty, but you have no idea of her rapacity. Ah; how our customers would love us if they always won! Yet the richer they are, the higher the society in which they move, God forgive me! the more I distrust them, the more I fear I may not be paid. Yes, there are days when, apart from the large banking houses, I could wish that my connection was purely a provincial one.'

Just then a clerk came in, handed him some papers that he had asked for that morning, and then went out.

'See here!' he resumed, 'here is a receiver of dividends at Vendôme, a man named Fayeux. Well, you can have no idea of the number of orders that I receive from him. To be sure, these orders, taken singly, are modest ones, coming as they do from folks of the petty *bourgeoisie*, shopkeepers and farmers. But there are so many of them. Really, the best of our business, the very foundation of it, will be found among the people of modest means, the crowd of nobodies who speculate.'

This somehow reminded Saccard of Sabatani, whom he had seen in the cashiers' office.

'I see that you have Sabatani now,' said he.

'I have had him for a year, I believe,' replied the broker, with an air of amiable indifference. 'He's a pleasant fellow, isn't he? He began in a small way, he is very prudent, and he will end by making something.'

What he did not say, what he no longer even remembered, was that Sabatani had merely deposited two thousand francs with him by way of 'cover.' Hence the moderate ventures at the outset. Undoubtedly, like many others, the Levantine expected that the insignificance of this 'cover' would be forgotten; and he evinced great prudence, increasing his orders in a stealthy gradual fashion, pending the day when, with a heavy settlement to meet, it would be necessary for him to disappear. But how could one distrust such a charming fellow, whose friend one has become? How could one doubt his solvency when one sees him gay, well-dressed, 'got up' in that elegant style which is indispensable, the very uniform, as it were, of robbery at the Bourse?

'Very pleasant, very intelligent,' repeated Saccard, suddenly resolving to remember Sabatani whenever he might need a discreet and unscrupulous fellow. Then, rising and taking leave, he said: 'Well, good-bye; when our stock is ready, I will see you again, before trying to get it quoted.'

And as Mazaud shook hands with him on the threshold, saying: 'You are wrong; you had better see Gundermann for your syndicate,' he again shouted in a fury: 'No, never!'

On leaving the broker's private room, he recognised Moser and Pillerault in the cashiers' office; the first was pocketing with a woeful air his fortnight's profits of seven or eight thousand francs; while the other, who had lost, paid over ten thousand francs with a loud voice, and a proud, aggressive air, as if after a victory. The luncheon and Bourse hour was approaching, and the office would then partly empty. Meantime, from the 'account' office, the door of which was ajar, there came a sound of laughter, provoked by a story which Gustave was telling Flory—a story of a boating party, at which a coxswain of the softer sex had fallen into the Seine.

On reaching the street, Saccard consulted his watch. Eleven o'clock—what a lot of time he had lost! No, he would not go to Daigremont's; and although he had flown into a passion at the very mention of Gundermann's name, he suddenly decided to go to see him. Besides, had he not warned him of his visit on that occasion at Champeaux' restaurant, when he had spoken to him of his great scheme by way of silencing his malicious laugh? He even excused the visit on the plea that he did not wish to get anything out of the man, but simply desired to confront and triumph over one who ever affected to treat him as an urchin. And so, as a fresh shower began to lash the pavement with a flood of water, he leaped into a cab, bidding the Jehu drive him to the Rue de Provence.

Gundermann there occupied an immense mansion, just large enough for his innumerable family. He had five daughters and four sons, of whom three daughters and three sons were married, and these had already given him fourteen grandchildren. At the evening meal, when all were gathered together, there were, counting his wife and himself, thirty-one at table. And, excepting two of his sons-in-law, who did not live in the house, all had their apartments there, in the left and right wings facing the garden; for the central block was entirely occupied by the spacious banking offices. In less than a century a monstrous fortune of a milliard of francs[13] had been amassed by this one family, thanks partly to thrift, and partly to fortunate combinations of circumstances. This wealth seemed a sort of predestination, which keen intelligence, persistent labour, prudent and invincible effort—continually directed to the same end—had largely assisted. Every river of gold now flowed into that sea; other millions were absorbed by those which Gundermann already possessed; it was a swallowing-up of the public wealth by the ever-increasing wealth of a single individual; and Gundermann was the true master, the omnipotent king, feared and obeyed by Paris and by the world.

As Saccard ascended the broad stone stairway, the steps of which were worn by the continual ascent and descent of scores of feet—more worn indeed than the thresholds of many old churches—he felt inextinguishable hatred for this man rising within him. Ah! the Jew! Against the Jew he harboured all the old racial resentment, to be found especially in the South of France; and it was something like a revolt of his very flesh, a repugnance of the skin, which, at the idea of the slightest contact, filled him with disgust and anger, a sensation which no reasoning could allay, which he was quite unable to overcome. And the singular thing was that he, Saccard, the terrible company promoter, the spendthrift with unclean hands, lost all self-consciousness as soon as a Jew was in question, and spoke of him with the harshness, the revengeful indignation of an honest man who lives by the labour of his arms, unstained by any usurious dealings. He indicted the whole Hebrew race, the cursed race without a country, without a prince, which lives as a parasite upon the nations, pretending to recognise their laws, but in reality only obeying its Jehovah—its God of robbery, blood, and wrath; and he pointed to it fulfilling on all sides the mission of ferocious conquest which this God has assigned to it, establishing itself among every people, like a spider in the centre of its web, in order to watch its prey, to suck the blood of one and all, to fatten itself by devouring others. 'Did anyone ever see a Jew working with his fingers?' he would ask.[14] Were there any Jewish peasants and working men? 'No,' he would say; 'labour disgraces, their religion almost forbids it, exalting only the exploitation of the labour of others. Ah! the rogues!' Saccard's rage was all the greater because he admired them, envied their prodigious financial faculties, that innate knowledge of arithmetic, that natural facility evinced by them in the most complicated operations, that scent and that luck which assure triumph in everything they undertake. 'Christians,' he would say, 'make sorry financial rogues, they always end by coming to grief; but take a Jew who does not even understand book-keeping, throw him into the troubled waters of any shady affair, and he will not only save himself, but bring out all the profit on his back.' It was the gift of the race, the reason why it ever subsisted among all the other nationalities that start up and disappear. And he would passionately predict the final conquest of every nation by the Jews, when they should at last have secured possession of the entire fortune of the globe, a feat which it would not take them long to accomplish, since they were allowed every day to freely extend their kingdom, and one could already see in Paris a Gundermann reigning on a firmer and more respected throne than the Emperor's.

When, after climbing the stairs, he was on the point of entering the spacious ante-room, he felt an inclination to turn back, for he saw that it was full of *remisiers* and other applicants, a tumultuous swarming crowd of men and women. The *remisiers* especially were struggling for first place, in the improbable hope of carrying off an order; for the great banker had his own agents; but it was already an honour, a recommendation, even to be received by him, and each of them wished to be able to boast of it. Accordingly the 'waits' were never long, the two office attendants had little else to do than to organise the procession—a continuous procession it was, a real gallop through the swinging doors. And thus, in spite of the crowd, Saccard was almost immediately admitted with the stream.

Gundermann's private office was a vast apartment, of which he simply occupied a little corner at the farther end, near the last window. Seated at a simple mahogany writing table, he was so placed as to turn his back to the light, his face remaining completely in the shade. Up at five o'clock every morning, he was at work when Paris was still asleep; and when at about nine the scramble of appetites began, rushing past him at a gallop, his day's work was already done. In the middle of the office, and at larger tables, stood two of his sons, and one of his sons-in-law who assisted him, rarely sitting down, but moving about hither and thither amid a world of clerks. All this, however, was the inner working of the establishment. The crowd from the street went straight across the room to him, the master, seated in his modest corner, as for hours and hours he held this open reception with an impassive gloomy air, often contenting himself with a mere sign, and only now and again speaking a word when he wished to appear particularly amiable.

As soon as he perceived Saccard, a faint, somewhat sarcastic smile lighted up his face.

'Ah! so it's you, my friend,' he said. 'Be seated a moment, if you have anything to say to me. I will be at your disposal directly.'

Then he pretended to forget him. Saccard, however, was not impatient, for he felt interested in the procession of *remisiers*, who, at each other's heels, entered the room with the same profound bow, drawing from their irreproachable frock coats the same little cards setting forth the same Bourse quotations, which they presented to the banker with the same suppliant and respectful gestures. Ten of them, twenty of them, passed by; the banker each time took the list, glanced at it and then returned it; and nothing equalled the patience he displayed beneath this avalanche of offers, unless indeed it were his absolute indifference.

At last Massias appeared, with the gay yet anxious air of a good dog who is often whipped. At times folks received him so badly that he could have cried. That day, undoubtedly, his stock of humility was exhausted, for he ventured to insist in the most unexpected fashion.

'See! monsieur, Mobiliers are very low. How much shall I buy for you?'

Without taking the proffered list, Gundermann raised his sea-green eyes upon this young man, who was so familiar, and roughly answered: 'I say, my friend, do you think it amuses me to receive you?'

'Well, monsieur,' retorted Massias, turning pale, 'it amuses me still less to come every morning for nothing, as I have done for three months past.'

'Then don't come again.'

The *remisier* bowed and withdrew, after exchanging with Saccard the furious, distressful glance of one who has suddenly become conscious that he will never make his fortune.

Saccard meantime was asking himself what interest Gundermann could have in receiving all these people. Evidently he had a special power of isolating himself; he remained absorbed, continued thinking. Moreover, in all this there must be some question of discipline, a habit of passing the market in review every morning, which invariably conduced to some little profit or other. In a greedy fashion Gundermann deducted eighty francs from the amount claimed by some jobber to whom he had given an order the day before, and who, it should be said, was certainly robbing him.

Then a dealer in curiosities arrived, bringing an enamelled gold box of the last century, which had been considerably restored, a trick which the banker immediately scented. Next came two ladies, an old one with the beak of a night-bird, and a young one, a very beautiful brunette; they wished to show him at their house a Louis XV. *commode*, which he promptly refused to go and see. Then came a jeweller with some rubies, a couple of inventors, some Englishmen, Germans, and Italians, folks of both sexes and every language. And meantime the procession of *remisiers* went on just the same, between the other visits, endless to all appearance, with an incessant repetition of one and the same gesture—the mechanical presentation of the list; while, as the hour for the opening of the Bourse approached, the clerks crossed the room in greater numbers than ever, bringing telegrams, or coming to ask for signatures.

But the tumult reached a climax when a little boy of five or six, riding astride a stick, burst into the office, playing a trumpet and followed by two other children—little girls, one three years old, and the other eight—who besieged their grandfather's arm-chair, tugged at his arms, and hung upon his neck; to all which he placidly submitted, kissing them with all the Jewish passion for one's offspring—the numerous progeny which yields strength, and which one defends.

Suddenly, however, he seemed to remember Saccard: 'Ah! my good friend, you must excuse me; you see that I haven't a minute to myself. Come now, explain your business to me.'

And he was beginning to listen to him, when an employee, who had introduced a tall, fair gentleman, came to whisper a name in his ear. He rose promptly, yet without haste, and went to confer with the gentleman in question at another window, while one of his sons continued receiving the *remisiers* and *coulissiers* in his stead.

In spite of his secret irritation, Saccard was beginning to experience a feeling of respect. In the tall, fair gentleman he had recognised the ambassador of one of the Great Powers, full of arrogance at the Tuileries, but here standing with his head slightly inclined, smiling like one who solicits some favour. At other times officials of high rank in the public service, the Emperor's ministers themselves, would be received standing in this way, in this room as public as a square, and resounding with the noisy mirth of children. And here was affirmed the universal sovereignty of this man, who had his own ambassadors in every court of the world, his consuls in every province, his agents in every city, and his vessels on every sea. He was not a speculator, a soldier of fortune manœuvring with the millions of others, dreaming, like Saccard, of heroic combats in which he should prove conqueror and win colossal booty for himself, thanks to the aid of mercenary gold enlisted under his orders; he was, as he quietly said, a simple money merchant, but the most shrewd, most careful there could be. Nevertheless, to establish his power, it was essential that he should rule the Bourse; and so with each settlement there was a new battle, in which the victory infallibly remained with him, thanks to the decisive power of his big battalions. For a moment, Saccard, as he sat watching him, was overwhelmed by the thought that all the money which this man set in motion was his own, that he held in his cellars an inexhaustible supply, in which he trafficked like a shrewd and prudent merchant, like an absolute master, obeyed at a glance, bent on hearing everything, seeing everything, doing everything himself. A milliard of one's own thus manipulated is an invincible force.

'We shan't have a minute, my good friend,' said Gundermann, when he came back. 'I am going to breakfast; come with me into the next room. Perhaps they will leave us in peace there.'

It was the little dining-room of the mansion, the one used for the morning meal, and where the entire family was never gathered together. That day there were only nineteen at table, eight of them children. The banker sat in the middle, and all he had in front of him was a bowl of milk.

He remained for a moment with his eyes closed, exhausted by fatigue, his face very pale and contracted; for he suffered from a complaint of the liver and the kidneys. Then, when with trembling hands he had lifted the bowl to his lips, and had drunk a mouthful, he sighed: 'Ah! I am tired out to-day.'

'Why do you not take a rest?' asked Saccard.

Gundermann turned his eyes upon him in astonishment, and naïvely answered: 'But I can't.'

In fact, he was not allowed even to drink his milk in peace, for the reception of the *remisiers* had begun again; the gallop now went on across the dining-room, while the members of the family, men and women, accustomed to all this stir and bustle, laughed and ate heartily of the cold meats and pastries, and the children, excited by two thimblefuls of pure wine, raised a deafening din.

Meantime Saccard, who was still watching him, marvelled at seeing him slowly swallow his milk with such an effort that it seemed as if he would never manage to empty the bowl. He had been put on a milk diet; he was no longer allowed to touch even a bit of meat or pastry. And that being the case, thought Saccard, of what use was his milliard to him? Moreover, women had never tempted him; for forty years he had remained strictly faithful to his wife; and now virtue was compulsory on his part, irrevocably definitive. Why then should he rise at five o'clock, ply this awful trade, weigh himself down with such immense fatigue, lead a galley-slave's life which no beggar would have accepted, with his memory crammed with figures, and his skull fairly bursting with a whole world of cares? Why, too, add so much useless gold to so much gold already possessed, when one may not buy and eat so much as a pound of cherries, or carry a passing girl off to some waterside wineshop, when one may not enjoy any of the things that are sold, nor even idleness and liberty? And Saccard, who despite his terrible appetites made due allowance for the disinterested love of money, simply for the power that it gives, felt seized with a sort of holy terror as he gazed upon that face, not that of the classical miser who hoards, but that of the blameless workman, without a fleshly instinct, who in his ailing old age had become as it were an abstract of himself, and obstinately continued building his tower of millions, with the sole dream of bequeathing it to his descendants, that they might raise it yet higher, until it should overshadow the entire earth.

At last Gundermann leaned over, and let him explain in an undertone the projected launching of the Universal Bank. Saccard, however, was sparing of details, simply alluding to the schemes in Hamelin's portfolio, for from the first words he had felt that the banker was trying to draw him, with the predetermination to refuse him his support.

'Another bank, my good friend, another bank!' he repeated in his sneering way. But the affair into which I would sooner put my money would be a machine, yes, a guillotine, to cut off the heads of all the banks already established.... A rake, eh? to clean out the Bourse. Your engineer hasn't something of that sort among his papers, has he?' Then, affecting a paternal air, he continued with tranquil cruelty: 'Come, be reasonable; you know what I told you. You are wrong to go into business again; I render you a real service in refusing to launch your syndicate; you will inevitably come

61

to grief, it is mathematically certain, for you are much too enthusiastic, you have too much imagination; and besides, matters always end badly when one deals with other people's money. Why doesn't your brother find you a good post, eh? a prefecture, or else a financial receivership—no, not a receivership, that also is too dangerous. Beware, my good friend, beware.'

Saccard had risen, quivering: 'You have made up your mind, then; you won't take any stock, you won't be with us?'

'With you? Never in my life. You will be cleared out within three years.'

There was a spell of silence, instinct with conflict; a sharp exchange of defiant glances.

'Then, good afternoon. I have not breakfasted yet, and am very hungry. We shall see who will be cleared out.'

And thereupon Saccard left the great financier in the midst of his tribe; and whilst they finished noisily stuffing themselves with pastry, the master went on receiving the last belated brokers, wearily closing his eyes every now and then, and draining his bowl with little sips, his lips all white with milk.

Throwing himself into his cab, Saccard gave his own address, Rue Saint-Lazare. One o'clock was striking, the day was lost; he was going home to lunch quite beside himself. Ah! the dirty Jew! There indeed was a fellow whom he would have been pleased to crunch with his teeth as a dog crunches a bone! Certainly he was a terrible morsel, too big to eat. But could one ever tell? The greatest empires had crumbled, a time always comes when the powerful succumb. And without eating him entirely at the first bite, might he not manage to get his teeth into him, tear from him some shreds of his milliard? That done, yes, he might afterwards eat him—why not?—and in the person of their undisputed king destroy those Jews who thought the feast to be entirely intended for themselves. These reflections, this wrath with which he had come away from Gundermann's, filled Saccard with a furious hankering, an imperative desire for traffic, immediate success. He would have liked to found his banking-house, set it working, triumph and crush all rival houses at a wave of his hand. All at once, the thought of Daigremont came back to him; and without debating the matter, swayed by an irresistible impulse, he leaned forward and called to the driver to go up the Rue Larochefoucauld. If he wanted to see Daigremont, he must make haste and postpone lunch till later, for he knew that it was Daigremont's habit to go out at about one o'clock. No doubt this Christian was worse than any two Jews, and passed for an ogre who devoured the young enterprises entrusted to his care. But at that moment Saccard would have negotiated with Cartouche[15] himself in order to conquer, and even on condition of dividing the spoil. Later on, they would see, he himself would prove the stronger.

Meanwhile the cab, after ascending the steep hill with some difficulty, stopped in front of the lofty monumental entrance of one of the last grand mansions of this neighbourhood, which once had some very fine ones. The detached buildings, at the rear of a vast paved courtyard, wore an air of royal grandeur; and the garden beyond, in which centenarian trees were still growing, remained a veritable park, isolated from the populous streets. All Paris knew that mansion for its splendid entertainments, and especially for the admirable collection of pictures assembled there, which not a grand-duke on his travels failed to visit. Married to a woman who was famous for her beauty, like his pictures were for theirs, and who had achieved a great success in society as a vocalist, the master of the house led a princely life, was as proud of his racing stable as of his gallery, belonged to one of the principal clubs, paraded the most costly women, and had a box at the Opera, a chair at the Hôtel Drouot,[16] and a foot-stool at the questionable resorts most in vogue. And all this profuse life, this luxury coruscating in an apotheosis of caprice and art, was entirely paid for by speculation, by a fortune which was incessantly on the move, and which seemed infinite like the sea, though, like the sea, it had its ebb and flow—balances in one or the other sense of two and three hundred thousand francs at each fortnightly settlement.

When Saccard had climbed the majestic entrance steps, a valet announced him, and escorted him through three reception rooms filled with marvels, to a little smoking room where Daigremont was finishing a cigar before going out. Already forty-five years of age, and struggling against stoutness, he was of high stature and very elegant, with his hair carefully trimmed, and wearing only a moustache and imperial, like a fanatic of the Tuileries. He affected great amiability, having absolute confidence in himself, a firm conviction of conquering.

He at once darted forward. 'Ah! my dear friend, what is becoming of you?' said he. 'Only the other day I was thinking about you. But are you not now my neighbour?'

He calmed down, however, and set aside this effusive manner, which he kept for the common herd, when Saccard, deeming it useless to beat about the bush, forthwith broached the object of his visit, expatiating on his great enterprise, and explaining that, before establishing the Universal Bank with a capital of twenty-five millions of francs, he wished to form a syndicate of friends—bankers and manufacturers—who would pressure the success of the issue by agreeing to take four-fifths of the shares, that was, some forty thousand. Daigremont had become very serious, and listened to him, and watched him, as if searching to the depths of his brain, to ascertain what effort, what labour useful to himself, he might yet get out of this man whom he had known so active, so full of marvellous qualities amidst all his blundering fever. At first he hesitated. 'No, no,' said he, 'I am overwhelmed already; I do not wish to take anything fresh in hand.'

Then, tempted nevertheless, he asked some questions, wished to know what projects the new venture would patronise, projects which Saccard was prudent enough to speak about with the extremest reserve. And when Daigremont had been made acquainted with the first enterprise which it was intended to launch, that idea of syndicating all the Mediterranean transport companies under the name of the United Steam Navigation Company, he seemed very much struck with it, and suddenly yielded.

'Well, I consent to go in. But on one condition only. How do you stand with your brother, the minister?'

Saccard was so surprised at the question that he frankly displayed his rancour. 'With my brother? Oh! he does his business, and I do mine. He hasn't very fraternal feelings, that brother of mine.'

'Then so much the worse!' flatly declared Daigremont. 'I won't be with you unless your brother is with you too. You understand, I won't have you two at loggerheads together.'

With an angry gesture of impatience Saccard began protesting. What need had they of Rougon? Would it not be seeking chains with which to bind themselves hand and foot? But at the same time the voice of prudence, stronger than his irritation, repeated to him that it was at least necessary that they should assure themselves of the great man's neutrality. And yet, after all, he brutally refused. 'No, no, he has always been too hoggish with me. I will never take the first step.'

'Listen,' resumed Daigremont. 'I expect Huret here at five o'clock with respect to a commission he has undertaken for me. You will hurry off to the Corps Législatif, take Huret into a corner, tell him your plans, and he will at once speak of the matter to Rougon, find out what the latter thinks of it, and we shall have the answer here at five o'clock. That's it, eh? An appointment here at five o'clock?'

With his head low, Saccard reflected. '*Mon Dieu!*' said he, 'if you insist upon it.'

'Oh, absolutely! Without Rougon, nothing; with Rougon, anything you like.'

'All right, I will go then.'

They had shaken hands vigorously, and Saccard had started off, when the other called him back. 'Ah, I say, if you find things promising, just call on your way back upon the Marquis de Bohain and Sédille; tell them that I am going in, and ask them to join—I want them with us.'

At the door Saccard found his cab, which he had kept, although he had only to go down to the end of the street to get home. He now dismissed the vehicle, in the idea that he could have his own horse in the afternoon; and then he hurried back to get something to eat. They had long since given him up; however, the cook served him a bit of cold meat, which he devoured whilst quarrelling with the coachman; for when the latter had been summoned, and had given an account of the veterinary surgeon's visit, it appeared that the horse must be allowed three or four days' rest. Thereupon Saccard, with his mouth full, accused the coachman of neglect, and threatened him with Madame Caroline, who would see to it all. Finally, he shouted for him to go for another cab. Just then a diluvian shower again swept the street, and he had to wait more than a quarter of an hour for a vehicle, into which he stepped, under the torrential downpour, shouting the address: 'To the Corps Législatif!'

His plan was to arrive before the sitting, so that he might get hold of Huret, and quietly interview him. Unfortunately an exciting debate was feared that day, for a member of the Left was to bring up the eternal question of Mexico, and Rougon no doubt would be obliged to reply.

As Saccard entered the Salle des Pas Perdus,[17] he was lucky enough to meet the deputy, and led him into one of the little reception-rooms near by, where they found themselves alone, thanks to the great excitement prevailing in the lobbies. The opposition was growing more and more formidable, a wind of catastrophe was beginning to blow—a wind destined to increase and sweep everything away. Thus Huret, who was very preoccupied, did not at first understand Saccard, and the latter had to repeat his request. On the deputy realising what was wanted of him, his dismay increased: 'Oh, my dear friend, how can you think of such a thing!' he exclaimed. 'Speak to Rougon at such a moment as this! He will send me to the deuce, you may be sure of it.'

Then his anxiety as to his personal interests became manifest. His very existence depended on the great man, to whom he owed his selection as an official candidate, his election, his situation as a kind of general servant living on the crumbs of his master's favour. By following this calling for a couple of years, he had, thanks to bribes and pickings prudently realised, been able to increase his extensive Calvados estates, intending to retire and enthrone himself there after the Downfall.

His fat, cunning, peasant-like face had now darkened, and expressed all the embarrassment he felt at this sudden request for intervention, which gave him no time

64

to consider whether he would gain or lose thereby. 'No, no! I cannot,' he repeated. 'I told you your brother's decision; I cannot disturb him again. The devil! think of me a little. He's by no means gentle when he's bothered; and, plainly now, I've no desire to pay for you at the cost of my own credit.'

Thereupon, Saccard, understanding, strove to convince him that millions of money were to be gained by the launching of the Universal Bank. With broad touches and glowing words, which transformed a pecuniary affair into a poet's tale, he explained all the superb enterprises which were in view, and dwelt on their certain and colossal success. Daigremont, whose enthusiasm was roused, would place himself at the head of the syndicate. Bohain and Sédille had already asked to come into it. It was impossible that he, Huret, should not be one of them: the others absolutely wanted him to join them on account of his high political position. They even hoped that he would consent to become a member of the board of directors, for his name was a guarantee of method and probity.

At this promise that he should be made a director, the deputy looked Saccard full in the face. 'Well, what is it that you want of me, what reply do you wish me to get from Rougon?' he asked.

'Oh! for my part,' replied Saccard, 'I would willingly have dispensed with my brother. But Daigremont insists on a reconciliation. Perhaps he is right—so I think that you ought simply to speak of our affair to the terrible fellow, and obtain, if not his help, at least a promise that he won't oppose us.'

Huret, his eyes half closed, still seemed undecided.

'You see, if you can only draw an amiable word from him—just an amiable word, you understand—Daigremont will be satisfied with it, and we will settle the matter this afternoon between us three.'

'Well, I will try,' suddenly declared the deputy, affecting a peasant's bluntness, 'but I shall only do so for your sake, for he is not a pleasant customer by any means—no indeed, especially when the Left is tormenting him. At five o'clock, then?'

'At five o'clock.'

For nearly an hour longer Saccard lingered at the Palais Bourbon, greatly disturbed by the rumours of battle which were afloat. Hearing one of the great orators of the Opposition announce that he meant to speak, he momentarily felt a desire to go in search of Huret again, and ask him if it would not be prudent to postpone the interview with Rougon until the next day. Then, fatalist that he was, believing in chance, he trembled lest he might compromise everything if he altered existing arrangements. Perhaps, too, in the scramble, his brother would the more readily speak the desired word. And thereupon, in order to let things take their course, he started off, and again got into his cab, which was already recrossing the Pont de la Concorde, when he recollected the desire expressed by Daigremont: 'Driver,' he called, 'Rue de Babylone.'

It was in the Rue de Babylone that the Marquis de Bohain lived, occupying a grand mansion's former dependencies—a pavilion which had once sheltered stablemen, but had now been transformed into a very comfortable modern house, the luxurious appointments of which were coquettishly aristocratic. The Marquis's wife, by the way, was never seen; her health was bad, he said; infirmities kept her in her apartments. Nevertheless, the house and furniture were hers; he lived with her only as a lodger, having nothing of his own save his clothes, a trunkful, which he could have carried away on a cab. He and she had been legally separated, so far as estate went, since he had begun living by speculation. On two disastrous occasions already he had flatly

65

refused to pay up what he owed, and the official receiver, after looking into matters, had not even taken the trouble to send him any stamped paper. The sponge was passed over the claims against him. He pocketed as long as he won, but as soon as he lost he did not pay; folks knew it, and resigned themselves to it. On the other hand, he bore an illustrious name, and his presence and manners were of a kind to adorn a board of directors, so that new companies in search of a little gilding disputed with each other for his services, and he never knew a slack time. At the Bourse he had his chair on the Rue Notre-Dame-des-Victoires side frequented by the rich speculators, who pretended to take no interest in the little rumours of the day. They respected and frequently consulted him. He had often influenced the market. And, briefly, he was quite a personage.

Though Saccard knew the Marquis well, he was nevertheless impressed by the loftily polite reception accorded him by this handsome old man of sixty, whose small head was perched upon a colossal body, a brown wig setting off his pale face, the expression of which was exceedingly aristocratic.

'Monsieur le Marquis, I come as a veritable solicitor,' said Saccard, explaining the motive of his visit, but without entering into details.

At his first words, however, the Marquis stopped him. 'No no, all my time is taken. I have at this moment a dozen proposals which I must refuse.'

Then, as Saccard added, smiling, 'Daigremont sent me; he thought of you,' he immediately exclaimed, 'Oh! is Daigremont in it? Well, well, if Daigremont is with you, so am I. Rely on me.'

Then, as his visitor wished to furnish him with at least a little information, so that he might know what sort of an undertaking he was joining, he closed his mouth, with the amiable, easy-going manner of a *grand seigneur*, who does not descend to such details, and has a natural confidence in people's probity.

'Not another word, I beg of you. I do not wish to know. You need my name, I lend it to you, and I am very glad to do so; that is all. Simply tell Daigremont to arrange the matter to his liking.'

On stepping into his cab again, Saccard, feeling quite gay, laughed inwardly. 'He will cost us dear,' he thought, 'but he is really charming.' Then he added aloud: 'Driver, Rue des Jeûneurs.'

It was here that Sédille had his warehouses and offices on a vast ground-floor at the far end of a courtyard. After thirty years' toil, Sédille, who was a native of Lyons and had retained some workshops there, had at last succeeded in making his silk business one of the best known and best established in Paris, when a passion for gambling, due to chance circumstances, broke out and spread within him with the destructive violence of a conflagration. A couple of strokes, which one after the other yielded him considerable profit, made him altogether lose his head. What was the use of giving thirty years of one's life to the earning of a paltry million, when, in a single hour, by a simple transaction at the Bourse, one can put the same amount in one's pocket? From that time he gradually ceased to take any interest in his business, which simply continued working thanks to pre-acquired motive power. He lived in the sole hope of some triumphant stroke of speculation; and, having fallen on a vein of persistent ill-luck, soon sank in gambling all the profits of his business. The worst of such a fever as this is that a man becomes disgusted with legitimate gains, and finally even loses an exact idea of money. And ruin lay inevitably at the end, for in vain did the Lyons workshops bring Sédille in a couple of hundred thousand francs a year, since speculation swept away three hundred thousand.

Saccard found him agitated and anxious, for this merchant gambler lacked phlegm and philosophy. He lived in a state of remorse, always hoping, always dejected, sick with uncertainty, and all this because he was still honest at heart. The settlement at the end of April had proved disastrous to him. However, his fat face, fringed with large fair whiskers, flushed at the first words: 'Ah! my dear fellow, if it is luck that you bring me, you are welcome!' Then seized with a fit of terror, he added: 'But no, no, do not tempt me. I should do better to shut myself up with my goods, and never stir from my counting-house.'

Wishing to let him calm himself, Saccard began speaking to him of his son Gustave, whom he had seen, he said, that morning at Mazaud's. But to the merchant this was another subject of chagrin, for he had dreamt of transferring the responsibility of his establishment to this son, and the latter despised commercial pursuits, and cared only for mirth and festivity, having the white teeth of a parvenu's son, teeth only fit to devour the fortune that might some day fall to them. Still, his father had placed him with Mazaud to see if he would nibble at finance.

'Since the death of his poor mother,' murmured the manufacturer, 'he has given me very little satisfaction. But in a broker's office he will perhaps learn some things that may be useful to me.'

'Well,' resumed Saccard abruptly, 'are you with us? Daigremont told me to come and tell you that he was going in.'

Sédille raised his trembling arms to heaven, and, in a voice expressive both of desire and fear, replied: 'Why, yes, I am with you. You know very well that I can't do otherwise than go in with you! If I should refuse and your enterprise should prosper, I should fall ill with regret. Tell Daigremont that I will go in.'

When Saccard found himself in the street again, he pulled out his watch, and saw that it was scarcely four o'clock. The time that he had before him, and the desire that he felt to walk a little, induced him to dismiss his cab. He repented of it almost immediately, however, for he had not reached the boulevard when a fresh shower, a deluge of water mingled with hail, again forced him to take refuge in a doorway. What cursed weather, when one had to scour Paris! After watching the rain fall for a quarter of an hour, he grew impatient again, and hailed an empty cab which was passing. It was a victoria, and in vain did he tuck the leather apron about his legs, for he was quite drenched when he reached the Rue Larochefoucauld, a good half-hour before his time.

The valet stated that his master had not yet returned, but conducted him to the smoking-room, where with slow short steps he paced up and down looking at the pictures. Then as a superb female voice, a contralto of deep and melancholy power, suddenly broke the silence of the mansion, he approached the open window to listen: it was Madame Daigremont rehearsing at her piano a composition which she doubtless meant to sing that evening in some *salon*. Lulled by the music, Saccard began thinking of the extraordinary stories that had been told him of Daigremont: the story of the Adamantine Company especially, that loan of fifty millions, all the securities of which he had kept in hand, selling them and re-selling them five times in succession, through agents of his own, until he had created a market, established a price for them. Then had come the genuine sale, followed by the inevitable fall from three hundred to fifteen francs, enormous profits being made out of a little world of simpletons, who were ruined at one blow. Ah! Daigremont was indeed a strong, a terrible man. Meantime his wife's voice still rang out, exhaling a wild, loving plaint of tragic intensity; while Saccard, stepping back to the middle of the room, halted before a Meissonier, which he valued at a hundred thousand francs.

Just then, however, some one came in, and on turning he was surprised to recognise Huret. 'What! here already? It is not yet five o'clock. Is the sitting over, then?'

'Over! what an idea! They are still squabbling.'

And thereupon he explained that, as the deputy of the Opposition was still speaking, Rougon would certainly not be able to answer until the next day. On realising that, he had ventured to tackle the minister, during a short adjournment, between two doors.

'Well,' asked Saccard nervously, 'and what did my illustrious brother say?'

Huret did not answer immediately. 'Oh! he was as surly as a bear. I will own that I relied on the exasperation in which I found him, for I hoped that he would simply tell me to be off. Well, I told him of your affair, and said that you did not wish to undertake anything without his approval.'

'And then?'

'Then he seized me by both arms, and shook me, shouting in my face: "Let him go and get hanged!" and there he planted me.'

Saccard, who had turned pale, gave a forced laugh. 'That was pleasant,' said he.

'Why yes, pleasant indeed,' answered the deputy, in a tone of conviction. 'I did not ask for so much; with that we can go ahead.' Then as in the next room he heard the footfall of Daigremont, who had just returned, he added in a low voice: 'Let me arrange it all.'

It was becoming evident that Huret greatly desired to see the Universal Bank established, and to become connected with it. No doubt he had already satisfied himself as to what kind of part he might play in the affair. Consequently, as soon as he had shaken hands with Daigremont, he put on a radiant expression, and waved his arm in the air. 'Victory!' he exclaimed, 'victory!'

'Ah! really. Tell me about it.'

'Well! the great man did as he was bound to do. He answered me, "Let my brother succeed!"'

Daigremont was in an ecstasy, so charming did he find the phrase 'Let him succeed!' It implied everything: 'If he is so stupid as not to succeed, I shall drop him; but let him succeed, and I will assist him.' Really it was quite exquisite!

'And, my dear Saccard, we shall succeed,' said Daigremont. 'Be easy on that point. We are going to do everything that is necessary to that end.'

Then, the three men having sat down, in order to decide upon the principal points, Daigremont rose up and went to close the window; for his wife's voice, gradually swelling in volume, was giving vent to a sob of infinite despair, which prevented them from hearing one another. And even with the window closed, the stifled lamentation resounded like an accompaniment while they decided upon founding a financial establishment to be called the Universal Bank, with a capital of twenty-five millions of francs, divided into fifty thousand shares of five hundred francs each. It was further agreed that Daigremont, Huret, Sédille, the Marquis de Bohain, and a few of their friends, should form a syndicate to take four-fifths of the stock in advance, and divide it among themselves, so that in the first place the success of the issue would be assured, whilst later on, keeping the shares in their possession, they would be able to create a scarcity in the market, and send the price up at will. However, everything nearly fell through when Daigremont demanded a premium of four hundred thousand francs to be divided among the forty thousand shares of the syndicate, at the rate of ten francs a share. Saccard protested, declaring that it was not reasonable to make the cow bellow before milking her. Matters were bound to be difficult at the outset; why make the situation any worse? Nevertheless he had to yield, in view of the attitude of Huret, who quietly regarded the matter as quite natural, saying that it was always done.

They were separating, having fixed an appointment for the next day, an appointment at which Hamelin the engineer was to be present, when Daigremont suddenly clapped his hand to his forehead with an air of despair. 'And Kolb, whom I was forgetting!' he said. 'Oh! he would never forgive me; he must be one of us. My little Saccard, if you want to oblige me, you will go to his place directly. It isn't six o'clock yet; you will still find him there. Yes, go yourself and not to-morrow, but to-night, because that will have an effect on him, and he may be useful to us.'

With all docility Saccard started off again, knowing that lucky days do not come twice over. But he had again dismissed his cab, having hoped to go home—a distance of a few steps—on leaving Daigremont's; and so, as the rain seemed to have stopped at last, he descended the street on foot, happy to feel under his heels the pavement of Paris, which he was reconquering. In the Faubourg Montmartre a few drops of rain made him take to the covered passages, the Passage Verdeau, the Passage Jouffroy and the Passage des Panoramas, which last brought him out again into the Rue Vivienne.

Here at the moment when he was about to enter Kolb's he once more started and stopped. A soft, crystalline music, coming as it were from the bowels of the earth, like the voices of legendary fairies, enveloped him; and he recognised the musical voice of gold, the continual jingle which pervaded this neighbourhood of trade and speculation, and which he had already heard in the morning. The end of the day was like its beginning; and the caressing sound of this voice made him radiant, it seemed like the confirmation of a good omen.

Kolb happened to be downstairs in the casting shop, and, as a friend of the house, Saccard went down to join him there. In the bare basement, ever lighted by large flaming gas-jets, the two founders were emptying by the shovelful several zinc lined boxes, filled that day with Spanish coins which they threw into the melting-pot on the great square furnace. The beat was intense; they had to shout to make themselves heard amid this harmonica-like music vibrating under the low vaulted ceiling. Freshly cast ingots, golden paving-stones, having all the glittering brilliancy of new metal, stood in rows upon the table of the assayer, who determined the standard. And since morning more than six millions of francs had passed through the founders' hands, assuring the banker a profit of no more than three or four hundred francs; for the difference realised, between two quotations is of the smallest, being measured by thousandths, so that in gold arbitrage, as the traffic is called, a profit only accrues when large quantities of metal are dealt with. Hence this tinkling of gold, this streaming of gold, from morning till night, from year's end to year's end, in the depths of that cellar, whither the gold came in coins, and whence it went away in ingots, to come back again in coins and go away again in ingots indefinitely, with the sole object of leaving in the trader's hands a few particles of the precious metal.

As soon as Kolb—a little man with a very dark complexion, whose nose, shaped like an eagle's beak, and emerging from a thick beard, proclaimed his Jewish origin—had understood Saccard's offer, which the gold almost drowned with a sound of hail, he accepted it. 'Certainly,' he cried. 'I am very glad to be in it, if Daigremont is! And thank you for having put yourself out on my account.'

However, they scarcely heard each other, and relapsed into silence, lingering there a moment longer, deafened, but experiencing a sensation of beatitude amid that clear provoking jingling, which made their flesh quiver, like some *altissimo* note prolonged upon the strings of violins to the point of provoking spasm.

Outside, although the fine weather had returned, although it was now a clear May evening, Saccard, worn out with fatigue, once more took a cab to go home. It had been a hard, but a well-filled day.

CHAPTER IV
THE BANK IS FOUNDED

Difficulties arose, the affair dragged along, and in fact five months rolled by without anything being settled. The latter days of September had already been reached, and it enraged Saccard to find fresh obstacles continually arising, a whole series of secondary questions, which it was necessary to solve beforehand, if they wished to establish anything serious and substantial. His impatience became so great, that at one moment he was on the point of renouncing the idea of a syndicate, haunted and seduced by the sudden thought of carrying out the affair with the Princess d'Orviedo alone. She had the millions necessary for the first launching; why should she not put them into this superb affair, leaving the smaller investors to come in later on, at the time of the future increase of capital which he had already in view? He thought of this in all good faith, convinced that he was offering her an investment in which she could increase her fortune tenfold—that fortune of the poor, which she was scattering in charities ever on a more extensive scale.

So one morning he went up to the Princess's rooms, and, like a friend who is also a man of business, he explained to her the motive and the mechanism of the bank which he dreamed of. He told her everything, spread the contents of Hamelin's portfolio before her, did not omit one of the many Oriental enterprises. Yielding to the faculty he possessed of becoming intoxicated by his own enthusiasm, and of acquiring faith by his burning desire to succeed, he even revealed the mad dream of the Papacy established at Jerusalem, spoke of the final triumph of Catholicism, the Pope enthroning himself in the Holy Land, dominating the world, and assured of a royal budget, thanks to the creation of the Treasury of the Holy Sepulchre.

The Princess, an ardent devotee, was solely struck by this supreme project, this crowning of the edifice, the chimerical grandeur of which was in keeping with the disorderly imagination which prompted her to throw away her millions in good works of colossal and useless luxury. The French Catholics had just been startled and irritated by the treaty which the Emperor had concluded with the King of Italy, and by which he pledged himself, under certain conditions, to withdraw the French troops from Rome. It was very certain that this meant the abandonment of Rome to Italy; and the Catholics already saw the Pope driven away, reduced to soliciting alms, and wandering through the cities of Europe leaning on a beggar's staff. But what a prodigious *dénouement* that would be: the Pope again finding himself Pontiff and

King at Jerusalem, installed and sustained there by a bank in which the Catholics of the whole universe would regard it an honour to become shareholders! It was so beautiful a conception that the Princess declared it the grandest idea of the century, worthy to incite the enthusiasm of any well-born person possessed of faith. Success seemed to her absolutely certain, and her esteem for the engineer Hamelin, whom she treated with consideration, knowing him to be a constant worshipper, increased. Nevertheless, she flatly refused to go into the affair; she intended to remain faithful to her oath to restore her millions to the poor, without ever deriving from them a single copper of interest, for she desired that this money, the fruit of gambling, should be lost, drunk up by poverty, like some poisoned water that must disappear. The argument that the poor would profit by the speculation did not touch her; it even irritated her. No, no! the accursed source must be dried up, exhausted; she had undertaken no other mission.

Disconcerted, Saccard could only profit by her sympathy to obtain from her an authorisation which he had hitherto vainly solicited. It had been his idea to install the Universal Bank in the mansion itself; or, at least, Madame Caroline had suggested this idea to him; for he himself saw things on a grander scale, and would have liked a palace forthwith. However, they might content themselves with roofing the court, yard with glass and transforming it into a central hall; whilst the entire ground floor, the stables, and coach-houses might be fitted up as offices. Then on the first floor he would give up his *salon*, which would do duty as a board-room, whilst his dining-room and six other rooms could be turned into additional offices. For himself, he should merely retain a bed-chamber and dressing-room, taking his meals and passing his evenings upstairs with the Hamelins; so that at small expense they would provide the Bank with somewhat limited but very respectable quarters. The Princess, as proprietor, had at first refused her consent, through her hatred of all traffic in money. Never, said she, should her roof shelter such abomination. But when she found that religion entered into the matter, she was moved by the grandeur of the purpose, and consented. It was an extreme concession, and she felt a little shudder pass through her at the thought of that infernal machine, a financial establishment, a house of speculation and jobbery, with its machinery of ruin and death, being set up underneath her.

Finally, a week after this abortive effort, Saccard had the joy of seeing the affair, so long thwarted by obstacles, concluded in a few days' time. Daigremont called to tell him that he had secured all needful support, and that they could go ahead. Then, for the last time, they went together over the proposed bye-laws, and drew up the articles of association. And it was a great time too for the Hamelins, whose circumstances were growing difficult again. Hamelin had for years had but one dream—to become the consulting engineer of a great financial establishment; as he expressed it, he undertook to bring the water to the mill. So, little by little, Saccard's fever had gained upon him, and he now burned with the same zeal and impatience. Madame Caroline, on the contrary, after her first enthusiasm at the idea of the beautiful and useful things which they were going to accomplish, seemed to grow colder and wore a dreamy air, now that they were reaching the briars and bogs of execution. Her great good sense, her upright nature, scented all sorts of dark and unclean holes; and she particularly trembled for her brother, whom she adored and whom she sometimes laughingly called 'a big stupid' in spite of all his science; not that she in the least doubted the perfect honesty of their friend, whom she saw so devoted to their fortune; but she experienced a singular sensation, as if the earth were moving under her feet, and feared lest she should fall and be swallowed up at the first false step.

That morning, Saccard, when Daigremont had gone, went up to the workroom with a beaming face. 'At last, it is settled!' he cried.

Hamelin, in a transport, stepped forward with moist eyes, and grasped his hands, as if he would crush them. And as Madame Caroline simply turned towards him, a little pale, Saccard added: 'Well, and you, is that all you have to say to me? Doesn't this news please you?'

Thereupon she smiled pleasantly. 'Why, yes, I am very glad, very glad, I assure you.'

And when he had given her brother particulars respecting the syndicate now definitely formed, she intervened with her peaceful air: 'So it is permissible, eh? for several persons to meet and divide stock among themselves, before it has been issued?'

He made a violent gesture of affirmation. 'Why, certainly, it is permissible! You don't think us silly enough to risk a failure? To say nothing of the fact that we need the support of men of standing, men who can control the market should matters be difficult at the outset. And now, at any rate, four-fifths of our shares are placed in sure hands. We can proceed to sign the articles of association at the notary's.'

She was daring enough to oppose him. 'I thought that the law required the subscription of the entire capital before that was done?'

This time, greatly surprised, he looked her in the face. 'You read the Code then?' he asked.

She coloured slightly, for he had guessed the truth. On the previous day, yielding to her uneasiness, that secret fear without any precise cause, she had read the law which regulated joint-stock companies. Still, just for a moment, she was on the point of denying it. Then she confessed with a laugh: 'Yes, it's true; I read the Code yesterday; and after my perusal, I found myself examining into my own honesty and that of others, just as after reading medical books one fancies oneself afflicted with every disease.'

He, however, took offence; for the circumstance that she had wished to inform herself showed that she distrusted him, and was prepared to watch him, with her searching intelligent woman's eyes.

'Ah!' he replied, with a gesture which swept all vain scruples away, 'do you suppose that we are going to conform to the trumperies of the Code? Why! we could not take two steps; we should be met by obstacles at every turn, while others, our rivals, would go ahead at full speed and outstrip us. No, no, I certainly shan't wait till all the capital is subscribed; moreover, I prefer to reserve some shares for ourselves, and I shall find a man with whom I will open an account, and who, in short, will be our man of straw.'

'It is forbidden,' she declared, simply, in that beautiful, grave voice of hers.

'Oh yes, it is forbidden, but all companies do it.'

'They do wrong, then, since it isn't right.'

Calming himself by a sudden effort of will, and smiling in his turn, Saccard thereupon thought it best to turn to Hamelin, who, in his embarrassment, was listening without intervening. 'I hope that you don't doubt me, my dear friend; I am an old stager of some experience; you can trust yourself in my hands, so far as the financial side of the affair is concerned. Bring me good ideas, and I will undertake to make them yield all desirable profit with the least possible risk. I believe that a practical man can say nothing better.'

72

The engineer, with his invincible timidity and weakness, turned the matter into a joke, in order to avoid giving a direct answer. 'Oh! you will have a real censor in Caroline,' said he. 'She is a born schoolmistress.'

'But I am quite willing to join her class,' declared Saccard gallantly.

Madame Caroline herself had begun laughing again. And the conversation continued in a familiar good-natured way.

'You see,' she said, 'I love my brother very much, and I like you yourself more than you think, and it would give me great sorrow to see you engage in shady transactions with nothing but disaster and grief at the end of them. Thus I may say, now that we are upon the matter, that I have a great terror of speculation and Bourse gambling. I was so glad, therefore, to read in the eighth clause of the proposed bye-laws which you made me copy that the company forbade itself all dealings "for account." That was a prohibition of gambling, was it not? And then you disenchanted me by laughing at me and explaining that it was simply a show clause, a formula which all companies made it a point of honour to insert in their bye-laws, but which none of them ever observed. Do you know what I should like? Why, that instead of these shares, these fifty thousand shares which you are going to issue, you should issue only debentures. Oh! you see that I have become very learned since I read the Code; I am no longer ignorant that folks do not gamble in debentures, that a debenture-holder is a simple lender who receives a certain percentage for his loan without being interested in the profits, whereas the shareholder is a partner who runs the risk of profit and loss. So, why not debentures? That would tranquillise me so much; I should be so happy!'

She jocularly exaggerated the supplicating tone of her request in order to conceal her real anxiety. And Saccard answered in the same tone, with comical passion: 'Debentures, debentures! No, never! What would you have us do with debentures? They are so much dead matter. You must understand that speculation, gambling, is the central mechanism, the heart itself, of a vast affair like ours. Yes, it attracts blood, takes it from every source in little streamlets collects it, sends it back in rivers in all directions, and establishes an enormous circulation of money, which is the very life of great enterprises. But for this, the great movements of capital and the great civilising works that result therefrom would be impossible. It is the same with joint-stock companies. Has there not been a great outcry against them? Has it not been said again and again that they are gambling, cut-throat institutions? But the truth is that without them we should have no railways nor any of the huge modern enterprises that have made the world a new one; for no single fortune would have sufficed to carry them through, just as no single individual or group of individuals would have been willing to run the risk. The risk and the grandeur of the object are everything. There must be a vast project, the magnitude of which will strike the imagination; there must be the hope of a considerable gain, of some stroke that will increase the investment tenfold, provided it is not swept away; and then passions kindle, life abounds, each brings his money, and you can knead the earth over again. What evil do you see in that? The risks incurred are voluntary, they are spread over an infinite number of persons, they are unequal, limited by the fortune and audacity of each. One man loses, but another wins; all hope to secure a lucky number, but must always expect to draw a blank; and humanity has no more obstinate, no more ardent dream, than that of trying fortune, of striving to obtain everything from its capricious decisions, of becoming a king, a demi-god!'

Little by little, Saccard had ceased laughing, and straightening himself upon his short legs, he became inflamed with a lyric ardour, indulging the while in gestures that scattered his words to the four corners of heaven. 'See!' he cried, 'we, with our Universal Bank, are we not going to open up a broad horizon, pierce through that old world of Asia, that unlimited field for the pickaxe of progress and the dreams of the goldfinder? Certainly there was never a more colossal ambition, and, I grant it, never were the chances of success or failure more obscure. But, precisely for that reason, we are within the very terms of the problem, and shall arouse, I am convinced, extraordinary infatuation among the public as soon as we become known. Our Universal Bank will, in the first place, be one of the orthodox establishments which transact all banking and discount business, which receive funds on deposit, and contract, negotiate, or issue loans. But what I especially wish to make of it, is a machine to launch your brother's grand projects: that will be its real *rôle*, the *rôle* in which it will find increasing profits and a gradually commanding power. We establish it, in short, in order that it may assist the financial and industrial companies which we shall organise in foreign countries, the companies whose shares we shall place, and which will owe us life and assure us sovereignty. And now that we are already in sight of this dazzling future of conquest, you come and ask me if it is allowable to form a syndicate and grant a premium to the syndicators, a premium which will be charged among the initial expenses. You worry yourself about inevitable petty irregularities, such as unsubscribed shares, which the Bank will do well to retain under cover of a man of straw; in short, you start on a campaign against gambling—gambling, good heavens! which is the very soul, the furnace, of the mechanical giant that I dream of! Know then that all this is nothing! that this paltry little capital of twenty-five millions is a simple faggot thrown under the machine to heat it! that I hope to double, quadruple, quintuple this capital as fast as our operations extend! that we must have a hail of gold, a dance of millions, if we wish to accomplish over yonder the prodigies we have predicted! Ah! I won't say there will be no breakage—one can't move the world, you know, without crushing the feet of a few passers-by.'

She looked at him, and, in her love of life, of all that was strong and active, she ended by finding him handsome, seductive, by reason of his fervour and faith. Accordingly, without espousing his theories, at which the uprightness of her clear intelligence revolted, she pretended to be vanquished.

'Well, then, say that I am only a woman, and that the battles of existence frighten me. Only do try to crush as few people as possible, and especially crush none of those I love.'

Saccard, intoxicated by his own outburst of eloquence, as triumphant at the mere exposition of his vast plans as though the work were already done, made a display of great good-nature. 'Oh, don't be afraid!' said he; 'if I play the ogre, it is for fun. We shall all be rich.'

Then they talked quietly of the arrangements which had to be made, and it was agreed that Hamelin should proceed to Marseilles and thence to the East, to hasten the launching of their grand enterprises.

Rumours were already spreading, however, about the Parisian market; the name of Saccard emerged from the troubled depths in which it had temporarily sunk; and the reports which circulated, at first in a whisper, but gradually in a louder key, so clearly trumpeted approaching success that once again, as at the Parc Monceau in former days, his ante-room became filled every morning with applicants. He saw

Mazaud call, as if by chance, to shake hands with him and talk over the news of the day; he received other brokers, Jacoby the Jew with the thundering voice, and his brother-in-law, Delarocque, a stout red-haired man who made his wife very unhappy. The *coulisse* came also, personified by Nathansohn, a little fair-haired, active man, borne onward on the wave of fortune. And as for Massias, resigned to the hard lot of an unlucky *remisier*, he already appeared every morning, though as yet there were no orders to be received. Day by day the crowd increased.

One morning at nine o'clock Saccard found the ante-room full. Not having yet engaged any special staff, he had to content himself with such assistance as his valet could give, and, as a rule, he took the trouble to usher in his visitors himself. That day, as he opened the door of his private room, Jantrou wished to be admitted, but among those waiting Saccard caught sight of Sabatani, for whom he had been searching for two days past.

'Excuse me, my friend,' said he, stopping the ex-professor in order to receive the Levantine first.

Sabatani, with his disturbing, caressing smile and adder-like suppleness, left the speaking to Saccard, and the latter, like one who knew his man, plainly set forth his proposition. 'My dear fellow,' said he, 'I have need of you. We want the loan of your name. I will open an account with you, set you down as the buyer of a certain number of our shares, which you will pay for simply by a manipulation of accounts. You can see that I come straight to the point, and treat you as a friend.'

The young man looked at him with his handsome velvet eyes gleaming softly in his long dark face.

'The law, dear master, formally specifies that payment must be made in cash. Oh! it is not for myself that I tell you that. You treat me as a friend, and I am very proud of it. Anything you like.'

Thereupon Saccard, to be agreeable to him, spoke of the esteem in which he was held by Mazaud, who was now willing to take his orders without cover. 'And, by the way,' he added, 'we shall also need signatures to make certain operations regular—transfers, for instance. Can I send you the papers to sign?'

'Why, certainly, dear master. Anything you like!'

He did not even raise the question of payment, knowing that such services are priceless; and, as the other added that they would give him a franc per signature to compensate him for his loss of time, he acquiesced with a simple nod of the head. Then, with his familiar smile, he said: 'I hope, too, dear master, that you won't refuse me your advice. As you will be so well placed, I shall come to you for information.'

'Quite so,' concluded Saccard, who understood. 'Till we meet again, be careful of yourself; don't listen too readily to the ladies.'

Then, with a laugh, for Sabatani was reported to be for some mysterious reason a remarkable favourite with the fair sex, he dismissed him by a private exit, which enabled him to send people away without making them pass through the ante-room again.

Having gone to open the other door, he next called Jantrou, who, as he saw at a glance, was in sore straits, at the very end of his tether, clad in a frock-coat, the sleeves of which had been worn threadbare by long leaning on *café* tables during his endless 'wait' for a situation. The Bourse continued to be a hard-hearted mother to him, and yet he bore himself jauntily, with his fan-shaped beard, still cynical and lettered, at times dropping a flowery phrase, betokening the former university man.

'I meant to write to you shortly,' said Saccard. 'We are drawing up a list of employees, upon which I have inscribed your name among the first, and I expect I shall place you in the issue office.'

Jantrou stopped him with a gesture. 'You are very kind, and I thank you. But I have a proposal to make to you.'

He did not explain himself forthwith, but, starting with generalities, inquired what part the Press would play in the launching of the Universal Bank. The other took fire at the first words, declared that he was for advertising on the largest scale, and would devote all available money to it. Not a trumpet was to be disdained; not even the penny trumpets; for he laid it down as an axiom that every noise was good from the simple fact that it was a noise. The ideal would be to have every paper at one's service; only that would cost too much.

'Is it your idea, then, to organise our advertising?' he at last inquired. 'Perhaps that wouldn't be a bad scheme. We will talk it over.'

'Yes, later, if you like. But what would you say to a paper of your own, completely your own, and which I should manage for you? Every morning there would be a page reserved for you, articles that would sing your praises, or paragraphs reminding people of you, with allusions to you in contributions altogether foreign to financial matters—in short, a regular campaign, in which, *à propos* of everything and nothing, you would be incessantly exalted on the slaughtered bodies of your rivals. Does that tempt you?'

'Why yes, if it doesn't cost the devil.'

'No, the price will be reasonable.'

And at last he named the paper he had in view—'L'Espérance,' which had been founded two years previously by a little group of Catholic notabilities, the violent members of the party, who waged ferocious war upon the Empire. The success of their efforts was however absolutely null, and every week there circulated a fresh report of the paper's disappearance.

'Oh, it doesn't print two thousand copies!' cried Saccard.

'But it will be our business to raise its circulation.'

'And besides, it is impossible: it drags my brother in the mud; I cannot afford to offend him at the very outset.'

Jantrou gently shrugged his shoulders. 'There is no need to offend anyone. You know as well as I do that, when a financial house has a paper of its own, it is of little consequence whether this paper supports or attacks the Government; if it is an officious journal, the house is certain to be included in all the syndicates organised by the Minister of Finance to insure the success of the State and Communal loans; while if it is an opposition print, the same minister is very considerate in his treatment of the bank which it represents, prompted by a desire to disarm it and win it over, which often finds expression in still more favours. So don't trouble yourself as to the politics of "L'Espérance." Have a paper, it is a power.'

Silent for a moment, Saccard, with that alertness of intellect which in a trice enabled him to appropriate another's idea, examine it, and adapt it to his needs, to the point of making it entirely his own, swiftly thought out a complete plan: he would buy 'L'Espérance,' silence its bitter attacks, lay it at the feet of his brother—who would be obliged to show his gratitude—but at the same time keep it Catholic, as a menace, a machine ever ready to resume its terrible campaign in the name of the interests of religion. And, if the folks in power were not amiable with him, he would brandish

Rome in their faces, and risk the grand Jerusalem stroke. It would be a pretty trick to finish with.

'Should we be free to do as we chose?' he asked abruptly.

'Absolutely free. They have had enough of it; the paper has fallen into the hands of a needy fellow who will hand it over to us for ten thousand francs or so. We can then do what we like with it.'

Saccard reflected a minute longer. 'Well, it is settled,' he eventually said. 'Make an appointment and bring your man here. You shall be director, and I will see to centralising all our advertising in your hands. I wish it to be something unheard of, enormous—oh! later on when we have the wherewithal to set the machine going properly.'

He had risen. Jantrou also rose, concealing the joy he felt at finding bread, beneath a bantering laugh, the laugh of one who has lost caste, and is weary of all the mire of Paris.

'At last, then, I shall return to my element, my dear *belles lettres*!'

'Don't engage anybody as yet,' said Saccard, as he escorted him to the door. 'And while I think of it, just make a note of a *protégé* of mine, Paul Jordan, a young man whom I find remarkably talented, and in whom you will have an excellent literary contributor. I will write him a letter and tell him to call upon you.'

As Jantrou was going out by the private door, this happy arrangement of the two outlets struck him. 'Why, this is convenient,' said he, in his familiar style. 'One can conjure people away. When beautiful ladies come, like the one I saluted just now in the ante-room, the Baroness Sandorff——'

Saccard did not know that she was there, and with a shrug of his shoulders he sought to express his indifference; but the other chuckled, refusing to believe in such disinterestedness. Then the two men exchanged a vigorous handshake, and Jantrou went off.

When he was alone, Saccard instinctively approached the mirror, and brushed back his hair, in which not a white thread as yet appeared. He had not, however, spoken falsely to Jantrou, for women scarcely entered his thoughts, now that business had again taken entire possession of him; and he merely yielded to the involuntary gallantry which makes it impossible for a Frenchman to find himself alone with a woman without fearing that she will look upon him as a blockhead if he does not conquer her. And so, as soon as he had ushered in the Baroness, he showed himself remarkably attentive.

'Be seated, madame, I pray you.'

Never had he seen her so strangely seductive, with her red lips, and her burning eyes with bruised lids, set deeply under thick eyebrows. What could she want of him? And he was much surprised, almost mortified, when she had explained to him the motive of her visit.

'*Mon Dieu!* monsieur, I beg your pardon for disturbing you without advantage to yourself; but between people who move in the same circle it is necessary one should render each other these little services. You lately had a cook, a *chef*, whom my husband is on the point of engaging. I have therefore simply come to inquire about him.'

Thereupon he allowed himself to be questioned, answering with the greatest obligingness, and at the same time never taking his eyes off her; for he fancied that all this was a mere pretext: in her heart she cared little or nothing about the cook, she evidently came for something else. And, in fact, by manœuvring, she finally referred to a common friend, the Marquis de Bohain, who had spoken to her of the Universal Bank. So much trouble and worry were attached to investments, said she, it was so difficult to find reliable securities. And at last he understood that she would willingly take some shares, with the premium of ten per cent. given to the syndicators; and he understood still better that, if he should open an account with her, she would not pay.

'I have my private fortune, she said, 'my husband never meddles with it. It gives me a deal of worry, but supplies a little amusement also, I confess. People are astonished—are they not?—to see a woman busy herself with money matters, especially a young woman, and they are tempted to blame her. There are days when I am in mortal embarrassment, having no friends who are willing to advise me. Last fortnight, for want of proper information, I lost a considerable sum. Ah! now that you will be in such a good position to know things, if you would be obliging, if you would only——'

Through the woman of society pierced the gambler, the fierce mad gambler. Such was the passion of this daughter of the Ladricourts, one of whose ancestors had taken Antioch, this diplomat's wife before whom the foreign colony of Paris bent almost double—a passion which led her, like some equivocal applicant, to the offices of everyone who dabbled in finance. Her lips bled, her eyes flamed more brightly, her desire shot forth, seemingly stirring all her ardent nature. And he was simple enough to believe that she was prepared for everything, provided that he admitted her into his great enterprise, and gave her some useful financial tips when opportunity offered.

'Why, I ask nothing better, madame,' said he, 'than to lay my experience at your feet.'

He had drawn his chair nearer, and he took her hand. But at this she at once seemed sobered. Ah! no, she had not yet come to that point! And she rose up in a revolt of birth and breeding.

'So you say, monsieur, that you were satisfied with your *chef*?' she exclaimed.

Quite astonished, Saccard rose in his turn. Had she hoped that he would put her name on the list and give her information for nothing? However, he merely replied: 'Very well satisfied, I assure you. It was only a change in my household arrangements which led me to part with him.'

The Baroness Sandorff hesitated, though scarcely for a second. Then she responded with a simple inclination of her head to the respectful bow with which he bade her good-day; and he was accompanying her to the little door when it was suddenly opened in a familiar manner. The intruder was Saccard's son Maxime, who was to breakfast with him that morning. He stepped aside, likewise bowing, and allowed the Baroness to pass. When she had gone, however, he gave a slight laugh, followed by a few bantering words.

Then seating himself in a large arm-chair, and taking up a newspaper, he added: 'Don't mind me; finish your receiving, if I am not in the way. I have arrived too early, but the fact is I wanted to see my doctor, and I did not find him at home.'

Just then the valet came in to say that the Countess de Beauvilliers requested to be received. Saccard, a little surprised, although he had already met his 'noble neighbour,' as he called her, at the Institute of Work, gave orders for her immediate admittance; then, recalling the valet, he told him to send everybody else away, as he was tired and very hungry.

When the Countess entered, she did not even see Maxime, who was hidden by the back of the large arm-chair. And Saccard was still more astonished to find that she had brought her daughter Alice with her. This lent additional solemnity to the visit: these two women so sad and so pale, the mother slender, tall and very white, with a past-century air, and the daughter already ageing, with a neck elongated to the point of ugliness. He set chairs for them with a bustling politeness, the better to show his deference. 'I am extremely honoured, madame,' said he; 'can I have the happiness to be of any use to you?'

With great timidity, which her haughty manners failed to conceal, the Countess finally explained the motive of her visit.

'Monsieur,' she said, 'it is in consequence of a conversation I lately had with my friend, the Princess d'Orviedo, that the idea occurred to me of calling on you. I confess to you that I hesitated at first, for at my age one cannot easily change one's ideas, and I have always been very much afraid of certain things of nowadays which I do not understand. At last, however, I have talked matters over with my daughter, and I believe it is my duty to stifle my scruples, so that I may try to assure the happiness of my children.'

And she continued; saying how the Princess had spoken to her of the Universal Bank, certainly a financial establishment like the rest of them in the eyes of the profane, but endowed in the eyes of the initiated with an irreproachable excuse, an object so meritorious and lofty as to silence the most timorous consciences. She named neither the Pope nor Jerusalem; those were matters not to be spoken of, scarcely to be whispered among the faithful; therein lay the mystery destined to excite enthusiasm; but each of her words, allusions, and hints revealed a hope and faith which imparted a true religious flame to her belief in the success of the new bank.

Saccard himself was astonished at her suppressed emotion, at the trembling in her voice. As yet he had only spoken of Jerusalem in the poetical phases of his fever. In his heart he distrusted that mad project, scenting something ridiculous in it, and quite prepared to abandon it and laugh at it if it should be greeted with jests. And the emotional application of this pious woman who brought her daughter with her, the earnest way in which she gave him to understand that she and all her kindred, the entire French nobility, would believe and become infatuated with the scheme, struck him forcibly, gave substance to what had been purely a dream, and infinitely enlarged his field of evolution. Was it true, then, that he had a lever here, the employment of which would permit him to move the world? With his gift of rapid assimilation, he at once entered into the situation, talking in mysterious terms of this final triumph which he would pursue in silence; and his speech was full of fervour, for he had really just acquired faith—faith in the excellence of the instrument placed in his hands by the crisis through which the Papacy was passing. He indeed had the happy faculty of believing, as soon as the success of his plans required it.

'In short, monsieur,' continued the Countess, 'I have decided upon a thing which has hitherto been repugnant to me. Yes, the idea of making money work, of putting it out at interest, had never entered my head. Mine are the old ways of viewing life, scruples that are becoming a little stupid, I know; but what would you have? One cannot easily throw off the ideas acquired in childhood, and I imagined that land alone, extensive estates, ought to support people like ourselves. Unfortunately, large estates——'

She blushed slightly, for she was coming to the confession of the ruin which she had so carefully concealed. 'Large estates can now scarcely be found in France; we have been sorely tried, and now we have but one farm left.'

Thereupon Saccard, to spare her further embarrassment, began blazing away. 'But nowadays, madame, no one lives on land. The landed fortune of olden times is an out-of-date form of wealth, which has ceased to have its *raison d'être*. It was the very stagnation of money, the value of which we have increased tenfold by throwing it into circulation, and by inventing paper money, and securities of all sorts, commercial and financial. It is by this means that the world is to be renewed, for nothing would be possible—neither the applications of science nor the final universal peace—without money, liquid money which flows and penetrates everywhere. Oh! landed wealth! it has gone to keep company with the old stage-coaches. With a million in land a man dies; whereas with a fourth of that capital invested in good enterprises at fifteen, twenty, and even thirty per cent., he lives.'

Gently, and with infinite sadness, the Countess shook her head. 'I scarcely understand you, and, as I have told you, I am a survivor of an epoch in which these things were feared, as things wicked and forbidden. However, I am not alone; above all, I must think of my daughter. In the last few years I have succeeded in laying aside, oh! a little sum——'

Her blush appeared again.

'Twenty thousand francs, which lie idle at home in a drawer. Later on perhaps I might feel remorseful at having left them thus unproductive; and since your enterprise has a good object, as my friend has confided to me, and since you are going to labour for what we all wish, and wish most ardently, I will make the venture. In short, I shall be grateful to you if you can reserve for me some shares in your bank, say to the amount of ten or twelve thousand francs. I wanted my daughter to accompany me, for I will not conceal from you that this money is hers.'

So far Alice had not opened her mouth, but had kept quite in the background, in spite of her look of keen intelligence. Now, however, she made a gesture of loving reproach. 'Oh, mine, mamma! Have I anything that is not yours?'

'And your marriage, my child?'

'But you know very well that I do not wish to marry.'

She had said this too quickly; the chagrin of her solitude cried out in her shrill voice. Her mother silenced her with a distressful glance; and they looked at each other for a moment, unable to lie, compelled as they were to share each other's daily sufferings and secrets.

Saccard was greatly moved. 'Madame,' said he, 'even though there were no more shares left, I would find some for you. Yes, if necessary, I will take them from my own. Your application touches me infinitely; I am highly honoured by your confidence.' And at that moment he really believed that he was making the fortune of these unfortunates; he associated them for a share in the golden rain that was about to pour upon him and around him.

The ladies had risen and were retiring. Only at the door did the Countess venture on a direct allusion to the grand affair, which they did not speak of. 'I have received,' she said, 'from my son Ferdinand, who is at Rome, a distressing letter respecting the sadness which the announcement of the withdrawal of our troops has produced there.'

'Patience!' declared Saccard, in a tone of conviction. 'We are here to save everything.'

They exchanged profound bows, and he accompanied them to the landing, passing this time through the ante-room, which he fancied was empty. But, as he came back, he noticed, on a bench, a tall, withered fellow of fifty, clad like a working man in his Sunday best, and accompanied by a pretty girl of eighteen, slender and pale.

'What! What do you want?'

The girl had risen first, and the man, intimidated by this abrupt reception, began to stammer a confused explanation.

'I had given orders that everybody was to be sent away!' added Saccard. 'Why are you here? Tell me your name at least.'

'Dejoie, monsieur, and I have come with my daughter Nathalie——'

Then he again became confused, so much so that Saccard in his impatience was about to push him to the door, when he finally understood that Madame Caroline had known the fellow for a long time and had told him to wait.

'Ah! you are recommended by Madame Caroline! You should have said so at first. Come in, and make haste, for I am very hungry.'

On returning to his room, he allowed Dejoie and Nathalie to remain standing; nor did he even sit down himself, wishing to despatch them more quickly. Maxime, who had risen on the departure of the Countess, was no longer discreet enough to hold aloof, but scrutinised the new-comers with an air of curiosity. And Dejoie told his story at length.

'This is how it is, monsieur. After I served my term in the army I was engaged as office-porter by M. Durieu, Madame Caroline's late husband, when he was a brewer. Then I entered the employ of M. Lamberthier, the salesman at the Central Markets; after which I worked for M. Blaisot, a banker, whom you must have known. He blew his brains out two months ago, and so I am now out of work. I must tell you first of all that I had married. Yes, I married my wife, Josephine, when I was with M. Durieu, and when she was cook to Monsieur's sister-in-law, Madame Leveque, whom Madame Caroline knew very well. Then, when I was with Monsieur Lamberthier, she could not get a situation there, but got suited at a doctor's in Grenelle, Monsieur Renaudin. Then she went to the linen-draper's shop, the Trois-Frères, in the Rue Rambuteau, where by ill-luck I could never get a situation——'

'In short,' interrupted Saccard, 'you come to ask me for employment, don't you?'

Dejoie, however, was determined to explain the great grief of his life, the ill-fortune which had led him to marry a cook with whose employers he had never succeeded in obtaining a situation. It was as if they had not been married, never having a home they could call their own, but having to meet at wine-shops, and kiss each other behind kitchen-doors. However, a daughter was born, Nathalie, whom he had been obliged to put out to nurse until she was eight years old, until indeed he was tired of living alone, and took her to join him in his little bachelor lodging. And in this wise he had become the little one's real mother, bringing her up, taking her to school, watching over her with infinite care, his heart overflowing the while with growing adoration.

'Ah! I may certainly say, monsieur,' he continued, 'that she has given me satisfaction. She's educated, and well behaved. And, as you can see yourself, she's as nice-looking as can be.'

Indeed Saccard found this blonde flower of the Paris pavements quite charming with her slight graceful figure and large eyes shining from under quivering ringlets of light hair. She complacently allowed her father to admire her, virtuous as yet, having no reason to be otherwise, yet allowing a ferocious, quiet egotism to be seen in the limpid brilliancy of her eyes.

'And so, monsieur,' continued Dejoie, 'she's now of an age to marry, and a capital suitor has just come forward, the eon of a pasteboard maker, our neighbour. But he wants to set up in business himself, and asks for six thousand francs. It isn't much; he might expect a girl who would bring him more. I must tell you that I lost my wife four years ago and that she left us her savings, her little profits as a cook, you see. Well, I have four thousand francs, but that's not six thousand, and the young man is in a hurry. Nathalie too——'

The girl, who stood listening, smiling, with a clear, cold decided look, here expressed assent with her chin. 'Of course,' said she, 'I want to end the matter, one way or another.'

Saccard again interposed. He had already gauged the man—his intellect might be limited, but he was upright, had a kindly heart, and was accustomed to military discipline. Moreover, it sufficed that he had presented himself with Madame Caroline's recommendation.

'Very well, my friend,' said the financier, 'I am about to purchase a newspaper, and I will engage you as office attendant. Let me have your address, and now good-day.'

Dejoie did not take his departure, however, but with fresh embarrassment resumed: 'It's very kind of you, monsieur. I'll accept the situation gratefully, for sure enough I shall have to work when I have arranged Nathalie's matter. But I came for something else. Yes, I have heard through Madame Caroline and other people too, that you are about to start a big enterprise, monsieur, and will be able to place your friends and acquaintances in a position to make as much money as you may choose them to make. So if you would be kind enough, monsieur, to interest yourselves in us, if you would consent to let us have some of your shares——'

A second time was Saccard moved, more moved even than he had been on the first occasion when the Countess likewise had intrusted her daughter's dowry to him. Did not this simple man, this microscopical capitalist, with savings scraped up copper by copper, personify the believing, truthful multitude, the great multitude that means abundant, substantial custom, the fanatical army that endows a financial establishment with invincible power? If this worthy fellow hurried to him in this fashion, before a single announcement had been made, a single advertisement issued, what would it be when the offices opened? He smiled with emotion upon this first little shareholder, in whose coming he beheld an omen of immense success.

'Agreed, my friend, you shall have some shares,' said he.

Dejoie's face became radiant, as though some great unhoped-for favour had been promised him. 'You are very kind, monsieur. And with my four thousand francs I shall be able, shan't I? to gain two thousand more, in six months' time or so, and then we can make up the amount we want. And since you consent, monsieur, I would rather settle the matter at once. I've brought the money.'

He fumbled in his pocket and pulled out an envelope which he offered to Saccard, who stood there motionless, silent, struck with admiration at this final proof of confidence. And he, the terrible corsair, who had levied tribute on so many fortunes, ended by bursting into a hearty laugh, honestly resolved that he would enrich this trusting man as well as all the others.

'But, my good fellow,' he said, 'things are not managed in that way. Keep your money. I will put your name down, and you will pay up at the proper time and place.'

Thereupon he finally dismissed them, after Dejoie had made Nathalie thank him, which she did with a smile of content lighting up her hard, yet candid eyes.

82

When Maxime at last found himself alone with his father he remarked with that insolently jeering air of his: 'And so now you dower young girls?'

'Why not?' Saccard answered gaily. 'It's a good thing to invest in other people's happiness.' Then before leaving his room he turned to set some papers in order, and all at once exclaimed: 'And you, by the way, don't you want some shares?'

Maxime, who was slowly walking up and down, turned round with a start, and planted himself in front of his father. 'Oh no, indeed! Do you take me to be a fool?' he asked.

Saccard made an angry gesture, for he found the answer sadly disrespectful and witty. He was on the point of shouting that the affair was really a superb one, and that he, Maxime, credited him with little common sense if he imagined him to be a mere thief like others; but as he looked at the young fellow, a feeling of pity came over him for this poor boy of his, who at five and twenty was already exhausted, worn-out, settled down, and even avaricious—so aged by vice, so anxious as to his health that he no longer ventured on any expenditure or enjoyment without carefully calculating the profits that might accrue to him. And thereupon, thoroughly consoled, quite proud of the passionate imprudence which he himself displayed at the age of fifty, he once more began laughing, and tapped his son on the shoulder: 'Come, let's go to breakfast, my poor youngster, and mind you are careful of your rheumatism.'

Two days later, October 5, Saccard, accompanied by Hamelin and Daigremont, repaired to the offices of Maître Lelorrain, notary, in the Rue Sainte-Anne, and there executed the deed which established the joint stock company of the Universal Bank, with a capital of five and twenty millions of francs, divided into fifty thousand shares of five hundred francs each, a fourth part of the amount alone having to be paid on allotment. The offices of the company were fixed at the Orviedo mansion in the Rue St. Lazare, and a copy of the bye-laws, drawn up in accordance with the deed, was deposited at Maître Lelorrain's office. Then, on leaving the notary's, as it happened to be a very bright, sunny autumn day, the three gentlemen lighted cigars, and slowly sauntered homeward by way of the boulevard and the Rue de la Chaussée d'Antin, feeling well pleased with life, and as merry as boys escaped from school.

The initial general meeting was not held until the following week, in a hall in the Rue Blanche which had formerly been used for public balls, and in which a scheming individual was now endeavouring to start a fine art exhibition. The members of the syndicate had already disposed of those shares which they had taken, but did not wish to keep for themselves; and there came to the meeting one hundred and twenty-two shareholders, representing nearly forty thousand shares, which should have given a total of two thousand votes, since twenty shares were necessary to entitle one to sit and vote. However, as no one shareholder was allowed more than ten votes, whatever might be the amount of stock held by him, the exact total number of votes proved to be sixteen hundred and forty-three.

Saccard positively insisted upon Hamelin presiding. He himself had voluntarily disappeared among the crowd. He had put down the engineer's name and his own for five hundred shares apiece, which were to be paid for, temporarily at all events, by a manipulation of accounts. All the members of the syndicate were present: Daigremont, Huret, Sédille, Kolb, and the Marquis de Bohain, each with the group of shareholders marching under his orders. Sabatani, one of the largest subscribers, was also noticed there, together with Jantrou, accompanied by several of the higher officials of the bank, who had entered upon their duties a couple of days previously.

And all the decisions which had to be arrived at had been so well foreseen and settled beforehand, that never was there a shareholders' meeting at which more splendid calmness, simplicity, and harmony were displayed. The sincerity of the declaration that the entire capital had been subscribed, and that one hundred and twenty-five francs per share had been paid on allotment, was endorsed by an unanimous vote; and then with all solemnity the company was declared to be established. Immediately afterwards came the appointment of the board of directors, which was to consist of twenty members, who, in addition to attendance fees, calculated at an annual total of fifty thousand francs, were, according to the bye-laws, to receive ten per cent. upon the net profits.

This was not to be despised, so each member of the syndicate had insisted upon having a seat on the board; and naturally, at the head of the list of those who were elected, came Daigremont, Huret, Sédille, Kolb, the Marquis de Bohain, and Hamelin, whom his colleagues wished to appoint chairman, followed by fourteen others of minor importance, selected from among the most subservient and ornamental of the shareholders. At last Saccard, who so far had remained in the background, came forward on Hamelin proposing him for the post of general manager. A murmur of sympathy greeted the mention of his name, and he also obtained a unanimous vote.

It then only remained for them to elect the two auditors, whose duty it would be to examine and report on the balance sheets and in this way check the accounts supplied by the management—functions, at once delicate and useless, for which Saccard had designated a certain Sieur Rousseau and a Sieur Lavignière, the first completely under the influence of the second, who was a tall, fair-haired fellow with very polite manners and a disposition to approve of everything, being consumed with a desire to become a member of the board when the latter, later on, should express satisfaction with his services. Rousseau and Lavignière having been appointed, the meeting was about to end, when the chairman thought it his duty to refer to the premium of ten per cent. granted to the members of the syndicate, in all four hundred thousand francs, which, at his suggestion, the meeting charged to the preliminary expenses account. It was a trifle; it was necessary to make an allowance to the promoters; and, this point being settled, whilst the crowd of petty shareholders hurried away like a flock of sheep, the larger subscribers lingered behind, shaking hands with one another on the footway with smiling faces.

On the very next day the directors met at the Orviedo mansion, in Saccard's former *salon*, now transformed into a board room. A huge table, covered with a green velvet cloth and encompassed by twenty arm-chairs upholstered in the same material, occupied the centre of the apartment, where there was also a couple of bookcases, the glass doors of which were provided with silk curtains, also green. Deep red hangings darkened the room, whose three windows overlooked the garden of the Beauvilliers mansion, whence came a kind of twilight, the peacefulness as it were of some old cloister, sleeping in the greeny shade of its trees. Altogether the apartment had a severe, aristocratic appearance, conveying an impression of antique honesty.

The board had met to select its officers, and when four o'clock struck almost all the members were present. With his lofty stature and little pale aristocratic head, the Marquis de Bohain was quite typical of 'old France;' whilst Daigremont, with his affability, personified the lofty fortune of the Empire in all the splendour of its success. Sédille, less worried than usual, began talking to Kolb of an unexpected turn which business was taking on the Vienna market; and around them the other directors, the band, stood listening, trying to glean some information, or else chatting together about their own affairs, being there merely to make up the requisite number, to pick up their share of the spoils on the days when there might be booty to divide. As usual, it was Huret who came late, out of breath, after escaping at the last moment from some committee of the Chamber on which he served. He apologised, and then they all seated themselves in the arm-chairs ranged round the table.

The eldest of the directors, the Marquis de Bohain, had taken his seat in the presidential arm-chair, which was higher and more lavishly gilded than the others. Saccard, as general manager, had placed himself at the other end of the table in front of him; and upon the Marquis announcing that they were first about to select a chairman, Hamelin at once rose up to decline nomination. He had reason to believe, said he, that several gentlemen present had thought of him for the chairmanship, but he wished to call their attention to the fact that he must start for the East immediately, that he was altogether without experience in banking, Bourse, and book-keeping matters, and that the chairmanship altogether carried with it a weighty responsibility which he was unable to accept. Saccard listened to him in great surprise, for only the day before the matter had been quite decided between them; and he at once divined that Madame Caroline had brought her influence to bear upon her brother. They had, he knew, had a long conversation together that morning. And so, as he was unwilling to have any other director as chairman—any independent individual who might embarrass him—he ventured to intervene, explaining that the office was mainly one of honour, and that it sufficed for the chairman to put in an appearance at the general meetings, and there support the proposals of the board and deliver the customary speeches. Moreover, said he, they were going to elect a vice-chairman, who would be empowered to sign for the board. As for the rest, the purely technical parts of their business, the account-keeping, the Bourse, the thousand and one details connected with the inner management of a great financial establishment, would not he, Saccard, be there, he the manager, expressly appointed to attend to the matters in question? According to the bye-laws he had to direct all the office work, see that money was collected and paid, attend to current affairs, carry out the decisions of the board—in a word, act as the company's executive officer. All this seemed sensible enough. Nevertheless, Hamelin resisted for a considerable time longer, and it became necessary for Daigremont and Huret to insist in the most pressing fashion, whilst the majestic Marquis de Bohain affected to take no interest in the matter.

At last the engineer yielded and was named chairman; and then the vice-chairmanship was bestowed on an obscure agriculturist, the Viscount de Robin-Chagot, formerly a Counsellor of State and a gentle niggardly fellow, who would prove a first-rate signing machine. As for the secretary, it was proposed that he should be selected not from among the board members but from among the bank staff, and thereupon the head of the issue department was chosen. Then, as dusk was falling in the spacious, severe-looking room, a greeny dusk of infinite sadness, the work accomplished was judged good and sufficient, and they separated after fixing their meetings at two a month—the petty board on the 15th, and the full board on the 30th.

Saccard and Hamelin went up together to the workroom, where Madame Caroline was awaiting them. By her brother's embarrassment she clearly realised that he had once more yielded through weakness; and for a moment she was quite angry with him.

'But come now, this isn't reasonable!' exclaimed Saccard. 'Remember that the chairman receives thirty thousand francs a year—which amount will be doubled when our business shall have extended. You are not rich enough to despise such an advantage. And besides, what is it that you fear, tell me?'

'Why, I fear everything,' answered Madame Caroline. 'My brother won't be here and I myself understand nothing about money matters. And about those five hundred shares which you have put him down for, without his paying for them at once, isn't that irregular? Would he not find himself in trouble if the enterprise should come to grief?'

Saccard had begun laughing. 'A fine affair!' said he. 'Five hundred shares, a first call of sixty-two thousand five hundred francs! Why, if he won't be able to pay that out of his first profits before six months are over our heads, we might just as well, all of us, throw ourselves into the Seine at once, rather than take the trouble to launch anything at all. No, you can be easy, speculation only devours fools.'

She retained her severity of demeanour in the growing darkness which was filling the room. However, a couple of lamps were brought, and a broad light then illumined the walls, the large plans, the bright water-colours, which so often made her dream of the countries over yonder. The plains were still barren, the mountains still barred the horizon, and once more she conjured up a vision of the distressful wretchedness of that old world asleep on its treasures, but which science was going to reawaken in its filth and its ignorance. What great and beautiful and good things there were to be accomplished! Little by little, her vision showed her the generations of the future, a stronger and happier humanity springing from the ancient soil which progress would once more plough.

'Speculation, speculation!' she mechanically repeated, struggling with her doubts. 'Ah! the idea of it fills my heart with disturbing anguish.'

Saccard, who was well acquainted with her usual train of thought, had watched that hope in the future dawning on her face. 'Yes,' said he, 'speculation. Why does the word frighten you? Speculation—why, it is the one inducement that we have to live; it is the eternal desire that compels us to live and struggle. Without speculation, my dear friend, there would be no business of any kind. Why on earth would you have me loosen my purse strings and risk my fortune, if you do not promise me some extraordinary enjoyment, some sudden happiness which will open heaven to me? With the mere legitimate, moderate remuneration of labour, the mere living wage— with nothing but well-balanced equilibrium in all transactions, life becomes a desert of dreary flatness, a marsh in which all forces slumber and stagnate. But, all at once, just make some dream flare up on the horizon, promise men that with one sou they shall gain a hundred, propose to all these sleepers that they shall join you in the chase after the impossible, and gain millions in a couple of hours, amidst the most fearful hazards—why then the race at once begins, all energies are increased tenfold, and amidst the scramble of people toiling and sweating for their own gratification, birth is given to great and beautiful living things. It is the same as in love. In love as in speculation there is much filth; in love also, people think only of their own gratification; yet without love there would be no life, and the world would come to an end.'

Madame Caroline was not prudish, and made up her mind to laugh. 'And so,' said she, 'your conclusion is that we must resign ourselves since all this enters into Nature's plan. You are right, life is by no means clean.'

Genuine bravery came to her at the thought that each forward step in the world's history and development is made through blood and mire. One must have will-power, determination. Meantime her eyes, straying along the walls, had not ceased gazing at the plans and drawings, and the future appeared to her with its ports, canals, highways, railways, rural districts with immense farms equipped like factories, new, healthy, and intelligent cities, where the human race would live to a great age and in the enjoyment of much knowledge.

'Well,' she resumed gaily, 'I must give way, I suppose, as usual. Let us try to do a little good, that we may be forgiven.'

Her brother, who had remained silent, now drew near and embraced her. She threatened him with her finger. 'Oh! you,' said she, 'you are a coaxer. I know you well. To-morrow, when you have left us, you will trouble yourself but little as to what may go on here; and as soon as you have buried yourself in your work over yonder, you will find everything going well and be dreaming of triumph, whilst here, perhaps, the soil will be cracking beneath us.'

'But,' cried Saccard in a jocular way, 'since it's understood that he will leave you here like a gendarme to lay hold of me if I behave badly.'

All three burst out laughing.

'Yes,' said Madame Caroline, 'you may rely upon it, I shall lay hold of you. Remember what you have promised, to ourselves to begin with, and then to so many others, my worthy Dejoie for instance, whom I strongly recommend to you. Ah! and our neighbours also, those poor Beauvilliers ladies, whom I saw to-day superintending their cook whilst she washed some of their linen, by way of reducing the laundry bill, no doubt.'

For another moment all three continued talking in a very friendly way, and Hamelin's departure was definitely settled. Then, as Saccard went down again to his private room, he learnt from his valet that a woman had been obstinately waiting to see him, although she had been told that there was a board meeting that afternoon, and that he would in all probability be unable to receive her. At first, feeling quite tired, Saccard became angry, and gave orders to send her away; then the thought that he ought to be grateful for success and the fear that he might change his luck should he close his door caused him to alter his mind. The stream of applicants was increasing day by day, and the swarming of this throng brought him intoxication.

His private room was lighted by a single lamp and he could not see his visitor very clearly.

'It was Monsieur Busch who sent me, monsieur,' she began.

His anger kept him standing, and he did not even tell the woman to sit down. By that shrill voice emanating from an unsightly mass of flesh he had recognised Madame Méchain. There was a pretty shareholder for you—a creature who bought securities by the pound weight!

She, however, calmly explained that Busch had sent her to get some information respecting the issue of the Universal Bank shares. Were there any still available? Could one hope to secure some with the premium accorded to the members of the syndicate? But all this was surely a pretext, a dodge to get in to see the house, to spy out what was being done there, and to feel him, Saccard; for her tiny eyes, gimlet-holes as they seemed, pierced in her puffy face, were ferreting everywhere, and incessantly returning to him, as though to probe him to the very soul. Busch, indeed, after long and patient waiting, ripening the famous affair of the abandoned child, was now making up his mind to act, and had sent her out to reconnoitre.

'There are none left,' answered Saccard brutally.

She realised that she would learn nothing further, and that any attempt that day would be imprudent. And so, without waiting for him to push her out, she at once stepped towards the door.

'Why don't you ask me for some shares for yourself?' he resumed with the intention of offending her.

Thereupon, in her lisping, pointed voice in which there was a touch of mockery, she replied: 'Me! Oh! that isn't my style of business—I—wait.'

And, at that moment, catching sight of the huge, worn leather bag which never left her, he felt a shudder pass through him. To think of it, on a day when everything had gone off so well, when he had at last felt so happy at beholding the long-desired birth of that great financial establishment, this woman came to him. Would she, rascally old creature that she was, prove to be the wicked fairy, the fairy who in the familiar tales throws a spell over princesses in their cradles? That bag which she had been carrying through the offices of his nascent bank was—he realised—full of depreciated securities, stock that had ceased to be quoted. And he understood, so he fancied, that she meant to wait as long as might be necessary in order to bury his own shares in it, when the fall of his enterprise should come. Her reply was like the cry of the raven that starts with the army when it sets out on the march, that follows it until the night of the carnage, then hovers and swoops down, knowing there must be dead to eat.

'*Au revoir*, monsieur,' added La Méchain, as she retired panting and very polite.

CHAPTER V
THE LITTLE MONSTER

A month later, in the early days of November, the installation of the Universal Bank was not yet finished. Carpenters were still putting up wainscotings, and painters were applying putty to the enormous glass roof with which the courtyard had been covered.

This delay was due to Saccard, who, dissatisfied with the smallness of the quarters, prolonged the work for the sake of adding unreasonable luxuries to it; and, not being able to set back the walls in order to realise his continual dream of the enormous, he had at last become angry, and thrown upon Madame Caroline the duty of finally dismissing the contractors. She it was, therefore, who superintended the placing of the last wickets. There was an extraordinary number of these. The courtyard, transformed into a central hall, was surrounded by them; grated wickets they were, severe and dignified, surmounted by beautiful brass plates, bearing inscriptions in black letters. In short, the installation, although effected in rather limited quarters, was a very happy one. On the ground floor were the departments which were to be in constant relation with the public, the different cash, issue, and other offices, where every current banking operation went on; and upstairs was the inner mechanism, so to speak, of the establishment, the managing, correspondence, and accountant's offices—that for disputed claims, and that of the staff. Altogether more than two hundred employees moved about in this restricted space. And what struck one as soon as one entered, even amidst the bustle of the workmen driving in their last nails while the gold jingled in the wooden bowls, was an air of severity, of ancient probity, vaguely suggestive of a sacristy, and due undoubtedly to the premises—to that old, dark, damp mansion, standing silent in the shadow of the trees of the neighbouring garden. It seemed to you, indeed, as though you were entering a house of piety.

One afternoon, on returning from the Bourse, Saccard himself experienced this sensation, which surprised him. It consoled him, however, for the absence of gilding, and he expressed his satisfaction to Madame Caroline. 'Well, all the same, for a beginning it is very nice,' said he. 'It has a family air; it's a real little chapel. Later on we shall see. Thank you, my beautiful friend, for all the trouble you have taken in your brother's absence.'

And as he made it a principle to utilize unexpected circumstances, he thenceforward exercised his ingenuity in developing the austere appearance of the house. He imposed upon his employees the manners of young priests; they spoke only in measured tones; they received and paid out money with quite priestly discretion.

Never had Saccard in his tumultuous life so actively expended his energy. In the morning at seven o'clock in advance of all the clerks, and before the office porter had even lighted his fire, he was already at his desk, opening his correspondence, and answering the most pressing letters. Then, until eleven o'clock, there was an interminable gallop—the principal friends and customers of the house, brokers, *remisiers*, the whole host of the financial world, to say nothing of the procession of heads of departments, coming for orders. He himself, as soon as he had a minute's rest, rose and made a rapid inspection of the various offices, where the employees lived in terror of his sudden appearances, which never occurred at the same hours two days running. At eleven o'clock he went up to breakfast with Madame Caroline, ate heartily and drank heartily, with the ease of a thin man whom food does not inconvenience; and the full hour which he spent there was not wasted, for that was the time when, as he put it, he confessed his beautiful friend—that is, asked her for her opinion about men and things, although as a rule he did not know how to profit by her great good sense. At noon he went off to the Bourse, wishing to be one of the first to arrive there, in order to see and talk. However, he did not gamble openly, but repaired to the spot as to a natural place of appointment, where he was certain to meet the customers of his bank.

Moreover, his influence was already felt at the Bourse; he had re-entered the building as a conqueror, a substantial man, supported henceforth by real millions; and the shrewd ones talked in low tones as they looked at him, whispering extraordinary rumours, and predicting his approaching sovereignty. Towards half-past three he was always back at the bank again, settling down to the irksome task of signing, and so trained in this mechanical movement of the hand that, his head free and speaking at his ease, he summoned employees, gave answers, and decided important matters without once ceasing to sign. Then, until six o'clock, he again received visitors, finished the work of the day, and prepared that of the morrow. And when he went up again to Madame Caroline, it was for a more copious meal than that at eleven o'clock— delicate fish and particularly game, with caprices in the matter of wine that led him to dine on one evening with Burgundy, on another with Bordeaux, and on another with Champagne, according to the fortune that had attended him that day.

'Dare to say that I am not well-behaved!' he cried sometimes, with a smile. 'Instead of frequenting clubs and theatres, I live here, like a good *bourgeois*, beside you. You must write that to your brother to reassure him.'

He was not as well-behaved as he pretended, having about that time taken a fancy to a little singer at the Bouffes; but he lived in such a desire, such an anxiety, for success, that all other appetites were bound to remain diminished and paralysed until he should feel himself triumphant, fortune's undisputed master.

'Bah!' Madame Caroline would answer, 'my brother has always been so staid that staidness is to him a natural condition, and not a merit, I wrote to him yesterday that I had induced you not to re-gild the board-room. That will please him much more.'

It was about this time, one very cold afternoon in the early days of November, at the moment when Madame Caroline was giving the head painter an order to merely clean the paint in the board-room, that a servant brought her a card, saying that the person who had delivered it strongly insisted upon seeing her. The card, a dirty one, bore the name of Busch, coarsely printed. She did not know the name; still she gave orders for the person to be shown up to her brother's room, where she usually received.

If for six long months Busch had remained patient, and had not utilised the extraordinary discovery which he had made of Saccard's natural son, it was in the first place for the reasons that he had originally advanced—the comparatively trifling result that there would be in simply obtaining payment of the six hundred francs, which the notes given to the mother represented, and the extreme difficulty of blackmailing Saccard in order to obtain more, that is, a reasonable sum of a few thousand francs or so. A widower, free from all 'incumbrances,' and but little afraid of scandal—how could one terrorise him, how make him pay a stiff price for that ugly present, a natural child, who had grown up in the mud, and was fated possibly to become a brute and an assassin? La Méchain had certainly made out a long bill of expenses, about six thousand francs: first small sums lent to Rosalie Chavaille, her cousin, the little one's mother; then what the poor woman's sickness had cost her, her burial, the care of her grave, and finally what had been spent for Victor himself, since he had fallen to her charge, in the way of food, clothing, and a multitude of other things. But if Saccard should not prove an affectionate father, was it not likely that he would send them about their business? For there was nothing in the world to prove that he was the father except the resemblance between himself and the child; and at most they might merely get from him the amount represented by the notes, provided always that he did not contend that they were barred by the statute of limitation.

Another reason why Busch had delayed action so long was that he had just spent several weeks of frightful anxiety by the side of his brother Sigismond, who was in bed stretched low by consumption. For a fortnight especially, this terrible 'stirabout' had neglected everything, forgotten the thousand and one complicated skeins which he was unravelling, no more appearing at the Bourse, and no longer pursuing a single debtor—never indeed leaving the bedside of his patient, but watching over him, caring for him, and changing his linen like a mother. Becoming prodigal, he who was so stingy, he summoned the best doctors of Paris, and would have paid an enhanced price for drugs if by this means they could only have been rendered more efficacious; and, as the doctors had forbidden all work, and Sigismond in this respect was obstinate, he carefully hid all the young fellow's papers and books. A war of ruses was then carried on between them. As soon as his nurse, overcome by fatigue, fell asleep, the young man, drenched with perspiration and devoured by fever, would manage to find a bit of pencil, and on the margin of a newspaper would again begin making his calculations, distributing wealth according to his dream of justice, and assuring to one and all a due share of happiness and life. And Busch, on waking, was irritated to find him worse, and felt heartbroken at the thought that he thus bestowed on his chimera the little life that was left him. He allowed him to play with these stupid theories, as he called them, just as one allows a child to play with jumping-jacks, when he was in good health; but to kill himself with such mad, impracticable ideas, really it was imbecile! At last, however, having consented to be prudent through affection for his elder brother, Sigismond had recovered some strength and was beginning to get up.

Then it was that Busch, going back to his work, declared that it was time to settle the Saccard matter, especially as Saccard had re-entered the Bourse as a conqueror, and had again become a personage of indisputable solvency. The report which Busch had received from La Méchain, whom he had sent to the Rue Saint Lazare, was excellent. Nevertheless, he still hesitated to attack his man in front, and was delaying matters in the hope of discovering some method by which he might conquer him, when a word dropped by La Méchain with regard to Madame Caroline, the lady who kept the house, and of whom all the shopkeepers in the neighbourhood had spoken to her, started him on a new plan of campaign. Was this lady perchance the real mistress, the one who held the keys of the cupboards and of the heart? He frequently obeyed what he called the stroke of inspiration, yielding to sudden divination, starting upon the chase with a mere indication due to his scent, and then collecting facts which would bring him certainty, and enable him to form a resolution. Thus it was that he betook himself to the Rue Saint Lazare to see Madame Caroline.

Upstairs in the work-room, she stopped short in surprise at sight of this stout, ill-shaven man, with a flat dirty face, greasy frock-coat, and white cravat. He, on the other hand, searched her very soul, finding her such as he desired her to be, so tall and healthy-looking, with her wonderful white hair, which, so to say, illumined her young face with gaiety and gentleness; and he was especially struck by the expression of her rather large mouth, such an expression of kindliness that he at once made up his mind.

'Madame,' said he, 'I wished to see Monsieur Saccard, but they just told me he was not in.'

He lied; he had not even asked for Saccard, for he knew very well that he was not in, having watched his departure for the Bourse.

'And so,' he resumed, 'I ventured to apply to you, really preferring this, for I am not ignorant who it is that I address. It is a question of a communication so serious and so delicate——'

Madame Caroline, who had so far not asked him to sit down, pointed out a chair with anxious alacrity.

'Speak, monsieur, I am listening.'

Carefully lifting the skirts of his coat, which he seemed to be afraid of soiling, Busch settled in his own mind that this woman must be Saccard's mistress.

'You see, madame,' said he, 'it is not an easy thing to say, and I confess to you that at the last moment I ask myself if I really ought to confide such a matter to you. I hope that you will see in the step I am taking nothing but a desire to enable Monsieur Saccard to repair old wrongs.'

With a gesture she put him at his ease, having, in her turn, understood with what sort of personage she had to deal, and desiring to curtail all useless protests. For the rest, he did not insist, but began to tell the old story in great detail—the seduction of Rosalie in the Rue de la Harpe, the birth of a child after Saccard's disappearance, the death of the mother in poverty and debauchery, and the fate of Victor left in the charge of a cousin too busy to watch him, and growing up in the midst of abomination. She listened to him, astonished at first by this romance which she had not expected, for she had imagined that it was a question of some shady financial transaction; and afterwards she visibly softened, moved by the mother's sad fate and the abandonment of the child, deeply stirred in the maternal instinct which was so strong within her, childless though she was.

'But,' said she, 'are you certain, monsieur, of the things that you tell me? Very strong proofs are needed, absolute proofs, in support of such stories.'

He smiled. 'Oh, madame, there is a certain proof, the extraordinary resemblance of the child to Monsieur Saccard. Besides, there are the dates—everything agrees and proves the facts beyond a doubt.'

She was trembling, and he observed it. After a pause he continued: 'You will understand now, madame, how embarrassing it was for me to address myself direct to Monsieur Saccard. I would say that I have no personal interest in the matter; I only come in the name of Madame Méchain, the cousin, whom chance alone has put on the track of the father; for, as I have had the honour to tell you, the twelve notes of fifty francs each given to the unfortunate Rosalie were signed with the name of Sicardot, a thing which I do not permit myself to judge—excusable, *mon Dieu*! in this terrible life of Paris. Only Monsieur Saccard, you see, might have misunderstood the nature of my intervention. And it was then that I was inspired with the idea of seeing you first, madame, so that I might be guided entirely by you as to the best course to follow, knowing what an interest you take in Monsieur Saccard. There! you have our secret. Do you think that I had better wait for him and tell him all to-day?'

Madame Caroline evinced increasing emotion. 'No, no, later on,' she replied.

But she herself did not know what to do, so strange was the story told her. Meanwhile, Busch continued to study her, well pleased with the extreme sensibility that placed her in his power, perfecting his plans, and henceforth feeling certain that he should be able to get from her far more than Saccard would ever have given.

'You see,' he murmured, 'it is necessary to come to some decision.'

'Well, I will go—yes, I will go to this Cité you speak of. I will go to see this Madame Méchain and the child. It is better, much better, that I should first see things for myself.'

She thought aloud; she had just decided to make a careful investigation before saying anything whatever to the father. Then, if she were convinced of the truth of the story, there would be time to tell him. Was she not there to watch over his house and his peace of mind?

'Unfortunately, the case is pressing,' replied Busch, bringing her little by little to the desired point. 'The poor boy is suffering. He is in abominable surroundings.'

She had risen. 'I will put on my bonnet and go at once,' said she.

In his turn he had to leave his seat, and he added carelessly: 'I say nothing of the little bill there will be to settle. Of course, the child has been an expense; and there was also some money lent during the mother's life. Oh! I don't know how much. I would not undertake that part of the matter. However, all the papers are there.'

'Very well, I will see them.'

Then he seemed to be moved himself.

'Ah! madame, if you knew all the queer things that I see in the course of business! The most respectable people have to suffer later on through their passions, or, what is worse, through the passions of their relatives. For instance, I could give you an example. Your unfortunate neighbours, those Beauvilliers ladies——'

With a sudden movement he had approached one of the windows, and was now darting inquisitive glances into the neighbouring garden. Undoubtedly, since his very arrival, he had been planning this attempt at spying, anxious as he always was to know his battle-ground. He had made a correct guess in the matter of the acknowledgment of ten thousand francs, signed by the Count de Beauvilliers in favour of Léonie Cron; the information he had received from Vendôme corroborated his theory of the adventure; the seduced girl, consumed by a desire to come to Paris, had left the paper as security with the usurer Charpier for some trifling loan, and then had taken herself off. But, although he had speedily found the Beauvilliers, he had employed La Méchain in scouring Paris for six months without managing to put his hand upon Léonie. She had first become maid of all work to a process-server, and he had traced her to three other situations, but, dismissed for misbehaviour, she had at last disappeared, and in vain had he searched every gutter. This exasperated him the more, as he could make no attempt upon the Countess until he could secure the girl and utilise her to threaten a scandal. However, he still nursed the affair; and, standing at Madame Caroline's window, he felt happy at being able to spy into the garden of the mansion, of which latter he had previously seen nothing save the façade in the street.

'Are those ladies also threatened with some annoyance?' asked Madame Caroline, with anxious sympathy.

He affected ignorance. 'No, I do not think so. I was simply referring to the sad situation in which the Count's misconduct has left them. Yes, I have friends at Vendôme; I know their story.' And as he finally made up his mind to leave the window, he felt, amid the emotion which he feigned, a sudden and singular reaction upon himself. 'And after all,' said he, 'if there were only money losses! But it is when death enters a house!'

This time real tears moistened his eyes. He had just thought of his brother, and was choking. She fancied that he had recently lost a relative, and discreetly refrained from questioning him. She had not been deceived as to the abject calling of this personage who inspired her with such a feeling of repugnance; and these unexpected tears determined her more than his shrewdest tactics would have done; her desire increased to hasten off to the Cité de Naples at once.

'Then, madame, I rely upon you?' said Busch.

'I start immediately,' she answered.

An hour later, having taken a cab, she was wandering about behind the Butte Montmartre, unable to find the Cité. At last, in one of the deserted streets running out of the Rue Marcadet, an old woman pointed it out to the cabman. At the entrance it was like some broken-up country road blocked with mud and refuse, and leading across a tract of waste land. It was only after an attentive glance that you distinguished the miserable shanties, compounded of earth, old boards, and zinc, and looking like heaps of rubbish around the inner courtyard. At the street corner, a one-storey house built of freestone, but repulsively decrepit and filthy, seemed to command the entrance, like a gaol. And here, indeed, lived La Méchain, like a vigilant proprietress, ever on the watch, exploiting in person her little population of starving tenants.

As soon as Madame Caroline had stepped from the cab, she saw La Méchain appear on the threshold, with her enormous figure swaying in an ancient blue silk dress, frayed at the folds and cracked at the seams, and with cheeks so puffy and red that her tiny nose, almost lost to sight, seemed to be cooking between two live coals. At this sight Madame Caroline hesitated, filled with a sudden feeling of uneasiness, but all at once the woman's gentle voice, which had the shrilly charm of a shepherd's pipe, reassured her.

'Ah! madame, Monsieur Busch sends you; you came for little Victor. Come in, come in. Yes, this is really the Cité de Naples. The street is not classified; we have no numbers yet. Come in. We must talk it all over first. *Mon Dieu*, it is so annoying, it is so sad!'

And then Madame Caroline had to accept a dilapidated chair, in a dining-room black with grease, where a red-hot stove kept up a stifling temperature and odour. La Méchain next had a deal to say about the visitor's luck in finding her there, for she had so much business to attend to in Paris that she seldom reached home before six o'clock. It became necessary to interrupt her.

'Excuse me, madame, I came about this poor child.'

'Precisely, madame, I am going to show him to you. You know that his mother was my cousin. Ah! I can say that I have done my duty. Here are the papers, here are the accounts.'

Going to a cupboard, she thereupon took from it a package of papers, carefully arranged, and enclosed in a blue wrapper such as lawyers use. And she talked on endlessly about the unhappy Rosalie, who had undoubtedly ended by leading a fearful life, though originally she had been a good hard-working girl.

'You see, madame, I lent her all this money in sums of forty sous and a hundred sous at a time. Here are the dates: June 20, forty sous; June 27, forty sous again; July 3, one hundred sous. And see, she must have been ill about this time, for here is an endless line of items of one hundred sous. Then I had Victor to dress. I have placed a V before all the expenditures made for the boy. To say nothing of the fact that, when Rosalie died—oh! in a very dreadful way—he fell completely into my charge. So, look, I have put down fifty francs a month. That is very reasonable. The father is rich; he can easily give fifty francs a month for his boy. In short, it makes five thousand four hundred and three francs, which, with the amount of the notes, six hundred francs, would make a total of six thousand francs. Yes, everything for six thousand francs; there you have it!'

In spite of the nausea, which was making her turn pale, Madame Caroline remarked: 'But the notes do not belong to you; they are the child's property.'

'Ah! excuse me,' replied La Méchain sharply, 'I advanced money upon them. To oblige Rosalie, I discounted them for her. You see my endorsement on the back. It is very good of me not to claim interest. You will reflect, my good lady; I am sure that you won't cause a poor woman like me to lose anything.'

Upon a weary gesture from the good lady, who accepted the statement of account, she became calm again. And once more she found her little piping voice to say: 'Now I will have Victor called.'

But in vain did she in turn despatch three urchins who were prowling about; in vain did she plant herself on the threshold and make vigorous gestures; it became certain that Victor refused to stir. One of the brats even brought back a dirty word for sole reply. Thereupon she started off herself, as if to lead the youngster back by the ear. But she reappeared alone, having reflected, thinking it a good plan, no doubt, to exhibit him in all his abominable horror.

'If Madame will take the trouble to follow me,' said she.

And on the way she furnished some particulars about the Cité de Naples, which her husband had inherited from an uncle. This husband probably was dead; no one had ever known him, and she never spoke of him except to explain the origin of her property. A sorry business, which would be the death of her, she said, for she found

94

more trouble than profit in it, especially now that the Prefecture was tormenting her, sending inspectors to require repairs and improvements, under the pretext that people were dying like flies on her premises. However, she energetically refused to spend a copper. Would they not soon require chimney-pieces ornamented with mirrors in rooms which she let for two francs a week! But she did not speak of her own greediness in collecting the rents, throwing families into the street the moment they failed to pay the usual two francs in advance, doing her own police work, and so feared that beggars without a shelter would not have dared to sleep for nothing against one of her walls.

With her heart oppressed, Madame Caroline examined the courtyard, a devastated piece of ground, full of mounds and hollows, and transformed by accumulated filth into a perfect cloaca. Everything was thrown into it; there was neither pit nor cesspool in the Cité, so that this yard had become an ever-growing dunghill, poisoning the air; and fortunately it was now cold weather, for on warm sunny days the stench generated pestilence. With anxious feet, Madame Caroline tried to avoid the heaps of vegetables and bones, while casting glances at the dwellings on either side. These were indescribable dens, some half tumbling down, others in ruins strengthened with the most extraordinary materials. Several were simply covered with tarred paper. Many had no doors, but afforded a glimpse of dark cave-like holes, whence came a nauseous breath of poverty. Families of eight and ten persons were huddled in these charnel-houses, often without even a bed—men, women, and children, rotting like decayed fruit, given over from early childhood to the most monstrous promiscuity. And thus bands of emaciated, puny brats, eaten up by disease, continually filled the courtyard, poor creatures growing on this dunghill like mushrooms. When an epidemic of typhoid fever or small-pox arose, it at once swept half the Cité into the cemetery.[18]

'I explained to you, madame,' continued La Méchain, 'that Victor has not had good examples before his eyes, and that it is time to think of his education, for he is almost in his teens. During his mother's life, you know, he saw things that were not at all proper, for she didn't stand on ceremony when she got drunk. Then, too, I have never had time to keep a sufficiently watchful eye upon him, because of my business in Paris. I tried to send him to school, but he would play on the Fortifications all day long, and twice I had to go to claim him because he had stolen—oh! trifles only. But you will see for yourself; at the age of twelve he is already a man. Finally, so that he might work a little, I gave him to Mother Eulalie, a woman who hawks vegetables about at Montmartre. He goes with her to market, and carries one of her baskets. The misfortune is that just now she is laid up, as she has something the matter with her. But here we are, madame; be good enough to enter.'

Madame Caroline shrank back. It was one of the foulest holes, at the very end of the courtyard, behind a real barricade of filth, a hovel scarce rising above the soil, a heap of plaster sustained by pieces of board. There was no window. The door—an old glass door it was lined with a sheet of zinc—was left open to let in the light, and the cold wind entered in a frightful fashion. In one corner she saw a palliasse thrown upon the beaten ground. There was no other recognisable piece of furniture among the jumble of broken casks, torn-down trellis-work, and half-rotten baskets which served as chairs and tables. A sticky moisture oozed from the walls, whilst a crack, a greenish split in the black ceiling, allowed the rain to come in just at the foot of the mattress. And the smell, the smell especially was frightful. Here was human degradation and absolute destitution in all their horror.

'Mother Eulalie,' cried La Méchain, 'here's a lady who's interested in Victor. What ails the brat that he doesn't come when he is called?'

A shapeless bundle of flesh stirred upon the mattress, under a shred of old printed calico which served as a covering; and Madame Caroline at last distinguished a fat woman of about forty. Her face was not ugly, and with little blonde ringlets around it still looked fairly fresh.

'Ah!' the sick woman moaned, 'by all means let the lady come in if she means us well, for this cannot possibly continue! When one thinks, madame, that I haven't been able to get up for a fortnight on account of my illness! Of course, I haven't a copper left. Impossible to continue business. I had a few things, which Victor went to sell; and I really believe that to-night we should have died of hunger.' Then, raising her voice, she added: 'Come now, it's stupid! Come out, little one! The lady wishes you no harm.'

And Madame Caroline trembled at seeing a bundle, which she had taken for a heap of rags, rise up from a basket. It was Victor, clad in the remnants of a pair of trousers and a linen vest. The light from the doorway fell full upon him, and she stood there with open mouth, astounded at his extraordinary resemblance to Saccard. All her doubts vanished; the paternity was undeniable.

'I don't want to be bored about going to school,' he declared.

But she still looked at him with a growing feeling of uneasiness. Besides the resemblance which had struck her, there was something alarming about the appearance of this urchin, with one half of his face larger than the other, and his nose twisted to the right; for he seemed prodigiously developed for his age—not very tall certainly, but thickset, full-grown already, like a precocious beast. Although his complexion was yet fresh and pure, his bold devouring eyes and sensual mouth were those of a man; and he embarrassed and terrified the beholder, like the sight of some monstrosity.

But the worst was to come, for when Madame Caroline questioned him, the answers he gave, the admissions he made, though Mother Eulalie in her shame sought to tone them down, were horrible and revolting beyond expression. Madame Caroline shuddered. Her heart failed her in a frightful attack of nausea.

She left twenty francs, hurried away, and again sought refuge in the house of the proprietress, in order to make up her mind and come to a definite understanding with the woman. The sight of such abandonment had suggested an idea to her—the Institute of Work. Had it not been expressly created for such falls, for the wretched children of the gutter, whom it was sought to regenerate by hygiene and the teaching of a trade? Victor must be extricated from this mire as quickly as possible, placed in that home, and have a new existence given him. She was still trembling at all that she had seen. And into the decision that she had arrived at there entered a woman's delicacy: to say nothing yet awhile to Saccard, to wait until the monster should be somewhat cleansed before exhibiting him; for the sight of this frightful offspring had filled her with something like shame for the father; she suffered at the thought of how ashamed of such a child he would be. A few months, however, would undoubtedly suffice to effect a great change, and then she would speak out, well pleased with her good work.

It was difficult to make La Méchain understand, however.

'*Mon Dieu*! Madame, as you please,' said she. 'Only I want my six thousand francs at once. Victor shall not stir from my house until I have my six thousand francs.'

This decision filled Madame Caroline with despair. She did not possess the amount, and, of course, did not want to ask the father for it. In vain did she argue and plead.

'No, no!' said La Méchain. 'If I no longer had my security, I might say good-bye to the money. I know that!' At last, however, realizing that the sum was a large one and that she might get nothing at all, she made an abatement. 'Well, give me two thousand francs at once. I will wait for the rest.'

But Madame Caroline's embarrassment remained the same, and she was asking herself where she could possibly get two thousand francs, when the idea struck her of applying to Maxime. She did not pause to think it over. He would surely consent to share the secret; he would not refuse to advance such a small sum, which his father would certainly repay him. And thereupon she went away, saying that she would return the next day to fetch Victor.

It was only five o'clock, and she was in such a fever to finish the matter that, on getting into her cab, she gave the driver Maxime's address in the Avenue de l'Impératrice. When she arrived, the valet told her that his master was at his toilet, but that he would all the same announce her.

For a moment she stifled in the reception-room into which she was ushered. The house was small, but furnished with an exquisite refinement of luxury and comfort. Hangings and carpets had been lavished upon it; and amid the warm silence of the rooms a delicate odour of ambergris was diffused. All was pretty, soft, and discreet here, although there was no sign of woman; for the young widower, enriched by his wife's death, had arranged his life for the sole worship of self, declining, like a man of experience, to allow anyone to share it again. Owing the enjoyments of life to one woman, he was determined not to let them be spoilt by another. He had long since abandoned his idea of entering the Council of State; he no longer even kept a racing stable, weary as he was of horses as well as women. And he lived alone, idle, perfectly happy, spending his fortune with art and precaution, evincing the ferocity of a perverse 'kept' masher who has turned serious.

'If Madame will allow me,' the valet returned to say, 'Monsieur will receive her in his room directly.'

Madame Caroline was on familiar terms with Maxime, now that whenever he went to his father's to dine he found her installed there as a faithful housekeeper. On entering his room, she saw that the curtains were drawn. Six candles, burning on the mantel-shelf and a stand, illumined with a quiet light this silky, downy nest, the more than effeminate chamber of a beautiful woman. With its deep seats and immense soft downy bed, this was his favourite room, where he had lavished delicacies, marvellous furniture, and precious *bibelots* of the last century, all blended, lost amidst the most delightful confusion of stuffs imaginable.

However, the door leading to the adjoining dressing-room was wide open, and Maxime appeared, saying: 'What has happened, then? Papa isn't dead, eh?'

With his pretty face, girlish but no longer fresh, his eyes blue and clear, hiding the emptiness of his brain, he had just left the bath, and, his skin cool and balmy, had slipped on an elegant white flannel costume. Through the door could still be heard the dripping from one of the bath taps, and a strong flowery perfume ascended from the soft warm water.

'No, no; it is not so serious,' she answered, put out by the quietly jesting tone of the question. 'And yet what I have to say to you embarrasses me a little. You will excuse me for thus falling in upon you——'

'It's true I dine out, but I have time enough to dress. Come, what is the matter?'

He waited, and now she hesitated, and began to stammer, greatly struck by all the luxury and enjoyable refinement which she perceived about her. Cowardice seized upon her; and she could not find courage to tell the whole story. Was it possible that existence, so stern to the child of chance over yonder, in the sink of the Cité de Naples, had shown itself so prodigal to this one, living amid such well-ordered wealth? So much vile wretchedness, hunger, and filth on the one hand, and on the other such exquisite refinement, abundance, and beautiful life. Could money, then, be education, health, intelligence? And if the same human mud remained beneath, did not all civilisation consist in the superiority of smelling nice and living well?

'*Mon Dieu!*' said she, 'it is such a story! But I believe I do right in telling it to you. For that matter, I am obliged to; I have need of you.'

Maxime at first listened to her standing; then he sat down in front of her, his legs giving way, such was his surprise. And when she had finished, he exclaimed: 'What, what! So I am not the only son! A frightful little brother falls on me from the sky, without so much as shouting "Look out!"'

She thought he spoke from an interested motive, and made an allusion to the question of inheritance.

'Oh! an inheritance from papa!' said he.

And he made a gesture of ironical carelessness, which she did not understand. What—what did he mean? Did he not believe in his father's great qualities, his certainty of attaining to fortune?

'No, no, I have my pile,' he added. 'I need nobody. But really this is such a queer affair that I cannot help laughing at it.'

And he did laugh, but in a vexed, anxious, hollow fashion, thinking only of himself, not yet having had time to consider what good or harm this event might bring him. He felt that he lived altogether apart from the others, and dropped a remark in which he brutally gave expression to his real feelings: 'After all, what do I care?'

Having risen, he passed into the dressing-room, and came back directly with a tortoiseshell polisher, with which he began gently rubbing his nails. 'And what are you going to do with your monster?' he asked. 'He cannot be put in the Bastille, like the Man with the Iron Mask.'

She then spoke of La Méchain's accounts, explained her idea of placing Victor at the Institute of Work, and asked for the two thousand francs.

'I don't wish your father to know anything of the matter yet awhile,' said she. 'You are the only person to whom I can apply; you must advance this money.'

But he flatly refused. 'To papa—not if I know it! not a sou! Listen, it is an oath! Even if papa only needed a sou to pay a bridge-toll, I would not lend it to him. Understand! there are some silly things that are altogether too silly; I do not wish to be ridiculous.'

Again she looked at him, disturbed by his ugly insinuations. In this exciting moment, however, she had neither the wish nor the time to make him talk. 'And to me,' she abruptly rejoined—'will you lend these two thousand francs to me?'

'To you, to you——'

He continued polishing his nails with a light, pretty movement, while examining her with his clear eyes, which searched women to their heart's blood. 'To you, yes; after all—I am willing. You are one of the gullible ones, you will pay me back.'

Then, after going to take two notes of a thousand francs each from a little desk, and giving them to her, he grasped her hands and held them for a moment in his own, with an air of friendly gaiety, like a step-son who feels some sympathy for his step-mother. 'You have some illusions respecting papa,' said he. 'Oh! don't protest; I don't want to meddle with your affairs. Women are so queer; it amuses them sometimes to devote themselves, and of course they are quite right in taking their pleasure where they find it. All the same, if some day you should be ill rewarded, come and see me, we will have a chat.'

When Madame Caroline was once more in her cab, still stifling from the soft warmth of the little residence and the heliotrope perfume which had penetrated her garments, she shuddered as though she had just left some house of ill-repute, frightened also by the son's reticence and jocularity with regard to his father, which increased her suspicion of a past life such as none would confess to. However, she did not wish to know anything; she had the money, and quieted herself by planning the work of the morrow, so that by night time the child might be saved from his vices.

Accordingly, early in the morning, she already had to start out, for there were all sorts of formalities to be fulfilled in order to ensure her *protege's* admission into the Institute of Work. Naturally, her position as secretary of the Committee of Superintendence, to which the Princess d'Orviedo, the founder of the Institute, had appointed ten ladies of high social standing, facilitated the accomplishment of these formalities; and in the afternoon she had only to go to the Cité de Naples to fetch Victor. She took some suitable garments with her, and was not really without anxiety as to the resistance which the boy might offer—he who would not hear speak of going to school. However, La Méchain, to whom she had sent a telegram, and who was waiting for her, informed her on the threshold of a piece of news by which she herself had been upset. Mother Eulalie had died suddenly in the night, from some cause which the doctor had been unable to precisely fix—a congestion, perhaps, some distemper produced by her corrupted blood. This tragedy had quite stupefied the boy, filled him with a secret fear, so that he consented to dress and seemed even pleased with the idea of living in a house with a beautiful garden. There was nothing to keep him at the Cité any longer since the 'fat 'un,' as he called Mother Eulalie, was going to rot in the grave.

Meanwhile, La Méchain, while writing her receipt for the two thousand francs, laid down her conditions. 'It is agreed, isn't it? you will complete the six thousand in one payment, six months from now. Otherwise, I shall apply to Monsieur Saccard.'

'But you will be paid by Monsieur Saccard himself,' said Madame Caroline. 'To-day I am simply his substitute, that is all.'

There was no affection in the farewells exchanged between Victor and his old cousin; a kiss upon the hair, and then the urchin was all haste to get into the cab, while La Méchain, scolded by Busch for having consented to accept merely an instalment of her claim, remained secretly annoyed at seeing her security thus escape her. 'Now, madame, be honest with me,' said she, 'otherwise I shall find a way to make you repent.'

On the way from the Cité de Naples to the Institute of Work on the Boulevard Bineau, Madame Caroline was only able to extract monosyllables from Victor, who with glittering eyes devoured the route, the broad avenues, the passers-by and handsome houses. He did not know how to write and could scarcely read, having always played the truant from school in order to loaf about the Fortifications; and his face, the face of a child who has precociously matured, only expressed the exasperated appetites of his race, a violent, pressing longing for enjoyment, aggravated by the wretchedness and the abominable examples amidst which he had grown up. On the Boulevard Bineau his eyes, like those of a young wild beast, glowed more brightly when, having alighted from the cab, he began crossing the central courtyard, edged on one side by the boys' and on the other by the girls' department. He had already darted a searching look at the spacious play-grounds planted with beautiful trees, at the faïence-walled kitchens, from whose open windows came the smell of meat, at the marble-decorated dining halls, as long and as lofty as the naves of chapels, at all the regal luxury which the Princess, obstinately bent on restitution, had desired to bestow upon the poor. Then, on reaching the farther end of the court, on entering the building where the managerial offices were installed, on being led from department to department so that the customary formalities of admission might be fulfilled, he listened to the clatter of his new shoes along the endless corridors, up and down the broad stairways, across all the vestibules flooded with air and light, and decorated in palatial style. His nostrils quivered; all this would be his.

Returning to the ground floor, however, in order that some document might be signed, Madame Caroline led him along a fresh corridor, and suddenly stopped before a glass door through which he could see a workshop, where some lads of his own age, standing at benches, were receiving instruction in wood-carving.

'You see, my little friend,' said she, 'they work here, because it is necessary to work if one wishes to secure good health and happiness. There are classes in the evening, and I hope you will be steady, and study well. You will, won't you? You will be able to decide your own future here, a future such as you have never dreamt of.'

Victor frowned, a dark expression came over his face. He did not answer, and henceforth his eyes—the eyes of a young wolf—only cast envious, thieving glances at all the lavish display of luxury. To have, to enjoy it all, but without work; to seize and feast upon it, tooth and nail—that was what he wanted. And from that moment he was there only as a rebel, a prisoner who dreams of robbery and escape.

'Everything is now settled,' resumed Madame Caroline; 'we are going up to the bathroom.'

It was the regulation that each inmate should take a bath on his arrival, and the baths were installed upstairs in little rooms adjoining the infirmary, beyond whose two small dormitories, one for boys and one for girls, the linen-room was situated. Six sisters of charity reigned in this superb linen-room, around which ran tiers of presses all of varnished maple, and also in the model infirmary, whose immaculate brightness, whiteness, and cheerful cleanliness were typical of health. And at times, too, some ladies of the Committee of Superintendence would come and spend an hour here in the afternoon, less to exercise any supervision than to help on the work by their own devoted assistance.

That day it chanced that the Countess de Beauvilliers and her daughter Alice were in a room separating the dormitories of the infirmary. The Countess often brought the girl there in order to divert her mind, in order that she might experience the pleasure which the practice of charity affords. And on this occasion Alice was helping one of the sisters to prepare some slices of bread and jam for two little convalescent girls who were allowed a snack between meals.

'Ah!' exclaimed the Countess at sight of Victor, who was given a seat whilst his bath was being got ready, 'here is a new one!'

As a rule, she behaved very ceremoniously towards Madame Caroline, merely saluting her with an inclination of the head, never speaking to her, for fear perhaps lest she might be obliged to enter into neighbourly intercourse with her. However, the sight of this boy whom Madame Caroline had brought to the Institute, the active kindness with which she attended to him, doubtless touched Madame de Beauvilliers and helped to draw her from her reserve. So they began talking together in an undertone.

'If you only knew, madame, from what a hell I have just taken him!' said Madame Caroline. 'I recommend him to your kindness as I have recommended him to all the ladies and gentlemen.'

'Has he any relatives? Do you know them?'

'No, his mother is dead. He has only me.'

'Poor boy! Ah! what misery there is!'

In the meantime Victor did not take his eyes off the slices of bread and jam. Ferocious greed had lighted up his eyes, and from the jam which was being spread on the bread with a knife his glances strayed first to Alice's tapering white hands, then to her slender neck, in turn to all parts of her figure—the spare figure of a sickly girl wasting away in the vain waiting for wedlock. Ah! if he had only been alone with her, how he would have given her a good butt in the stomach with his head and sent her reeling against the wall, so that he might have taken the bread and jam from her. However, the girl had noticed his gluttonous glances, and after consulting the sister of charity with her eyes, exclaimed: 'Are you hungry, my little friend?'

'Yes.'

'And you don't dislike jam?'

'No.'

'So it would suit you if I got a couple of slices ready for you to eat when you have taken your bath?'

'Yes.'

'A great deal of jam on very little bread, that's what you want, isn't it?'

'Yes.'

She laughed and joked, but he remained grave and open-mouthed, with his greedy eyes devouring both herself and her bread and jam.

At that moment, however, loud shouts of joy, quite a violent uproar, arose from the boys' ground, where four o'clock playtime was beginning. The workshops were emptying, and the youngsters had half an hour before them to stretch their legs and eat a morsel. 'You see,' resumed Madame Caroline, leading Victor to a window, 'although they work here, they also play. Do you like work?'

'No.'

'But you like play?'

'Yes.'

'Well, if you want to play you will have to work. Everything will come all right; you will be sensible, I am sure of it.'

He returned no answer. A flush of pleasure was heating his face at the sight of his released companions shouting and skipping hither and thither. Then his eyes reverted to the promised slices of bread and jam, which the girl had finished preparing and was

101

laying on a plate. Yes, liberty and dainties all the time, he wanted nothing else. However, his bath was now ready, and so he was led away.

'That little fellow won't be easy to manage, I fancy,' gently said the sister; 'I distrust them when they haven't a straight face.'

'Yet this one isn't ugly,' murmured Alice. 'To see him look at you, you would think he was eighteen.'

'That is true,' rejoined Madame Caroline, with a slight shudder; 'he is very advanced for his age.'

Before going away the ladies wished to have the pleasure of seeing the little convalescent girls eat their bread and jam. One of them especially was very interesting, a little fair-complexioned thing of ten years old, who already had knowing eyes, a womanly look, the sickly precocity peculiar to the Parisian *faubourgs*. Moreover, hers was the old story: a drunken father who had gone off with a mistress, and a mother who had likewise taken to drink and chosen a paramour. Yet the wretched woman was allowed to come and see her child, for she herself had begged that she might be taken from her, having retained an ardent feeling of maternal love amidst all her degradation. And she happened to be there that very afternoon—a thin, yellow-skinned, worn-out creature with eyelids reddened by tears—and she sat beside the white bed where, propped up by pillows, her little one, neat and clean, lay eating her bread and jam in a pretty, graceful way.

The woman recognised Madame Caroline, for she had previously called at Saccard's for help. 'Ah! madame,' said she, 'so here's my poor Madeleine saved again. She has all our misfortunes in the blood, you see, and the doctor well told me that she wouldn't live if she continued to be hustled about at home, whereas here she has meat and wine, and air and quietness. I pray you, madame, tell that good gentleman that I don't spend an hour of my life without blessing him.'

A sob checked her utterance; her heart was melting with gratitude. It was Saccard whom she alluded to, for, like most of the parents who had children at the institution, she knew him alone. The Princess d'Orviedo did not show herself, whereas he had long lavished his efforts, peopling the establishment, picking little wretches of all kinds out of the gutters in order that this charitable machine, in some degree his own creation, might the sooner set to work. And, moreover, he had, as usual, grown quite enthusiastic, taking five-franc pieces from his own pocket and distributing them among the sorry parents whose little ones he saved. And to all those wretched folk he remained the one true benefactor.

'And you will tell him, won't you, madame? that there is a poor woman praying for him somewhere. Oh! it isn't that I'm religious. I don't want to be; I've never been a hypocrite. No, between the churches and us it is all over, for we not merely don't think of them any more, but it's of no use to waste one's time in them. Still, that doesn't alter the fact that there's something up above us, and when somebody has been good to you it relieves you, you know, to call down the blessings of Heaven upon him.'

Tears started from her eyes and rolled down her withered cheeks. 'Listen to me, Madeleine, listen,' she resumed.

The little girl, who looked so pale in her snow-white chemise as she lay there licking the jam off the bread with the tip of her greedy tongue, her eyes beaming the while with happiness, raised her head and became attentive, but without interrupting her feast.

'Every evening,' continued the mother, 'before you go to sleep in bed, you must join your hands like this, and say: "Pray, God, grant Monsieur Saccard a reward for all his kindness, and give him a long life and happiness." You hear, Madeleine; you promise me you will say it?'

'Yes, mother.'

During the following weeks Madame Caroline's mind was sorely troubled. She had no longer a clear opinion of Saccard. The story of Victor's birth and abandonment, of that poor creature Rosalie's sad affair, of the unpaid notes of hand, and of the fatherless child growing up in the midst of mire—all that lamentable past made her feel sick at heart. She brushed aside the visions of it that arose before her in the same way as she had refrained from provoking Maxime's indiscreet revelations. Plainly enough, there were certain old-time mud stains in all this business, the thought of which frightened her, and the full knowledge of which would have brought her, she felt it, too much grief. And then how strange the contrast. There was that woman in tears, joining her little girl's hands, and teaching her to pray for that very same man. There, in this case, was Saccard worshipped as an incarnation of beneficent Providence; and verily he had given proof of true kindness of heart, had actually saved souls from perdition, by the passionate scheming activity which he evinced, raising himself to virtue whenever the task before him was a fine one. And thus Madame Caroline ended by refusing to judge him, and, like a learned woman who has read and thought too much, sought to quiet her conscience by saying that he, like all other men, was compounded of good and evil.

Three months slipped by, during which she went to see Victor twice every week; and at last, how it came about she hardly knew, she one day again found herself Saccard's mistress. Was it that this child Victor had become as it were a bond, a link, inevitably drawing her, his mother by chance and adoption, towards the father who had abandoned him? Yes, it is probable that in her case there was far less sensuality than a kind of sentimental perversion. In her great sorrow, at being childless herself, the charge of this man's son amid such poignant circumstances had certainly affected her to the point of annihilating her will. And, moreover, her self-surrender was explained by her craving for maternity. Then, too, she was a woman of clear good sense; she accepted the facts of life without wearing herself out in trying to explain their thousand complex causes. The unravelling of heart and brain, the minute splitting and analysing of hairs, was, to her mind, a pastime fit only for idle worldlings with no household to manage, no child to love, intellectual humbugs who ever seek excuses for their frailty in what they call the 'the science of the soul.'

She, with her vast erudition, who formerly had wasted her time in a burning desire to know the whole vast world and join in the disputes of philosophers, had emerged from this phase of her life with a feeling of great contempt for all such psychological recreations, which threaten to supersede both the pianoforte and the embroidery frame, and of which she would laughingly remark that they had depraved far more women than they had reclaimed. And so, whenever she felt a gap within her, whenever her free will succumbed, she preferred to have the requisite courage to realise the fact and accept it, and relied upon the work of Life to efface the fault, to repair the evil, even as the ever-rising sap closes the gash in the heart of an oak tree, supplying in time fresh wood and bark.

Thus, if she was now Saccard's mistress, without having desired it, without feeling sure if she esteemed him, she did not experience any feeling of ignominy, but buoyed herself up by judging him to be not unworthy of her, attracted as she was by the qualities he showed as a man of action, by the energy to conquer that he evinced, by the belief that he was good and useful to others. In the need we all feel of purifying our errors, her first feeling of shame had passed away, and nothing now appeared more natural, more peaceful than their *liaison*. Reason, not passion, seemed to link them together; he was happy at having her with him of an evening when he did not go out; and she, with her keen intelligence and uprightness, showed herself almost maternal, evinced a calming affection. And for Saccard, that freebooter of the Parisian streets, whose roguery in all sorts of shady financial affairs had brought him many a scorching and drubbing, the affection of this adorable woman, who, her six and thirty years notwithstanding, was still so young and healthy under the snowy mass of her abundant white hair, who displayed such valiant good sense, such true wisdom in her faith in life, such as it is, and despite all the mud that its torrent rolls along—this affection was really an undeserved stroke of luck, a reward stolen like all others.

Months passed by, and it must be admitted that throughout all the difficult beginnings of the Universal Bank Madame Caroline found Saccard very energetic and very prudent. Indeed, her suspicions of shady transactions, her fears that he might compromise her brother and herself entirely disappeared when she saw him so obstinately, so incessantly struggling with difficulties, expending his energy from morning till night in order to ensure the perfect working of this huge new machine, whose mechanism was grinding and grating and seemed likely to burst. And she felt grateful to him for it all, she admired him.

The Universal was not progressing as he had hoped it would, for it had against it the covert hostility of great financiers. Evil reports were spread abroad and obstacles were constantly cropping up, preventing the employment of its capital, frustrating all profitable endeavours on a large scale. Accordingly Saccard made a virtue of necessity—of the slow progress to which he was reduced—taking but one step forward at a time, and on solid ground, ever on the look-out for pitfalls, too much absorbed in striving to avoid a fall to dare to launch out into hazardous speculation. He impatiently champed the bit, stamping like a race-horse who is allowed a mere trot. However, never were the beginnings of a financial house more honourable or more correct, and the Bourse talked of it all in astonishment.

In this wise, then, they reached the date of the first general meeting of shareholders. April 25 had been chosen for this meeting, and on the 20th Hamelin, hastily recalled by Saccard, who was stifling in his narrow sphere, arrived from the East expressly to preside over it. He brought excellent news with him; the agreements for the formation of the United Steam Navigation Company were concluded, and he, moreover, had in his pocket the firmans granting the working of the Carmel silver mines to a French company; to say nothing of the National Turkish Bank, the foundations of which he had just laid at Constantinople, and which would become a branch of the Universal. As for the big question of the Asia Minor Railway, this was not yet ripe and must be kept in reserve. Besides, he meant to return to the East directly after the meeting, in order to continue his studies. Saccard, who was delighted, had a long conversation with him, at which Madame Caroline was present, and he easily persuaded them that an increase of capital would be absolutely necessary if they wished to provide for all these enterprises. The large shareholders, Daigremont,

Huret, Sédille, and Kolb, who had been consulted, had already approved of an increase, so that a couple of days sufficed to mature the suggestion and lay it before the board on the very eve of the meeting of shareholders.

This special board-meeting was a solemn affair. All the directors attended in that large severe-looking room on the first floor, where the light acquired a greenish tinge through the proximity of the lofty trees in the garden of the Beauvilliers mansion. As a rule, there were two board-meetings every month: the petty, but more important meeting on or about the 15th, when only the real leaders, the true managers, of the enterprise would attend; and the full meeting on the 30th, when the silent and purely ornamental directors came to signify their approval of all that had been prearranged and to give the signatures required of them. On this occasion the Marquis de Bohain arrived one of the first, testifying with an aristocratic weary air to the approval of the entire French nobility. And the Viscount de Robin-Chagot, the penurious, gentle vice-chairman, who had been selected to school those of the directors to whom the position of affairs had not been communicated, drew them aside, and in a few words informed them of the orders of the general manager, the real master of one and all. It was an understood thing, and with a nod they all promised compliance.

At last the proceedings commenced. Hamelin acquainted the board with the report which he was to read at the shareholders' meeting. This was the big task on which Saccard had long been at work, and which he had at last drafted in a couple of days, supplementing it with information which Hamelin had furnished on his arrival. Yet, while the engineer read it aloud, he listened modestly, with an air of keen interest, as though he had not previously been acquainted with a single word of it.

The report began by recapitulating the business done by the Universal Bank since its foundation. Its transactions were good ones, but they were mainly little every-day matters in which money was promptly turned over—all the usual routine, in fact, of financial houses. Still, some rather large profits had been made in the matter of the Mexican loan which had been floated during the preceding month, after the Emperor Maximilian's departure for Mexico. A queer affair was this, disgracefully mismanaged, with plenty of pickings in the way of premiums for enterprising speculators; and Saccard greatly regretted that lack of money had kept him from wading yet more deeply in these troubled waters. However, if the bank's transactions had simply been commonplace ones, at least it had managed to live. Since its foundation on October 5, until December 31, it had realised profits amounting to rather more than four hundred thousand francs. This had enabled the management to pay off one-fourth of the preliminary expenses, to give the shareholders five per cent., and to carry ten per cent. to a reserve fund. Moreover, the directors had received the ten per cent. guaranteed to them by the articles of association, and there remained about sixty-eight thousand francs, which it was proposed to carry forward until the next distribution of profits. Nothing could have been more strictly commonplace and honourable than all this. It was the same with regard to the price at which Universal shares were quoted at the Bourse; they had risen from five hundred to six hundred francs, not suddenly, but in a slow normal fashion, just like the shares of any respectable banking house. And for two months now the price had remained stationary, there being no reason for any increase, given the humdrum daily round in which the newly-born concern seemed to be falling asleep.

But the report passed on to the future, and here everything suddenly expanded; a vast horizon of a series of great enterprises was spread before the view. Especial attention was called to the United Steam Navigation Company, whose shares were to be issued by the Universal Bank. This company, with a capital of fifty millions of francs, was to monopolise the entire transport service of the Mediterranean. It would amalgamate those two great rival concerns, the Phocæan Company, with its service to Constantinople, Smyrna, and Trebizond by way of the Piræus and the Dardanelles, and the Maritime Company, with its service to Alexandria by way of Messina and Syria; to say nothing of the various minor houses which would be absorbed in the enterprise—Combarel and Co., with their service to Algeria and Tunis; Veuve Henri Liétard, who ran another service to Algeria, but by way of Spain and Morocco; and, finally, Messrs. Féraud-Giraud Brothers, whose vessels plied along the coasts of Italy to Naples, Civita Vecchia, and the ports of the Adriatic. By making one company of all these rival concerns, which were killing one another, the entire Mediterranean would be conquered. By the centralization of capital they would be able to build superior vessels, of unsurpassed speed and comfort; and they would further be able to increase the frequency of the services and the number of the ports of call, so that the East would soon become a mere suburb of Marseilles. And to what importance would the company not attain when the Suez Canal was finished and it became possible for it to organise services to India, Tonquin, China, and Japan! Never had a greater and a safer enterprise been conceived.

Then came the question of supporting the National Turkish Bank, concerning which the report supplied an abundance of technical particulars, fully demonstrating what a secure and substantial enterprise this would be. And the recital of the contemplated operations concluded with the announcement that the Universal would also give its patronage to the Carmel Silver Mining Company, which was to be established with a capital of twenty millions of francs. Specimens of ore, which chemists had analysed, had been found to contain a large proportion of silver. But, more even than science, the antique poesy clinging to the Holy Places summoned up a vision of silver pouring forth in a miraculous stream—a divine, dazzling vision which Saccard had alluded to at the end of a sentence with which he was very pleased.

Finally, after all these promises of a glorious future, the report concluded by recommending an increase of capital. It should be doubled, raised from five and twenty to fifty millions of francs. The suggested system of issue was of extreme simplicity, in order that everybody might understand it. Fifty thousand new shares would be created, and reserved share by share for the holders of the original stock, so that there would not even be any public subscription. Only these new shares were to be issued at five hundred and twenty francs apiece, inclusive of a premium of twenty francs. This would yield a million, which could be carried to the reserve fund. It was reasonable and prudent that this little tax should be levied on the shareholders, since they would be favoured by the new issue. Moreover, only a fourth part of the value of the shares, *plus* the premium, was payable on allotment.

A hum of approval arose when Hamelin ceased reading. It was perfect; not the faintest objection could be raised. Throughout the perusal Daigremont, to all appearance very much interested in his finger-nails, had smiled at sundry vague thoughts that occurred to him; whilst deputy Huret, leaning back in his arm-chair with closed eyes, almost fell asleep under the impression that he was at the Chamber of Deputies. And meantime Kolb, the banker, quietly and openly devoted himself to making a long calculation on some of the sheets of paper which, like every director, he had before him.

However, Sédille, who was always anxious and distrustful, made up his mind to ask a few questions. What would become of those new shares which the shareholders, relinquishing their right, might not choose to take up? Would the bank keep them on its own account, and, if so, would this not be illegal, as the declaration of increase of capital, required by law, could not be made at the notary's until the entire additional capital had been subscribed? On the other hand, if the Bank meant to get rid of these shares, to whom and how did it expect to sell them? However, at the first words spoken by the silk manufacturer, the Marquis de Bohain, observing Saccard's impatience, intervened, and declared, with his grand aristocratic air, that the board left these matters of detail to its chairman and manager, who were both so devoted and so competent. And after this only congratulations were heard, and the meeting broke up with everybody in rapturous delight.

The shareholders' meeting on the morrow supplied occasion for some really touching demonstrations. It was again held in that hall in the Rue Blanche where the proprietor of a public ball had gone bankrupt; and prior to the chairman's arrival the most favourable reports began to circulate among the crowd of shareholders. One rumour in particular was transmitted in whispers from ear to ear: Rougon, the minister, the manager's brother, whom the growing Opposition was now virulently attacking, was disposed to favour the Universal if the Bank's newspaper 'L'Espérance,' a former organ of the Catholic party, would only defend the Government. One of the deputies of the Left had lately raised that terrible cry 'The second of December[19] is a crime!' which had resounded from one to the other end of France like an awakening of the public conscience. And it was necessary to answer it by great deeds—such as the launching of the approaching Universal Exhibition, which, it was expected, would increase business tenfold. Besides, people would make piles of money in Mexico and elsewhere now that the triumph of the Empire was at its zenith.

In one little group of shareholders, whom Jantrou and Sabatani were schooling, a good deal of laughter was indulged in at the expense of another deputy of the Left who, during the discussion of the army budget, had let his fancy run riot to the point of suggesting that the Prussian recruiting system should be adopted in France. The Chamber had been much amused by this. How the terror of Prussia had been troubling certain brains since that Denmark affair, under the influence of the secret resentment that Italy had harboured against France since Solferino! However, all the hubbub of private conversation, all the loud buzzing that prevailed in the hall, was suddenly hushed when Hamelin and the other officials entered. Displaying even more modesty than at the board meeting, Saccard had withdrawn from all prominence, hidden himself away among the throng; and he contented himself with giving the signal for applauding the report, which embodied the first balance-sheet, duly checked and approved by Lavignière and Rousseau the auditors, and finally proposed the doubling of the Bank's capital. The meeting alone had power to authorise this increase, upon which it decided with enthusiasm, quite intoxicated as it was by the millions of the United Steam Navigation Company and the National Turkish Bank, and realising, moreover, that it was necessary to place the capital on a par with the importance which the Universal was now about to acquire. As for the Carmel silver mines, the announcement concerning them was greeted with a religious thrill. And when votes of thanks had been accorded to the chairman, directors, and manager, and the shareholders separated, they all began dreaming of Carmel and of that miraculous rain of silver which would pour down from the Holy Places amidst a halo of glory.

A couple of days later Hamelin and Saccard, on this occasion accompanied by the Viscount de Robin-Chagot, the vice-chairman, returned to Maître Lelorrain's offices in the Rue Ste. Anne to make the needful declaration of the increase of capital, which, they alleged, had been entirely subscribed. But the truth was that some three thousand shares, declined by the original shareholders to whom by right they belonged, had been left on the Bank's hands and turned over to the Sabatani account by some jugglery in the book-keeping. It was the original irregular device, repeated and aggravated—the system of concealing a certain number of Universal shares in the Bank's own coffers, as a kind of reserve, which would enable it to speculate and throw itself into the thick of the fight at the Bourse so as to keep up prices should any coalition of 'bears' be formed to beat them down.

Hamelin, though he disapproved of these illegal tactics, had ended by completely trusting the management of financial operations to Saccard. There was a conversation between them and Madame Caroline on this subject, but in reference only to the shares which Saccard had compelled the Hamelins to take for themselves. Five hundred of the first issue and five hundred of the second had been allotted to them, a thousand shares in all, one-fourth of the value of which was demandable, together with the premium of twenty francs per share on the last five hundred. The brother and sister insisted on paying the amount in question, one hundred and thirty-five thousand francs, out of an unexpected legacy of three hundred thousand francs which had come to them from an aunt, who had recently died, ten days after her only son, the same fever carrying them both off. Saccard allowed his friends to pay as they desired to do so; however, he did not explain in what manner he expected to release his own shares.

'Ah, this inheritance!' said Madame Caroline, laughing. 'It is the first piece of luck that has come to us. I really believe that you bring us luck. Why, what with my brother's salary of thirty thousand francs, his liberal allowance for travelling expenses, and all this gold that has just rained down upon us—probably because we no longer needed it—we are now quite rich!'

She looked at Saccard with hearty gratitude, henceforth vanquished, absolutely confident in him, each day losing some of her clear-sightedness amidst the growing affection with which he inspired her. Then, carried away by her gay frankness despite everything, she added: 'No matter. If I had earned this money, I shouldn't risk it in your enterprises, I assure you. But, you see, we scarcely ever knew that aunt of ours; we never gave a thought to her money. It's like money picked up in the street, something which seems to me not to be quite honestly come by, something which I feel a trifle ashamed about, and so, you understand, I don't set much store by it, and shan't be so sorry if it's lost.'

'Precisely!' exclaimed Saccard, jesting in his turn. 'It will increase and multiply and give you millions. There is nothing like stolen money to yield a profit. Within a week from now you'll see—you'll see what a rise there will be.'

And indeed Hamelin, having been compelled to delay his departure, witnessed with surprise a rapid rise in the price of Universal. At the settlement at the end of May they commanded more than seven hundred francs. This was the usual result which attends an augmentation of capital: the classic whip-stroke, the trick of stimulating success, of urging the quotations into a brisk canter whenever there is a new issue. But the rise was also in a measure due to the genuine importance of the enterprises which the Bank was about to launch. The large yellow bills, placarded all over Paris, announcing the approaching opening of the Carmel silver mines, had ended by turning every head, kindling the first symptoms of a passionate intoxication which was destined to grow and sweep all common sense away. The ground was prepared; for there, all ready, was that compost of the Empire, compounded of fermenting remnants and heated by maddened appetites, a soil favourable to one of those wild growths of speculation which every ten or fifteen years block and poison the Bourse, leaving only ruin and blood behind them.[20] Swindling financial concerns were already springing up like mushrooms; great companies, by the example they set, were urging people into risky speculative ventures; an intense gambling fever was breaking out amidst the uproarious prosperity of the reign, amidst all the dazzling whirl of pleasure and luxury, of which the approaching Exhibition promised to be the final splendour, the deceptive transformation scene, as at the close of some extravaganza. And amidst the vertigo that had seized upon the mob, amidst the scramble of all the fine chances that were freely offered, the Universal was at last setting in motion, like some powerful machine which was destined to infatuate and crush everybody, and which violent hands were heating incautiously, immoderately, to the point almost of explosion.

When her brother had again started for the East, Madame Caroline once more found herself alone with Saccard, and they resumed their life of close, almost conjugal, intimacy. She obstinately continued to manage his household and effect economies like a faithful stewardess, albeit there was now a great change in his fortune, as in hers. And in the smiling peacefulness of her existence, her temper ever even, she experienced but one worry—her conscientious scruples with regard to Victor, her hesitating doubt as to whether she ought to conceal the child's existence from his father any longer. They were very dissatisfied with the boy at the Institute of Work, where he was ever committing depredations. However, the six months' trial had now taken place, so ought she to produce the little monster, though he was not yet cleansed of his vices? At thought of him, she at times experienced genuine suffering.

One evening she was on the point of speaking. Saccard, ever dissatisfied with the petty quarters in which the Universal was lodged, had just prevailed on the board to rent the ground floor of a house next door, in order to enlarge the offices, pending the time when he might venture to propose the building of the palatial pile which he dreamt of. So it again became necessary to have doorways cut through the walls, partitions removed, and wickets set in place. And on the evening in question, when Madame Caroline returned from the Boulevard Bineau in despair over the abominable conduct of Victor, who had almost eaten the ear of one of his playmates, she requested Saccard to come up with her to their rooms.

'I have something to say to you,' she remarked.

But, once upstairs, when she saw him, one shoulder white with plaster, go into an ecstasy over a fresh idea of enlargement which had just occurred to him—that of covering the courtyard of the next house with glass, as he had done in the case of the Orviedo mansion—she lacked the courage to upset him, as she must do should she reveal her deplorable secret. No, she could continue waiting; that frightful little scapegrace must be reformed. The thought of the suffering of others took all strength away from her; and so she simply said: 'Well, my friend, it was precisely about that courtyard. The very same idea had occurred to me.'

CHAPTER VI
A GREAT STROKE

The offices of 'L'Espérance,' the Catholic journal in distress, which, at Jantrou's suggestion, Saccard had purchased to assist him in launching the Universal Bank, were situated in the Rue Saint Joseph, in an old, dark, damp building, of which they occupied the first floor, at the rear of the courtyard. A passage led from the ante-room, where the gas was always kept burning; and on the left came, first, the office of Jantrou, the director, and then a room which Saccard had reserved for himself; whilst on the right were the contributors' room, the sub-editor's room, and others. Across the landing were the manager's and cashier's offices, which an inner passage, behind the staircase, connected with the editorial rooms.

That day, Jordan, who was finishing an article in the contributors' room, which he had entered at an early hour in order not to be disturbed, went out just as the clock struck four to find Dejoie, the office porter, who, by a broad gas flame, although it was radiant daylight out of doors, was greedily reading the Bourse bulletin, which had just arrived, and at which he invariably got the first look.

'I say, Dejoie, was it Monsieur Jantrou who just came in?'

'Yes, Monsieur Jordan.'

The young man hesitated, experienced a feeling of uneasiness, which for a few seconds kept him there. In the difficult beginnings of his happy household, some old debts had fallen upon him; and, in spite of his luck in finding this paper to take his articles, he was passing through a period of cruel embarrassment, the greater as his salary had been attached, and as that very day he had to pay a fresh note of hand, or otherwise an execution would be promptly levied on his few sticks of furniture. Twice already he had vainly applied to the director for an advance, for Jantrou had fallen back upon the attachment placed in his hands.

However, the young fellow at last made up his mind, and was approaching the door, when the porter added:

'Monsieur Jantrou is not alone.'

'Ah! who is with him?'

'He came in with Monsieur Saccard, and Monsieur Saccard told me to let no one enter except Monsieur Huret, whom he is waiting for.'

Jordan breathed again, relieved by this delay, so painful did he find it to ask for money. 'All right, I will go back to finish my article. Let me know when the director is alone,' said he.

Just as he was stepping away, however, Dejoie detained him, with a shout of extreme delight: 'You know that Universal have reached 750.'

The young man made a gesture as though to say that it was all one to him, and then returned to the contributors' room.

Almost every day Saccard thus went up to the newspaper office on leaving the Bourse, and often even made appointments in the room which he had reserved for himself there, in order to negotiate certain special and mysterious affairs. Jantrou, moreover, although officially only the director of 'L'Espérance,' for which he wrote political articles in the finished, florid style of a University man, articles which his opponents themselves recognised as the 'purest atticism,' was in addition the financier's secret agent, entrusted with the discharge of delicate duties. And among other things he had just organised a vast advertising scheme in connection with the Universal Bank. Of the little financial sheets that swarmed all over France, he had chosen and 'bought' a dozen. The best belonged to doubtful banking-houses, whose very simple tactics consisted in publishing and supplying copies of these prints for two or three francs a year, a sum which did not even represent the cost of postage; but then they recouped themselves in another way, dealing in the money and securities of the customers which the papers brought them. It was pretended that the sole object of these papers was to publish the Bourse quotations, the winning numbers in the bond drawings, all the technical information useful to petty capitalists, but gradually puffs were slipped in among the other 'copy,' in the form of recommendation and advice, at first modestly and reasonably, but soon immoderately and with quiet impudence, so as to sow ruin among credulous readers.

From among the mass of the two or three hundred publications which were thus ravaging Paris and France, Jantrou, with keen scent, had just chosen those which had not as yet lied too boldly, and were not, therefore, in too bad odour. But the big affair which he contemplated was the purchase of one of them, the 'Côte Financière,' which already had twelve years of absolute honesty behind it; only such honesty threatened to be very expensive, and he was waiting till the Universal should be richer and find itself in one of those situations when a last trumpet blast determines the deafening peals of triumph. However, he had not confined himself to gathering together a docile battalion of these special organs, which in each successive number celebrated the beauty of Saccard's operations; he had also contracted with the principal political and literary journals, keeping up in their columns a running fire of amiable paragraphs and laudatory articles, at so much a line, and assuring himself of their aid by presents of shares when new issues were placed on the market. And then, too, there was the daily campaign carried on under his orders in 'L'Espérance,' not a violent campaign of approbation, but an explanatory and even argumentative one, a slow fashion of seizing hold of the public and strangling it.

It was to talk about the paper that Saccard had shut himself up with Jantrou that afternoon. In the morning issue he had found an article by Huret teeming with such extravagant praise of a speech made by Rougon in the Chamber the day before, that he had entered into a violent rage, and was waiting for the deputy, to have an explanation with him. Did they suppose that he was his brother's hireling? Was he paid to compromise the journal's line of conduct by unreserved approval of the Minister's slightest acts? Jantrou smiled silently when he heard him speak of the journal's line of conduct. Still, as the storm did not threaten to burst upon his own shoulders, he listened to him calmly, examining his finger-nails the while. With the cynicism of a disillusioned man of letters, he had the most perfect contempt for literature, for both 'one' and 'two,' as he said, alluding to the pages of the paper upon which the articles, even his own, appeared; and he only began to evince any interest on reaching the advertisements. He now wore the newest of clothes—closely girt in an elegant frock coat, his button-hole blooming with a brilliant rosette of various colours; in summer carrying a light-coloured overcoat on his arm, in winter buried in a furcoat costing a hundred louis; and showing himself especially careful with regard to his head-gear, his hat always being irreproachable, glittering indeed like a mirror. But with all this there were still certain gaps in his elegance; a vague suspicion of uncleanliness persisting underneath, the old filth of the ex-professor fallen from the Bordeaux Lycée to the Paris Bourse, his skin penetrated, stained by the dirt in which he had lived for ten years; so that, amid the arrogant assurance of his new fortune, he still frequently evinced base humility, making himself very small and humble in the sudden fear of receiving some kick from behind, as in former times.

He now made a hundred thousand francs a year, and spent double the amount, nobody knew how, for he paraded no mistress, but was probably consumed by some awful vice, the secret cause which had driven him from the University. Absinthe, moreover, had been gradually devouring him ever since his days of poverty, and in the luxurious club-house of to-day continued the work begun in the low-class cafés of former times, mowing off his last hairs, and imparting a leaden hue to his skull and face, of which his black, fan-shaped beard remained the sole glory. And Saccard having again invoked 'L'Espérance's' line of conduct, Jantrou stopped him with a gesture, with the weary air of a man who, not liking to waste his time in futile passion, had made up his mind to talk of serious matters, since Huret did not put in an appearance.

For some time the ex-professor had been nursing some new advertising ideas. He thought first of writing a pamphlet, some twenty pages long, about the great enterprises which the Universal Bank was launching—a pamphlet, however, which should have all the interest of a romance, and be couched in a dramatic and familiar style; and he wished to inundate the provinces with this pamphlet, to have it distributed gratuitously in the remotest country districts. Then he proposed to establish an agency, which should draw up and 'manifold' a daily bulletin of the Bourse, sending a hundred copies of it to the best papers in the various departments of France. This bulletin would be given away or sold at a nominal price, and in this wise they would soon have in their hands a powerful weapon, a force which every rival banking-house would have to recognise. Knowing Saccard, he thus primed him with his ideas, returning to the attack until the other had adopted them, made them his own, enlarged them to the point of really re-creating them.

In talk like this the minutes slipped away, and they came at last to the apportionment of the advertising funds for the next quarter, to the subsidies to be paid to the principal newspapers, to the terrible financial scribe employed by a hostile house whose silence it was necessary to purchase, and the course which they should take with regard to the approaching sale by auction of the fourth page of a very old and highly-respected print. And, amidst their prodigality with regard to all the money that they thus uproariously scattered to the four corners of heaven, you could detect what immense disdain they felt for the public, what contempt in which they, intelligent business men, held the dense ignorance of the masses—the masses which were ready to believe all stories, and were so incompetent to understand the complex operations of the Bourse that the most shameless traps caught passers-by, and made millions of money rain down.

Whilst Jordan was still striving to concoct fifty lines of 'copy' with which to complete his two columns, he was disturbed by Dejoie, who called him. 'Ah!' said the young fellow, 'is Monsieur Jantrou alone now?'

'No, monsieur, not yet. But your wife is here, and wants to see you.'

Very anxious, Jordan hurried out. For a few months past, since La Méchain had at last discovered that he was writing over his own name in 'L'Espérance,' he had been pursued by Busch for payment of the six notes of fifty francs each which he had formerly given to a tailor. He could have managed to pay the three hundred francs which the notes represented, but what exasperated him was the enormity of the costs, that total of seven hundred and thirty francs and fifteen centimes to which the debt had risen. He had entered into a compromise, however, and pledged himself to pay a hundred francs a month; and, as he could not manage it, his young household having more pressing needs, the costs rose higher yet every month, and the intolerable annoyances were ever beginning afresh.

Just then he was again passing through a serious crisis. 'What's the matter?' he asked his wife, whom he found in the ante-room.

But, before she could answer, the door of the director's office was thrown open, and Saccard appeared, shouting: 'I say, Dejoie—and Monsieur Huret?'

'Why, monsieur, he isn't here,' stammered the bewildered attendant; 'I cannot make him hurry.'

The door was closed again with an oath, and Jordan, having taken his wife into one of the adjoining offices, was there able to question her at his ease.

'What's the matter, darling?' he again asked.

Marcelle, usually so gay and brave, whose little, plump, dark person and clear countenance, with laughing eyes and healthy mouth, expressed happiness even in trying times, now seemed utterly upset. 'Oh, Paul, if you only knew!' she replied. 'A man came—oh! a frightful, ugly man—who smelt bad, and had been drinking, I think. Well, he told me that the matter was ended, that the sale of our furniture was fixed for to-morrow. And he had a placard, which he wanted to stick up at the street door.'

'But it is impossible!' cried Jordan. 'I have received nothing; there are other formalities to be observed.'

'Oh! you know still less about these matters than I do. When papers come, you do not even read them. Well, to keep him from putting up the placard I gave him forty sous, and hurried off to tell you.'

They were in despair. Their poor little home in the Avenue de Clichy! Those few little bits of furniture, of mahogany and blue rep, which they had purchased with such difficulty at so much a month, and of which they were so proud, although they sometimes laughed at them, finding them in execrable *bourgeois* taste! Still they loved them, because ever since their wedding night they had formed part of their happiness in those two little rooms over yonder, those little rooms which were so sunny, so open to space, with a view stretching away even to Mont Valérien. And he who had driven in so many nails, and she who had shown so much ingenuity to give the apartments an artistic appearance! Was it possible that all was going to be sold, that they were to be driven from that pretty nook, where even poverty was delightful to them?

'Listen,' said he, 'I was thinking of asking for an advance; I will do what I can, but I haven't much hope.'

Then, in a hesitating way, she confided her idea to him. 'This is what I have been thinking of,' said she. 'Oh! I would not have done it without your consent, as you may judge from the fact that I have come here to talk with you about it. Yes, I desire to apply to my parents.'

He promptly refused. 'No, no, never! You know very well that I don't wish to be under any obligation to them.'

The Maugendres certainly behaved in a decorous fashion. But Jordan retained in his heart a recollection of the coldness which they had shown him after the suicide of his father, whose fortune had been swept away in speculation. He remembered that they had then only consented to the long-planned marriage of their daughter because she was determined on it, and that they had taken all sorts of offensive precautions against himself, among others that of not giving a sou of dowry, convinced as they were that a fellow who wrote for the newspapers would devour everything. Later on, said they, their daughter would inherit their property. And so the young couple, she as well as he, had taken a certain pride in starving without asking anything of her parents apart from the meal which they took with them once a week, on Sunday evenings.

'I assure you,' she replied, 'our reserve is ridiculous, since I am their only child, since the whole must come to me some day! My father tells every one who will listen to him that he has acquired an income of fifteen thousand francs by his awning manufactory at La Villette; and then, too, there is their little residence, with its beautiful garden, to which they have retired. It is stupid for us to let ourselves be worried like this when they have a surfeit of everything. They have never been cruel to us, you know. I tell you that I am going to see them.'

She evinced a cheerful bravery, displayed a determined air, very practical in her desire to bring happiness to her dear husband, who worked so hard without yet having obtained anything from either the critics or the public, excepting a good deal of indifference and a few smacks. Ah! money, she would have liked to bring it to him by the bucketful, and he would be very stupid to be over particular about it, since she loved him and owed him everything. It was her fairy story, her 'Cinderella:' the treasures of her royal family, which with her little hands she deposited at the feet of her ruined prince, to keep him on in his march to glory and the conquest of the world.

'Come,' she gaily said, kissing him, 'I really must be of some use to you; all the pain must not be yours.'

He yielded; it was agreed that she should go straightway to the Rue Legendre, at Batignolles, where her parents lived, and that she should bring the money back to the office, in order that he might try to pay it that very evening. And, as he accompanied her to the stairs, as much agitated as though she were starting on a very dangerous expedition, they had to step aside to make room for Huret, who had at last arrived. When Jordan returned to finish his article in the contributors' room, he heard a violent hubbub of voices in Jantrou's office.

Saccard, now grown powerful, the master once more, wished to be obeyed, knowing that he held them all by the hope of gain and the terror of loss in that colossal game of fortune which he was playing with them.

'Ah! so here you are,' he shouted on seeing Huret. 'Did you stop at the Chamber to offer the great man your article in a gilt frame? I've had enough, you know, of this swinging of incense-burners under his nose, and I have been waiting for you to tell you that it must be stopped—that in future you must give us something else.'

Quite amazed, Huret looked at Jantrou. But the latter, thoroughly determined not to get himself into trouble by coming to the deputy's succour, had begun to pass his fingers through his handsome beard, his eyes wandering away.

'What! something else?' finally asked Huret; 'but I give you what you asked for. When you purchased "L'Espérance," the organ of extreme Catholicism and Royalty, which was carrying on such a bitter campaign against Rougon, you yourself asked me to write a series of laudatory articles in order to show your brother that you did not intend to be hostile to him, and in this wise to indicate the new policy of the paper.'

'The policy of the paper, precisely,' replied Saccard with increased violence; 'it is the policy of the paper that I accuse you of compromising. Do you think that I wish to be my brother's vassal? Certainly I have never been sparing of grateful admiration and affection for the Emperor; I don't forget what we all owe to him, what I in particular owe to him. But to point out the mistakes that are made is not the same thing as to attack the Empire; on the contrary, it is the duty imposed on every faithful subject. That, then, is the paper's policy—devotion to the dynasty, but entire independence with regard to Ministers, to all the ambitious individuals ever bestirring themselves and fighting together for the favour of the Tuileries!'

And then he launched into an examination of the political situation, in order to prove that the Emperor had bad advisers. He accused Rougon of having lost his authoritative energy, his former faith in absolute power, of compounding with liberal ideas for the sole purpose of retaining his ministerial portfolio. For his part, striking his chest with his fist, he declared himself to be unchangeable, a Bonapartist from the very first, a believer in the *coup d'état*, with the conviction that the salvation of France lay, to-day as well as formerly, in the genius and strength of a single man. Yes, rather than assist the evolution of his brother, rather than allow the Emperor to commit suicide by new concessions, he would rally the uncompromising believers in dictatorship together, make common cause with the Catholic party, in order to prevent the rapid downfall which he foresaw. And let Rougon take care, for 'L'Espérance' might resume its campaign in favour of Rome!

Huret and Jantrou listened to him, astonished at his wrath, never having suspected that he possessed such ardent political convictions. And it occurred to the former to try to defend the last acts of the Government.

'Well, my dear fellow,' said he, 'if the Empire is moving towards liberty, it is because all France is pushing it firmly in that direction. The Emperor is borne along with the current, and Rougon is obliged to follow him.'

But Saccard was already passing to other grievances, without a thought of making his attacks in any degree logical.

'And see,' said he, 'it is the same with our foreign situation; why, it is deplorable! Since the Treaty of Villafranca which followed upon Solferino, Italy has harboured resentment against us for not having finished the campaign and given her Venice; so that now she is allied with Prussia, in the certainty that the latter will help her to beat Austria. When war breaks out, you'll see what a row there'll be, and what a fix we shall be in; especially as we have made the great mistake of letting Bismarck and King William seize the Duchies in the Denmark affair, in contempt of a treaty which France herself had signed. It is a slap in the face, there's no denying it, and there is nothing for us to do now but to turn the other cheek. Oh! war is certain; you remember how French and Italian securities fell last month, when there was some talk of a possible intervention on our part in German affairs. Within a fortnight, perhaps, Europe will be on fire.'

More and more surprised, Huret became excited, contrary to his habit. 'You talk like the Opposition papers,' said he; 'but you certainly don't want "L'Espérance" to follow the lead of the "Siècle" and the others. There is nothing left for you but to insinuate, like those rags do, that, if the Emperor allowed himself to be humiliated in the Schleswig-Holstein affair, and let Prussia grow with impunity, it is because he had for many months kept an entire army corps in Mexico. Come, be a little fair; the Mexican affair is over, our troops are coming back. And then I do not understand you, my dear fellow. If you wish to keep Rome for the Pope, why do you seem to blame the hasty peace of Villafranca? Venice given to Italy means the Italians in Rome within two years; you know that as well as I do, and Rougon knows it too, although he swears the contrary in the tribune.'

'Ah! you see what a trickster he is!' shouted Saccard superbly. 'Never will they touch the Pope, do you hear me? without the whole of Catholic France rising up to defend him. We should carry him our money, yes! all the money of the Universal. I have my plan, our affair lies there, and really, if you keep on exasperating me, you will make me say things that I do not want to say as yet.'

Jantrou, very much interested, had suddenly pricked up his ears, beginning to understand, trying to profit by the remarks thus casually dropped.

'Well,' replied Huret, 'I want to know what to depend upon with regard to my articles, and we must come to an understanding. Are you for intervention or against intervention? If we are for the principle of nationalities, by what right are we to meddle with the affairs of Italy and Germany? Do you wish us to carry on a campaign against Bismarck? Yes! in the name of our menaced frontiers.'

But Saccard, erect, beside himself, burst out: 'What I want is that Rougon shall not make a fool of me any longer. What! after all that I have done! I buy a newspaper, the worst of his enemies; I make it an organ devoted to his policy; I allow you to sing his praises for months, and yet never has the beggar given us a single lift. I have still to receive the first service from him.'

Thereupon the deputy timidly remarked that the Minister's support had singularly aided the engineer Hamelin in the East, opening all doors to him, and exercising pressure upon influential personages.

'Oh, stuff and nonsense! He could not do otherwise. But has he ever sent me a word of warning the day before a rise or a fall, he who is so well placed to know everything? Remember, I have a score of times charged you to sound him, you who see him every day, and you have yet to bring me a useful bit of information. Yet it would not be such a serious matter—a simple word for you to repeat to me.'

'Undoubtedly. But he doesn't like that sort of thing; he says it is all jobbery, which a man always repents of.'

'Nonsense! Has he any such scruples with Gundermann? He plays the honest man with me, and he gives tips to Gundermann.'

'Oh, Gundermann, no doubt! They all need Gundermann; they could not float a loan without him.'

At this Saccard clapped his hands with a violent gesture of triumph. 'There we are, then; you confess it! The empire is sold to the Jews—the dirty Jews! All our money is doomed to fall into their thieving paws. There is nothing left for the Universal but to collapse before their omnipotence.'

And then he exhaled his hereditary hatred, again brought forward his charges against that race of traffickers and usurers for centuries on the march through the nations, sucking their blood, like the parasites of scab and itch, and, although spat upon and beaten, yet marching on to the certain conquest of the world, which they would some day possess by the invincible power of gold. And he was especially furious against Gundermann, giving way to his old resentment, to his unrealisable mad desire to strike that Jew down; and this in spite of a presentiment that he was the limit against which he (Saccard) would fall should he ever engage in a struggle with him. Ah, that Gundermann! a Prussian in the house, albeit born in France; for his sympathies were evidently with Prussia; he would willingly have supported her with his money, perhaps he was secretly supporting her even now! Had he not dared to say one evening, in a *salon*, that, if war should ever break out between Prussia and France, the latter would be vanquished?

116

'I have had enough of it; do you understand, Huret? and get this well into your head: that if my brother is of no service to me, I do not intend to be of any further service to him; When you have brought me a good word from him—I mean a "tip" that we can turn to account—I will allow you to resume your dithyrambs in his favour. Is that clear?'

It was too clear. Jantrou, who had again found his Saccard under the political theorist, had once more begun to comb his beard with his finger tips. But all this did not suit the wily peasant-like prudence of Huret, who was greatly annoyed, for he had staked his fortune upon the two brothers, and would have liked to quarrel with neither of them.

'You are right,' he murmured; 'let us act discreetly, especially as we must wait to see what will happen. And I promise you to do everything to obtain the great man's confidence. The first news that he gives me, I will jump into a cab and bring it to you.'

Having played his part, Saccard was already in a good humour again. 'It is for you all that I am working, my good friends,' said he. 'For my part, I have always been ruined, and I have always devoured a million a year.'

Then, reverting to the advertising, he continued: 'I say, Jantrou, you ought to make your Bourse bulletin a little more lively. Yes, you know, give us some jokes, some puns. The public like that sort of thing; there is nothing like wit to help them to swallow things. That's it, eh? some puns!'

It was the director's turn to be vexed. He prided himself on his literary distinction. But he had to promise. And thereupon, as he invented a story of some fashionable women who had offered to allow advertisements to be tattooed on their persons, the three men, laughing loudly, again became the best friends in the world.

Meanwhile Jordan had at last finished his article, and was impatiently awaiting his wife's return. Other contributors arrived; he chatted with them, and then went into the ante-room. And there he was a little scandalised to find Dejoie, with his ear against the door of the director's room, listening to all that was being said in it, while his daughter Nathalie kept watch.

'Do not go in,' stammered the attendant. 'Monsieur Saccard is still there—I thought I heard them call me.'

The truth was that, bitten by a fierce longing for gain ever since he had bought eight fully paid-up shares in the Universal with the four thousand francs which his wife had saved and left to him, he lived only for the delightful emotion of seeing these shares 'go up' in value; and ever on his knees before Saccard, drinking in his most trifling remarks, as though they had been oracular utterances, he could not resist his desire to become acquainted with his real thoughts, to hear what the demi-god said in the secrecy of his sanctuary. Moreover, there was no egotism in this; his only thought was for his daughter, and he had just become excited by the calculation that, at seven hundred and fifty francs apiece, his eight shares already represented a profit of twelve hundred francs, which, added to the capital sum, made five thousand two hundred francs. Another rise of a hundred francs, and he would have the six thousand francs he desired, the dowry which his neighbour, the mill-board maker, insisted upon as a condition of his son's marriage with the girl. At this thought, Dejoie's heart melted; and he gazed with tearful eyes at the child whom he had brought up, and whose real mother he had been in the happy little home which they had made together since he had taken her from her nurse.

However, he was very much put out at being surprised by Jordan, and sought to hide his indiscretion by saying whatever entered his head: 'Nathalie, who just came up to see me, met your wife out of doors, Monsieur Jordan.'

'Yes,' said the young girl; 'she was turning into the Rue Feydeau. Oh, she was running so fast!'

Her father allowed her to go out as she pleased, certain of her good behaviour, said he. And he did right to rely upon her, for she was really too cold, too determined to ensure her future happiness, to compromise by folly the marriage which had been so long looked forward to. With her slender figure, and her large eyes lighting up her pretty, pale, smiling face, she loved herself with egotistical obstinacy.

Jordan, surprised and at a loss to understand, exclaimed: 'What! you saw her in the Rue Feydeau?'

But he had not time to question the girl further, for at that moment Marcelle entered, out of breath. He forthwith took her into the adjoining office, but, finding the law-court reporter there, had to come out again and content himself with sitting down beside her on a little bench at the end of the passage.

'Well?'

'Well, dear, it is done, but not without trouble.'

Despite her satisfaction, he saw clearly that her heart was full; and she rapidly told him everything in a low voice, for in vain did she vow to hide certain things from him; she could keep no secrets.

For some time the Maugendres had been changing in their manner towards their daughter. She found them less affectionate, more preoccupied, slowly becoming the prey of a new passion—the passion for gambling. It was the usual story: the father, a stout, calm, bald man, with white whiskers; the mother, lean and active, earner in part of the common fortune; both living in too profuse a style on their fifteen thousand francs a year, and sorely worried at having nothing left to do. He, indeed, had nothing to occupy his attention, except the collection of his money. Formerly he had thundered against all speculation, and shrugged his shoulders with mingled wrath and pity in speaking of the poor fools who allowed themselves to be plucked in stupid, unclean, thieving Bourse transactions. But about this time, a considerable sum of money owing to him having been repaid, he conceived the idea of lending it against securities. That was not speculation, but a simple investment; only from that day forward he had contracted the habit of attentively reading the Bourse quotations in his paper after breakfast. And in this wise the evil took root; the fever gradually seized upon him at sight of the mad dance of securities, on breathing the poisonous atmosphere of the gambling world, and his mind became haunted by the thought of millions made in an hour, whereas he himself had spent thirty years in getting a few hundred thousand francs together. He could not help talking to his wife about it at each meal; what strokes he would have made if he hadn't sworn that he would never gamble! And he explained the operation; he manipulated his funds with all the skilful strategy of a carpet general, always ending by vanquishing his imaginary opponents, for he prided himself on having become wonderfully expert in such matters as options and lending money on securities.

His wife, growing anxious, declared that she would rather drown herself at once than see him risk a copper; but he reassured her. What did she take him for? Never in his life would he do such a thing! Yet an opportunity had offered; both had long desired to build a little greenhouse in their garden—a greenhouse costing from five to six thousand francs; and thus one evening, his hands trembling with a delightful emotion, he laid upon his wife's work table six notes of a thousand francs each, saying that he had just won them at the Bourse; a stroke which he had felt sure of, an indulgence which he promised he would never allow himself again, and on which he had only ventured because of the greenhouse. She, a prey to mingled anger and astonished delight, had not dared to scold him, and the following month he launched out into some transaction in options, explaining to her that he feared nothing since he limited his loss. Besides, there were some excellent chances among the lot, and it would have been very stupid of him to let others alone profit by them. And thus—it was fatal—he began to speculate, in a small way at first, but gradually more boldly, whilst she, tortured by anxiety, like a good prudent housewife, yet with her eyes sparkling at the slightest gain, continued to predict that he would die a beggar.

But it was especially Captain Chave, Madame Maugendre's brother, who blamed his brother-in-law. He, who could not live on his pension of eighteen hundred francs a year, speculated at the Bourse to be sure; but then he was the shrewdest of the shrewd; he went there as a clerk goes to his office, and embarked solely in cash transactions, brimming over with delight when he took his twenty-franc piece home in the evening. These were daily operations of the most certain sort, and so modest that there was no possibility of catastrophe. His sister had offered him a home in her house, which was too large now that Marcelle had married; but wishing to be free, he had refused, and tenanted a single room in the rear of a garden in the Rue Nollet. For years he had been cautioning Maugendre, telling him not to gamble, but to take life easily; and when the latter had cried, 'But you?' he had made a vigorous gesture. Oh! he! that was different; he hadn't got an income of fifteen thousand francs! If he gambled, it was the fault of that dirty Government which begrudged to its old soldiers the delights of their old age. His great argument against gambling was that the gambler is mathematically bound to lose: if he wins, he has to deduct brokerage and stamp tax; if he loses, he has to pay these taxes in addition to his loss. So that, even admitting that he wins as often as he loses, he is still out of pocket to the extent of the stamp tax and the brokerage. At the Paris Bourse these taxes annually produce the enormous total of eighty millions of francs. And he brandished those figures—eighty millions gathered in by the State, the brokers, and the bucket-shops!

Seated on the little bench at the end of the corridor, Marcelle told her husband a part of this story.

'I must say, dear, that my visit was ill-timed. Mamma was quarrelling with papa on account of some loss which he has met with at the Bourse. Yes, it appears that he never leaves it now. It seems so queer to me, he who formerly used to say that all men ought to earn their money by steady work. Well, they were disputing, and there was a newspaper, the "Côte Financière," which mamma was flourishing under his nose, telling him that he didn't know anything, that she had foreseen the fall herself. Then he went for another paper, "L'Espérance," in fact, and wanted to show her the article from which he had got his information. Indeed, the house is full of newspapers; they stuff themselves with them from morning till night, and I believe—God forgive me!— that mamma is beginning to speculate too, in spite of her furious air.'

Jordan could not help laughing, so amusingly did she mimic the scene amidst all her sorrow.

'Well, I told them of our worry, and asked them to lend us two hundred francs to stop the proceedings. And if you had only heard how they cried out! Two hundred francs, when they had lost two thousand at the Bourse! Was I laughing at them? Did I want to ruin them? Never had I seen them in such a state. They who were so kind to me, who would have spent their all in making me presents! They must really be going mad, for there is no sense in making their lives wretched in this fashion when they could be so happy in their beautiful house, with nothing to worry them, no care but to live at their ease on the fortune which they so painfully earned.'

'I certainly hope that you did not insist,' said Jordan.

'Why, yes, I did insist; and then they fell upon you. You see that I tell you everything; I had promised myself to keep this from you, and now it escapes me. They repeated to me that they had foreseen how it would be, that writing in the newspapers isn't a proper business for anyone, and that we should end by dying on the straw. Finally, as I was getting angry in my turn, and was just about to leave, the Captain came in. You know that Uncle Chave has always been very fond of me. Well, in his presence, they became reasonable, especially as he triumphed over papa by asking him if he meant to keep on getting himself robbed like that. Then mamma took me aside, and slipped fifty francs into my hand, saying that with that we could obtain a few days' delay, enough time to turn round.'

'Fifty francs! a pittance! And you accepted them?'

Marcelle had grasped his hands tenderly, calming him with her quiet good sense.

'Come, don't be angry. Yes, I accepted them, and I understood so well that you would never dare to take them to the process-server that I went at once myself to his office, you know, in the Rue Cadet. But just imagine! he refused to take the money, explaining that he had formal orders from M. Busch, and that M. Busch could alone stop the proceedings. Oh! that Busch! I hate nobody, but how he exasperates and disgusts me! Still, all the same, I ran off to his office in the Rue Feydeau and he had to content himself with the fifty francs; so there, here we are, with a little peace before us for a fortnight.'

Deep emotion had contracted Jordan's face, while the tears that he was restraining moistened his eyelids. 'You did that, little wife, you did that?' said he.

'Why yes, I did not wish you to be annoyed any further. What harm does it do to me to get a scolding if you are allowed to work in peace?'

She was laughing now, and forthwith she began to tell the story of her arrival at Busch's office amid all his dusty, grimy papers; the brutal way in which he had received her, his threats that he would not leave them a rag on their backs if the whole debt were not paid at once. The queer part was that she had given herself the treat of exasperating him by disputing his legal right to recover the debt, those three hundred francs represented by the notes, which costs had run up to no less than seven hundred and fifty francs and fifteen centimes, whereas he had probably found the papers in some bundle of old rags which hadn't perhaps cost him a hundred sous. On hearing this he had almost choked with fury; in the first place, said he, he had paid a very high price for the notes; and there was his lost time, and all the running about during a couple of years to discover the person who had signed them, and the intelligence that he had had to display in this hunt. Was he not to be repaid for all that? So much the worse for those who allowed themselves to be caught! All the same, however, he had ended by taking the fifty francs, for his prudent system was always to compromise.

'Ah! little wife, how brave you are, and how I love you!' said Jordan, impulsively kissing Marcelle, although the sub-editor was just passing. And then, lowering his voice, he asked: 'How much have you left at home?'

'Seven francs.'

'Good!' he rejoined, feeling quite happy, 'we can go two days on that, so I won't ask for an advance, which would surely be refused. Besides, it worries me so to ask. To-morrow I will go to see if the "Figaro" will take an article from me. Ah! if I had only finished my novel, and if that would sell a little!'

Marcelle kissed him in her turn. 'Yes, things will go on all right. Now you will come home with me, won't you? That will be so nice of you, and for to-morrow morning we'll buy a red herring at the corner of the Rue de Clichy, where I saw some splendid ones. To-night we have potatoes and bacon.'

Having asked a comrade to look at his proofs, Jordan started off with his wife. Saccard and Huret were also going away just then. In the street a brougham had stopped outside the newspaper office, and they saw the Baroness Sandorff step out. She bowed with a smile, and then went hurriedly up the stairs. She now sometimes visited Jantrou in this fashion, just by way of asking him if he knew of anything. In spite of his sudden rise, she still treated him as she had done in the days when he had presented himself at her father's house, bending double and soliciting orders. Her father had been a frightfully brutal man, and she could not forget how she had once seen him, when enraged by a heavy loss, kick Jantrou out of the door. And now that the ex-professor was at the fountain-head of information, she had again become familiar, and sought to extract tips from him.

'Well, is there nothing new?' she asked, when she had reached his office, where she would not even sit down.

'No, indeed; I know nothing.'

But she continued to look at him with a smile, persuaded that he was unwilling to speak. Then, to force him to be confidential, she began to talk of that stupid war, which was about to set Austria, Italy, and Prussia fighting. The world of speculation was panic-stricken; there had been a terrible fall in Italian funds, as well as in all securities for that matter. And she was very much worried, for she did not know how far she ought to follow the movement, already having heavy engagements for next settling-day.

'Doesn't your husband give you any information?' asked Jantrou jestingly. 'He is certainly in a good position to do so, at the Embassy.'

'Oh! my husband,' she murmured, with a disdainful gesture: 'my husband, I get nothing out of him.'

He continued to laugh at her expense, going so far as to allude to the Public Prosecutor, Delcambre, who was said to pay her losses when she consented to pay them at all. 'And your friends, don't they know anything, either at Court or at the Palais de Justice?'

She pretended not to understand, but, without taking her eyes off him, rejoined, in a supplicating tone: 'Come, be amiable yourself. You know something.'

'Amiable, why should I be?' said he, laughing, with an embarrassed air. 'You are scarcely amiable with me.'

Straightway she became grave again, and a stern expression came into her eyes. That man, whom her father had received with kicks—ah! never! And she turned her back upon him to go away when, out of spite, seeking to wound her, he added: 'You just met Saccard at the door, didn't you? Why didn't you question him? He wouldn't refuse you.'

She suddenly stepped back. 'What do you mean?'

'Why, whatever you please. Oh, don't pretend to be mystified!'

A feeling of revolt filled her; all the pride of her race, still alive, rose out of the troubled depths, the mire in which her gambling passion was slowly, gradually drowning it. However, she did not indulge in an outburst, but in a clear, severe tone of voice simply said: 'Ah! my dear sir, what do you take me for? You are mad. No, I have nothing in common with your Saccard, because I didn't choose.'

Thereupon he saluted her with a profound bow. 'Well, madame, you made a very great mistake. You, who are always seeking "tips," could easily obtain them from that gentleman.'

At this she made up her mind to laugh; however, when she shook hands with him, he felt that hers was quite cold.

The month of June went by; on the 15th Italy had declared war against Austria. On the other hand, Prussia in scarcely a couple of weeks had, by a lightning march, invaded Hanover and conquered the two Hesses, Baden, and Saxony, surprising the unarmed populations in full peace. France had not budged; well-informed people whispered very softly at the Bourse that she had had a secret understanding with Prussia ever since Bismarck had met the Emperor at Biarritz, and folks talked mysteriously of the 'compensations' which she was to receive for her neutrality. But none the less, the fall in public funds, and almost all securities, went on in the most disastrous fashion. When the news of Sadowa, that sudden thunderbolt, reached Paris on the 4th of July, there was a collapse of every kind of stock. Folks believed in an obstinate prolongation of the war; for though Austria was beaten by Prussia, she had defeated Italy at Custozza, and it was already said that she was gathering the remnants of her army together, abandoning Bohemia. Orders to sell rained upon the *corbeille*; and buyers were not to be found.

On July 4, Saccard, calling at the office of the paper rather late, about six o'clock, did not find Jantrou there, for the editor's passions were now leading him into very disorderly courses. He would suddenly disappear for a time, returning invariably with a worn-out look and dim, bleared eyes. Women and drink were playing havoc with him. At the hour when Saccard arrived the office was emptying. There was scarcely a soul left there excepting Dejoie, who was dining at a corner of his little table in the ante-room; and Saccard, after writing a couple of letters, was in his turn about to take himself off when Huret, as red as a turkey-cock, rushed in like a whirlwind, not even taking the trouble to close the doors behind him.

'My dear fellow, my dear fellow!' he began; but he was almost stifling, and had to stop and carry both hands to his chest. 'I have just left Rougon,' he added at last; 'I had to run, because I hadn't got a cab. But eventually I found one. Rougon has received a despatch from over yonder; I've seen it! Such news! such news!'

With a violent wave of the arm, Saccard cut him short, and hastened to close the door, for he had caught sight of Dejoie, who was already on the prowl, with ears on the alert.

'Well, what?' he then asked.

'Well, the Emperor of Austria hands Venetia over to the Emperor of the French and accepts his mediation, so that Napoleon is now about to address himself to the Kings of Prussia and Italy with the view of bringing about an armistice.'

A moment's silence ensued.

'That means peace, eh?' said Saccard.

'Evidently.'

Thunderstruck, no idea as yet occurring to him, Saccard gave vent to an oath. 'D— — it! And everybody at the Bourse is speculating for a further fall!' Then, in a mechanical way, he added: 'And does nobody know this news?'

'No, it's a confidential despatch. There won't even be any announcement in the "Moniteur" to-morrow morning. In all probability, Paris will know nothing for four and twenty hours.'

Then the flash of lightning, the sudden inspiration, came to Saccard. He again rushed to the door and opened it to see if anyone were listening. He was quite beside himself, and when he came back he planted himself in front of the deputy and seized hold of both lapels of his coat. 'Keep quiet, not so loud!' said he. 'We are masters of the situation if Gundermann and his gang are not warned. Not a word, do you hear?—not a word to a living soul, to any of your friends, to your wife even! It happens luckily! Jantrou isn't here, the secret will be ours alone, and we shall have time to act. Oh, I don't mean to work merely for my own profit! You are in it, all our colleagues of the Universal too. Only a secret must never be confided to a lot of people. Everything would be lost if there were the slightest indiscretion before the opening of the Bourse to-morrow.'

Huret, who was greatly disturbed, quite upset in fact, by the magnitude of the stroke which they were about to attempt, promised to speak to no one. And then, deciding that they must open the campaign at once, they divided the work between them. Saccard had already taken up his hat when a last question came to his lips.

'So it was Rougon who told you to bring me this news?'

'To be sure,' replied Huret.

He had hesitated, however, in giving this answer, and, in point of fact, he lied. The despatch had simply been lying on the Minister's table, and curiosity had prompted him to read it while he was left alone in Rougon's room for a few moments. However, as his interest lay in furthering a cordial understanding between the two brothers, his lie seemed to him a very adroit one, the more so as he knew that they had little desire to see each other and talk about such things.

'Well,' said Saccard, 'there's no denying it, he's done me a good turn this time. And now let's be off!'

Dejoie was still the only person in the ante-room. He had striven to hear them, but had been unable to catch a single distinct word. Nevertheless, they divined that he was in a feverish state; and indeed he had scented the huge prey they were after. It might be invisible, but there was a smell of money in the air, and to such a degree did it disturb him that he impulsively rushed to the window on the landing to see them cross the courtyard.

The difficulty lay in acting with the greatest possible speed and the greatest possible caution at one and the same time. And so, on reaching the street, they parted company—Huret undertaking to deal with the 'Petite Bourse,' held on the Boulevards in the evening, whilst Saccard, late though it was, rushed off in search of brokers and jobbers to give them orders for the purchase of stock. He wished to divide and scatter these orders as much as possible, in order not to arouse any suspicion; and, moreover, he wished to meet these brokers and jobbers as though by chance instead of hunting them up at home, which might have appeared singular. Luck came to his help. While walking down the Boulevard he met Jacoby, with whom he joked and chatted for a while, and before leaving him he managed to give him a rather heavy order without provoking undue astonishment. A hundred steps further on he fell in with a tall, fair-haired girl whom he knew to be the mistress of another broker, Delarocque, Jacoby's brother-in-law; and as she said that she expected to see him a little later, Saccard asked her to give him his card, on which he wrote a few words in pencil.

Then, knowing that Mazaud meant to attend a banquet of old schoolfellows that evening, he contrived to be at the restaurant where it was held when the broker arrived there, and reversed the orders which he had given him earlier in the day. But his greatest piece of luck was to come. About midnight, whilst he was on his way home, he was accosted by Massias, who was just leaving the Théâtre des Variétés. They walked towards the Rue St. Lazare together, and on the way Saccard had all the time necessary to pose as an eccentric fellow who believed in a rise. Oh! not at once, of course. However, playing his part, he ended by giving Massias numerous orders for Nathansohn and other *coulissiers*, saying as he did so that he was acting on behalf of a group of friends, which after all was true. When he went to bed, he had taken up position as a 'bull,' with orders representing more than five millions of francs.

At seven o'clock the next morning Huret called on Saccard and acquainted him with what he had done at the Petite Bourse held on the Boulevard in front of the Passage de l'Opéra. Here he had bought as much as he could, but in a prudent way, so as not to bring about any undue rise in prices. His orders represented a million francs; and both, judging the stroke to be so far too modest a one, resolved to renew the campaign. For this they had all the morning before them. Before doing anything, however, they rushed upon the newspapers, trembling with the fear that they might find the news printed in them—a paragraph, a mere line which would annihilate all their plans. But no! the Press knew nothing. It believed in the continuation of the war, and every paper was full of telegrams giving detailed accounts of the battle of Sadowa. If no report should leak out before two in the afternoon, if they should have an hour before them when the Bourse opened, they would, as Saccard put it, make a clear sweep at the cost of the Jews. And then they again parted company, each on his own side hastening to bring fresh millions into the field.

Saccard spent that morning in tramping the streets and sniffing the air, experiencing such a desire to walk that he sent his brougham home after his first call. Whilst in the Rue Vivienne he looked in at Kolb's, where the jingle of gold fell delightfully on his ears, like some promise of victory; and he had sufficient strength of mind to say nothing to the banker, who, he found, knew nothing himself. Then he went up to Mazaud's, not to give any fresh order, but simply to feign anxiety respecting the one that he had given the night before; and here also they were still in utter ignorance of the truth. Little Flory alone caused him some anxiety by the persistent way in which he hovered about him, but the sole cause of this was the young clerk's profound admiration for the financial intelligence of the manager of the Universal Bank. As his friend Mademoiselle Chuchu was becoming a source of considerable expense to him, he had begun to speculate in a small way on his own account, and longed to know what orders the great man might give, so as to follow his lead.

At last, after a hasty repast at Champeaux', where he experienced profound delight at hearing the pessimist lamentations of Moser, and even Pillerault, both of whom predicted a further fall in prices, Saccard found himself upon the Place de la Bourse. It was only half-past twelve; but, as he put it, he wished to see everyone arrive. The heat was overpowering; fierce sun-rays streamed down, whitening the steps, whose reflections imparted to the peristyle the oppressive, burning temperature of an oven.

The unoccupied chairs were crackling in this fiery air, whilst the speculators stood up seeking the protection of the narrow shadows which the columns cast.

Under a tree in the garden Saccard caught sight of Busch and La Méchain, who, on perceiving him, began talking with animation; and he even fancied that they were about to approach him when all at once they changed their minds. Was it possible that the news was known by these low ragpickers of the Bourse, who were ever scouring the gutters for such securities as might fall into them? For a moment he shuddered. But he heard himself called by name, and recognised Maugendre and Captain Chave seated on a bench and quarrelling together; for the former was now always jeering at the captain's paltry ventures, which resulted in the gain of no more than a louis a day, just as might have been the case in some little country *café* after innumerable hard-fought games of piquet. Come, now, said Maugendre, could he not venture on a serious stroke that afternoon in all security? Was not a fresh fall certain, as sure to come as the sun was shining above them? And he called upon Saccard to corroborate him. Was it not certain that there would be a fall? For his own part, he had staked heavily on the fall, so convinced of its coming that he would have ventured his entire fortune. Saccard responded to this direct question by smiling and tossing his head in an indefinite sort of way, feeling meantime a twinge of remorse at the thought that he could not warn this poor man whom he had known so industrious and clear-headed in the days when he sold awnings. However, he had sworn to be dumb, and was swayed by the ferocity of the gambler who has resolved that he will do nothing that may interfere with luck.

Just then, too, a fresh incident diverted his attention. The Baroness Sandorff's brougham passed by. He watched it, and saw that on this occasion it drew up in the Rue de la Banque. And all at once he bethought himself of Baron Sandorff, the Councillor at the Austrian Embassy. The Baroness must surely know the news, and would doubtless spoil everything by some piece of feminine clumsiness. He had already crossed the street, and began prowling around the brougham, which stood there motionless and silent, destitute of all signs of life, with the coachman stiffly erect upon his box. However, one of the windows was at last lowered, and thereupon Saccard gallantly bowed and drew near.

'Well, Monsieur Saccard,' said the Baroness, 'prices are still falling, I suppose?'

He fancied that she was preparing a trap for him. 'Why, yes, madame,' he replied.

Then as she looked at him anxiously, with the wavering expression which he had so often known among gamblers, he realised that she herself knew no more than the others. A stream of hot blood thereupon ascended to his brain, filling him with a sensation of beatitude.

'So you have nothing to tell me, Monsieur Saccard?' she resumed.

'Why, no, madame, nothing but what you must already know.'

And thereupon he left her, thinking as he walked away: 'You have been none too amiable with me, and it will amuse me to see you get a ducking.'

As he was returning to the Place de la Bourse again, the sight of Gundermann, whom he espied in the distance emerging from the Rue Vivienne, made his heart flutter once more. There could be no doubt of it; distance might shorten the great Baron's figure, but it was indeed he, walking slowly as was his wont, carrying his pale head erect without looking at anybody, as though, in the midst of all that crowd, he were alone in his royalty. And Saccard watched him with a feeling of terror, seeking to interpret each movement that he made. On seeing Nathansohn approach him, he imagined that all was lost. But his hopes revived when he saw the *coulissier* draw back with a discomfited air. No, there was certainly nothing unusual about the great banker; he had his every-day look. And all at once Saccard's heart leapt with joy, for Gundermann had just entered the confectioner's shop to make his customary purchase of sweetmeats for his little grand-daughters; and that was a sure sign of his knowing nothing, for he never set foot in the shop on days of crisis.

One o'clock struck and the bell announced the opening of the market. It was a memorable Bourse, one of those great days of disaster—disaster caused by a totally unexpected rise—which are so rare that they remain legendary. At the outset, amid the overpowering heat, prices fell yet lower. Then some sudden isolated purchases—the desultory fire of skirmishers, as it were, before the opening of a battle—provoked astonishment. But amidst the general distrust, things still remained dull and heavy, when all at once the number of purchases began to increase, demands sprang up in all directions, and Nathansohn at the *coulisse* under the colonnade, and Mazaud, Jacoby, and Delarocque in the *corbeille* within the building, were to be heard shouting that they would take any stock at any price. And then there was a tremor, a sudden ground-swell as it were, though nobody yet dared to rush into the fight, so inexplicable was this sudden change in the tone of the market.

Prices had but slightly risen, and Saccard had time to give Massias fresh orders for Nathansohn. Then, as little Flory passed by on the run, he asked him to hand Mazaud a *fiche* on which he had written a request to the broker to continue buying, to keep on at it indeed until he sent him word to stop. Flory read what was written on the *fiche* as he trotted off, and, fired with confidence, followed the great man's lead, at once effecting some purchases on his own account. And at a quarter to two o'clock the thunderbolt fell in the midst of the crowded Bourse. Austria surrendered Venetia to the Emperor; the war was over. Whence had the news arrived? Nobody knew; but it came simultaneously from every tongue, and, indeed, from the very flagstones. Someone had brought it, and all repeated it in a growing clamour, like the loud voice of an equinoctial tide. Prices then began to rise with furious bounds amidst the frightful uproar; and before the bell rang out the closing hour there was a difference of forty, fifty francs in many quotations. It was an indescribable *mêlée*—one of those battles in which confusion prevails, when soldiers and officers alike rush hither and thither, thinking only of saving their skins, but unable to do so because they are blinded, deafened, and no longer possess any clear idea of the situation. Perspiration streamed from the foreheads of the combatants, whilst the relentless sun beat upon the steps, wrapping the Bourse in the blaze of a conflagration.

When settling day came round, and it was possible to form an idea of the disaster, it proved an immense one. The battle-field was strewn with wounded and ruined. 'Bear' Moser was one of the most severely hit. Pillerault, who on this one occasion had despaired of a rise, paid dearly for his weakness. Maugendre was out of pocket to the tune of fifty thousand francs, his first serious loss. The Baroness Sandorff had such heavy differences to make good that Delcambre, it was reported, refused to pay for her; and she turned quite white with rage and hatred at the mere mention of her husband, the Embassy councillor, who had held the despatch in his own hands before Rougon had ever seen it, and yet had not said a word to her on the subject. But the big bankers, the Jewish bankers especially, had been subjected to a terrible defeat—a real massacre, so to say. It was asserted that Gundermann, for his part, had lost eight millions of francs. And this astounded people. How was it that he had not been warned—he, the undisputed master of the market, to whom Cabinet Ministers were but clerks and states, dependencies? There had evidently been one of those extraordinary combinations of circumstances which bring about great strokes of chance. It was an unforeseen, an idiotic disaster that had befallen the market, a disaster outside the pale of logic and reason.

However, the story spread, and Saccard passed for a great man. He had raked in nearly all the money lost by the 'bears.' Personally, he had put a couple of million francs in his pockets. The rest was to be placed in the coffers of the Universal Bank, or rather in the hands of the directors. With great difficulty he succeeded in persuading Madame Caroline that Hamelin's share of the plunder so legitimately gained from the Jews was a million. Huret, having helped in the work, had taken care to secure for himself a princely share of the booty. As for the others, the Daigremonts, the Bohains, they needed no pressing to accept what was offered them. Thanks and congratulations were voted to the eminent manager unanimously. And one heart especially was warm with gratitude to Saccard, the heart of little Flory, who had gained ten thousand francs, a small fortune, which would enable him to live with Chuchu in a little nest in the Rue Condorcet, and join Gustave Sédille and other friends at expensive restaurants in the evening. As for Jantrou, it was found necessary to make him a considerable present, as he was very angry at not having been forewarned. Dejoie alone remained in the dumps, fated to experience eternal regret at having one evening scented fortune vaguely, mysteriously passing by in the air, all to no purpose.

This, Saccard's first triumph, seemed as it were some florescence of the Empire which now had attained its apogee. He became a part of the splendour of the reign, one of its glorious reflections. On the very evening when he waxed powerful and wealthy amidst so many shattered fortunes, at the very hour when the Bourse became but a field of ruin, all Paris adorned itself with bunting and illuminated as on the occasion of some great victory; and festivities at the Tuileries and rejoicings in the streets proclaimed Napoleon III. the master of Europe—so high and mighty that emperors and kings chose him as arbiter in their quarrels, and handed provinces over to him that he might dispose of them between them. No doubt there were protests at the Chamber of Deputies; prophets of misfortune confusedly predicted a terrible future. Prussia increased, strengthened by all that France had tolerated, Austria beaten, and Italy ungrateful. But bursts of laughter and shouts of anger drowned those anxious voices; and on the morrow of Sadowa, Paris, the centre of the world, set all her avenues and monuments ablaze with illuminations, pending the coming of those black, icy nights, those gasless nights, through which the red fuses of shells were destined to wing their flight.

Overflowing with success, Saccard that evening walked the streets, the Place de la Concorde, the Champs Élysées, all the footways where *lampions* were lighted. Carried along in the full-tide stream of promenaders, his eyes dazzled by the day-like brilliancy, it was possible for him to imagine that folks had illuminated in his honour. For was he not also an unexpected conqueror, one who rose to increased power in the midst of the disasters of others? A single annoyance tempered his satisfaction—the anger displayed by Rougon, who, in a terrible fury, on realising the origin of the Bourse stroke, had given Huret his dismissal. So the great man had not shown himself a good brother by sending him (Saccard) the all-important news. Must he dispense with that high patronage? must he even attack the omnipotent Minister? All at once, while he was standing in front of the Palace of the Legion of Honour, which was surmounted by a gigantic cross of fire, glowing brightly against the black sky, he boldly resolved to do so on the day when he should feel himself sufficiently strong. And then, intoxicated by the songs of the crowd and the flapping of the flags, he retraced his steps through flaming Paris to the Rue Saint Lazare.

Two months later, in September, Saccard, rendered audacious by his victory over Gundermann, decided that he must give fresh impulse to the Universal. At the shareholders' meeting held at the end of April the balance-sheet had shown for the year 1865 a profit of nine million francs, inclusive of the premium of twenty francs on each of the fifty thousand new shares issued when the capital had been doubled. The preliminary expenses had now been entirely paid, the shareholders had received their five per cent., and the directors their ten per cent.; whilst, in addition to the regulation percentage, a sum of five million francs had been carried to the reserve fund. With the remaining million they had contrived to pay a dividend of ten francs per share. This was a fine result for an institution which had not yet been two years in existence. Saccard, however, worked in a feverish way, cultivating the financial soil on a violent system, heating it, overheating it at the risk of burning the crop; and thus he prevailed, first on the directors, and then on a special shareholders' meeting held on September 15, to authorise a fresh increase of capital. In fact, the capital was again doubled—raised from fifty to a hundred millions of francs—by the creation of one hundred thousand new shares, exclusively reserved to existing shareholders, share per share. However, these new shares were issued at no less than six hundred and seventy-five francs, inclusive of a premium of one hundred and seventy-five francs which was to be paid into the reserve fund. The Universal's growing successes, the profitable strokes which it had already made, and especially the great enterprises which it was about to launch—such were the reasons brought forward to justify this enormous increase of the capital, twice doubled at short intervals; for it was certainly necessary to endow the Bank with an importance and strength commensurate to the interests it represented. Moreover, this increase of capital had an immediate effect; the shares, which for some months had remained stationary, their average quotation at the Bourse being seven hundred and fifty francs, rose to nine hundred francs in three days.

Hamelin, who had not been able to return from the East to preside over the extraordinary meeting of shareholders, wrote his sister an anxious letter, in which he expressed his fears respecting this mode of conducting the affairs of the Universal, this fashion of madly forcing the pace. He well divined that false declarations had again been made at Maître Lelorrain's office. And, indeed, all the new shares had not been subscribed, as the law required, and the Bank remained in possession of those refused by its shareholders. The instalments on allotment not being paid, these shares were transferred by some jugglery in the book-keeping to the Sabatani account. Moreover, by borrowing the names of some of its directors and employees, the Bank had subscribed a portion of its own issue, so that it now held nearly thirty thousand of its shares, representing seventeen and a half millions of francs.

Not only was this illegal, but the situation might become dangerous, for experience has proved that every financial establishment which speculates in its own stock is lost. Nevertheless, Madame Caroline answered her brother gaily, twitting him with having now become the trembler, to such a point that it was she, formerly the suspicious one, who had to reassure him. She said that she was always on the watch, and could detect nothing suspicious; on the contrary, she was wonderstruck by the great things, all so clear and logical, which she was witnessing. The truth was that she, of course, knew nothing of the things which were hidden from her, and was, moreover, blinded by her admiration for Saccard, the sympathetic emotion into which she was thrown on beholding that little man's activity and intelligence.

In December Universal shares commanded more than a thousand francs. And in presence of this triumph there was a flutter among the big-wigs of the banking world. Gundermann, who was still to be met at times on the Place de la Bourse entering the confectioner's shop to buy sweetmeats with an automatic step and absorbed air, had paid the eight millions which he had lost without complaining, without a single of his intimates hearing a word of anger or rancour fall from his lips. As a rule, whenever he lost in this fashion, which rarely happened, he would say that it served him right and would teach him to be less careless; and folks would smile at this, for carelessness on Gundermann's part was scarcely to be imagined. But the hard lesson he had received must this time have remained upon his heart; the idea that he, so cold, so phlegmatic, so thoroughly a master of men and things, should have been beaten by that break-neck fellow, that passionate lunatic Saccard, must surely have been unendurable to him. And, indeed, from that very moment he began to watch, certain that in time he should have his revenge. In presence of the general infatuation for the Universal, he at once took up position, knowing, as he did, by long observation, that success achieved with unnatural rapidity, that lying prosperity conduct to the most complete disasters. However, the figure of a thousand francs, at which the shares were now quoted, was still a reasonable one, and he waited for further developments before beginning to 'bear' the stock.

His theory was that no man could bring about events at the Bourse, that at the utmost one could foresee them and profit by them when they came to pass. Logic was sole ruler; truth, in speculation as in other things, was an omnipotent force. As soon as the price of Universals should have risen to an unduly exaggerated figure there would come a collapse; a fall would take place, it was a mathematical certainty; and he would simply be there to see his calculations realised and pocket his profits. And he already decided that he would open the campaign when the quotations should have risen to fifteen hundred francs. At that price he would begin selling Universals, moderately at first, but to an increasing extent as each settling day came by, in accordance with a predetermined plan. He did not need to form any syndicate of 'bears,' his own efforts would suffice; sensible people would clearly divine the truth and follow his play. That noisy Universal, that Universal which was so rapidly taking up a big position in the market, which was rising like a menace against the great Jew bankers—he would coldly wait till it should crack of itself, and then with a shove of the shoulder he would throw it to the ground.

Later on, folks related that it was Gundermann himself who secretly facilitated Saccard's purchase of an old building in the Rue de Londres, which he had the intention of demolishing in order to raise upon the site the monument of his dreams, the palace in which he purposed installing his bank in the most sumptuous style. He had succeeded in winning over the directors with regard to this matter, and the workmen began their task in the middle of October.

On the day when the foundation stone was laid with great ceremony, Saccard repaired to the newspaper office at about four o'clock, and whilst awaiting the return of Jantrou, who had gone to carry some reports of the solemnity to friendly contemporaries, he received a visit from the Baroness Sandorff. She had at first asked for the editor, and then, as though by chance, came upon the manager of the Universal, who gallantly placed himself at her disposal with regard to any information that she might desire, and ushered her into his own private room at the end of the passage. And this interview proved decisive.

It happened, however, that Madame Caroline, who had been shopping in the neighbourhood, called at the office at this very time. She would occasionally come up in this way, either to give Saccard an answer about some matter or other, or to ask for news. Moreover, she knew Dejoie, for whom she had found a situation there, and usually stopped to chat with him for a moment, well pleased with the gratitude which he displayed towards her. On this occasion she did not find him in the ante-room, and so turned into the passage, where she ran against him just as he was returning from listening at Saccard's door. This was now quite a disease with him; he trembled with fever, and applied his ear to every keyhole in the hope of overhearing some Bourse secret.

'He is in, isn't he?' said Madame Caroline, trying to pass on.

But Dejoie stopped her, stammering, lacking the time to prepare a lie. 'Yes, he's there, but you can't go in.'

'Can't go in. Why is that?'

Then he, who knew nothing of her position with regard to Saccard, allowed her to divine the truth.

For a moment Madame Caroline remained motionless. In the dim passage the livid pallor of her face could not be detected. She had just felt so keen, so cruel a pain in her heart that she could not remember having ever suffered so much before; and it was the stupor caused by this frightful pang which nailed her there. What should she do?—force her way in, create a scandal?

Whilst she still stood there, dazed, destitute of will, Marcelle, who had come to fetch her husband, approached her gaily. 'Oh, is it you, dear madame?' the young woman exclaimed. 'Just fancy, we are going to the theatre this evening. Oh! it's quite an affair, for we can't afford expense. But Paul has discovered a little restaurant where we shall feast ourselves at thirty-five sous a head.'

Just then Jordan entered the passage and laughingly interrupted his wife. 'Two courses, a decanter of wine, and as much bread as one can eat,' said he.

'And then,' continued Marcelle, 'we shan't take a cab. It is so amusing to walk home at a late hour. As we are rich to-night, we shall spend a franc on an almond cake to take home with us. It will be a perfect *fête*, a reckless jollification.'

She went off, delighted, on her husband's arm; and Madame Caroline, who had returned to the ante-room with them, now found sufficient strength to smile. 'I hope you will amuse yourselves,' she murmured in a trembling voice.

Then she in her turn departed. She loved Saccard, and carried away with her a feeling of astonishment and grief—grief, as it were, for some shameful sore which she was unwilling to reveal.

CHAPTER VII

REVELATIONS

Two months later, one grey, mild November afternoon, Madame Caroline went up to the room where her brother's plans were kept, immediately after breakfast, in order to set to work. Her brother, when at Constantinople, busy with his great scheme of the Oriental railways, had asked her to go through all the notes he had made at the time when they had travelled through Asia Minor together, and to draw up a kind of memoir, which would be an historical *résumé* of the question. During two long weeks already she had been trying to give her whole mind to this task. It was so warm that day that she let the fire go out and opened the window, whence, before sitting down, she gazed for a moment at the tall bare trees of the Beauvilliers garden, which had a violet hue against the pale grey sky.

She had been writing for nearly half an hour when the need of some document forced her to engage in a long search among the portfolios heaped upon her table. She rose, stirred up some other papers, and sat down again with her hands full; and whilst she was classifying various loose documents she came upon some religious pictures, an illuminated view of the Holy Sepulchre, and a prayer surrounded by emblems of the Passion, guaranteed to ensure salvation in those distressful moments when the soul is in peril. She then remembered that her brother, like the pious fellow he was, had bought the pictures at Jerusalem. Emotion suddenly overcame her, and tears moistened her cheeks. Ah! that brother of hers, so intelligent, so long unappreciated, how happy he was in being able to believe, in being able to refrain from smiling at that *naïf* view of the Holy Sepulchre, executed in the style of the pictures which are used to decorate sweetmeat boxes! And how happy he was, too, in being able to derive a serene strength from his faith in the efficacy of that rhymed prayer, which, poetically, was on a par with the verses found in Christmas crackers! She again beheld him, ever trustful, too easily imposed upon perhaps, but so upright and tranquil, never revolting, never struggling even. And she, who had been struggling and suffering for two months past, she who no longer believed, whose mind was scorched by reading, worn out by reasoning, how ardently in her hours of weakness did she not wish that she had remained simple and ingenuous like him, so that she might lull her bleeding heart to sleep by thrice repeating, morn and eve alike, that childlike prayer, around which were depicted the nails and the lance, the crown and the sponge of the Passion!

On the morrow of the day when chance had so brutally made her acquainted with the truth concerning Saccard and the Baroness Sandorff she had exerted all her will power to resist her desire to watch them. She was not this man's wife, and did not wish to carry jealousy to the point of scandal. She was no longer twenty, but six and thirty, and the terrible experience of her married life had made her tolerant. Still it was in vain that she practised abnegation; her nature revolted, and she experienced intense suffering. There were times when she longed to sever the ties which bound her to Saccard, to provoke a violent scene and hurl in his face the wrong that he had done her. However, she succeeded in mastering herself, in forcing herself to remain not only silent, but calm and smiling; and never indeed in her existence, hitherto so hard, had she been in greater need of strength than now.

Still holding the religious pictures, she bent her eyes upon them for a moment longer, smiling the sorrowful smile of one who cannot believe, and her heart melting with affection for her brother. But a moment later she no longer beheld them. Her mind had wandered away, as it always did directly she ceased to occupy it, and she was again thinking of Saccard, of what he had done the day before, of what he might that day be doing. He seemed to be leading his usual life, devoting his mornings to his worrying duties at the Bank, his afternoons to the Bourse, his evenings to the invitations to dinner which he received, to the first performances given at the theatres, to the society of actresses whom she was not jealous of, to everything, in fact, which is supposed to make up a life of pleasure. And yet she felt that some new interest absorbed him, an interest, no doubt, in that woman, whom he met somewhere. No doubt she had prohibited herself from trying to ascertain where and when it was that they met; yet it all made her distrustful and suspicious, and, as her brother laughingly expressed it, she had begun playing the gendarme again, even with regard to the affairs of the Bank, which she had previously ceased watching, so great at one moment had her confidence become. At the present time, however, she was struck and grieved by certain irregular practices; and then was quite surprised to find that she really cared nothing about the matter at bottom, lacking the strength alike to speak and act, so completely did a single anguish fill her heart—anguish for that betrayal, which she would have condoned, but the thought of which stifled her, despite all her efforts. And now, ashamed at last to find her tears flowing again, she went and hid the religious pictures, deeply regretting that she, who had no faith, could not go and kneel in some church, and find relief by weeping and praying.

Having at last calmed herself, she set to work on the memoir again, and had been writing for some ten minutes or so when the valet came to inform her that Charles, Saccard's coachman who had been dismissed on the previous day, absolutely insisted upon speaking to her. Saccard himself had detected the fellow stealing the horses' oats. She hesitated for a moment, and then consented to see him.

Tall, good-looking, with shaven face and confident, conceited gait, Charles came into the room and insolently exclaimed: 'I've come, madame, about the two shirts of mine which the laundress has lost, and won't make an allowance for. Madame surely doesn't suppose that I can put up with such a loss. And, as Madame is responsible, I wish Madame to pay me for my shirts. Yes, I want fifteen francs.'

She was very severe in all these household matters. Perhaps she would have paid the fifteen francs to avoid any discussion. But she was disgusted by the effrontery of this man, who had been caught thieving only the day before.

'I owe you nothing, and I shall give you nothing,' said she; 'besides, Monsieur warned me, and absolutely forbade me to do anything for you.'

Charles took a step forward with a threatening air. 'Oh, Monsieur said that, did he? I suspected as much, and Monsieur made a great mistake, for now we shall have some fun. For I know all about Monsieur and his goings on. Yes, indeed, I know all about them!'

Madame Caroline had risen to her feet, intending to order him out of the room; but before she could do so he had forced the whole horrid story upon her unwilling ears. She tried to get rid of him by handing him the fifteen francs that he had asked for, and he took them and even became polite; but nothing could stop his venomous tongue. And thus she learnt everything; the meetings of Saccard and the Baroness, and a horribly scandalous scene in which Delcambre, the Public Prosecutor, long the woman's lover, had taken part.

But at last the coachman went off, and after remaining for a few moments motionless Madame Caroline sank with a prolonged wail on to a chair beside her work-table, giving free course to the tears which had so long been stifling her. For a long while she wept in silent agony, but the time came when amidst all her grief for self, her grief for the wrong which had been done her, she felt the many suspicions, the many fears respecting other matters that she had sought to bury, reviving.

She had forced herself to tranquillity and hope in the affairs of the Universal, becoming in her loving blindness an accomplice in all that was not told her and that she did not seek to learn. And now, in a fit of violent remorse, she reproached herself for writing that reassuring letter to her brother at the time of the last shareholders' meeting. For, since jealousy had again opened her eyes and ears, she had known that the irregular practices were continuing, ever growing worse and worse. The Sabatani account had increased to a yet higher figure, the Bank was speculating more and more extensively under cover of Sabatani's name, to say nothing of the monstrous lying puffs which were being disseminated, the foundations of sand and mud on which had been reared that colossal edifice, whose rise, so rapid that it seemed miraculous, inspired her with far more terror than delight. And it was especially the terrible pace which distressed her—the continual gallop at which the Universal was driven along, like some engine stuffed full of coals and set upon diabolical rails that it might rush on until a final great shock should make everything burst and smash.

She was not a simpleton, a booby, who could be deceived; albeit ignorant of the technicalities of banking, she fully understood the reasons of this overdriving, this feverishness destined to intoxicate the mob and plunge it into epidemical madness. Each morning must bring its rise; it was necessary to keep on inspiring a belief in fresh successes, in streamlets of gold converted into great rivers, oceans of the precious metal. Her poor brother, so credulous, fascinated, carried away—did she mean to betray him, to abandon him to the mercy of that flood which threatened to drown them all some day? At thought of her inaction, her powerlessness, she was once more filled with despair.

Meantime the twilight was darkening the workroom; there was not even a reflection from the fire-place to illumine it, for she had let the fire go out; and in the increasing gloom Madame Caroline wept more and more bitterly. It was cowardly to weep in this fashion, for she was perfectly conscious that all these tears were not due to her anxiety about the affairs of the Universal. Assuredly it was Saccard alone who was forcing that terrible gallop, lashing the monster on and on with extraordinary ferocity and moral unconsciousness, careless as to whether he killed it or not. He was the only guilty one, and she shuddered as she tried to read him, to read that murky financier's soul, of which even he himself was ignorant, a miry Infinite of all degradations, hidden one from another by the darkness in which they were enveloped. Though there were things which she did not yet clearly distinguish, she suspected them and trembled at them. But the mere discovery of so many sores, the fear of a possible catastrophe, would not have sufficed to bow her in this fashion over that table, weeping and strengthless; it would, on the contrary, have set her erect, eager for struggle and cure. She knew herself; she was a warrior. No, if she sobbed so bitterly, like a weak child, it was because she loved Saccard, and because Saccard at that very moment was betraying her. And this avowal which she was obliged to make to herself filled her with shame, redoubled her tears until she almost choked. 'To think that I have no pride left, my God!' she stammered aloud; 'to be so weak and miserable! to be unable when I would!'

But just then she was astonished to hear a voice address her in the darkness. It was the voice of Maxime, who had just entered, like one at home. 'What! you in the dark and crying?' said he.

Confused at being thus surprised, she strove to master her sobs, while he added: 'I beg your pardon, but I thought that my father had come back from the Bourse. A lady asked me to bring him to dinner at her house.'

However, the valet now brought a lamp, and, after placing it on the table, withdrew. The whole of the spacious room was illumined by the soft light that fell from the shade.

'It is nothing,' Madame Caroline tried to explain—'merely a woman's fretting, and yet I seldom give way to my nerves.'

Her eyes dry and her figure erect, she was already smiling with the brave mien of a fighter. For a moment the young man looked at her, as she thus proudly drew herself up with her large clear eyes, her thick lips, her expression of virile kindness, which her thick crown of hair softened and endowed with a great charm; and he found her still young, white-haired though she was, her teeth also very white—indeed an adorable woman, who had become beautiful. And then he thought of his father and shrugged his shoulders with contemptuous pity. 'It is on account of him, is it not,' said he; 'that you have put yourself in this fearful state?'

She wished to deny it, but she was choking, tears were again coming to her eyelids.

'Ah! my poor lady,' resumed Maxime; 'I told you, you will remember, that you entertained illusions about papa, and that you would be ill rewarded. It was inevitable.'

Thereupon she remembered the day when she had gone to borrow those two thousand francs of the young man in order to pay part of Victor's ransom. Had he not then promised to have a chat with her whenever she might desire to know the truth? Was not this an opportunity to learn all the past by questioning him? And an irresistible need of knowing urged her on. Now that she had commenced the descent she must go to the bottom. That course alone would be brave, worthy of her, useful to all.

Still the inquiry was repugnant to her, and, instead of boldly starting upon it, she took a circuitous course, as though with the object of changing the conversation. 'I still owe you two thousand francs,' said she; 'I hope you are not too angry with me for keeping you waiting.'

He made a gesture as though to imply that she might take all the time she needed, and then abruptly said: 'By the way, and my little brother, that monster?'

'I am greatly grieved about him. I have so far said nothing about him to your father. I should so much like to cleanse the poor boy a little, so that it might be possible for your father to love him.'

A burst of laughter from Maxime disturbed her, and as she gave him a questioning look he exclaimed: 'Well, I think that you are wasting time and trouble in that respect also! Papa will hardly understand your taking all this trouble. He has experienced so many family annoyances.'

She was still looking at him, so demurely egotistical in his enjoyment of life, so disengaged from all human ties, even from those which a life of pleasure creates. He had smiled, alone enjoying the covert maliciousness of his last words. And she was conscious that she was at last about to discover the secret of these two men.

'You lost your mother at an early age?' she said.

'Yes, I scarcely knew her. I was still at Plassans, at school, when she died here in Paris. Our uncle, Doctor Pascal, has kept my sister Clotilde with him there; I have only once seen her since.'

'But your father married again?'

He hesitated. A kind of ruddy vapour seemed to dim his empty eyes, usually so clear.

'Oh! yes, yes; he married again, the daughter of a magistrate, one Béraud du Châtel—Renée her name was; she was not a mother to me, but a good friend.' Then, sitting down beside her in a familiar way, he went on: 'You see, one must understand

134

papa. *Mon Dieu*! he isn't worse than others. Only children, wives—in short, all around him—hold in his mind a second place to money. Oh! let us understand each other; he doesn't love money like a miser, for the sake of having a huge pile of it and hiding it in his cellar. No; if he wishes to make it gush forth on every side, if he draws it from no matter what sources, it is to see it flow around him in torrents; it is for the sake of all the enjoyments he derives from it—luxury, pleasure, power. What can you expect? It is in his blood. He would sell us—you, me, no matter whom—if we were a part of some bargain. And he would do it as an unconscious and superior man; for he is really the poet of the million, so mad and rascally does money make him—oh! rascally on a very grand scale!'

This was just what Madame Caroline had understood, and while listening to Maxime she nodded her head in token of assent. Ah! money, that all-corrupting poisonous money, which withered souls and drove from them all kindness, tenderness, and love for others! Money alone was the great culprit, the agent of all human cruelties and abominations. At that moment she cursed it, execrated it, in the indignant revolt of her woman's nobility and uprightness. Ah! if she had had the power, she would with a gesture have annihilated all the money in the world, even as one would crush disease with a stamp of the heel in order to preserve the world in health.

'And your father married again,' she slowly repeated after a pause, with a tinge of embarrassment in her voice as vague memories began awaking within her. Who was it that had alluded to the story in her presence? She could not have told. But doubtless it had been some woman, some friend, in the early days of her residence in the Rue Saint Lazare, when Saccard had rented the first floor of the mansion. Had there not been some question of a marriage which he had contracted, some marriage for money, some shameful bargain? And later on had not crime quietly taken its seat at the hearth, abominable depravity, tolerated, suffered to abide there without let or hindrance?

'Renée,' replied Maxime in a very low tone, and as though despite himself, 'was only a few years older than me.'

He raised his head and looked at Madame Caroline. And then, suddenly throwing off all self-restraint, with unreasoning confidence in this woman, who seemed to him so healthy and so sensible, he told the story of the shameful past, not in consecutive phrases, it is true, but in shreds—involuntary, imperfect confessions which it was for her to connect together. So, in this wise, Madame Caroline learnt the frightful story: Saccard selling his name, marrying a girl in trouble for money's sake; completing the unhinging of the poor child's ailing mind by means of this same money, by the mad, prodigal, dazzling life he led; and then, because he was in need of money and required her signature, closing his eyes to whatever she might do. Ah! money, money the King, money the deity, beside which tears and blood were as nothing! Money adored for its infinite power far above all vain human scruples! And in proportion as the might of money increased in her eyes, and Saccard stood revealed to her in all his diabolical grandeur, Madame Caroline was seized with real terror, frozen, distracted by the thought that she too had become this monster's prey, after so many others.

'There!' said Maxime, concluding. 'It pains me to see you like this; it is better that you should be warned. But don't let this make trouble between you and my father. I should be very grieved if such were the case, for you would be the one to weep over it, not he. And now do you understand why I refuse to lend him a sou?'

As she did not answer, for her throat was contracted and a terrible pang tortured her heart, he rose, and glanced at a mirror, with the tranquil ease of a handsome man who is certain of his correctness in life. Then, coming back, he stood before her.

'Such examples age you quickly, do they not?' he said. 'For my part, I promptly settled down; I married a young girl who was ill and is now dead; I swear to-day that no one shall ever induce me to act foolishly again. No! But papa, you see, is incorrigible, because he has no moral sense.'

He took her hand, and, holding it for a moment in his own, felt that it was quite cold.

'I am going, since he doesn't come back. But pray don't grieve like this. I thought you so strong! And you ought to thank me, for there is only one thing that is stupid in life—to let oneself be duped.'

Finally he started off, but at the door he stopped to add, with a laugh: 'I was forgetting; tell him that Madame de Jeumont expects him to dinner.'

Left to herself, Madame Caroline did not stir. Bowed down on her chair in the spacious room, which had sunk into an oppressive silence, she gazed fixedly at the lamp with dilated eyes. It seemed to her that the veil had been suddenly torn aside. All that she had hitherto been unwilling to distinguish plainly, which she had only tremblingly suspected, now appeared before her in its frightful crudity, so clear that it would henceforth be impossible to doubt it, to gloss it over. She beheld Saccard naked, with the ravaged, complicated soul of a man of money, murky and rotting. For him there were neither bonds nor barriers; he rushed on to the satisfaction of his appetites with the unbridled instincts of a man who knows no other limit than powerlessness. He had sold his son, his wife, all who had fallen into his clutches; he had sold himself, and he would sell her too, and sell her brother, dispose of their hearts and their brains for money. He was nothing but a maker of money, one who threw beings and things into the melting-pot to coin them into money. In a brief interval of lucidity she saw the Universal diffusing money like perspiration in all directions—a lake, an ocean of money, into the midst of which, all at once, with a frightful crash, the whole house would topple down. Ah! money, horrible money, that smirches and devours!

Madame Caroline rose up in angry haste. No, no, it was monstrous; it was all over; she could no longer remain near that man. She would have forgiven him his betrayal; but loathing seized upon her at thought of all that old-time filth; terror distracted her at thought of the crimes which were possible in the future. There was nothing left for her but to start off at once if she did not wish to be splashed with mud herself, crushed beneath the ruins. And a pressing desire came to her to go far, far away, to join her brother in the distant East, less to warn him than to disappear herself. Yes, she must start, start at once! It was not yet six o'clock; she could take the *rapide* for Marseilles at seven fifty-five; for it seemed to her that to see Saccard again would be beyond her strength. She would make whatever purchases were necessary at Marseilles before embarking. A little linen in a trunk, one spare dress, and she would be off. In a quarter of an hour she could be ready.

Then the sight of her work on the table, the memoir which she had begun writing, made her pause for a moment. But what would be the use of taking that with her, since the whole thing was rotten at the foundation and was bound to fall? Nevertheless she began carefully arranging the documents and memoranda, like a good housewife who never likes to leave things in disorder. And the task occupied her for some moments, calming the first fever of her decision. She was again fully mistress of herself, when she gave a last glance round the room before leaving it. But just then the valet came in again, bringing a number of papers and letters.

In a mechanical kind of way Madame Caroline looked at the superscriptions, and perceived in the pile a letter from her brother addressed to herself. It came from Damascus, where Hamelin was then staying, making arrangements for the proposed branch line from that city to Beyrout. At first she began to glance over the letter, standing near the lamp, and resolving that she would read it more carefully later on in the train. But each sentence held her attention, she was unable to skip a word; and she finally sat down again at the table, and gave herself up to the absorbing perusal of this long letter, which filled twelve pages.

Hamelin happened to be in one of his gayest moods. He thanked his sister for the last good news which she had sent him from Paris, and sent her still better news in return, for everything, said he, was going to his liking. The first balance-sheet of the United Steam Navigation Company promised well; the new steamships were realising large receipts, thanks to their perfect equipment and superior speed. He jokingly said that folks travelled in them for pleasure, and pointed to the sea-ports invaded by tourists from the Western world, and declared that he could not make a journey by highway or byway without coming face to face with some Parisian of the Boulevards. As he had foreseen, it was really the East opened up to France. Cities, said he, would before long spring up on the fertile slopes of the Lebanon range. But particularly did he give a vivid picture of the lonely Carmel gorge, where the silver mine was now being actively worked. The savage site was being humanised; springs had been discovered amidst the gigantic pile of fallen rocks which barred the valley on the north; and fields were being formed, wheat was replacing the mastic-trees, whilst a whole village had sprung up near the mines, at first merely some wooden cabins, huts to shelter the workmen, but now little stone-built houses with gardens—the beginning of a city which would continue growing so long as the veins were not exhausted. There were now nearly five hundred inhabitants on the spot, and a road had just been finished connecting the village with Saint Jean d'Acre. From morning till night the extraction machines were roaring, waggons set out amid the loud cracking of whips, women sang, and children played and cried where formerly there had been a desert and death-like silence, which only the eagles had broken with the sound of their slowly beating pinions. And myrtle and broom still perfumed the atmosphere, which was so delightfully pure.

On the subject of the first railway which he had to lay, the line from Broussa to Beyrout by way of Angora and Aleppo, Hamelin wrote at great length. All the formalities had been concluded at Constantinople. He was delighted with certain happy alterations which he had made in the line of route, so as to overcome the difficult passage through the Taurus passes; and of these passes and of the plains that stretched away at the foot of the mountains he wrote with the rapture of a man of science who had found new coal deposits there, and expected to see the country covered with factories. He had located his guiding points, and chosen the sites of his stations, some in the midst of the wild solitudes—one here, another farther on. Cities would spring up around those stations at the intersection of the natural highways. The seed was already sown for the crop of men and grand things of the future; everything was already germinating; within a few years there would here be a new world. And he concluded with a loving kiss for his dear sister, happy at being able to associate her in this resurrection of a people, telling her that much of it would be due to her, to her who had so long helped him, buoyed him up by her fine bravery and health.

Madame Caroline had finished her perusal, the letter lay open on the table, and she remained there thinking, her eyes once more fixed upon the lamp. Then her glances involuntarily rose and strayed round the walls, lingering for a moment on each of the plans, each of the water-colour drawings she saw there. The pavilion for the manager of the United Steam Navigation Company was now built at Beyrout, and was surrounded by vast store-houses. That deep, wild gorge of Mount Carmel, blocked up with brambles and stones, was now being peopled; the huge nest, as it were, of some new-born race. Those levellings in the Taurus range were changing the aspect of the horizon, opening the way for free commerce. And from all those geometrically outlined designs, secured to the walls by a few tacks, there sprang up before her a complete vision of the far-off country where she had formerly travelled, and which she had loved so dearly for its beautiful sky of unchanging blue and its ever fertile soil.

Again she beheld the gardens of Beyrout rising up in tiers, the valleys of Mount Lebanon with their great forests of olive and mulberry trees, the plains of Antioch and Aleppo with their immense orchards of delightful fruits. Again she beheld herself with her brother continually journeying through that marvellous country, whose incalculable wealth was lost, ignored, or misapplied, which had had no roads, no industry, no agriculture, no schools, but had been solely the abode of idleness and ignorance. Now, however, all was springing to life again, thanks to an extraordinary flow of fresh sap. This vision of the East of to-morrow already set prosperous cities, cultivated fields, happy people before her eyes. And she saw them, and heard the busy hum of the workshops; and realised that this old soil, so long asleep, was reawakened at last, and was entering upon the work of parturition.

Then Madame Caroline acquired the sudden conviction that money was the dung-heap in which grew the humanity of to-morrow. Some of Saccard's remarks, scraps of his theories respecting speculation, came back to her mind. She recalled that idea of his that without speculation there would be no great fruitful enterprises, just in the same way as without love, though love may have its horrid aspects, there would be no life. If life is to continue in the world, there *must* be passion. If her brother over yonder in the East was in such high spirits, shouting victory amidst the workshops and yards which were being got in order, and the buildings which were springing from the soil, it was because the passion for gambling was making money rain down and rot everything in Paris. Poisonous and destructive money became the ferment of all social vegetation, served as the necessary compost for the execution of the great works which would draw the nations nearer together and pacify the earth.

She had cursed money, and now she fell in awe-stricken admiration before it; for was not money the sole force that can level a mountain, fill up an arm of the sea—briefly, render the earth inhabitable by men, who, once relieved of labour, would become but the conductors of machines. From this force, which was the root of all evil, there also sprang everything that was good. And, shaken to the depths of her being, she no longer knew what to do, for although she had already decided that she would not go away, since success seemed complete in the East and it was at Paris that the battle raged, she was yet unable to calm herself, to heal her bleeding heart.

She rose, and with her forehead pressed against a pane of one of the windows commanding the garden of the Beauvilliers mansion, she looked out. It was now night; and she could only distinguish a faint gleam in the lonely little room in which the

Countess and her daughter confined themselves, so that they might economise firing and avoid soiling the other apartments. Behind the thin muslin curtains she could vaguely distinguish the figure of the Countess, who was mending some linen, whilst Alice was busy with some water-colour sketches, which she painted hurriedly by the dozen and secretly sold. A misfortune had lately happened to them; their horse had contracted some illness, and for a fortnight they had been confined to the house, obstinately refusing to show themselves on foot in the streets, and reluctant to hire another horse from a livery stable. Nevertheless, amidst the poverty which they so heroically concealed, they were now buoyed up, inspirited by one hope—a hope that the rise in the value of Universal shares would continue, that their gain, already very considerable, would fall upon them in a golden rain when the day came for them to realise their shares at the highest possible figure. The Countess promised herself a really new dress, and dreamt of being able to give four dinners a month without having to live on bread and water for a fortnight in order to do so. Alice, too, no longer laughed with an affected air of indifference when her mother spoke to her of marriage, but listened with a slight trembling of the hands, beginning to believe that this dream would perhaps be realised, and that, like others, she might have a husband and children of her own.

As Madame Caroline stood looking at the little lamp which lighted them, she felt great calmness, a soft affectionate feeling, penetrating her, struck as she was by the circumstance that money, merely the hope of money, sufficed for the happiness of those poor creatures. If Saccard should enrich them, would they not bless him—would he not remain charitable and good in the estimation of both of them? So goodness was to be found everywhere, even in the worst, who are always good to someone, and who always, amidst the curses of a crowd, have humble, isolated voices thanking and adoring them. At this thought her mind turned towards the Institute of Work. On the day before she had, on Saccard's behalf, distributed some toys and sweetmeats there, in celebration of an anniversary; and she smiled involuntarily at the recollection of the children's noisy joy. For the last month Victor had given greater satisfaction; she had read some notes about him when calling on the Princess d'Orviedo, with whom, twice a week, she had a long chat respecting the institution. But as the image of Victor suddenly appeared to her, she felt astonished at having forgotten him in her crisis of despair, when she had made up her mind to flee from Paris. Could she have thus abandoned him—compromised the success of the good action which she had carried so far with so much trouble? A more and more penetrating feeling of gentle affection came upon her as she gazed into the obscurity of the tall trees, a flood of ineffable renunciation, of divine tolerance, which enlarged her heart; and it seemed to her that the common little lamp of the Beauvilliers ladies was now shining forth like a star.

When Madame Caroline came back to her table she was shivering a little. What! was she cold then? The idea amused her, she who boasted of passing the winter without fires. She felt, however, as though she had come from an icy bath, rejuvenated and strong, with her pulse very calm. It was thus with her on the mornings when she rose feeling particularly well. Then it occurred to her to put a log in the fire-place; and, seeing that the fire was out, she amused herself in lighting it again, without ringing for a servant. It was quite a job, for she had no small wood, but she at last managed to ignite the logs by means of some old newspapers, which she burned one after another. On her knees before the hearth she laughed all alone; and for a moment she remained there, feeling happy and surprised. She had again passed through one of her great crises, and now she again hoped. For what? She knew nothing of the eternal unknown that lay at the end of life, at the end of humanity. To live, that must suffice, in order that life might continually bring her the cure for the wounds which life inflicted. Once more did she remember the catastrophes of her existence—her frightful marriage, her poverty in Paris, her abandonment by the only man whom she had loved; and after every fall she had recovered that tenacious energy, that immortal joy which ever placed her on her feet again amid the ruins. Had not everything just collapsed again? She could no longer esteem Saccard, confronted as she had been by his frightful past, even as holy women are confronted by the unclean wounds which they go, morning and evening, to dress, not hoping ever to heal them. But, albeit she knew the truth, she was going to continue her wonted life. She was going to live in a fire, in the panting forge of speculation, under the incessant threat of a final catastrophe, in which her brother might lose his honour and his life. Nevertheless, there she stood, almost reckless, as on the morning of a fine day, tasting the joy of battle in confronting danger. Why? for nothing in reason, but for the sole pleasure of being! Her brother told her truly she was the incarnation of invincible hope.

When Saccard returned he found Madame Caroline buried in her work, finishing in her firm handwriting a page of the memoir on the Oriental railways. She raised her head and smiled at him peacefully, while his lips lightly touched her beautiful, radiant, white hair.

'You have been very busy, my friend?'

'Oh, endless business! I saw the Minister of Public Works; I went to meet Huret, then I had to return to the Ministry, where I only found a secretary, but at last I have the promise they want over yonder.'

Having handed him Hamelin's letter, which delighted him, she watched him as he exulted over the approaching triumph, and said to herself that she would henceforth look after him more closely in order to prevent the follies of which he would otherwise certainly be guilty. However, she could not bring herself to treat him with severity.

'Your son came here to invite you to dinner,' she said, 'on behalf of Madame de Jeumont.'

'Oh, she had already written to me!' he exclaimed. 'I forgot to tell you that I am going there this evening. It bores me terribly, tired as I am.'

Then he went off, after once more kissing her white hair. She returned to her work again, with her wonted kindly, indulgent smile. She had forced herself to subdue her feelings. Was she not, after all, but a friend—a friend in all things? The thought of jealousy caused her shame. She wished to rise superior to the pain it might bring her. For, despite everything, she loved him with all her courageous, charitable heart. It was the triumph of love—that fellow Saccard, that financial bandit of the streets, loved so completely, so absolutely by that adorable woman because she beheld him, brave and active, creating a world, making life.

CHAPTER VIII
THE BOOM BEGINS

It was on April 1, in the midst of *fêtes*, that the Universal Exhibition of 1867 was opened with triumphal splendour. The Empire's great 'season' was beginning, that supreme gala season which was to turn Paris into the hostelry of the entire world—a hostelry gay with bunting, song, and music, where there was feasting and love-making

140

in every room. Never had a *régime* at the zenith of its power convoked the nations to such a colossal spree. From the four corners of the earth a long procession of emperors, kings, and princes started on the march towards the Tuileries, which were all ablaze like some palace in the crowning scene of an extravaganza.

And it was at this same period, a fortnight after the Exhibition opened, that Saccard inaugurated the monumental pile in which he had insisted upon lodging the Universal. Six months had sufficed to erect it; workmen had toiled day and night without losing an hour, performing a miracle which is only possible in Paris; and a superb façade was now displayed, rich in flowery ornamentation, suggestive in some respects of a temple, in others of a music hall—a façade of such a luxurious aspect that passers-by stopped short in groups to gaze upon it. And within all was sumptuous; the millions in the coffers seemed to have streamed along the walls. A grand staircase led to the board-room, which was all purple and gold, as splendid as the auditorium of an opera house. On every side you found carpets and hangings, offices fitted up with a dazzling wealth of furniture. Fastened in the walls of the basement, where the share offices were installed, were huge safes, with deep oven-like mouths, and transparent glass partitions enabled the public to perceive them, ranged there like the barrels of gold that figure in the folk-tales, and in which slumber the incalculable treasures of the fairies. And the nations with their kings on their way to the Exhibition would be able to come and view them, for all was ready, the new building awaited them, to dazzle them, catch them one by one, like an irresistible golden trap scintillating in the sunlight.

Saccard was enthroned in a most sumptuously adorned office with Louis Quatorze furniture of Genoa velvet and gilded woodwork. The staff had again been increased; it exceeded four hundred employees; so now it was quite an army that Saccard commanded with the pomp of a tyrant who is both adored and obeyed, for he was very open-handed in the matter of presents and gratuities. And, despite his mere title of manager, it was he in reality who reigned, above the chairman of the board, above the board itself, which simply ratified his orders. Madame Caroline was consequently ever on the alert, busy in finding out his decisions, to try and thwart them if she thought it necessary. She disapproved of this new, unduly magnificent establishment, though she could not blame it in principle, having recognised the necessity of having larger quarters in the fine days when she had been all confidence, and had joked her brother for growing anxious. The argument she now used in combating all this luxury was that the Bank lost its aspect of honest modesty, of deep religious gravity. What would the customers, accustomed to the monkish solemnity, the discreet half-light prevailing on the ground floor of the Rue Saint Lazare, think on entering this palace in the Rue de Londres, with its lofty storeys enlivened with sound and flooded with light? Saccard answered that they would be overwhelmed with admiration and respect, that those who brought five francs would take ten from their pockets, swayed by self-pride and intoxicated with confidence. And he was right in thus estimating the effect of all this tinsel. The success of the building was prodigious; as an effective advertisement it surpassed Jantrou's most extraordinary puffs. The pious little capitalists of the quiet parts of Paris, the poor country priests arriving in the morning from the railway stations, stood gaping beatifically before the doors, and came out flushed with pleasure at the thought of having their funds in such a palace.

In reality, the point which more particularly vexed Madame Caroline was that she could no longer constantly be in the establishment exercising supervision. She was only able to go to the Rue de Londres at long intervals on some pretext or other. She now lived alone in the workroom at home, and scarcely saw Saccard, except in the evening. He had kept his rooms in the Rue Saint Lazare, but the entire ground floor, as well as the offices on the first floor, remained closed; and the Princess d'Orviedo, happy in reality at being freed from the remorse of having that bank, that money shop, installed underneath her, did not even try to re-let the premises, indifferent as she was to the question of making money, even in the most legitimate way. The empty house, echoing to every passing vehicle, seemed like a tomb. Madame Caroline now only heard that quivering echo ascending through the ceilings from the closed wickets whence for two years there had ever come a faint jingling of gold. Her days now seemed to her of greater length and increasing dulness. Yet she worked a great deal, always kept busy by her brother, who required her to do no end of writing for him. At times, though, she would pause in her work and listen, instinctively feeling anxious, desirous of knowing what was going on at the Bank. But she heard nothing, not a breath; the rooms below were stripped of their furniture, empty, dark, securely locked. Then a little shiver would come upon her and she would forget herself for a few minutes in her anxiety. What were they doing in the Rue de Londres? Was not the crack appearing at that very moment—the crack which would cause the collapse of the whole edifice?

A report, vague and faint as yet, was spreading to the effect that Saccard contemplated a fresh issue of shares. He wished to raise the Bank's capital from one hundred to one hundred and fifty millions. It was a time of particular excitement, the fatal time when all the prosperities of the reign, the vast works which had transformed the city of Paris, the frenzied circulation of money, the *furore* of luxury and greed, were bound to culminate in a high fever of speculation. Each wished to have his share of wealth and risked his fortune on the *tapis vert*, in order to increase it tenfold and reap enjoyment like so many others who had enriched themselves in a single night. The banners of the Exhibition flapping in the sunlight, the illuminations and orchestras of the Champ de Mars, the crowds from all over the world which streamed along the streets, completed the intoxication of the Parisians, made them dream alike of inexhaustible wealth and sovereign dominion. During the clear evenings, from all the huge city *en fête*, seated at table in exotic restaurants, amid a colossal fair where pleasure was freely sold under the stars, there arose the supreme fit of madness, the joyous, voracious folly which seizes upon great capitals threatened with destruction. And Saccard, with the scent of a cut-purse, had so clearly divined the advent of this paroxysm, this desire of one and all to empty their pockets and throw their money to the winds, that he had just doubled the amount allowed for advertising, urging Jantrou to raise the most deafening din.

Day by day, ever since the opening of the Exhibition, the voice of the Press had been like a peal of bells ringing the praises of the Universal. Each morning brought its clash of cymbals to make the world turn round and look: some extraordinary news 'par,' some story of a lady who had forgotten a hundred shares in a cab; some extract from an account of a journey in Asia Minor, in which it was explained that the first Napoleon had predicted the advent of the establishment in the Rue de Londres; some leading article in which the *rôle* of this financial house was considered from a political point of view in connection with the approaching solution of the Eastern question, to say nothing of the constant notes in the financial journals, all enlisted and marching together in a compact mass. Jantrou had made annual contracts with the small financial prints, which assured him a column in every number; and in utilising this column he displayed astonishing fertility and variety of imagination, going so far even as to attack the Bank, for the sake of refuting the attack and triumphing afterwards. The famous pamphlet which he had meditated had just been launched through the entire world to the extent of a million copies. His new agency was also established—that agency which, under the pretext of sending a financial bulletin to the provincial newspapers, made itself absolute master of the market in all the important towns. And finally 'L'Espérance,' shrewdly conducted, was daily acquiring greater political importance. Much attention had been attracted by a series of articles issued after the decree of January 19, which to the old formula of an address from the Corps Législatif substituted the right of interpellation—a fresh concession on the part of the Emperor on his path to the re-establishment of Parliamentary liberty. Saccard, who inspired these articles, did not venture to openly attack his brother, who, despite everything, was still Minister of State, resigned, such was his passion for power, to defend to-day that which he had condemned yesterday; still it could be seen that the financier was on the look-out, watching Rougon in his false position, caught as he was between the Third Party hungering for his inheritance, and the Clericals who had leagued themselves with the despotic Bonapartists against the establishment of a liberal empire. Indeed, insinuations were already beginning; the paper was again becoming a mouthpiece of militant Catholicism, commenting tartly on each one of the Minister's acts. The accession of 'L'Espérance' to the ranks of the Opposition journals would mean popularity, and would finish carrying the name of the Universal to the four corners, not only of France, but of the world.

Then, as an effect of all the formidable advertising, the probability of an increase of capital, the rumour of a new issue of fifty millions, fevered even the most sensible of that agitated society, ripe for every folly. From humble dwellings to aristocratic mansions, from the dark dens of door-porters to the drawing-rooms of duchesses, all heads took fire; the general infatuation became blind faith, heroic and ready for battle. Folks enumerated the great things done by the Universal—its first startling successes, its unexpected dividends, such as no other company had distributed in the early phases of its existence. They recalled that happy idea of the United Steam Navigation Company, which had so speedily yielded a magnificent profit, and whose shares already commanded a premium of a hundred francs. Then there was the Carmel silver-mine, with its miraculous yield of the precious metal, to which a reverend preacher had referred during Lent from the pulpit of Notre-Dame, calling it a gift from the Most High to trusting Christians.[21] And, besides this, there was another company established to work the immense deposits of coal which had been discovered; and yet another which was going to work the vast Lebanon forests, felling a certain number of trees every year, to say nothing of the establishment of that substantial concern, the National Turkish Bank at Constantinople.

There had not been one check; good fortune, ever on the increase, changed everything that the Universal touched into gold. There was already a large *ensemble* of prosperous creations, providing an immovable basis for future operations and justifying the rapid increase of the capital. Then there was the future which opened before overheated imaginations—the future so big with great enterprises that it necessitated that call for another fifty millions, the mere announcement of which was sufficient to upset men's brains. In this respect there was an unlimited field for Bourse and drawing-room rumours; however, the approaching grand affair of the Oriental

Railway Company stood out amid all other projects, found its way into all conversations, decried by some and exalted by others.

The women especially became excited, and carried on enthusiastic propaganda in favour of the scheme. In boudoirs and at gala dinners, behind flowery *jardinières* at the late hour of tea,[22] even in the depths of alcoves, there were charming, persuasive, caressing creatures who thus catechised men: 'What! you have no Universals? But they are the only shares worth having! Make haste and buy some Universals if you wish me to love you!' It was the new Crusade, they said, the conquest of Asia, which the Crusaders of Peter the Hermit and Saint Louis had been unable to effect, and which they, these ladies, undertook to accomplish with their little purses of chain gold. They all pretended to be well-informed, and talked in technical terms of the main line which would be opened first from Broussa to Beyrout by way of Angora and Aleppo. Later on would come the branch line from Smyrna to Angora; later, that from Trebizond to Angora by way of Erzeroum and Sivas; later still, that from Damascus to Beyrout. And then they smiled, and winked, and whispered that perhaps there would be another one, oh! a long time hence, from Beyrout to Jerusalem, by way of the old cities of the coast—Saida, Saint Jean d'Acre, and Jaffa. And afterwards, *mon Dieu*! who could tell? there might be one from Jerusalem to Port Said and Alexandria. To say nothing of the fact that Bagdad was not far from Damascus, and that, if a line should be carried to that point, why, Persia, India, and China would some day be united to the West.

At a word from their pretty lips it seemed as though the treasures of the Caliphs were found again and were shining resplendently, as in some tale of the 'Arabian Nights.' The jewels and gems of dreamland rained into the coffers of the palace in the Rue de Londres; whilst Carmel supplied smoking incense and a vague, delicate background of Biblical legends, hallowing the mighty appetite for gain. Did it not mean Eden reconquered, the Holy Land delivered, religion triumphing in the very cradle of humanity? And then the ladies paused, refusing to say any more, but their eyes beaming at thought of that which it was necessary to hide. That could not even be whispered in a lover's ear. Many of these ladies were ignorant of the secret, but none the less pretended to know it. That was the mystery, the thing which perchance might never happen, and which perchance might some day burst upon the world like a thunderbolt: Jerusalem purchased from the Sultan, given to the Pope with Syria for a kingdom; the Papacy provided with a revenue supplied by a Catholic bank—the Treasury of the Holy Sepulchre—which would place it beyond the pale of political disturbances; briefly, Catholicism would be rejuvenated, would be no longer forced to any compromises, but would acquire renewed authority, and dominate the world from the summit of the height where Christ the man expired.

And of a morning now, in his luxurious Louis Quatorze office, Saccard was forced to forbid his door when he wished to work; for there were endless assaulting parties, or rather a court procession, coming, as it were, to a king's levée—courtiers, business people, applicants of all kinds soliciting and adoring his omnipotence. One morning, during the early days of July, he was particularly inflexible, giving the most stringent orders to admit no one. Whilst the ante-room was filling with people, who, despite the usher, persisted in waiting and hoping that they would be received, he shut himself up with two heads of departments to finish planning the new issue of shares. After examining various projects, he pronounced in favour of a combination which, thanks to this new issue of a hundred thousand shares, would permit the complete release of the two hundred thousand old ones, upon each of which only one hundred and twenty-five francs had been paid. This result was arrived at by issuing the new shares—which were reserved for existing shareholders—at the price of eight hundred and fifty francs; that is to say, five hundred francs for the share itself and three hundred and fifty francs premium, this premium effecting the proposed release. However, certain complications arose, due to the large amount of its own stock which the Bank held, and it was necessary to find a means of filling up certain gaps, the worry of which acted upon Saccard's nerves. The sound of the voices in the ante-room, moreover, irritated him. That cringing Paris, whose homage he usually received with the good-nature of a despot prone to familiarity, filled him on this occasion with contempt. And Dejoie, who served him as usher in the morning, having ventured to take a roundabout way and enter by a little door opening from a passage, he turned on him in a fury: 'What! I told you nobody, nobody; do you understand? Here! take my walking stick, place it at my door, and let them kiss it.'

Dejoie impassively ventured to insist. 'Excuse me, monsieur, it is the Countess de Beauvilliers. She begged so hard, and, as I know Monsieur wishes to be agreeable to her——'

'What!' cried Saccard in a fit of anger; 'let her go to the devil with the others.'

Then with a gesture of repressed wrath he immediately reconsidered the matter: 'Show her in,' said he, 'since it seems certain that I cannot be left in peace. And by the little door, mind, so that the whole flock may not enter with her.'

The welcome which he extended to the Countess de Beauvilliers was fraught with the abruptness of a man just recovering from excitement. Even the sight of Alice, who accompanied her mother, silently meditating, did not calm him. He had sent the two heads of departments away, and was only thinking of how soon he would be able to call them back so as to continue his work.

'Pray speak quickly, madame, for I am terribly busy.'

The Countess, always slow with her words and movements, always preserving the sadness of a fallen queen, stopped short in evident surprise. 'But if I disturb you, monsieur'—she began.

He had to offer them seats, and the girl, the braver of the two, sat down the first in a resolute way whilst her mother continued: 'I have come for some advice, monsieur. I am in a state of very painful uncertainty, and am afraid that I shall never be able to come to a decision by myself.'

Then she reminded him that at the time of the establishment of the Bank she had taken a hundred shares, which she had doubled at the time of the first increase of capital and again at the time of the second increase, so that she now held four hundred shares, upon which, inclusive of premiums, she had paid the sum of eighty-seven thousand francs. Twenty thousand francs of this amount had been supplied by her savings, and the rest—some seventy thousand—she had been forced to borrow on her farm, Les Aublets.

'And it now happens,' she continued, 'that I have just found a purchaser for the farm. And I understand that there is to be a new issue of shares. If that is so, I may perhaps place our entire fortune in your house.'

Saccard was now calming down, flattered at finding these two poor women, the last members of a great and ancient race, so trustful and anxious in his presence. He went into figures and rapidly supplied them with information.

'A new issue—yes, there is to be one, I am just attending to it,' he said. 'The shares will be priced at eight hundred and fifty francs, inclusive of premium. You say that you now have four hundred shares; well, two hundred of these new ones will be allotted to you; so that you will be required to pay one hundred and seventy thousand francs. But all your shares will be released, and you will have six hundred belonging to you entirely without any further liability with regard to them.'

They did not understand, and he had to explain to them how the premium would release the shares; and they turned a little pale at the big figures that were mentioned, oppressed by the thought of what an audacious stroke they would have to risk.

'As for the money,' murmured the mother at last, 'that will be all right. I am offered two hundred and forty thousand francs for Les Aublets, which were formerly worth four hundred thousand; so that, after repaying the sum I have already borrowed, there would be just enough left to pay for the shares. But what a terrible thing, *mon Dieu!* this fortune displaced, our whole existence ventured in this fashion!'

Her hands trembled, and there was a spell of silence, during which she reflected how this financial machinery had already drawn in both her savings and the seventy thousand francs that she had borrowed, and now threatened to take the entire farm. Her old respect for landed property, ploughed fields, meadows and forests, her repugnance for traffic in money—that base calling of the Jews, unworthy of her race— came back to her and filled her with anguish at this decisive moment, when everything was on the point of being consummated. Her daughter meantime looked at her in silence, with her pure yet ardent eyes.

Saccard gave an encouraging smile.

'Well,' said he, 'it is very certain that you will have to place confidence in us. But there are the figures. Examine them, and hesitation seems to me impossible. Suppose you decide to do it, then you will have six hundred shares, which will have cost you two hundred and fifty-seven thousand francs. Now they are quoted to-day at an average rate of thirteen hundred francs, which would give you a total of seven hundred and eighty thousand francs. You have already more than tripled your money. And it will continue; you will see how the quotations will go up after the new issue! I promise you that your shares will be worth a million before the end of the year.'

'Oh, mamma!' said Alice, allowing the words to escape her in a sigh, as if despite herself.

A million! The mansion in the Rue Saint-Lazare freed from its mortgages, cleansed of the mire of poverty! Life replaced on a proper footing; an end to the nightmare of those who have a carriage but lack bread! The daughter married, with a respectable dowry, able at last to have a husband and children, that joy which is permitted to the lowest, poorest creature of the streets! The son, whom the climate of Rome was killing, relieved, able to maintain his rank, pending the time when he might serve the great cause, which at present utilised him so little! The mother reinstated in her high position, able to pay her coachman, no longer hesitating to add a dish to her Tuesday dinners, no longer forced to fast for the rest of the week! That million flamed before them; it meant salvation, the realisation of their dream.

Conquered for her own part, the Countess turned to her daughter to ask for her adhesion: 'Well, what do you think of it?'

But the girl would say nothing more; she let her eyelids slowly fall to hide the glow of her eyes.

'Ah! true,' continued the mother, smiling in her turn, 'I had forgotten that you wished to let me remain sole mistress in the matter. But I know how brave you are, and all that you hope for.'

Then, addressing Saccard, she said: 'Ah! people speak so highly of you, monsieur. We can go nowhere without hearing the most beautiful and touching things about you. It is not only the Princess d'Orviedo, but all my friends, who are enthusiastic over your work. Many of them are jealous of me because I was one of your first shareholders, and if I were to take their advice I should sell even my mattresses in order to buy more shares.'

She jested in a mild, gentle way. 'I even think them a trifle crazy,' she continued— 'yes, really a trifle crazy. No doubt it is because I am no longer young enough to understand it all. But my daughter is one of your admirers. She believes in your mission, and carries on propaganda in all the houses where we visit.'

Quite charmed, Saccard looked at Alice, who at that moment was so animated, so penetrated with lively faith, that she actually seemed to him very pretty, albeit already faded, with yellow complexion, and scraggy neck. And he deemed himself very great and good at the idea of having brought happiness to that sad creature whom the mere hope of a husband sufficed to beautify.

'Oh!' said she in a very low, seemingly distant voice, "tis so beautiful to think of, that conquest yonder—yes, a new era, the Cross radiant——'

But that was the mystery of which no one spoke; and her voice sank lower yet, died away in a breath of rapture. Moreover, Saccard reduced her to silence by a friendly gesture, for in his presence he would not tolerate any mention of the grand affair, the supreme, hidden end. His gesture implied that it was necessary one should always aim at attaining that end, but that one should never open one's lips to speak about it. In the sanctuary the censers swung in the hands of the few initiated.

After an interval of feeling silence, the Countess at last rose. 'Well, monsieur,' said she, 'I am convinced. I shall send my notary word that I accept the offer which is made for Les Aublets. May God forgive me, if I do wrong!'

Standing before her, Saccard declared with mingled gravity and emotion: 'It is God himself who inspires you, madame; be certain of it.'[23]

And as he accompanied them into the little passage, avoiding the ante-room, which was still thronged with people, he met Dejoie, who was prowling about with an embarrassed air.

'What's the matter? Not someone else, I hope?'

'No, no, monsieur. If I dared to ask Monsieur's advice—it is for myself.'

And he manœuvred in such a way that Saccard found himself in his office again, while Dejoie stood on the threshold in a very deferential attitude.

'For you. Ah! true, you are a shareholder also. Well, my man, take the new shares which will be reserved for you; take them even if you must sell your shirts to do so. That is the advice which I give to all our friends.'

'Oh! monsieur, the slice is too big a one, my daughter and I are not so ambitious. At the outset I took eight shares with the four thousand francs which my poor wife saved up and left to us; and I still only have those eight, for at the time of the other issues, you see, when the capital was twice doubled, we hadn't the money to take up the shares which we were entitled to purchase. No, no, that is not the question; one need not be so greedy as that. I simply wanted to ask Monsieur, without offending him, if he is of opinion that I ought to sell?'

'What! that you ought to sell?'

Thereupon, with all sorts of circumlocutions, prompted by anxiety and respect, Dejoie explained his situation. At their present price of thirteen hundred francs his eight shares represented a total of ten thousand four hundred francs. So he could easily give Nathalie the dowry of six thousand francs which the pasteboard-maker required. But, in presence of the continual rise of the shares, an appetite for money had come to him also—an idea, vague at first and then all-absorbing, of securing a share of the spoil for himself, a little income of six hundred francs a year, which would enable him to retire. For that, a capital of twelve thousand francs would be required, which added to his daughter's portion of six thousand would make the, to him, enormous total of eighteen thousand francs; and he despaired of ever getting such an amount together, for to do so he must wait till the shares should rise to a value of two thousand three hundred francs.

'You understand, monsieur,' said he. 'If the shares won't rise any higher I prefer to sell, because Nathalie's happiness should come before everything, shouldn't it? But if they continue going up, why, I shall be heartsick at the thought of having sold them.'

'Come, my man, you are stupid!' exclaimed Saccard vehemently. 'Do you think that we are going to stop at thirteen hundred? Do *I* sell? You shall have your eighteen thousand francs, I answer for it. And now be off and turn out all those people—tell them that I have gone.'

When he found himself alone again, Saccard recalled the two heads of departments and was able to finish his work in peace.

It was decided that an extraordinary meeting of shareholders should be held in August in order to vote the fresh increase of capital. Hamelin, who was to preside, landed at Marseilles towards the end of July. For two months past his sister, in each letter that she had written him, had been more and more pressingly advising him to return. Amidst all the success of the Bank, which day by day was growing more pronounced, she experienced an instinctive feeling that danger was covertly approaching, an unreasoning fear which she did not even dare to speak of; and she preferred that her brother should be on the spot to see things for himself, for she had come to the point of distrusting her own mind, of fearing that she might be strengthless against Saccard and allow herself to be blinded to such a degree even as to betray this brother whom she loved so much. Ought she not to have confessed her *liaison* to him—that *liaison* which, in the innocence of his piety and science, passing through life in ignorance of so many of its aspects, he certainly did not suspect? This idea was extremely painful to her; and she at last sought refuge in cowardly compromises; she discussed with duty, which, now that she knew the man and his past, clearly ordered her to tell everything, that her brother might be on his guard. In her hours of strength she promised herself that she would have a decisive explanation, and would not suffer the uncontrolled disposal of such large sums of money by criminal hands, in which so many millions had already melted away to the ruin of such numbers of people. Was it not the only virile, honest course she could take, the only course worthy of her? Then her lucidity, however, left her; she grew weak and temporized, finding no grievances except the irregularities common to all financial houses, as he affirmed. Perhaps he was right in telling her with a laugh that the monster she dreaded was success, that success which in Paris resounds and strikes like a thunderbolt, and which left her trembling, as if under the suddenness and anguish of a catastrophe. She no longer knew what to do; there were even times when she admired him the more, full of that infinite affection which she retained for him, albeit she had ceased to esteem him. Never would she have thought her heart so complicated; she felt herself a woman; she feared lest she might not be able to act. And so she was very happy at her brother's return.

On the very afternoon of Hamelin's arrival Saccard arranged to see him in the work-room, where they were certain of not being disturbed, in order to submit to him the resolutions which the board of directors would have to approve of before they could be laid before the shareholders. By a tacit agreement, however, the brother and sister met shortly before the time agreed upon, and finding themselves alone together were in a position to talk freely. Hamelin had come back very gay, delighted at having brought his complicated railway affair to a successful issue in that Eastern country, which was slumbering in idleness and where political, administrative, and financial obstacles were ever cropping up to defeat all efforts. However, in his case, the success was complete; they would start on the first works, work-yards would be opened in all directions as soon as the company should be definitely formed in Paris, and he was so enthusiastic, so confident in the future, that Madame Caroline acquired yet another reason for preserving silence—it would cost her so much to spoil that beautiful delight. Nevertheless she expressed some doubts to put him on his guard against the infatuation which was carrying away the public. He checked her and looked her in the face. Did she know of anything suspicious? If so, why didn't she speak out? And she did not speak, she was unable to think of any precise charge.

When Saccard came into the room, not having yet seen Hamelin since his return, he threw his arms round his neck and embraced him with the exuberant affection of a man from the South. Then, when Hamelin had confirmed his last letters and given him particulars of the absolute success which had attended his long sojourn abroad, he waxed enthusiastic. 'Ah! my dear fellow,' said he, 'this time we are going to become the masters of Paris, the kings of the market. I have been working hard too; I have an extraordinary idea; you shall see.'

He forthwith explained his plan, which was, first, to raise the Bank's capital from one hundred to one hundred and fifty millions by issuing a hundred thousand new shares, and, secondly, to release the whole of the shares, the old as well as the new ones. He intended, he said, to offer the new shares at the price of eight hundred and fifty francs, employing the premium of three hundred and fifty francs per share to build up a reserve fund, which, with the amounts already set aside at each distribution, would reach the figure of five and twenty millions. And all that remained for him to do was to find an equal sum so as to have in hand the fifty millions that would be necessary to release the two hundred thousand old shares. It was here that his so-called extraordinary idea came in. It was to draw up an approximative estimate of the current year's profits, which in his opinion would at the least amount to thirty-six millions of francs. From these he could quietly take the twenty-five millions which he needed. And so, from December 31, 1867, the Universal would have a definitive capital of a hundred and fifty millions represented by three hundred thousand fully paid-up shares. They would afterwards unify the stock and make the shares payable to bearer in order to facilitate their free circulation on the market. That would be the stroke of genius entailing perfect triumph.

'Yes, a stroke of genius,' he repeated; 'the expression is none too strong.'

Hamelin, somewhat dazed, turned over the pages of Saccard's memoir on the subject, examining the figures. 'I hardly like this premature balance-sheet,' he said at last. 'These are real dividends that you will be giving your shareholders, since you will release their shares; and one must be certain that the amounts are really earned, for otherwise we might be rightly accused of distributing fictitious dividends.'

Saccard grew excited. 'What! But I am below the estimates! Just look and you will see if I have been reasonable; won't the steamers, the Carmel mine, and the Turkish bank yield larger profits than those which I have put down? You have brought me bulletins of victory from over yonder; everything is marching on, everything is prosperous, and yet you cavil about the certainty of success!'

Hamelin smiled, and calmed him with a gesture. Yes, yes! he had faith in the future. Only he preferred that things should take their regular course.

'And indeed,' said Madame Caroline, gently, 'why should you hurry? Could not we wait till April for this increase of capital? Or, since you need twenty-five millions more, why not issue the stock at a thousand or twelve hundred francs at once, for in that way you would not require to anticipate the profits of the current year?'

Saccard looked at her momentarily nonplussed, astonished that that this idea should have occurred to her.

'No doubt,' said he, 'if the shares were issued at eleven hundred francs, instead of at eight hundred and fifty, we should then have exactly the twenty-five millions we want.'

'Then settle things in that way,' she resumed: 'you can hardly fear that the shareholders will kick at it. They will pay eleven hundred francs as readily as eight hundred and fifty.'

'Oh yes, that is certain,' said Saccard. 'They'll pay whatever we like, and they'll even fight together to decide who shall pay most. They have quite lost their heads and would storm the building to bring us their money.'

All at once, however, he recovered his self-possession, and with a violent start of protest exclaimed: 'But come, what are you talking about? I don't want to ask them eleven hundred francs on any account. It would really be too foolish and too simple. Understand that in these financial matters it is always necessary to strike the imagination. The grand idea is to take money out of people's pockets before it has even got into them. They at once imagine that they are not parting with it. They fancy even that a present is being made to them. And besides, can't you see what a colossal effect will be produced by the newspapers notifying these anticipated profits, announcing with a flourish of trumpets these thirty-six millions gained in advance? Why, the whole Bourse will take fire; our shares will be quoted at over two thousand francs, and will keep on rising and rising till there will be no stopping them.'

He gesticulated as he spoke, erect, and stretching his little legs till he really became taller, his arms waving among the stars, like the inspired bard of Money, whose poetic flight, no failure, no ruin had ever been able to check. To urge on his enterprises, to keep them at a feverish gallop—that was his instinctive system, the course into which he dashed, both heart and soul. He had compelled success, kindled every greed by that lightning march of the Universal—three issues of shares in three years, the capital leaping from five and twenty to fifty, one hundred, and one hundred and fifty millions with a speed which seemed to denote miraculous prosperity. And the dividends also had increased by leaps and bounds—nothing the first year, then ten francs, then thirty-three francs per share, and now thirty-six millions to be apportioned amongst the entire stock and release it. And all this had been achieved amidst the deceptive overheating of the machine, the fictitious subscription of shares and their retention by the Bank, in order to make people believe that they had really been taken up. Yes, it had been achieved thanks to the impulse imparted by speculation at the Bourse, where each fresh increase of capital had determined such an exaggerated rise in the quotations.

Still deep in his examination of Saccard's scheme, Hamelin had not supported his sister in her remarks.

Shaking his head, he now reverted to questions of detail.

'None the less, I don't approve of your anticipated balance-sheet, since the profits have not actually been made. I am not now referring to our enterprises, although, like all human affairs, they may meet with accidents. But I see here the Sabatani account, three thousand and odd shares, representing more than two millions of francs. Now you place these to our credit, whereas we ought to be debited with them, for Sabatani is only our man of straw. We can say these things between ourselves, can we not? And stay! I also see here the names of several of our employees, even some of our directors, all of them *prête-noms*—oh! I can guess it easily enough, you need not tell me. It makes me tremble to see that we are keeping such a large number of our shares. We not only do not take in the cash which they represent, but we bring ourselves to a standstill so far as they are concerned, and we shall end by devouring ourselves some day.'

Madame Caroline gave him an encouraging look, for he was at last giving voice to her hidden fears; he was putting his finger on the cause of the secret uneasiness which had grown up within her as success increased. 'Oh! gambling! gambling!' she murmured.

'But we do not gamble,' cried Saccard. 'Only it is surely allowable for us to keep up the price of our stock, and we should be fools if we did not prevent Gundermann and others from bringing it down by playing against us for a fall. Although they have not quite dared to do so yet, it may come all the same. That is why I am rather glad we have a certain number of our shares in hand, and I warn you, if they force me to it, I am even ready to buy some of those in the market—yes, I'll even buy rather than see the quotations fall by a single centime.'

He spoke these last words with extraordinary vehemence, as if he were swearing that he would die rather than suffer defeat. However, by dint of effort he afterwards calmed himself, and began to laugh, though not without some peevishness. 'So distrust is coming back again, is it?' he said. 'I thought we had had an explanation once for all about all these matters. You consented to place yourselves in my hands, so let me go ahead. I seek nothing but your fortune, a great, great fortune.' He paused and lowered his voice as though frightened himself by the enormity of his desire. 'Do you know what I want?' he whispered. 'Why, I want the shares to be quoted at three thousand francs!'

He waved his hand, as though over yonder, in space, he could behold that triumphant quotation blazing in figures of fire which set the horizon of the Bourse all aglow and ascended to the heavens like stars.

'It is madness!' said Madame Caroline.

'As soon as prices exceed two thousand francs,' Hamelin declared, 'each fresh rise will constitute a danger; and for my own part I warn you that I shall sell my shares so as not to take part in such lunacy.'

By way of reply Saccard began to hum a tune. People always talk of selling and yet do not sell. He would enrich them, despite themselves. Then again he began to smile in a very affectionate, though somewhat mocking way. 'Trust me,' said he. 'It seems to me that I haven't managed your affairs so badly until now. Sadowa brought you a million.'

This was true; the Hamelins had forgotten it. Yet they had accepted that million fished out of the troubled waters of the Bourse. For a moment they remained silent, turning pale, with the heart-pang felt by those who are still honest but are no longer certain whether they have acted rightly. Had the leprosy of gambling seized upon them also? Were they, too, rotting in that maddening atmosphere of Money in which circumstances compelled them to live?

'No doubt that is so,' the engineer at last muttered; 'but if I had been here——'

Saccard would not let him finish. 'Nonsense,' said he. 'You need feel no remorse; it was only so much money regained from those dirty Jews!'

At this all three began to laugh; and Madame Caroline, having seated herself, made a gesture of tolerance and resignation. Could one let oneself be devoured and not devour others? It was life. To do otherwise would require virtues of too sublime a character, or else the solitude of a cloister, far from all temptation.

'Come, come!' Saccard continued gaily. 'Do not appear to spit upon money: in the first place, it would be idiotic to do so; and secondly, it is only the powerless who disdain power. It would be illogical to kill yourselves in labouring to enrich others without cutting off the share you are legitimately entitled to. Otherwise, you might just as well go to bed and sleep!' He dominated them and would not permit them to say another word. 'Do you know that you will soon have a pretty sum in your pockets?' he exclaimed. 'Wait a moment.' And then, with a school-boy's petulance, he rushed to Madame Caroline's table, and, taking a pencil and a sheet of paper, began covering the latter with figures. 'Wait!' he said again. 'I am going to draw up your account. Oh! I know it. At the outset you had five hundred shares, doubled a first time and then doubled again, so that you now hold two thousand. And you will have three thousand after our next issue.'

Hamelin tried to interrupt him.

'No, no!' said he. 'I know that you have the money to pay for them, what with the three hundred thousand francs that you inherited on the one hand, and your Sadowa million on the other. See! your first two thousand shares have cost you four hundred and thirty-five thousand francs, the other thousand will cost you eight hundred and fifty thousand francs, in all twelve hundred and eighty-five thousand francs. So you will still have fifteen thousand francs left you for pocket money, to say nothing of your salary, now thirty thousand francs a year, but which we shall raise to sixty thousand.'

Bewildered by his flow of words, they listened, and at last began to take an acute interest in these figures.

'You can see very well that you are honest,' he continued 'that you pay for what you take. But those matters are mere bagatelles. This is what I wanted to get at!'

So saying he sprang to his feet again and flourished his sheet of paper with an air of triumph. 'At three thousand francs apiece your three thousand shares will yield you nine millions,' he said.

'Three thousand francs apiece!' they exclaimed, protesting with a gesture against his mad obstinacy.

'Yes, of course!' said he. 'I forbid you to sell until that price is reached. I shall know how to prevent you—oh! by force if necessary, by the right a man has to prevent his friends from acting foolishly. Three thousand francs, that is the quotation I must have, and I will have it!'

What answer could they give to that terrible fellow, whose strident voice sounded like the crow of a cock proclaiming his triumph? They again laughed and affected to shrug their shoulders. Their minds were quite easy, they declared, for that wonderful price would never be reached. He, however, had again seated himself at the table, and was making fresh calculations, drawing up his own account. Had he paid for his three thousand shares? would he pay for them? That point remained obscure. It was even probable that he possessed a still larger number of shares; but the matter could not be easily elucidated, for he also served as one of the Bank's *prête-noms*, and how was one to distinguish the shares which really belonged to him among all those that were entered in his name? His pencil continued jotting down line after line of figures. Then all at once, with a rapid zig-zag stroke, he effaced everything and crumpled up the paper. The amount he had noted on it, with the two millions which he had picked up amid the blood and mire of Sadowa, constituted his share of the spoil.

'I must leave you, I have an appointment,' he said, taking up his hat. 'But it's agreed, isn't it? In a week's time we'll have the board meeting, and immediately afterwards the shareholders' meeting to vote on the new scheme.'

When Madame Caroline and Hamelin, bewildered and weary, again found themselves alone, they remained silent for a moment, seated opposite each other.

'What would you have?' at last said the engineer, responding to his sister's secret thoughts. 'We are in it and must remain in it. He is right in saying that it would be stupid of us to refuse this fortune. I have always looked on myself as a mere man of science who brings water to the mill; and I have brought it, I think, clear and abundant in the shape of excellent affairs, to which the Bank owes its rapid prosperity. And so, since no reproach can fall upon me, let us keep free from discouragement, let us work.'

She had risen from her chair, staggering and stammering: 'Oh, all that money! all that money!' And, choking with invincible emotion at the thought of those millions which were about to fall upon them, she hung upon his neck and wept. It was with joy undoubtedly, with happiness at seeing him at last worthily rewarded for his intelligence and labour; but with pain also, a pain of which she could not have told the exact cause, but in which there was a commingling of shame and fear. He began to make fun of her, and they once more affected cheerfulness; yet a feeling of uneasiness remained within them, a secret dissatisfaction with themselves, unconfessed remorse at being forced into this soiling complicity.

'After all, he is right,' repeated Madame Caroline; 'everybody does it. Such is life.'

The board meeting was held in the new room in the sumptuous building of the Rue de Londres. Here, there was no damp reception-room to which the pale reflections from a neighbouring garden imparted a greenish hue, but a vast apartment, lighted by four windows, overlooking the street, an apartment with a lofty ceiling and majestic walls, decorated with large paintings and streaming with gold. The chairman's arm-chair was a veritable throne, dominating the other arm-chairs, which, superb and grave, were ranged as if for a meeting of Cabinet Ministers around an immense table, covered with red velvet. And, above the monumental white marble chimney-piece, where trunks of trees blazed in winter time, there stood a bust of the Pope,[24] a shrewd amiable face which seemed to be smiling maliciously at the idea of finding itself in such a place.

Saccard had now acquired complete control over the board by buying most of its members. Thanks to him, the Marquis de Bohain, compromised in the matter of a *pot-de-vin*, the fraudulent appropriation of some money which he had pocketed and spent, was able to stifle the scandal by refunding the amount to the company he had robbed, and so he was now Saccard's very humble servant, albeit he still carried his head high like a perfect flower of nobility, the finest ornament of the board. Huret, too, since Rougon had dismissed him for revealing the despatch respecting the surrender of Venice, had been devoting himself entirely to the fortunes of the Universal, acting as the Bank's representative at the Corps Législatif, and fishing for it in the miry waters of politics, though retaining for himself the larger part of the profits accruing from his shameless jobbery, which some fine morning would probably land him in Mazas. And the Viscount de Robin-Chagot, the vice-chairman, pocketed a secret allowance of a hundred thousand francs for giving all the signatures that were asked of him during Hamelin's long absences. Banker Kolb also paid himself for his passive compliance by utilizing the Universal's influence abroad, and even by compromising it in his arbitrage operations. And Sédille, the silk merchant, shaken by a terrible settlement, had borrowed a large sum which he had been unable to refund. Daigremont alone remained absolutely independent, a circumstance which at times disturbed Saccard, although the amiable fellow continued treating him in a very charming way, inviting him to his entertainments, and readily signing everything that was submitted to him with the good grace of a Parisian sceptic, who as long as he makes money considers that everything is going on all right.

On this occasion, in spite of the exceptional importance of the business, the board was managed quite as easily as at other times. It had indeed become a matter of habit—all the real work was done at the petty meetings held on the 15th of the month; at the full meetings, which took place a fortnight later, there was merely a question of sanctioning the predetermined resolutions with due ceremony.

Such was the indifference now displayed by the directors, that the minutes of each successive meeting threatened to become mere repetitions of one another, trite records of unswerving, uniform approval; and so it became necessary to attribute scruples and remarks to sundry members of the board, to concoct indeed an entirely imaginary discussion, which nobody was surprised to find recorded, when, at the following meeting, the minutes were read over in all seriousness and duly signed.

Knowing the good and grand news that Hamelin had brought with him, Daigremont no sooner espied him than he rushed forward and heartily grasped his hands. 'Ah! my dear chairman,' said he, 'how glad I am to congratulate you!'

They all surrounded the engineer and welcomed him, including even Saccard, who behaved as though he had not seen him before; and when the meeting commenced, and Hamelin began to read the report which he was to present to the shareholders, they listened—a very unusual thing. The fine results already obtained, the magnificent promises for the future, the ingenious system for increasing the capital, and at the same time releasing the old shares, all announcements were received with admiring nods of the head. And nobody had any thought of asking for explanations. It was perfect. Sédille having pointed out an error in a figure, it was even agreed not to insert his remarks in the minutes in order not to disturb the beautiful unanimity of the gathering; and then everyone signed in rapid succession, under the influence of enthusiasm, and without making any observation.

The meeting was already over; they were on their feet, laughing and joking, amid the resplendent gildings of the room. The Marquis de Bohain described an imperial shooting party at Fontainebleau; while Deputy Huret, who had lately been to Rome, related how he had received the blessing of the Pope. Kolb had just disappeared, running off to keep some appointment. And to the other directors, the supernumeraries, Saccard, in a low tone, gave them his instructions respecting the attitude which they were to take up at the approaching meeting. Daigremont, however, worried by the Viscount de Robin-Chagot's inordinate praise of Hamelin's report, caught hold of the manager's arm as he passed by to whisper in his ear: 'Not too fast, eh?'

Saccard stopped short and looked at him. He remembered how he had originally hesitated to bring Daigremont into the affair, knowing that he was not over reliable in financial matters. And in a loud voice, so that all might hear, he now replied: 'Oh! who loves me must follow me!'

Three days later, the specially summoned meeting of shareholders was held in the grand Salle des Fêtes at the Hôtel du Louvre. They had not cared for that bare sorry-looking hall in the Rue Blanche for such a solemnity as this; they wanted the use of a gala gallery, still warm with life between some banquet and some wedding ball. According to the articles of association, it was necessary to hold at least twenty shares in order to be admitted; and the shareholders who attended were over twelve hundred in number, representing four thousand and odd votes. The formalities at the entrance, the presentation of tickets and signing of names in a special register, occupied over two hours. A tumult of gay chatter filled the gallery, in which were to be seen all the directors and many of the principal employees of the Universal. Sabatani was there talking to a group of acquaintances about his country, the East, in a languishing, caressing voice, relating marvellous tales about it, as though the region were some Tom Tiddler's ground where one need but stoop in order to pick up gold, silver, and precious stones; and Maugendre, who in June had made up his mind to buy fifty shares at one thousand two hundred francs apiece, convinced as he was of a further rise, stood listening to the Levantine open-mouthed and well pleased with the keenness of his scent. Meantime Jantrou, who, since he had become rich had been leading an altogether depraved life, chuckled to himself, his mouth twisted into an ironical grimace, and his head heavy with his orgy of the previous night.

When Hamelin had taken the chair and opened the meeting, Lavignière, who had been re-elected auditor and was soon to be raised to a position on the board—his dream—was called upon to read a report on the financial situation of the Bank, such as it would be at the end of next December. In order to comply with the statutes, Saccard had devised this plan of controlling, as it were, the anticipatory balance-sheet which the meeting would have to deal with. Lavignière reminded the shareholders of the balance-sheet of the previous year, presented at the ordinary meeting in April— that magnificent balance-sheet which had shown a net profit of eleven millions and a half, and after allowing five per cent. for the shareholders, ten per cent. for the directors, and ten per cent. also for the reserve fund, had admitted of the further distribution of a dividend of thirty-three per cent. Then, with a deluge of figures, he established that the sum of thirty-six million francs given as the approximate profits of the current year, far from seeming to him exaggerated, fell short of the most modest hopes. Undoubtedly he was sincere, and had conscientiously examined the documents submitted for his verification; but, in order to study a set of accounts thoroughly, it is necessary to draw up another set. Besides, the shareholders did not listen to him. Only a few devotees, Maugendre and others, petty holders who represented a vote or two, drank in his figures amid the persistent hum of conversation. For the others the auditors' report was not of the slightest consequence. It was only when Hamelin at last arose that a religious silence ensued. Not at once, however, for applause broke out even before he had opened his mouth, as a homage to the zeal and stubborn, brave genius of this man, who had gone so far in search of barrels of money to empty them upon Paris. After that came ever-increasing success, swelling into triumph. The audience hailed a fresh reminder of the balance-sheet of the previous year, which Lavignière had been unable to make them hear. But the estimates of the approaching balance-sheet especially excited their delight—millions for the Steam Navigation Company, millions for the Carmel silver-mine, millions for the Turkish National Bank; and the addition seemed endless, the thirty-six millions grouped themselves in an easy natural fashion, and then fell in a cascade with a ringing sound. But a further horizon was revealed, when the future operations were dealt with. The Oriental Railway Company appeared—at first the main line, the work in connection with which was about to begin; then the branch lines, the whole network of modern industry and enterprise thrown over Asia, humanity's triumphant return to its cradle, the resurrection of the old world. And in the far distance loomed up the mystery which they did not speak of, the crowning of the edifice which was to astonish the nations. When Hamelin at last came to the explanation of the resolutions which he intended to submit to the meeting there was perfect unanimity. A thunder of applause greeted the proposals to increase the capital and release the stock. Above all heads could be seen Maugendre's fat hands clapping vigorously. On the foremost benches, too, the directors and employees made a furious uproar, through which pierced the voice of Sabatani, who had risen to his feet and shouted 'Brava!' as though he had been at a theatre. All the resolutions were then adopted by acclamation.

Saccard, however, had planned an incident, which was introduced into the proceedings at this point. He was aware that he was accused of gambling, and wished to efface even the slightest suspicions from the minds of distrustful shareholders should there be any in the hall. Accordingly, Jantrou, whom he had coached, rose up, and addressing the chairman in his thick, husky voice, exclaimed: 'I believe, Mr. Chairman, that I am acting as the mouthpiece of many shareholders in inquiring if it is certain that the Bank possesses none of its own shares!'

Hamelin, who had not been forewarned, remained embarrassed for a moment. Then he instinctively turned towards Saccard, who had hitherto been hidden away in his seat, but who now suddenly rose, and, perched on tip-toe to increase his stature, replied in his strident voice: 'No, not one, Mr. Chairman!'

Bravoes, no one knew why, again burst forth at this announcement. Though Saccard really lied, it was nevertheless a fact that the Bank had not a single share standing in its own name, since Sabatani and the others covered it. And that was all; there was some further applause, and then they all made their exit amid gaiety and noise.

The report of this meeting, published in the newspapers, at once produced an enormous effect at the Bourse and all over Paris. For this moment Jantrou had kept in reserve a last shower of puffs, the loudest flourishes that had been blown for a long time on the trumpets of advertising. Moreover, he had at last just executed his grand stroke, the purchase of the *Côte Financière*, that substantial old journal which had twelve years of stainless honesty behind it. It had cost a great deal of money, but the serious customers, the trembling middle-class folks, the prudent people with huge fortunes, the mass of self-respecting men of money, had been gained by it. In a fortnight the figure of fifteen hundred francs was reached at the Bourse, and in the last days of August, by successive leaps, the shares rose to two thousand. The infatuation was still at fever-heat; the paroxysm became more and more intense each day. Folks bought and bought; even the most prudent went on buying, convinced that the shares would rise higher yet, go up indeed for ever and ever. It was as though the mysterious caverns of the Arabian Nights were opening, as though the incalculable treasures of the Caliphs were being offered to the greed of Paris. Such was the public enchantment that all the dreams which for months past had been spoken of in whispers now appeared to be on the point of realisation: the cradle of humanity was being reoccupied, the old historic cities of the coast were being resuscitated from their sand. Damascus, then Bagdad, then India and China, would be exploited by the invading troop of French engineers. The conquest of the East, which Napoleon had been unable to accomplish with his sword, was to be realised by a financial company sending an army of pickaxes and wheelbarrows thither. Asia would be conquered by dint of millions, and billions would be derived from it in return. And especially was this the hour of triumph for the crusade undertaken by the women at their little five-o'clock gatherings, at their grand midnight receptions, at table and elsewhere. They had clearly foreseen it all. Constantinople was taken; they would soon have Broussa, Angora, and Aleppo; later they would secure Smyrna, Trebizond, all the cities to which the Universal laid siege, until the day came when they should conquer the last one, the holy city which they did not name, but which was, as it were, the Eucharistic promise of the expedition. Fathers, husbands, and lovers, compelled to it by the passionate ardour of the women, went to give their brokers orders to the repeated cry of '*Dieu le veut!*'[25] And at last came the dreadful crush of the small and humble, of the tramping crowd that follows large armies, passion descending from the drawing-room to the kitchen, from the merchant to the workman and the peasant, and sweeping along in this mad gallop of millions innumerable poor subscribers with but one share or three or four or ten shares apiece, door-portresses nearly ready to retire, old maids living with their cats, provincial pensioners with allowances of ten sous a day, country priests whom almsgiving had left almost penniless; in fact, the whole emaciated hungry mass of infinitesimal capitalists, those whom a catastrophe at the Bourse sweeps away like an epidemic, and at one stroke stretches in paupers' graves.

And this exaltation of Universal shares, this ascension which carried them up as if on a divine wind, went on to the accompaniment of the yet louder and louder music that arose from the Tuileries and the Champ de Mars and of the endless festivities with which the Exhibition intoxicated Paris. The flags flapped more noisily in the oppressive atmosphere of the warm summer days; not an evening came but the burning city sparkled beneath the stars like a colossal palace in which debauchery went on until the dawn. The joy had spread from house to house; the streets were an intoxication; a cloud of yellow vapour—the steam of festivities, the sweat of revellers—travelled away to the horizon, rolling its coils over the house-roofs, wrapping Paris in the lurid night of Sodom, Babylon, and Nineveh.

Ever since May emperors and kings had been coming thither on pilgrimage from the four corners of the world—endless processions, well-nigh a hundred sovereigns, princes, and princesses. Paris was thoroughly satiated with Majesties and Highnesses;

it had welcomed the Emperor of Russia and the Emperor of Austria, the Sultan of Turkey and the Viceroy of Egypt; and it had thrown itself under the wheels of carriages in order to get a nearer view of the King of Prussia, whom Count von Bismarck followed like a faithful dog. Salutes of honour were continually thundering from the Invalides, while the dense crowd at the Exhibition made a popular success of the huge, sombre Krupp guns, which Germany exhibited there. Almost every week the Opera was lighted up for some official festivity. Folks stifled in the little theatres and the restaurants, all crowded to excess, and the Boulevard footways were no longer wide enough for the overflowing torrent of frail women. Napoleon III. himself wished to distribute the awards to the sixty thousand exhibitors in a ceremony which surpassed all others in magnificence—a 'glory,' as it were, burning on the brow of Paris, the resplendency of the reign, when the Emperor, amid illusive radiance, appeared as the master of Europe, speaking with the calmness of conscious strength and promising peace. Yet on the very morning of the ceremony, tidings of the frightful Mexican tragedy, the execution of Maximilian, had reached the Tuileries. French blood and treasure had been lavishly expended for naught; and the news was designedly concealed from the people in order that the festivities might not be saddened. Nevertheless it was the first stroke of the knell sounding solemnly already, albeit the reign had scarce passed its meridian, and dazzling sunlight still prevailed.

And amidst this glory it seemed as if Saccard's star rose higher still, attained also to yet greater brilliancy. At last, as had been his endeavour for so many years, he had made fortune a slave, a thing of his own, a thing one can dispose of, keep under lock and key, alive and real. So many times had falsehood dwelt in his coffers, so many millions had flowed through them, escaping by all sorts of unknown holes! But this was no longer the deceptive splendour of the façade; it was real sovereignty substantially based upon full sacks of gold; and he did not exercise this sway like a Gundermann, after long years of economy on the part of a whole line of bankers, he laid the proud unction to his soul that he himself had acquired it like a soldier of fortune who conquers a kingdom at a stroke. In the days of his land speculations in the Quartier de l'Europe he had often risen very high; but never had he felt conquered Paris fawning so humbly at his feet as now. And he recalled the day when, breakfasting at Champeaux', ruined once more, and doubting his star, he had cast hungry glances at the Bourse, furiously eager for his revenge, feverishly longing to begin everything, reconquer everything again. Accordingly, now that he had become the master once more, great was his appetite for enjoyment! In the first place, as soon as he believed himself omnipotent he got rid of Huret, and instructed Jantrou to launch against Rougon an article in which the Minister, in the name of the Catholics of France, was openly accused of playing a double game in the Roman question. This was the definitive declaration of war between the two brothers. Since the convention of September 15, 1864,[26] and especially since Sadowa, the French clerical party had pretended to be deeply anxious about the Pope's position; and so now 'L'Espérance' resumed its old Ultramontane politics and violently attacked the liberal Empire, such as the decrees of January 19[27] had begun to make it. A remark of Saccard's circulated in the Chamber: he had said that, in spite of his profound affection for the Emperor, he would resign himself to Henry V., the Count de Chambord, rather than allow the revolutionary spirit to lead France into catastrophes. Then, his audacity increasing with his victories, he no longer concealed his plan of attacking the great Jew bankers in the person of Gundermann, whose billion he meant to breach and breach until the time came for assault and final capture. As the Universal had acquired such miraculous development, why should it not, a few years hence, with the support of entire Christendom, become the sovereign mistress of the Bourse? And Saccard, with warlike bluster, affected the demeanour of a rival, a neighbouring king of equal power, whilst Gundermann, very phlegmatic, without even indulging in a grimace of irony, continued watching and waiting—to all appearances simply interested by the continual rise of Universal stock—like a man who has placed his firm reliance in patience and logic.

His passions had thus elevated Saccard, and his passions were fated to ruin him. Gorged though he was, he would have liked to have found a sixth sense to satisfy. Madame Caroline, who had come to that point that she always smiled, even when her heart was bleeding, remained a friend to whom he would listen with a kind of conjugal deference. But the Baroness Sandorff, icily cold despite her ardent eyes, no longer had any attraction for him. Besides, he was too busy, too absorbed to indulge in a *grande passion*. All he wanted, all he cared about, was some woman whom he might parade as a token of wealth, just like another man might flaunt a huge diamond pin in his cravat. That pin with some would be an advertisement; and it was for advertisement's sake and for the mere satisfaction of vanity that Saccard, on his side, wished to show himself to all Paris in the company of some woman of exceptional notoriety. When this idea came to him his choice at once fell upon Madame de Jeumont, at whose house he had dined on two or three occasions in Maxime's company. Although six and thirty, she was still handsome, with the regular, majestic beauty of a Juno, and she was particularly notorious, for she had attracted the attention of the Emperor, who had heaped gold upon her and had even created her husband a Knight of the Legion of Honour. It proved a costly whim for Saccard, but it keenly satisfied his vanity. One night a grand ball was given at the Ministry of Foreign Affairs, and the reception-rooms, all ablaze with the light of the chandeliers, were crowded with bare shoulders and dress coats, when Saccard entered in triumph, having Madame de Jeumont on his arm, whilst her husband followed behind them. At sight of them, the groups of guests were suddenly broken up, and a broad passage was left for this scandalous exhibition of unbridled licence and mad prodigality. It was the culminating moment of Saccard's existence. Amid the all-prevalent, intoxicating *odor di femina* and the lulling music of the distant orchestra, folks smiled and whispered together as the trio passed. In one *salon*, however, another stream of inquisitive guests had gathered around a colossal individual, who stood there, dazzling and superb, in a white cuirassier uniform. It was Count von Bismarck, who, with his tall figure towering above all others, with big eyes, thick nose and powerful jaw, crossed by the moustaches of a conquering barbarian, was laughing broadly at some jocular remark. Since Sadowa he had given Germany to Prussia; the treaties of alliance against France, so long denied, had been signed for months; and war—which had nearly broken out in May *à propos* of the Luxemburg affair—had now become inevitable. When Saccard in his triumph crossed the room with Madame de Jeumont on his arm and the husband following behind, Count von Bismarck for a moment ceased laughing like a good-humoured, playful giant, and gazed at them inquisitively as they passed.

CHAPTER IX
EXCELSIOR!

Once again Madame Caroline found herself alone. Hamelin had remained in Paris until the early days of November on account of the formalities connected with the final constitution of the company, with its capital of one hundred and fifty millions of francs; and he it was who by Saccard's desire went to Maître Lelorrain's, in the Rue Sainte-Anne, to make the fresh declarations which the law required, alleging that all the shares had been subscribed and the capital paid in, which was not true. Then he started for Rome, where he was to spend a couple of months, having some important matters which he did not speak of to study there—doubtless that famous visionary scheme of installing the Pope at Jerusalem, as well as a more weighty and practical idea, that of transforming the Universal into a Catholic bank, based on the interests of all Christendom, a vast machine which would crush the Jew bankers and sweep them off the face of the earth. And from Rome he meant to betake himself to the East again, having to return thither to attend to the railway line from Broussa to Beyrout. He went off delighted with the rapid prosperity of the Universal, and feeling absolutely convinced that it was firmly established, though at the same time he experienced some secret anxiety at its amazing success. In a conversation which he had with his sister on the day before his departure he only laid stress upon one point, which was that she must resist the general infatuation and sell their shares should the quotations ever exceed two thousand two hundred francs; for he wished to protest personally against a higher rise, deeming it both foolish and dangerous.

As soon as she was alone again, Madame Caroline felt yet more disturbed by the burning atmosphere in which she lived. The shares reached the price of two thousand two hundred francs during the first week in November; and all around her she found rapture, thanksgiving, and unlimited hope. Dejoie was brimming over with gratitude, and the Beauvilliers ladies now treated her as an equal, for was she not the friend of the demigod who was about to restore their ancient house? A chorus of benedictions went up from the happy multitude of speculators both great and small, for daughters were at last supplied with dowries, the poor were suddenly enriched, ensured of incomes in their old age, whilst the wealthy burned with insatiable delight at becoming more wealthy still. 'Twas an unique moment that followed the close of that Exhibition in Paris, now so thoroughly intoxicated with pleasure and power, a moment of faith in happiness, of conviction in endless good luck. All stocks and shares had gone up in price, the most valueless found credulous purchasers; a plethora of equivocal concerns inflated the market, congested it to the point of apoplexy; whilst, underneath, all sounded hollow, revealed the real exhaustion of a *régime* which had indulged in much enjoyment, which had spent milliards upon great public works, and had fattened many huge financial institutions whose gaping coffers were discharging their contents in all directions. Amid such general vertigo a smash up was bound to follow at the first crack, and Madame Caroline doubtless had some such anxious presentiment when she felt her heart pain her at each fresh leap in the price of Universals. No bad rumour as yet circulated; you detected but a slight quivering among the astonished, subdued 'bears.' Still she was perfectly conscious of a feeling of uneasiness, of something which was already undermining the edifice. What it was could not be told, as nothing precise manifested itself, and so she was forced to wait, face to face with the splendour of the triumph which was still increasing despite those slight shocks, those signs of instability portending a catastrophe.

Moreover, she now had another worry. The officials of the Institute of Work were at last satisfied with Victor, who had become silent and crafty; and if she had not yet told everything to Saccard it was from a singular feeling of embarrassment, which made her suffer from the shame that he would feel when she should tell her story, and caused her to postpone its narration from day to day. On the other hand, Maxime, to whom out of her own pocket she about this time refunded the two thousand francs which he had lent her, waxed merry over the balance of four thousand, for which Busch and La Méchain were ever clamouring. They were robbing her, said he, and his father would be furious. Accordingly, from that time forward she turned a deaf ear to the repeated demands of Busch, who insisted on being paid the remainder of the promised sum. After numerous applications he finally became angry, especially as his old idea of blackmailing Saccard had come back to him since the financier's rise to a position of wealth and influence, a position which placed him, Busch believed, at his mercy, as he must now necessarily fear scandal. So one day, exasperated at deriving nothing from such a fine affair, he resolved to apply to him direct, and wrote him a letter, asking him to be good enough to come to his office, to look into some old papers which had been found in a house in the Rue de la Harpe. He gave the number of the house and made so clear an allusion to the old story that he felt sure Saccard would be seized with anxiety and hasten to obey the summons. This letter, however, was forwarded to the Rue Saint-Lazare, and fell into the hands of Madame Caroline, who recognised the writing on the envelope. She trembled, and wondered for a moment whether she ought not to run to Busch's office and try to buy him off. Then she reflected that he had perhaps written to Saccard about something else, and that at any rate this would be a way of ending the matter. In her emotion she was even pleased to think that the task of revealing the affair should fall upon another. In the evening, however, when Saccard returned home and opened the letter in her presence she simply saw a grave expression come over his face, and thought that the letter must refer to some money complication. In reality he had experienced profound surprise, and his throat had contracted at the thought of falling into such filthy hands, which he could guess must be plotting some baseness. Still, he put the letter into his pocket with an easy gesture, and decided to call upon Busch as he was requested to do.

Several days passed, however, the second fortnight of November arrived, and each morning Saccard postponed his visit, more and more bewildered by the torrent which was bearing him along. The quotation of two thousand three hundred francs had just been reached and he was delighted, albeit feeling that resistance was being offered at the Bourse, and indeed becoming more and more pronounced as the rise continued. Evidently some group of 'bears' was taking up position, entering upon the struggle timidly as yet, venturing as a rule on mere outpost skirmishes, although on two occasions he found himself obliged to give orders to buy under cover of borrowed names, so that there might be no pause in the upward march of the quotations. The system of making the Bank buy up its own shares, speculate with them, and thus devour itself, was at last being put into practice.

One evening, thoroughly stirred by his passionate fever, Saccard could not help speaking of the matter to Madame Caroline. 'I fancy that things will soon be getting warm,' said he; 'we have become too strong, and they find us in their way. I can scent Gundermann. I know his tactics: he will begin selling regularly, so much to-day, so much to-morrow, increasing the amount until he succeeds in shaking us.'

Interrupting him, she said gravely: 'If he has any Universals he does right to sell.'

161

'What! he does right to sell!'

'No doubt, my brother told you so. All quotations above two thousand francs are absurd.'

He looked at her, and, quite beside himself, gave vent to an angry outburst: 'Sell them! Dare to sell your own shares! Yes, play against me, since you want me to be defeated!'

She blushed slightly, for, truth to tell, she had only the day before sold a thousand of her shares in obedience to her brother's orders; and this sale, like some tardy act of honesty, had eased her feelings. As Saccard did not put any direct questions to her, she did not confess the matter to him, but her embarrassment increased when he added: 'For instance, there were some defections yesterday, I am sure of it. Quite a large parcel of shares came into the market, and quotations would certainly have fallen if I hadn't intervened. It wasn't Gundermann who made such a stroke as that. His system is a slower one, though the result in the long run is more crushing. Ah! my dear, I am quite confident, but still I can't help trembling, for it's nothing to defend one's life in comparison with having to defend one's money and that of others.'

And indeed from that moment Saccard ceased to be his own master. He belonged to the millions which he was making, still triumphing, yet ever on the verge of defeat. He no longer even found time to see the Baroness Sandorff, who felt that he was breaking away from her and relapsed into her former ignorance and doubts. Since their intimacy had begun she had gambled with almost a certainty of winning and had made much money, but she now clearly saw that he was unwilling to answer her, and even feared that he might be lying to her. Either because her luck had turned, or he had indeed been amusing himself by starting her on a false scent, a day came when she lost by following his advice. Her faith was then badly shaken. If he thus misled her, who would guide her? And the worst was that the secret hostility to the Universal at the Bourse, so slight at first, was now growing day by day. There were still only rumours; no precise statement was made; no genuine fact impaired the Bank's credit. Only it was tacitly allowed that there must be something the matter, that the worm was in the fruit, though this did not prevent the rise of the stock from continuing, from becoming more and more formidable every day.

However, after a deal in Italians which proved disastrous, the Baroness, decidedly anxious, resolved to call at the office of 'L'Espérance' to try to make Jantrou talk.

'Come, what's the matter?' she said to him. 'You *must* know. Universals have just gone up another twenty francs and yet there are rumours afloat—no one can tell me exactly what, but at all events nothing very good.'

Jantrou's perplexity was, however, as great as her own. Placed at the fountain-head of information, in case of need manufacturing reports himself, he jokingly compared his position to that of a clock-maker who lives among hundreds of clocks and yet never knows the correct time. Thanks to his advertising agency, he was in everybody's confidence, but the result of this was that he could never form a firm opinion, for the information which he received on one hand was generally contradicted, reduced to nought, by that which he received on another.

'I know nothing,' he replied, 'nothing at all.'

'You mean that you don't want to tell me.'

'No, upon my word, I really know nothing. Why, I was even thinking of calling on you to question you! Has Saccard ceased to be obliging, then?'

She made a gesture which confirmed him in his suspicion; and, still looking at her, he went on talking, venting his thoughts aloud: 'Yes, it's annoying, for I relied on you. For, you see, if there is to be a catastrophe, one ought to be forewarned of it, so as to have time to turn round. Oh! I don't think there need be any hurry; the Bank still stands firm as yet. Only such queer things happen sometimes.' As he thus gazed at her and chattered, a plan suddenly took shape in his head, and all at once he resumed: 'I say, since Saccard drops you, you ought to cultivate Gundermann's acquaintance.'

Such was her surprise that for a moment she remained without speaking. 'Why Gundermann?' she asked at last. 'I know him a little; I've met him at the De Roivilles' and the Kellers'.'

'So much the better if you know him. Go to see him on some pretext or other, talk to him, and try to get on friendly terms with him. Just think of it—to become Gundermann's *confidante* and rule the world!'

'But why Gundermann?' she repeated.

Thereupon he explained that Gundermann was certainly at the head of the group of 'bears' who were beginning to manœuvre against the Universal. This he knew; he had proof of it. So, as Saccard was no longer obliging, would it not be simple prudence to make friends with his enemy, without, however, breaking with him? With a foot in each camp, she would be sure of being in the conqueror's company on the day of battle. And he suggested this treachery to her with an amiable air, like a good adviser. With a woman at work for him, he felt that he would be able to sleep in peace. 'Come, what do you say?' he added; 'let us make a bargain. We will warn each other, we will tell each other everything we hear.'

Thereupon he grasped her hand, which she relinquished to him, already losing her contempt for him, forgetting the lackey that he had been, no longer realising into what low debauchery he had fallen, his face bloated, his handsome beard reeking of absinthe, his new coat soiled with spots, his shiny hat damaged by the plaster of some disreputable stairway.

She called upon Gundermann the very next day. Since Universals had reached the figure of two thousand francs he had indeed been leading a bear movement, but with the utmost discretion, never going to the Bourse, nor sending even an official representative thither. His argument was that a share in any company is in the first place worth its price of issue, and secondly the interest which it may yield, this depending upon the prosperity of the company, the success attending its enterprises. There is therefore a maximum value which cannot be reasonably increased. As soon as that value is exceeded through popular infatuation, the prudent course is to play for a fall in the certainty that it must come. Still, despite his convictions, despite his absolute belief in logic, he was surprised by Saccard's rapid conquests, surprised to find that he had become such a power all at once, and was already beginning to frighten the big Jew bankers. It was necessary to lay this dangerous rival low as soon as possible, not only in order to regain the eight millions lost on the morrow of Sadowa, but especially in order to avoid having to share the sovereignty of the market with such a terrible adventurer, whose reckless strokes seemed to succeed in defiance of all common sense, as if by miracle. And so, full of contempt for passion, Gundermann, mathematical gambler, man-numeral that he was, carried his phlegm, his frigid obstinacy still further, ever and ever selling Universals despite their continuous rise, and losing larger and larger sums at each successive settlement, with the fine sense of security of a wise man who simply puts his money into a savings' bank.

When the Baroness at last managed to enter the banker's room amid the scramble of employees and *remisiers*, the hail of papers which had to be signed and of telegrams which had to be read, she found Gundermann suffering from a fearful cough which seemed to be tearing his throat away. Nevertheless he had been there since six o'clock in the morning—coughing and spitting, worn out with fatigue, it is true, but steadfast all the same. That day, as a foreign loan was to be issued on the morrow, the spacious room was invaded by an even more eager crowd than usual, and two of the banker's sons and one of his sons-in-law had been deputed to receive this whirlwind; whilst on the floor, near the narrow table which he had reserved for himself in the embrasure of a window, three of his grandchildren, two girls and a boy, were quarrelling with shrill cries over a doll, an arm and a leg of which had already been torn off and lay there beside them.

The Baroness at once brought forward the pretext which she had devised to explain her visit. '*Cher monsieur*,' said she, 'I have come to pester you, which needs a deal of courage. It is with reference to a charity lottery——'

He did not allow her to finish, for he was very charitable, and always bought two tickets, especially when ladies whom he had met in society thus took the trouble to bring them to him. However, he had to keep her waiting for a moment, for an employee came to submit some papers to him. They spoke of vast sums of money in hurried words.

'Fifty-two millions, you say? And the credit was?'

'Sixty millions, monsieur.'

'Well, carry it to seventy-five millions.'

Then he was returning to the Baroness, when he overheard a word or two of a conversation between his son-in-law and a *remisier*, and this started him off again. 'Not at all,' he interrupted. 'At the rate of five hundred and eighty-seven fifty, that makes ten sous less per share.'

'Oh! monsieur,' said the *remisier*, humbly, 'it would only make forty-three francs less!'

'What, forty-three francs! Why, it is enormous! Do you think that I steal money? Every one his due; I know no rule but that!'

At last, so that they might talk at their ease, he decided to take the Baroness into the dining-room, where the table was already laid for breakfast. He was not deceived by that pretext of a lottery, for, thanks to obsequious spies, who kept him informed, he knew how intimate she was with Saccard, and strongly suspected that she had come on some matter of serious interest. Consequently he did not stand on ceremony. 'Come now!' he exclaimed, 'tell me what you have to say.'

But she pretended surprise. She had nothing to say to him; she simply wished to thank him for his kindness.

'Then you have not been charged with a commission for me?' he asked, seemingly disappointed, as if he had thought for a moment that she had come with a secret mission from Saccard, some invention or other of that madman.

Now that they were alone, she looked at him with a smile, with that deceptive, ardent air of hers by which so many men had been caught. 'No,' she said, 'no, I have nothing to say to you, and since you are so very kind, I would rather ask something of you.' And then, leaning forward, she made her confession, spoke of her deplorable

164

marriage to a foreigner, who had understood neither her nature nor her needs; and explained how she had been obliged to have recourse to gambling in order to keep up her position. And finally, she expatiated on her solitude, on the necessity of being advised and guided through the quicksands of the Bourse, where so heavy a penalty attends each false step. 'But I thought,' he interrupted, 'that you were already advised by somebody.'

'Oh, somebody!' she murmured with a gesture of profound disdain. 'No, nobody—I have nobody. It is your advice that I should like to have, the advice of the master. And it really would not cost you anything to be my friend, just to say a word to me, merely one word every now and then. If you only knew how happy you would make me, how grateful I should be to you!'

Speaking in this wise, she sought to fascinate him by glance and gesture, but all to no avail. He remained cold, impassive, like one who has no passions. And whilst he listened to her he took some grapes, one by one, from a fruit-stand on the table, and ate them in a languid, mechanical way. This was the only excess which he allowed himself, the indulgence of his most sensual moments, the penalty for which was days of suffering, for his digestive organs were so impaired that a rigorous milk diet had been prescribed for him. Looking at the Baroness, he gave her the cunning smile of a man who knows that he is invincible; and without wasting further time, coming straight to the point, he said: 'Well, you are very charming, and I should really like to oblige you. So on the day, my beautiful friend, when you bring me some good advice, I promise to give you some in return. Come and tell me what others are doing, and I'll tell you what I shall do. It is understood, eh?'

He had risen, and she was obliged to return with him into the adjoining room. She had perfectly understood the bargain which he proposed, the spying and treachery which he required of her. But she was unwilling to answer, and made a pretence of reverting to the subject of the lottery; whilst he, with a shake of his head, seemed to be adding that he did not really need any help, since the logical, inevitable *dénouement* would come just the same, though perhaps not quite so fast. And when she at last went off his attention was immediately turned to other important matters, amid all the extraordinary tumult prevailing in that market of capital, what with the procession of Boursiers, the gallop of his employees, and the play of his grandchildren, who had just torn the doll's head off with shouts of triumph. Seated at his narrow table, he became absorbed in the study of a sudden idea, and heard nothing more.

The Baroness Sandorff returned twice to the office of 'L'Espérance' to acquaint Jantrou with what she had done, but she did not find him there. At last Dejoie admitted her one day when his daughter Nathalie sat talking with Madame Jordan on a bench in the passage. A diluvian rain had been falling since the day before; and in the wet gray weather the old building, overlooking a dark well-like courtyard, seemed frightfully melancholy. Such was the darkness that the gas had been lighted, and Marcelle, waiting for Jordan, who had gone in search of some money, to pay a new instalment to Busch, listened sadly to Nathalie as the latter chatted away like a vain magpie, with the dry voice and sharp gestures of a precocious Parisian girl.

'You understand, madame, papa won't sell. There is a lady who is urging him to do so, trying to frighten him. I do not give her name, because surely it is hardly her place to frighten people. It is I who am now preventing papa from selling. Sell indeed! when the price is still going up! To do that one would need to be a regular simpleton, don't you think so?'

'No doubt!' Marcelle simply answered.

'The price, you know, has now got to two thousand five hundred francs,' continued Nathalie. 'I keep the accounts because papa scarcely knows how to write. And so our eight shares represent twenty thousand francs already. That's nice, is it not? First of all, papa wanted to stop at eighteen thousand, that was his figure—six thousand for my dowry, and twelve thousand for himself, enough for a little income of six hundred francs a year, which he would have well earned with all these emotions. But is it not lucky that he didn't sell, since we have already got two thousand francs more? And now we want more still, we want enough to give papa an income of a thousand francs at the very least. And we shall get it; Monsieur Saccard has told us so. He is so nice, is Monsieur Saccard!'

Marcelle could not help smiling. 'Then you no longer intend to marry?' she said.

'Yes, yes, when the rise comes to an end. We were in a hurry, Theodore's father especially, on account of his business. But it would be silly, wouldn't it, to stop up the source when the money keeps pouring out of it? Oh! Theodore understands it all very well, especially as the larger papa's income gets, the more capital there will be for us by-and-by. That's worth considering—and so we are all waiting. We have had the six thousand francs for months, and I might have married, but we prefer to let them increase and multiply. Do you read the articles in the newspapers about the shares?'

Without waiting for a reply, she went on: 'Papa brings me the papers and I read them every evening. He has already seen them and I have to read them over to him again. One could never tire of them, they make such beautiful promises! I have my head so full of them when I go to bed that I dream about them all night. Papa tells me, too, that he sees things in his sleep which are very good signs. The night before last we had the same dream, of five-franc pieces which we were picking up by the shovelful in the street. It was very amusing.'

Again she paused in her cackle to ask: 'How many shares have you got?'

'We, not one!' answered Marcelle.

Nathalie's fair little face, crowned with light wavy hair, assumed an expression of intense compassion. Ah! the poor people who had no shares! And her father having called her to ask her to carry some proofs to a contributor, on her way back to the Batignolles, she went off, affecting the importance of a capitalist, who now came to the office almost every day in order to ascertain the Bourse quotations at the earliest possible moment.

Left alone on her bench, Marcelle fell back into a melancholy reverie, she who was usually so gay and brave. *Mon Dieu!* how dark it was, what a gloomy day it was! and to think that her poor husband was running about the streets in that diluvian rain! He had such contempt for money, felt such uneasiness at the very idea of occupying himself with it, that it cost him a great effort to ask it even of those who owed it to him! Then becoming absorbed, hearing nothing, she recalled her experiences since waking in the morning; while all around her feverish work went on in connection with the paper—contributors rushing past, 'copy' coming and going, doors slamming and bells ringing incessantly.

To her it had been an evil day. In the first place she had scarcely washed and was still in her morning wrap when at nine o'clock, just as Jordan had gone out to investigate an accident which he was to report, she was astounded to see Busch make his appearance, accompanied by two very dirty-looking men, perhaps process servers, perhaps bandits, she never could tell exactly which. That abominable fellow Busch, undoubtedly taking advantage of the fact that there was only a woman to contend with, declared that they meant to seize everything if she did not pay him on the spot. And she argued the matter in vain, being unacquainted with any of the legal formalities. He affirmed so stoutly that judgment had been signified and the placard posted that she was left in bewilderment, believing at last in the possibility of these things happening without one knowing of them. However, she did not surrender, but explained that her husband would not return even to lunch, and that she would allow nothing to be touched until he should come back. Then, between these three shady personages and this young woman with her hair hanging over her shoulders, there ensued a most painful scene, the men already making an inventory of the goods, and she locking the cupboards, and placing herself in front of the door as though to prevent them from taking anything away. To think of it! Her poor little home which she was so proud of, those few sticks of furniture which she was ever dusting and polishing, those hangings in the bedroom which she had put up herself! As she shouted to them with warlike bravery, they would have to pass over her body if they wished to take those things away. And she called Busch rogue and thief to his very face. Yes! a thief who wasn't ashamed to demand seven hundred and thirty francs and fifteen centimes, without counting the fresh costs, for a claim which he had picked out of some heap of rags and old iron bought for a hundred sous! To think that they had already paid the thief four hundred francs in instalments and that he talked of carrying off their furniture to pay himself the other three hundred and odd francs which he wished to rob them of! Yet he knew perfectly well that they were honest people and would have paid him at once had they only possessed the sum. And he profited by the circumstance that she was alone, unable to answer, ignorant of legal matters, to come there and frighten her and make her weep. He was a rogue, a thief, a thief! Quite infuriated, Busch shouted even louder than she did, slapping his chest and asking: Was he not an honest man? Had he not paid sterling money for the claim? He had fulfilled all the formalities of the law and meant to make an end of the matter. However, when one of the two dirty men began opening the chest of drawers in search of the linen, Marcelle's demeanour became so terrific, she threatened so stoutly to bring everyone in the house and in the street to the spot, that the Jew slightly calmed down; and at last after another half-hour's wild discussion he consented to wait until the morrow, furiously swearing, however, that he would then remove everything if she did not keep her promise to him. Oh! what burning shame it had been, a shame from which she still suffered—those horrid men in her rooms, wounding all her feelings, even her modesty, searching her very bed, and quite infecting the happy chamber, whose window she had been obliged to leave wide open after their departure.

But another and a deeper sorrow awaited Marcelle that day. The idea had occurred to her of at once hastening to her parents to borrow the needed sum of them: in this way, when her husband came back at night, she would not have to fill him with despair, but would be able to make him laugh by telling him of the scene of the morning. She already saw herself describing the great battle, the ferocious assault made upon their household, the heroic way in which she had repulsed the attack. Her heart beat very fast as she entered the little residence in the Rue Legendre, that comfortable house in which she had grown up, and where it now seemed to her she would find only strangers, so different, so icy was the atmosphere. As her parents were sitting down to table, she accepted their invitation to breakfast, in order to put them in better humour. Throughout the meal the conversation ran upon the rise in

Universals, the price of which had gone up another twenty francs only the day before; and Marcelle was astonished to find her mother more feverish, more greedy even than her father, she who at the outset had trembled at the very idea of speculation; whereas now, with the violence of a conquered woman, it was she who chided him for his timidity, in her anxious eagerness for great strokes of luck. They had scarcely begun eating, when she flew into a tantrum: she was astounded at hearing him talk of selling their seventy-five shares at the unhoped-for figure of two thousand five hundred and twenty francs, which would have yielded them a hundred and eighty-nine thousand francs, in truth a pretty profit, more than a hundred thousand francs above the price at which they bought the stock. Yet this did not satisfy her. 'Sell!' said she, 'when the "Côte Financière" promised the figure of three thousand francs!' Had he gone mad? For the 'Côte Financière' was known for its old-time honesty; he himself often repeated that with this newspaper as a guide one could sleep soundly. Oh! no, indeed, she would not let him sell! She would sooner sell their house to buy more shares. And Marcelle, silent, with her heart compressed at hearing them so passionately bandy these big figures, wondered how she might venture to ask for a loan of five hundred francs in this house which gambling had invaded, and where little by little she had seen rise the flood of financial newspapers that now submerged it, enveloped it with the intoxicating glamour of their puffs.

At last, at dessert, she ventured to speak out. She and her husband were in need of five hundred francs, they were on the point of being sold up, and surely her parents would not abandon them in such disaster. Her father at once lowered his head and darted a glance of embarrassment at her mother. But the latter was already refusing the request in a firm voice. Five hundred francs, indeed! where did she expect them to find them? All their capital was invested in their operations; and besides, she reverted to her old-time diatribes. When a girl has married a pauper, a man who writes books and articles, she must put up with the consequence of her folly, and not fall back for support upon her parents. No! she—the mother—had not a copper for idlers, who with their pretended contempt for money only dreamed of living on that of other people. And thereupon she allowed her daughter to depart; and Marcelle went off in despair, her heart bleeding at the great change that had taken place in her mother, formerly so reasonable and so kind.

Once in the street Marcelle had walked along in an almost unconscious state, her eyes fixed on the ground as though she hoped to find the money there. Then the idea of applying to Uncle Chave suddenly occurred to her, and she immediately betook herself to his little lodging in the Rue Nollet, so as to catch him before he went off to the Bourse. She found him smoking his pipe all alone; and on hearing of her trouble he became greatly distressed and even angry with himself, exclaiming that he never had a hundred francs before him, for he no sooner won a trifle at the Bourse than like a dirty pig he went and spent it. Then, on hearing of the Maugendres' refusal, he began to thunder against them, horrid beasts that they were! He no longer associated with them, said he, since the rise of their shares had driven them crazy. Hadn't his sister contemptuously called him a higgler by way of ridiculing his prudent system of operations, and this simply because he had advised her in a friendly spirit to sell and realise? Ah! well, she would get no pity from him when the fall came and she found herself in a pickle!

Once more in the street, with her pocket still empty, Marcelle had to resign herself to the unpleasant course of calling at the newspaper office to acquaint her husband with what had occurred that morning. It was absolutely necessary that Busch should be paid. Having heard her story, Jordan, whose book had not yet been accepted by any publisher, had started off to hunt for money, through the streets of muddy Paris in that rainy weather—not knowing where to apply—at friends' houses or at the offices of the newspapers he wrote for, but vaguely relying upon some chance meeting. Although he had begged her to go home again, she was so anxious that she had preferred to remain waiting for him on that bench.

Dejoie, seeing her alone after his daughter's departure, ventured to bring her a newspaper. 'If Madame would like to read this,' said he, 'just to while away the time.'

But she refused the offer with a wave of the hand; and, as Saccard arrived at that moment, she assumed a brave air, and gaily explained that she had sent her husband on a bothersome errand in the neighbourhood which she had not cared to undertake herself. Saccard, who had a feeling of friendship for the young couple, insisted that she should go into his office, where she could wait more comfortably. But she declined the offer, saying that she was very well where she was. And he ceased to press the matter, in the surprise he experienced at suddenly finding himself face to face with the Baroness Sandorff, who was leaving Jantrou's office. However, they both smiled, with an air of amiable understanding, like people who merely exchange a bow, in order not to parade their intimacy.

Jantrou had just told the Baroness that he no longer dared to give her any advice. His perplexity was increasing, since the Universal still stood firm in spite of the growing efforts of the 'bears.' Undoubtedly Gundermann would eventually win, but Saccard might last a long time, and perhaps there was yet a lot of money to be made by clinging to him. He, Jantrou, had decided to postpone any rupture and to keep on good terms with both sides. The best plan for her to adopt, he said, was to try to retain Saccard's confidence, and either keep the secrets which he might confide to her for herself, or else sell them to Gundermann, should it be to her advantage to do so. And Jantrou offered this advice in a jesting sort of way, without affecting any of the mysteriousness of a conspirator; whilst she, on her side, laughed and promised to give him a share in the affair.

'So now she is trying her fascinations on you!' exclaimed Saccard in his brutal way as he entered Jantrou's office.

The editor feigned astonishment. 'Whom are you talking about? Oh, the Baroness! But, my dear master, she adores you. She was telling me so just now!'

Saccard shrugged his shoulders. Love matters were of no interest to him just then. Walking to and fro, pausing at times in front of the window to watch the fall of that seemingly endless rain, he vented all his nervous delight. Yes, Universals had risen another twenty francs on the previous day. But how the deuce was it that people still persisted in selling? There would have been a rise of thirty francs but for a heap of shares which had fallen on the market soon after business began. He could not explain it, ignorant as he was that Madame Caroline, fighting against that senseless rise, in obedience to the orders left with her by her brother, had again sold a thousand shares. However, with success still increasing, Saccard ought not to have complained; and yet an inward trembling, produced by secret fear and anger, disturbed him. The dirty Jews had sworn to ruin him, he exclaimed; that rogue Gundermann had just put himself at the head of a syndicate of 'bears' in order to crush him. He had been told so at the Bourse, where folks declared that the syndicate disposed of three hundred millions of francs. Ah, the brigands! And there were other reports—reports which he did not venture to repeat aloud, but which were each day growing more precise, allegations with regard to the stability of the Universal, and predictions of approaching difficulties, though as yet the blind confidence of the public had not been shaken.

However, the door opened, and Huret with his air of feigned simplicity came in.

'Ah! so here you are, Judas!' said Saccard.

Having learnt that Rougon had decided to abandon his brother, Huret had become reconciled to the minister; for he was convinced that as soon as Saccard should have Rougon against him, a catastrophe would be inevitable. To earn his pardon, he had now re-entered the great man's service, again doing his errands and exposing himself to kicks and insults in order to please him. 'Judas!' he repeated, with the shrewd smile that sometimes lighted up his heavy peasant face; 'at any rate, a good-natured Judas, who comes to give some disinterested advice to the master whom he has betrayed.'

But Saccard, as if unwilling to hear him, shouted by way of affirming his triumph: 'Two thousand five hundred and twenty yesterday, two thousand five hundred and twenty-five to-day! Those are the last quotations, eh?'

'I know; I have just sold.'

At this blow the wrath which Saccard had been concealing under a jesting air burst forth. 'What! you have sold? So it's perfect then! You drop me for Rougon, and you go over to Gundermann!'

The Deputy looked at him in amazement. 'To Gundermann, why so? I simply look after my interests. I'm not a dare-devil, you know. I prefer to realise as soon as there is a decent profit. And that is perhaps the reason why I have never lost.'

He smiled again like a prudent, cautious Norman farmer, garnering his crop in a cool collected way.

'To think of it! A director of the Bank!' continued Saccard violently. 'Whom can we expect to have confidence? What must folks think on seeing you sell in that fashion when the shares are still rising? I am no longer surprised that people should assert that our prosperity is artificial, and that the day of the downfall is at hand. These gentlemen, the directors, sell, so let us all sell. That spells panic!'

Huret made a vague gesture. In point of fact, he did not care a button what might happen henceforth; he had made sure of his own pile, and all that remained for him to do now was to fulfil the mission entrusted to him by Rougon with as little unpleasantness for himself as possible. 'I told you, my dear fellow,' said he, 'that I had come to give you a piece of disinterested advice. Here it is. Be careful; your brother is furious, and he will leave you altogether in the lurch if you allow yourself to be beaten.'

Restraining his anger, Saccard asked impassively: 'Did he send you to tell me that?'

After hesitating for a moment, the Deputy thought it best to confess that it was so. 'Well, yes, he did. Oh! you cannot suppose that the attacks made upon him in "L'Espérance" have anything to do with his irritation. He is above such personal considerations. Still, it is none the less true that the Catholic campaign in your paper is, as you yourself must realise, of a nature to embarrass him in his present policy. Since the beginning of all these unfortunate complications with regard to Rome he has had the entire clergy on his back. He has just been obliged to have another bishop censured by the Council of State for issuing an aggressive pastoral letter. And you choose for your attacks the very moment when he has so much difficulty to prevent himself from being swamped by the Liberal evolution brought about by the reforms of January 19—reforms which, as folks say, he has only decided to carry out in order that he may prudently circumscribe them. Come, you are his brother, and can you imagine that your conduct pleases him?'

'Of course,' answered Saccard sneeringly, 'it is very wrong on my part. Here is this poor brother of mine, who, in his rage to remain a Minister, governs in the name of the principles which he fought against yesterday, and lays all the blame upon me because he can no longer keep his balance between the Right, which is angry at having been betrayed, and the Third Estate, which longs for power. To quiet the Catholics, he only the other day launched his famous "Never!" swearing that never would France allow Italy to take Rome from the Pope. And now, in his terror of the Liberals, he would like very much to give them a guarantee also, and thinks of ruining me to satisfy them. A week ago Émile Ollivier gave him a fine shaking in the Chamber.'

'Oh,' interrupted Huret, 'he still has the confidence of the Tuileries; the Emperor has sent him the star of the Legion of Honour in diamonds.'

But, with an energetic gesture, Saccard retorted that he was not to be duped. 'The Universal is growing too powerful, that is the worry, is it not? A Catholic bank, which threatens to conquer the world by money as it was formerly conquered by faith, can that be tolerated? All the Freethinkers, all the Freemasons, ambitious to become Ministers, shiver at the thought. Perhaps, too, there is some loan which they want to work with Gundermann. What would become of a Government that did not allow itself to be preyed upon by those dirty Jews? And so my fool of a brother, in order to retain power six months longer, is going to throw me as food to the dirty Jews, to the Liberals, to the entire riff-raff, in the hope that he will be left in peace while they are devouring me. Well, go back and tell him that I don't care a fig for him.'

He straightened up his short figure, his passion prevailing over his irony, in a trumpet-flourish of battle. 'Do you understand? I don't care a fig for him! That is my answer; I wish him to know it.'

Huret slightly stooped. As soon as folks lost their tempers in matters of business he had nothing more to say. And after all, in this particular affair, he was only a messenger. 'All right, all right,' he said, 'he shall be told. You will get your back broken, but that is your own look-out!'

An interval of silence followed. Jantrou, who had remained perfectly silent, pretending to be entirely absorbed in correcting some proofs, raised his eyes to admire Saccard. How fine the bandit was in his passion! These rascals of genius triumph at times when they reach this state of recklessness, and are carried along by the intoxication of success. And at this moment Jantrou was on Saccard's side, firmly believing in his star.

'Ah, I was forgetting,' resumed Huret; 'it seems that Delcambre, the Public Prosecutor, hates you. Well, you probably do not yet know it, but the Emperor this morning appointed him Minister of Justice.'

Saccard, who had been pacing up and down the room, stopped short. With darkened face he at last exclaimed:

'Another nice piece of goods! So they have made a Minister of that thing! But why should I care about it?'

'Well,' rejoined Huret, exaggerating his expression of feigned simplicity, 'if any misfortune should happen to you, as may happen to anybody in business, your brother does not wish you to rely upon him to defend you against Delcambre.'

'But, d—— it all!' shrieked Saccard, 'I tell you that I don't care a button for the whole gang, either for Rougon, or for Delcambre, or for you either!'

At that moment, fortunately, Daigremont entered the room. He had never before called at the newspaper office, so that his appearance was a surprise to them all and averted further violence. Studiously polite, he shook hands all round, smiling upon one and the other with the wheedling affability of a man of the world. His wife was going to give a *soirée* at which she intended to sing, and, in order to secure a good article, he had come to invite Jantrou in person. However, Saccard's presence seemed to delight him.

'How goes it, my great man?' he asked.

Instead of answering, Saccard inquired: 'You haven't sold, have you?'

'Sold! Oh no, not yet.' And there was a ring of sincerity in his laughter. He was made of firmer stuff than that.

'One ought never to sell in our position!' cried Saccard.

'Never. That is what I meant to say. We all of us have the same interests, and you know very well that you can rely on me.'

His eyelids had drooped, and he gave a side glance while referring to the other directors, Sédille, Kolb and the Marquis de Bohain, answering for them as for himself. Their enterprise was prospering so well, he said, that it was a real pleasure to be all of one mind in furthering the most extraordinary success which the Bourse had witnessed for the last half century. Then he found some flattering remark for each of them, Saccard, Huret, and Jantrou, and went off repeating that he should expect to see them all three at his *soirée*; Mounier, the tenor at the Opera, would, he said, give his wife her cue. Oh, the performance would be a very effective one!

'So that's all the answer you have to give me?' asked Huret, in his turn preparing to leave.

'Quite so,' replied Saccard in a curt, dry voice. And to emphasise his decision he made a point of not going down with Huret as he usually did.

Then, finding himself alone again with the editor, he exclaimed: 'This means war, my brave fellow! There is no occasion to spare anybody any further; belabour the whole gang! Ah, at last, then, I shall be able to fight the battle according to my own ideas!'

'All the same, it is rather stiff!' concluded Jantrou, whose perplexities were beginning again.

Meantime, on the bench in the passage, Marcelle was still waiting. It was hardly four o'clock, and Dejoie had already lighted the lamps, so early had it grown dark amid the grey, obstinate downpour. Every time that the good fellow passed her he found some little remark with which to entertain her. Moreover, the comings and goings of contributors were becoming more frequent; loud voices rang out in an adjoining room; there was all the growing fever which attends the making up of a newspaper.

After a time, suddenly raising her eyes, Marcelle saw Jordan in front of her. He was drenched, and looked overwhelmed, with that trembling of the lips, that slightly crazy expression which one notices in those who have long been pursuing some hope without attaining it. Marcelle realised that he had been unsuccessful.

'You could get nothing, eh?' she asked, turning pale.

'Nothing, my darling, nothing at all—nowhere, it wasn't possible.'

She uttered only a low lament, but it was instinct with all her agony of heart: 'Oh, my God!'

172

Just then Saccard came out of Jantrou's office and was astonished to find her still there. 'What, madame, has your truant husband only just come back? Ah! I told you that it would be better for you to wait in my office.'

She looked at him fixedly, and a sudden inspiration dawned in her large desolate eyes. She did not pause to reflect, but yielded to that reckless bravery which throws women forward in moments of passion. 'Monsieur Saccard,' said she, 'I have something to ask you. If you are willing, we will now go to your room.'

'Why, certainly, madame.'

Jordan, who feared that he could divine her purpose, tried to hold her back, stammering 'No, no,' in the sickly anguish which always came upon him when pecuniary matters were in question. However, she released herself, and he had to follow her.

'Monsieur Saccard,' she resumed as soon as the door was closed, 'for the last two hours my husband has been vainly running about, trying to find five hundred francs, and he doesn't dare to apply to you. So it is I who have come to ask you for them——'

And then, in a spirited way, with the amusing air of a gay, resolute little woman, she described the scene which had taken place in the morning—the brutal entrance of Busch, the invasion of her home by the three horrid men, the manner in which she had managed to repel the assault, and the promise which she had made to pay the money that very day. Ah! those pecuniary sores so common among the humble, those great sorrows caused by shame and powerlessness—the very existence of human beings continually put in question through the lack of a few paltry pieces of silver!

'Busch!' repeated Saccard. 'So it's that old swindler Busch, is it, who holds you in his clutches?'

Then, with affable good-nature, turning to Jordan, who remained silent and pale, feeling supremely uncomfortable, he said: 'Well, I will advance you the five hundred francs. You ought to have asked me for them in the first place.'

He had seated himself at his table to sign a cheque, when he stopped to reflect. He remembered the letter which he had received from Busch, the visit which he had to make to him, and which he had been postponing from day to day in his annoyance over the nasty affair that he scented. Why should he not at once go to the Rue Feydeau, taking advantage of the opportunity now that he had a pretext for going there?

'Listen,' said he, 'I know this rascal through and through. It is better that I should go to pay him in person, to see if I can't get your notes back at half price.'

Marcelle's eyes now sparkled with gratitude. 'Oh, Monsieur Saccard, how kind you are!' she exclaimed. And, addressing her husband, she added: 'You see, you big silly, that Monsieur Saccard has not eaten us!'

Yielding to an irresistible impulse, he threw his arms round her neck and kissed her, as though to thank her for being more energetic and skilful than himself in these material difficulties which paralysed his energy.

'No, no!' said Saccard, when the young man finally pressed his hand, 'the pleasure is mine; it is very pleasant to see you love one another so much. Go home, and be easy.'

In a couple of minutes his brougham, which was waiting for him, conveyed him to the Rue Feydeau, through muddy Paris, amid the jostling of umbrellas and splashing of puddles. But once upstairs he rang in vain at the dirty old door, on which was a plate bearing the inscription '*Disputed Claims*' in big letters. It did not open, there was no sound within, and he was on the point of going away, when, in his keen vexation, he

173

shook it violently with his fist. Then a halting step was heard, and at last Sigismond appeared.

'What! it is you! I thought that it was my brother, who had come up again and forgotten his key. I never answer the door myself. Oh, he won't be long, and you can wait for him if you wish to see him.'

With the same painful, unsteady step he returned, followed by Saccard, into the room which he occupied overlooking the Place de la Bourse. It was still quite light at that height above the mist, whence the rain was pouring into the streets. The room was frigidly bare with its little iron bedstead, its table and two chairs, and its few shelves of books. A small stove stood in front of the chimney-piece, and the fire, carelessly looked after, forgotten, had just gone out.

'Sit down, monsieur,' said Sigismond, 'my brother told me that he was only going out for a moment.'

Saccard declined the proffered chair, however, and stood looking at him, struck by the progress which consumption had made in this tall, pale fellow with child-like eyes—eyes with a dim, dreamy expression, passing strange under a forehead which seemed typical of energy and obstinacy. His long wavy hair fell on either side of his face, which had become extremely sunken and emaciated, elongated too and drawn, as it were, towards the grave.

'You have been ill?' remarked Saccard, at a loss what else to say.

Sigismond made a gesture of complete indifference. 'Oh, as usual,' he replied. 'This last week hasn't been a good one on account of the wretched weather. But I get on very well all the same. I no longer sleep, you know, so I can work, and if I have a little fever, why, it keeps me warm. Ah, there is so much to be done!'

He had again seated himself at his table, on which a book in the German language was lying open. 'I must apologise for sitting down,' said he; 'I remained up all night in order to read this book, which I received yesterday. A masterpiece, yes, the fruit of ten years' labour, ten years of the life of my master, Karl Marx. It is the treatise on Capital which he promised us so long ago. So now we here have our Bible.'

Saccard took a step forward to glance inquisitively at the book, but the sight of the Gothic characters at once repelled him. 'I shall wait until it is translated!' he exclaimed, laughing.

The young man shook his head as though to say that even when translated the book would be understood by few excepting the initiated. It was not a work of propaganda. But how wonderfully logical it was, with what a victorious abundance of proofs it showed that existing society, based upon the capitalistic system, would inevitably be destroyed! The ground clear, they would be able to rebuild.

'Then this is the sweep of the broom?' asked Saccard, still jesting.

'In theory, yes,' answered Sigismond. 'All that I one day explained to you, the whole evolution, is in these pages. It only remains for us to carry it out. And you are blind if you do not see the progress which the idea is already making every hour. Thus you, who, with your Universal, have stirred up and centralized hundreds of millions during the last three years, you really don't seem to suspect that you are leading us straight to Collectivism. I have followed your enterprise with passionate interest; yes, from this quiet out-of-the-way room I have studied its development day by day, and I know it as well as you do, and I say that you are giving us a famous lesson; for the collectivist State will only have to do what you are doing, expropriate you in bulk when you have expropriated the smaller capitalists in detail. And in this wise will be realised the

174

ambition of your huge dream, which is, I understand, to absorb all the capital in the world, to become the one bank, the one general warehouse of public wealth. Oh, I admire you very much; I would let you go on if I were the master, because you are beginning our work, like a forerunner of genius!'

Thereupon he smiled, with the pale smile of an invalid, as he noticed the attention of his questioner, who was very surprised to find him so familiar with the affairs of the day, and also very flattered by his intelligent praise. 'Only,' continued Sigismond, 'on the day when we expropriate you in the name of the nation, substituting for your private interests the interests of all, and transforming your great machine for sucking the blood of others into the regulator of social wealth, we shall begin by abolishing this.'

He had found a sou among the papers on his table and was holding it up between two fingers.

'Money!' exclaimed Saccard, 'abolish money! What fantastic madness!'

'We shall abolish coined money. Remember that metallic money will have no place, no *raison d'être* in a collectivist State. For purposes of remuneration we shall replace it by our labour notes, and if you look upon it as a measure of value we have another which will fulfil the same purpose, that which we shall obtain by determining the average day's labour in our workshops. This money, which masks and favours the exploitation of the workman, which enables people to rob him, by reducing his salary to the minimum sum which he must secure to avoid dying of hunger—this money must be destroyed. Is it not something frightful, this possession of money which creates a multitude of private fortunes, which prevents free and fruitful circulation, which begets scandalous sovereignties, makes a few men masters of both the financial market and social production? Each of our crises, all the anarchy of the time, come from that source. Money must be killed—yes, killed.'

Saccard grew angry, however. What! no more money, no more gold, no more of those shining stars which had illumined his life! In his eyes wealth had always taken the shape of bright new coins, raining like a spring shower amid the sunbeams, falling like hail upon the ground, and strewing it with heaps of silver, heaps of gold which were stirred with a shovel in order that one might have the pleasure of seeing them shine and hearing them jingle. And that gaiety, that incentive to effort and life, was to be abolished!

'It's idiotic, that is,' said he; 'yes, idiotic. It will never be done, you hear me.'

'Why never? Why idiotic? Do we use money in family life? In family economy you only find common effort and exchange. So of what use will money be when society shall have become one large family, governing itself?'

'I tell you that it is madness! Destroy money! Why, money is life itself! There would be nothing left, nothing!'

He was walking up and down, beside himself. And in this fit of passion, as he passed the window, he gave a glance outside as though to make sure that the Bourse was still there, for perhaps this terrible fellow had blown it down with a breath. But yes, it was still there, though very vague and dim in the depths of the twilight, looking, in fact, as if it were melting away under the rain, like a pale phantom Bourse on the point of vanishing into grey mist.

'However, it is stupid of me to discuss such a thing,' resumed Saccard. 'It is impossible. Abolish money! I should like to see you do it.'

175

'Bah!' murmured Sigismond, 'everything undergoes transformation and disappears. We already saw the form of wealth change when the value of land declined, and real estate, fields and forests became as nothing by the side of funded property, investments in State securities and industrial stocks and shares. And now this form of wealth is smitten with premature decay. Money was long considered to be worth its five per cent. per annum, but such is no longer the case; its value is steadily falling, so why should it not at last disappear, why should not a new form of wealth govern social relations? It is this wealth of to-morrow that our labour notes will bring.'

He had become absorbed in the contemplation of that sou, as if he dreamt that he held in his hand the last sou of the past ages, a sou that had outlived the defunct old time society. How many joys and how many tears had worn away the humble coin!

Then, growing sad as he thought of the seeming eternity of human desires, he resumed in a gentle voice: 'After all, you are right: we ourselves shall not see these things. It will take years and years. Can we even know whether the love of others will ever have sufficient vigour to take the place of egotism in the social organisation? Yet I had hoped for a nearer triumph. Ah, I should so much have liked to witness the dawn of justice!'

For a moment the bitterness born of the disease from which he suffered broke his voice. He who, in his denial of death, treated it as if it were not, made a gesture as if to brush it aside. And yet he was already resigned.

'I have performed my task,' said he; 'I shall, at all events, leave my notes, if I have not time to prepare the complete scheme of reconstruction which I dreamed of. The society of to-morrow must be the ripe fruit of civilisation, for if we do not retain the good features of emulation and control all will collapse. Ah, how clearly I can see that society even now, complete, such as I have managed to construct it after labouring through so many nights! All contingencies are foreseen; everything is solved; sovereign justice, absolute happiness, are ensured at last. It is all there—on paper, mathematical, final——'

His long, emaciated hands were straying among the papers on his table, and he grew quite excited, dreaming of the many milliards reconquered for humanity and equitably divided among all; of the joy and health which with a stroke of the pen he restored to suffering mankind, he who no longer ate, who no longer slept, but, without a want, was slowly dying in that bare room.

A harsh voice, however, suddenly made Saccard start. 'What are you doing here?'

It was Busch, who had just come back, and who in his perpetual fear that his brother might be sent into a fit of coughing by being made to talk too much was darting at his visitor the oblique glances of a jealous lover. However, he did not wait for Saccard's reply, but in a maternal, almost despairing fashion began to scold. 'What! you have let your fire go out again. Is there any sense in it, on such a cold damp day as this!'

And, already bending on his knees, despite the weight of his huge frame, he began breaking up some small wood and relighting the fire. Then he went to fetch a broom, swept up the litter, and saw to the medicine which his brother had to take every two hours. And it was only when he had prevailed on him to lie down on the bed to rest that he again became tranquil.

'If you will step into my office, Monsieur Saccard,' said he.

Madame Méchain was now there, seated on the only chair there was. She and Busch had just been down to make an important call, with the complete success of which they were delighted. At last, after a delay which had well-nigh driven them to despair, one of the affairs which they had most at heart had been set afoot again. For three years, indeed, La Méchain had been tramping the pavements in search of Léonie Cron, that girl in whose favour the late Count de Beauvilliers had signed an acknowledgment of ten thousand francs, payable on the day when she should attain her majority. Vainly had La Méchain applied to her cousin Fayeux, the dividend-collector at Vendôme, who had bought this acknowledgment for Busch in a lot of old debts belonging to the estate of a certain Charpier, a grain merchant and occasional usurer. Fayeux knew nothing, and simply wrote that Léonie Cron must be in the employ of a process-server in Paris; at all events, she had left Vendôme more than ten years before and had never returned, and it was impossible to obtain any information from any of her relatives, as they were all dead. La Méchain had managed to discover the process-server, and had even succeeded in tracing Léonie to a butcher's house, next to a fast woman's, and next to a dentist's; but then the thread abruptly broke, the scent was lost. It was like searching for a needle in a haystack. How can one hope to find a girl who has fallen, disappeared amid the mire of a great city like Paris? In vain had she tried the servants' agencies, visited the low lodging-houses, ransacked the haunts of vice, always on the watch, turning her head and questioning as soon as the name of Léonie fell upon her ears. And this girl, for whom she had searched so far, she had that very day, by chance, discovered in the Rue Feydeau itself, in a disreputable house, where she had called to hunt up an old tenant of the Cité de Naples who owed her three francs. A stroke of genius had led her to recognise the wench under the distinguished name of Léonide, and Busch, being notified, had at once returned with her to the house to negotiate. Stout, with coarse black hair falling to her eyebrows, and with a flat, flabby face, Léonie had at first surprised him; then, with a feeling of delight that she had fallen so low, he had offered her a thousand francs if she would relinquish to his hands her rights in the matter. She had accepted the offer with childish delight, like the simpleton she was; and by this means they would at last be able to carry out their scheme of hunting down the Countess de Beauvilliers. The long-searched-for weapon was in their grasp, a weapon hideous and shameful beyond their wildest hopes.

'I was expecting you, Monsieur Saccard,' said Busch. 'We have to talk. You received my letter, of course.'

Meantime La Méchain, motionless and silent, did not stir from the only chair in that little room, which was littered with papers and lighted by a smoky lamp. And Saccard, who had to remain standing and did not wish it to be supposed that he had come there in response to any threat, at once entered upon the Jordan matter in a stern, contemptuous voice.

'Excuse me,' said he, 'I came up to settle the debt of one of my contributors—little Jordan, a very nice fellow, whom you are pursuing with red-hot shot, indeed with really revolting ferocity. This very morning, it seems, you behaved towards his wife in a way in which no man of good breeding, would behave.'

Astonished at being attacked in this fashion when he was on the point of assuming offensive tactics himself, Busch lost his balance, forgot the other matter, and became irritated on account of this one. 'The Jordans!' said he; 'you have come on account of the Jordans. There is no question of any wife or any good breeding in matters of business. When people owe, they ought to pay, that is my rule. Scamps, who have been humbugging me for years past, from whom I have had the utmost trouble to extract

177

four hundred francs, copper by copper! Ah! thunder, yes! I will sell them up! I will throw them into the street to-morrow morning, if I don't have the three hundred and thirty francs and fifteen centimes which they still owe me upon my desk to-night!'

Thereupon, Saccard, in order to drive him quite wild, declared that he had already been paid his money forty times over, for the debt had certainly not cost him ten francs. These tactics succeeded, for Busch almost choked with anger. 'There it goes again! That is the only thing that any of you can find to say!' he exclaimed; 'and what about the costs, pray? This debt of three hundred francs which has increased to more than seven hundred? However, that does not concern me. When folks don't pay me, I prosecute. So much the worse if justice is expensive; it is their fault! But according to you, when I have bought a debt for ten francs, I ought to receive ten francs and no more! And what about my risks, pray, and all the running about that I have to perform, and my brain-work—yes, my intelligence? For instance, in this Jordan matter you can consult Madame, who is here. She has been attending to it. Ah, the journeys and the applications which she has made! She has worn out no end of shoe-leather in climbing the stairs of newspaper offices, where folks showed her the door as if she were a beggar, without ever giving her the address she wanted. Why, we have been nursing this affair for months, we have dreamed about it, we have been working on it as one of our masterpieces; it has cost me a tremendous sum, even if I only calculate the time spent over it at ten sous an hour!'

He was becoming excited, and with a sweeping gesture pointed to the papers that filled the room. 'I have here more than twenty millions of debts, of all ages, owed by people in all stations of life—some very small amounts, others very large ones. Will you pay a million for them? If so, I will willingly let you have them. When one thinks that there are some debtors whom I have been hunting for a quarter of a century! To obtain a few paltry hundred francs, and sometimes even less from them, I wait in patience for years until they become successful or inherit property. The others, the unknown and most numerous, sleep there—look! in that corner, where that huge heap is. That is chaos, or rather raw material, from which I must extract life—I mean my life, and Heaven alone knows after what an entanglement of search and worry! And when I at last catch one of these folks in a solvent condition, you expect me not to bleed him? But, come, you would think me a fool if I didn't do so; you would not be so stupid yourself!'

Without waiting to discuss the question any further, Saccard took out his pocket-book. 'I am going to give you two hundred francs,' said he, 'and you will give me the Jordan papers, with a receipt in full.'

Busch's exasperation made him start. 'Two hundred francs! Not if I know it! The amount is three hundred and thirty francs and fifteen centimes, and I want the centimes!'

But with the tranquil assurance of a man who knows the power which money has when it is spread out before one, Saccard, in a voice which neither rose nor fell, repeated: 'I am going to give you two hundred francs.'

Three times he spoke these words, and the Jew, convinced at heart that it would be sensible to compromise, ended by accepting the offer, but with a cry of rage and with tears starting from his eyes. 'I am too weak. What a wretched trade! Upon my word I am plundered, robbed. Go on while you are about it, don't restrain yourself, take some others too—yes, pick some out of the heap, for your two hundred francs.'

Then having signed a receipt and written a line to the process-server, for the papers were no longer at the office in the Rue Feydeau, Busch remained for a moment panting at his desk, so upset that he would have let Saccard then and there go off had it not been for La Méchain, who so far had neither made a gesture nor spoken a word.

'And the affair?' said she.

He suddenly remembered. He was going to take his revenge. But all that he had prepared, his narrative, his questions, the skilfully planned moves which were to make the interview take the course he desired, were swept away, forgotten in his haste to come to the brutal fact.

'The affair, true—I wrote to you, Monsieur Saccard. We now have an old account to settle together.'

He stretched out his hand to take the wrapper containing the Sicardot notes, and laid it open in front of him.

'In 1852,' he said, 'you stayed at a lodging-house in the Rue de la Harpe; you there signed twelve promissory notes of fifty francs each in favour of a girl of sixteen, Octavie Chavaille, whom you had ruined. Those notes are here. You have never paid a single one of them, for you went away without leaving any address before the first one matured. And the worst of it is you signed them with a false name, Sicardot, the name of your first wife.'

Very pale, Saccard listened and looked at him. In utter consternation he once more beheld the past, and it seemed as though some huge, shadowy, but crushing mass were falling upon him. In the fear of the first moment he quite lost his head, and stammered, 'How is it you know that? How did you get hold of those notes?'

Then, with trembling hands, he hastened to take out his pocket-book again, with the one thought of paying and regaining possession of those annoying papers. 'There are no costs, are there?' said he. 'It is six hundred francs. Oh! a good deal might be said, but I prefer to pay without discussion.'

And thereupon he tendered six bank-notes.

'By-and-by!' cried Busch, pushing back the money. 'I have not finished. Madame, whom you see there, is Octavie's cousin, and these papers are hers; it is in her name that I seek payment. That poor Octavie became a cripple, and had many misfortunes before she at last died at Madame's house in frightful poverty. If Madame chose, she could tell you things——'

'Terrible things!' emphasised La Méchain in her piping voice, breaking silence at last.

Saccard, quite scared, having forgotten her, turned and saw her sitting there all of a heap, like a half-empty wineskin. Bird of prey that she was with her shady trade in worthless securities, she had always made him feel uneasy, and now he found her mixed up in this unpleasant story.

'Undoubtedly, poor creature, it is very sad,' he murmured.

'But if she is dead, I really do not see——Here, at any rate, are the six hundred francs.'

A second time Busch refused to take the sum.

'Excuse me,' he said, 'you do not know all yet; she had a child. Yes, a child who is now in his fourteenth year—a child who so resembles you that you cannot deny him.'

'A child, a child!' Saccard repeated several times, quite thunderstruck.

Then, suddenly replacing the six bank-notes in his pocket-book, recovering his self-possession and becoming quite merry, he continued:

'But, I say, are you having a game with me? If there is a child, I shan't give you a copper! The little one is his mother's heir. He shall have the money and whatever more he wants besides. A child, indeed! Why, it makes me feel quite young again. Where is he? I must go to see him. Why didn't you bring him to me at once?'

In his turn stupefied, Busch now thought of how long he had hesitated and of the infinite pains that Madame Caroline had taken to hide Victor's existence from his father. And, quite nonplussed, he burst into complicated explanations, revealing everything—the six thousand francs claimed by La Méchain for keep and money lent, the two thousand which Madame Caroline had paid on account, the frightful instincts which Victor had displayed, and his removal to the Institute of Work. And at each fresh revelation Saccard gave a violent start. What! Six thousand francs, indeed! How was he to know, on the contrary, that they had not despoiled the little fellow? Two thousand francs on account! They had had the audacity to extort two thousand francs from a lady friend of his! Why, it was robbery, abuse of confidence! The little one, of course, had been brought up badly, and now he, Saccard, was expected to pay those who were responsible for his evil education! Did they take him to be a fool, then?

'Not a copper!' he cried. 'You hear me. You need not expect to get a copper from me!'

With a pale face, Busch rose and took his stand in front of his table. 'Well, we will see,' he exclaimed; 'I will drag you into court!'

'Don't talk nonsense. You know very well that the courts don't deal with such matters. And if you hope to blackmail me you deceive yourself, for I don't care one rap for anything you may say or do. A child! Why, I tell you it makes me feel quite proud!' Then, as La Méchain blocked up the doorway, he had to hustle her, climb over her in fact, in order to get out. She was suffocating, but managed to call to him in her flute-like voice as he went down the stairs, 'You rascal! You heartless wretch!'

'You shall hear from us,' howled Busch, shutting the door with a bang.

Such was Saccard's excitement that he gave his coachman orders to drive to the Rue Saint-Lazare at once. He was in a hurry to see Madame Caroline, whom he accosted without the slightest sign of embarrassment, at once scolding her for having given the two thousand francs. 'Why, my dear friend, one should never part with money in that fashion. Why did you act without consulting me?'

She, scared at finding that he knew the story at last, remained silent. It was really Busch's handwriting that she had recognised on that envelope, and now she had nothing more to hide, since another had just relieved her of the secret. Nevertheless, she still hesitated, in confusion for this man who questioned her so much at his ease.

'I wanted to spare you a chagrin,' she began. 'The poor child was in such a terrible state. I should have told you all long ago, but for a feeling——'

'What feeling? I confess that I do not understand you.'

She did not try to explain herself, to further excuse herself, invaded as she was by a feeling of sadness, of weariness with everything—she whom life usually found so courageous; while he, delighted, really rejuvenated, continued chattering.

'The poor little fellow! I shall be very fond of him, I assure you. You did quite right to take him to the Institute of Work, so that they might clean him up a little. But we will remove him from there and give him teachers. To-morrow I will go to see him— yes, to-morrow, if I am not too busy.'

The next day, however, there was a board meeting, and two days passed, and then a week, during which Saccard was unable to find a spare minute. He often spoke of the child, but kept on postponing his visit, always yielding to the overflowing river that carried him along.

In the early days of December, amidst the extraordinary fever to which the Bourse was still a prey, Universals had reached the price of two thousand seven hundred francs. Unfortunately, the alarming reports went on growing and spreading, and though the rise continued there was an intolerable feeling of uneasiness. The inevitable catastrophe was indeed openly predicted, and if the shares still went up— went up incessantly—it was by the force of one of those prodigious, obstinate infatuations which refuse to surrender to evidence. And Saccard now lived amid the glamour of his spurious triumph, with a halo around him as it were—a halo emanating from that shower of gold which he caused to rain upon Paris. Still, he was shrewd enough to feel that the soil beneath him was undermined, cracking, threatening to sink under his feet and swallow him up. And so, although he remained victorious after each settlement, he felt perfectly enraged with the 'bears,' whose losses must already be very heavy. What possessed those dirty Jews that they should fight on so tenaciously? Would he not soon annihilate them? And he was especially exasperated by the fact that, apart from Gundermann, who was playing his usual game, he could scent other sellers—soldiers of the Universal perhaps, traitors who, losing confidence, were going over to the enemy, all eagerness to realise their gains.

One day when Saccard was thus venting his displeasure in presence of Madame Caroline, she thought it her duty to tell him everything. 'You know, my friend,' said she, 'that I also have sold. Yes, I have just parted with our last thousand shares at the rate of two thousand seven hundred francs.'

He was overcome, as though confronted by the blackest of treasons. 'You have sold, you! you, my God!' he gasped.

She had taken hold of his hands and was pressing them, really grieved for him, but reminding him that she and her brother had long since warned him of their intention. Moreover, Hamelin, who was still at Rome, kept on writing to her in the most anxious strain about this exaggerated rise, which he could not understand, and which must be stopped, said he, even under penalty of tumbling into an abyss. Only the day before she had received a letter from him, giving her formal orders to sell. And so she had sold.

'You, you!' repeated Saccard; 'so it was you who were fighting me, you whom I felt in the dark! It is your shares that I have been obliged to buy up!'

He did not fly into a passion, as he usually did, and she suffered the more from his utter despondency; she would have liked to reason with him, to induce him to abandon that merciless struggle, which nothing but a massacre could terminate.

'Listen to me, my friend,' she said. 'Reflect that our three thousand shares have brought us more than seven millions and a half. Is not that an unhoped-for, an extravagant profit? Indeed, all this money frightens me, I cannot believe that it belongs to me. However, it is not our personal interest that is in question. Think of the interests of all those who have entrusted their fortunes in your hands, of all the millions which you are risking in the game. Why sustain that senseless rise? why stimulate it further? I hear people say on every hand that a catastrophe lies inevitably at the end of it all. You cannot keep on rising for ever; there is no shame in allowing the shares to revert to their real value, and, with the enterprise firm and stable, that will mean salvation.'

But he had already sprung to his feet.

'I mean that the quotations shall reach three thousand francs!' he cried. 'I have bought, and I will buy again, even if it kills me. Yes! may I burst and all burst with me, if I do not reach the figure of three thousand francs, and keep to it!'

After the settlement of December 15, Universals rose to two thousand eight hundred, and then to two thousand nine hundred francs. And on the 21st the quotation of three thousand and twenty francs was proclaimed at the Bourse, amid the uproar of an insane multitude. There was no longer any truth or logic in it all; the idea of value was perverted to the point of losing all real significance. A report was current that Gundermann, contrary to his prudent habits, had involved himself in frightful risks. For months he had been nursing a fall; and so each fortnight his losses had increased by leaps and bounds in proportion to the rise Indeed, people were beginning to whisper that his back might be broken after all. All brains were topsy-turvy; prodigies were expected.

And at that supreme moment, when Saccard, at the summit, felt the earth trembling under him, and secretly feared that he might fall, he was king. When his carriage reached the Rue de Londres, and drew up outside the triumphal palace of the Universal, a valet hastened down and spread out a carpet, which rolled across the footway from the vestibule steps to the gutter; and then Saccard condescended to alight from his brougham, and made his entrance into the Bank, like a sovereign, spared from treading on the common pavement of the streets.

CHAPTER X
THE BATTLE OF MILLIONS

That day, the last of the year, the day of the December settlement, the great hall of the Bourse was already full at half-past twelve o'clock, and the agitation as displayed by voice and gesture was extraordinary. For several weeks the effervescence had been increasing, and now came this last day of struggle with its feverish mob, through whose ranks the growl of conflict already sped, the growl of the decisive battle which was on the point of being fought. Out of doors there was a terrible frost; but the oblique rays of a clear winter's sun penetrated through the high windows, brightening the whole of one side of the bare hall with its severe-looking pillars and dreary arched roof, the cold aspect of which was increased by the grey allegorical paintings that decorated it. And from end to end of the arcades were the apertures of the air-stoves, disseminating warm breath amid the cold currents of air which were admitted by the grated doors ever and ever on the swing.

'Bear' Moser, looking even more anxious and yellow than usual, chanced to run against 'Bull' Pillerault, who stood in the hall, arrogantly planted on his long, heron-like legs. 'You know what they say,' began Moser. But he had to raise his voice in order to make himself heard amid the growing hubbub of conversation, a regular, monotonous rolling sound, like the clamour of overflowing water running on without cessation. 'They say that we shall have war in April. With all these formidable armaments matters cannot end otherwise. Germany won't leave us time to carry out the new Army Law which the Chamber is about to vote. And besides, Bismarck——'

Pillerault burst into a laugh. 'Oh, go to Jericho with your Bismarck! I myself had five minutes' conversation with him whilst he was here during the summer. He seemed a very pleasant fellow. If you are not satisfied with the crushing success of the Exhibition, what is it that you want? Why, my dear fellow, Europe is ours!'

182

Moser shook his head despondently, and again began venting his fears in sentences which were interrupted every second by the jostling of the crowd. The market might seem to be prosperous, but its prosperity was of a plethoric nature, of no more use than the surplus fat of those who are over-stout. Owing to the Exhibition, too many enterprises had sprouted up, people had become infatuated, and they were now reaching the pure madness of gambling. Take Universals, for instance; was it not madness to have run them up to such a price as three thousand and thirty francs?

'Ah, that's what you don't like!' exclaimed Pillerault; and, drawing nearer and emphasising every syllable, he continued: 'My dear fellow, we shall close this afternoon at three thousand and sixty. Mark my word, you fellows will all be knocked into a cocked hat.'

Although extremely impressionable, Moser indulged in a slight whistle of defiance. And to emphasise his pretended ease of mind he gazed up into the air, momentarily scrutinising a few women who, leaning over the railing of the gallery near the telegraph office, appeared greatly astonished by the aspect of this hall which they were not allowed to enter. Above them were scutcheons bearing the names of towns, and capitals and columns stretching away in pale perspective, which the infiltration of rain water had here and there stained yellow.

'What, is it you?' resumed Moser as, lowering his head, he recognised Salmon, who was standing before him, smiling his deep, eternal smile.

Then, quite disturbed, interpreting this smile as an approval of Pillerault's predictions, he resumed: 'Well, if you know anything, out with it. My reasoning is simple. I am with Gundermann because Gundermann, eh? is—Gundermann. Things always end well with *him*.'

'But how do you know that Gundermann is playing for a fall?' asked Pillerault with a sneer.

So scared was Moser by this question that his eyes dilated and started from his head. For months past it had been current gossip at the Bourse that Gundermann was watching Saccard, that he was fostering a fall in Universals pending the moment when, at the approach of some settling day, he would suddenly decide to strangle it by overwhelming the market with the weight of his millions. And so, if that last day of the year threatened to be so warm, it was because everybody believed and repeated that the battle was now at hand, one of those merciless battles in which one of the contending armies is left prostrate on the field, annihilated. However, can one ever be certain of anything in that sphere of falsehood and strategy? The surest things, the things prophesied with the most certainty, became, at the slightest breath, subjects of distressful doubt.

'You deny the evidence?' murmured Moser. 'To be sure, I haven't seen the orders, and one can assert nothing positively. What do you say, Salmon? Surely Gundermann cannot let go now!'

And he no longer knew what to believe at sight of the silent smile of Salmon, which seemed to him to grow keener and keener until it expressed extreme cunning.

'Ah!' he continued, protruding his chin in the direction of a stout man who was passing, 'if *he* would only speak, I should have no worry. He sees things clearly.'

It was the celebrated Amadieu, who still lived upon his success in the affair of the Selsis mines, the shares in which he had purchased at fifteen francs apiece in a fit of imbecile obstinacy, selling them later on at a profit of fifteen millions, the whole venture succeeding through pure luck without there having been either foresight or calculation on his part. He was nevertheless venerated for his great financial capacity; a whole court followed him, trying to catch his slightest words, and playing in the sense which they seemed to indicate.

'Bah!' exclaimed Pillerault, swayed by his favourite theory of recklessness, 'the best way, after all, is to follow one's idea, come what may. There is nothing but luck. A man is either lucky or unlucky. Well, then, he should not reflect. Every time that I have reflected, I have been nearly ruined. Look here! as long as I see that gentleman yonder at his post, looking as though he wants to devour everything, I shall go on buying.'

With a gesture, he had pointed to Saccard, who had just arrived and stationed himself in his usual place, against the pillar of the first arch on the left. In this wise, as was the case with all the managers of important establishments, his whereabouts was known. Clerks and customers knew for certain where to find him as soon as the Bourse opened. Gundermann, alone of all the chief financiers, affected never to set foot in the great hall; he did not even send an official representative thither; but one could divine the presence of an army which obeyed his command, so that, although absent, he nevertheless reigned as sovereign master, exercising authority through the legion of *remisiers* and brokers who brought his orders, to say nothing of his creatures, who were so numerous that you could never tell who might not be one of his mysterious soldiers. And it was against this indiscernible but ever active army that Saccard in person openly contended.

There was a bench behind him in the corner by the pillar, but he never sat down; treating fatigue with scorn, he remained standing during the two hours which the market lasted. In moments of unconstraint he would at the most rest his elbow against the stone-work, which, up to a height of five or six feet, had been darkened and polished by repeated rubbing; and, indeed, this was a characteristic feature of the dull, bare building, for on all sides, across the doors, along the walls and up the staircases, you perceived the same broad band of shiny dirt, a filthy 'dado' as it were, the accumulated sweat of generations of gamblers and thieves. And amidst these black-edged walls Saccard, in broadcloth and dazzling linen, scrupulously elegant, like all the *boursiers*, displayed the amiable, tranquil expression of a man who has no worry.

'You know,' said Moser, lowering his voice, 'it's said that he keeps up the rise by large purchases of stock. If the Universal gambles in its own shares, it is lost.'

Pillerault began protesting. 'More tittle-tattle!' said he. 'Can anybody say exactly who sells and who buys? As for Saccard, he's here for the customers of his Bank, which is only natural. And he's here, too, on his own private account, for I've no doubt he gambles with his own money.'

Moser did not insist. Nobody at the Bourse would, as yet, have ventured to say for certain what terrible game it was that Saccard was playing—the large purchases which he was making on behalf of the Bank under cover of men of straw, Sabatani, Jantrou and others, particularly employees of his establishment. Nothing but a rumour was current; a rumour whispered from ear to ear, contradicted of course, but ever reviving, though it was impossible to prove its accuracy. At first Saccard had only supported the quotations in a prudent way, as soon as possible reselling the stock which he purchased, so as to avoid tying-up too much capital and filling his coffers with shares. But now he was carried away by the struggle, and he had foreseen that it would be necessary to make very large purchases on this occasion if he wished to remain master of the battle-field. His orders were given, and he affected the smiling calmness of ordinary days, in spite both of his uncertainty as to the final result and of the worry

184

which he felt at thus proceeding farther and farther along a path which he knew to be frightfully dangerous.

All at once Moser, who had gone to prowl about behind the celebrated Amadieu, who was conferring with a little man with a hangdog look, came back very much excited, stammering: 'I have heard—heard with my own ears. He said that Gundermann's orders to sell exceeded ten millions. Oh, I shall sell, sell! I would sell even my shirt!'

'Ten millions! the devil!' murmured Pillerault, in a somewhat shaky voice. 'Then it is really war to the knife.'

And in the rolling clamour ever on the increase, swollen by all the private chats, there was nothing but talk of this ferocious duel between Gundermann and Saccard. The words were not to be distinguished, but the noise was made up of it; it was that alone that was growling so loud—talk of the calm, logical obstinacy which the one displayed in selling, of the feverish passion for buying of which the other was suspected. The contradictory rumours which were circulating, whispered at first, ended in trumpet-blasts. As soon as some opened their mouths, they shouted to make themselves heard amid the uproar; while others, full of mystery, leaned forward and whispered in the ears of their companions, even when they had nothing to say.

'Well, all the same, I shall keep to my arrangements and play for a rise!' resumed Pillerault, already strengthened in his opinions. 'With such a bright sunshine as this everything is bound to go up.'

'Come down, you mean,' retorted Moser with his doleful obstinacy. 'The rain isn't far off; I had an attack of my complaint last night.'

However, there was now so much sharpness about the smile of Salmon, who was listening to them in turn, that they both remained distrustful and annoyed. Could that devil of a fellow, so wonderfully smart, so deep, and so discreet, have discovered yet a third way of playing, something quite apart from either bulling or bearing?

Stationed in front of his pillar, Saccard meanwhile beheld the crowd of his flatterers and customers increasing around him. Hands were constantly being stretched out towards him, and he shook them all with the same felicitous readiness, each grasp of his fingers being instinct with a promise of triumph. Some people hastened up, exchanged a word with him, and then went off delighted. Many, however, persisted in staying, clung to him like leeches, quite vain that they should belong to his group. He often expended his amiability on persons whose names he could not remember. Thus he did not recognise Maugendre until Captain Chave had told him who he was. The Captain, now reconciled to his brother-in-law, was urging him to sell, but the pressure of Saccard's hand sufficed to inflame Maugendre with unlimited hope. Then there was Sédille, the member of the board, the great silk merchant who wanted a minute's private chat. His business was in jeopardy; his fortune was now so linked to the destinies of the Universal that if the quotations should start falling, as was possible, he would be ruined. And so, extremely anxious, devoured by his passion, having other worries, moreover, in connection with his son Gustave, who was not doing himself much good at Mazaud's, he felt the need of being reassured and encouraged. He spoke to Saccard, and the latter with a tap on the shoulder sent him off full of faith and ardour.

Then quite a procession set in—Kolb the banker, who had realised long since, but wished to remain friends with fortune; the Marquis de Bohain, who, with the haughty condescension of a *grand seigneur*, pretended that he frequented the Bourse out of mere curiosity and want of occupation; Huret, too, who had come to see if there were no more pickings to be made, for it was contrary to his nature to remain on bad terms with those who still breasted the current; he was far too supple to be otherwise than friendly with people, so long as they had not been swallowed up.

However, Daigremont put in an appearance, and thereupon all the others stepped aside. He was very powerful, and people noticed his amiability, the way in which he joked with Saccard with an air of trusting comradeship. The bulls were radiant, for he had the reputation of being an adroit man, who knew how to escape from houses as soon as the floorings began to crack; and this made it certain that the Universal was not yet cracking. And, finally, others moved to and fro, simply exchanging glances with Saccard—men in his service, the employees who were charged with giving orders, and who bought also on their own account, in the rage for gambling which, like an epidemic, was decimating the staff in the Rue de Londres, now always on the watch, with ears at every key-hole, on the hunt for tips.

In this wise Sabatani twice passed by, bearing himself with the effeminate grace of his semi-Oriental, semi-Italian nature, and pretending not even to see his patron; whilst a few steps away, Jantrou, standing motionless, with his back turned, seemed absorbed in reading the despatches from foreign money markets, posted there in grated frames. The *remisier* Massias, who, always on the run, jostled the group around Saccard, gave the latter a nod, as an answer doubtless respecting some commission which he had quickly executed. And as the opening hour approached, the endless tramping of the crowd, crossing the hall in either sense, filled it with the deep agitation and roar of a rising tide.

All were waiting for the first quotation.

Leaving the brokers' room, Mazaud and Jacoby had just come to the *corbeille* side by side, with an air of correct confraternity. Yet they knew each other to be adversaries in the merciless struggle which had been going on for weeks past, and which might end in the ruin of either one or the other of them. Mazaud, good-looking, short and slight of build, showed a gay vivacity, born of the good luck which had hitherto attended him, the luck by which he had inherited the business of his uncle at the early age of thirty-two; whilst Jacoby, a former managing clerk who had become a broker after long service, thanks to some customers who had financed him, had a huge belly and the heavy gait of a man of sixty. Tall, bald, and grizzled, he displayed the broad face of a good-natured fellow extremely fond of pleasure. And he and Mazaud, both with their note-books in their hands, began talking of the fine weather as though they had not held on the leaves of those books the millions with which they were going to attack each other in the destructive conflict between offer and demand.

'A fine frost, eh?'

'Yes, it was so delightful that I came on foot.'

Upon reaching the *corbeille*, the vast circular basin as yet unlittered by waste paper, they paused for a moment, leaning against the red velvet balustrade which encircled it, and continuing to exchange disjointed, commonplace remarks whilst darting stealthy glances around them.

Starting from the *corbeille* were four railed passages, so disposed that the whole formed a cross, or rather a four-pointed star of which the *corbeille* was the centre. These passages were sacred spots, to which the public was not admitted. In the spaces between them, in front of the*corbeille*, you perceived on one hand a compartment where the employees dealing with cash transactions were installed just under the three 'quoters,' who were perched upon high chairs behind huge registers; whilst, on the other hand, an open compartment, known from its shape, no doubt, as the 'Guitar,' enabled speculators and employees to place themselves in direct communication with the brokers. Behind the *corbeille*, in the space between the rear points of the star, was the crowded Rente market, where, as in the Cash department, each broker was represented by a special clerk; for the brokers themselves, disposed around the *corbeille*, were entirely absorbed by the great, savage business of gambling, and gave their personal attention to 'account' transactions exclusively.

Mazaud, however, seeing his authorised clerk Berthier making signs to him in the railed-off passage on his left hand, went to exchange a few words with him in a whisper. The authorised clerks alone had the privilege of entering these passages, and even then they had to keep at a respectful distance from the red velvet balustrade of the *corbeille*, which no profane hand was allowed to touch. Every day, on repairing to the Bourse, Mazaud was accompanied by Berthier and his Cash and Rente clerks, to whom the clearing-house clerk was often adjoined; to say nothing of the telegram clerk, Flory, whose beard was now overrunning his face to such a degree that little of his features excepting his soft lustrous eyes could be seen. Since winning ten thousand francs on the day after Sadowa, Flory, maddened by the demands of Mademoiselle Chuchu, who had become capricious and ravenous, had gambled wildly on his own account, calculating nothing himself, but ever watching Saccard's play, which he followed with blind faith. His acquaintance with the orders and telegrams which passed through his hands sufficed to guide him. And at this moment, having just run down from the telegraph office on the first floor, with both hands full of telegrams, he sent an attendant to call Mazaud, who left Berthier to come to the 'Guitar.'

'Am I to run through them and classify them to-day, monsieur,' asked Flory.

'Undoubtedly, if they are coming thus *en masse*. What are all those?'

'Oh, Universals—orders to buy, almost all.'

The broker, with a practised hand, turned the telegrams over, and was evidently well pleased. Very much involved with Saccard, whom he had long been carrying over for considerable sums, and from whom that very morning he had received orders to buy on a very large scale indeed, he had finally become the Universal's authorized broker. And, although so far not a prey to any great anxiety, he nevertheless felt relieved at noticing how persistent was the infatuation of the public, how obstinately people went on buying Universals in spite of the extravagance of the rise. One name particularly struck him, among those appended to the telegrams, that of Fayeux, the dividend-collector at Vendôme, who must have secured a vast number of petty buyers among the farmers, devotees, and priests of his province, for not a week passed but he thus sent orders after orders.

'Give those to the Cash-clerk,' said Mazaud to Flory. 'And don't wait for the telegrams to be brought down to you. Go up and wait, and bring them down yourself.'

Going at once to the Cash department, Flory leant over the balustrade, shouting, 'Mazaud! Mazaud!' at the top of his voice.

It was Gustave Sédille who approached, for employees lose their own names at the Bourse and take those of the brokers whom they represent. In this wise Flory himself was called Mazaud by the others. For two years Gustave Sédille had been out of the office, but he had lately returned to it in the hope of thereby inducing his father to pay his debts; and that afternoon, owing to the absence of the principal clerk, he found himself entrusted with the Cash-work, which amused him. Flory leant over to whisper in his ear, and they agreed between them that they would only effect the purchases for Fayeux at the last quotation, after using his orders for a private gamble of their own, first buying and then selling in the name of their usual man of straw, so as to pocket the difference, for a rise seemed to them to be certain.

Meantime Mazaud went back towards the *corbeille*. But at every step an attendant handed him a *fiche* on which an order had been scribbled in pencil by some customer who had been unable to approach. For these *fiches* each broker had his own special colour—red, yellow, blue or green—so that he might easily recognise them. Mazaud's were green, the colour of hope; and the little slips kept on accumulating between his fingers as the attendants continually went to and fro, taking them, at the end of the railed passages, from the employees and speculators who, in order to save time, were each provided with a supply of the little cards.

As Mazaud halted once more in front of the velvet-topped balustrade he again came upon Jacoby, who also carried a handful of *fiches*, red ones, the hue of freshly shed blood. These undoubtedly were orders from Gundermann and his followers, for everybody was aware that in the massacre now being prepared Jacoby would be the broker of the 'bears,' the executioner-in-chief of the Israelite banking world. He was at present listening to another broker, his brother-in-law, Delarocque, a Christian who had married a Jewess, a very bald, stout, thick-set, florid man, partial to clubland and known to receive the orders of Daigremont, who had lately fallen out with Jacoby as he had formerly fallen out with Mazaud. The story which Delarocque was telling—a story of equivocal character—lighted up his little blinking eyes, while he waved, in passionate pantomime, his memorandum-book, from which protruded his package of *fiches*, which were blue, the soft blue of an April sky.

'Monsieur Massias is asking for you,' an attendant came to say to Mazaud.

The latter quickly returned to the end of the railed passage. The *remisier*, now completely in the pay of the Universal, had brought Mazaud news from the *coulisse*, which had already begun business under the peristyle in spite of the terrible cold. A few speculators ventured to show themselves there, but went to warm themselves in the hall every now and then; whereas the *coulissiers*, wrapped in heavy overcoats, with their fur collars turned up, bravely kept their places in a circle, as usual, underneath the clock, and growing so animated, shouting and gesticulating so vehemently that they did not feel the cold. And one of the most active was little Nathansohn, now in a fair way to become a man of importance, for luck had favoured him since the day when, resigning his position as a mere petty clerk at the Crédit Mobilier, he had had the idea of renting a room and opening a wicket.

Speaking rapidly, Massias explained to Mazaud that, as prices seemed to have a downward tendency under the weight of the shares with which the 'bears' were overwhelming the market, Saccard had just had the idea of operating at the *coulisse*, in order to influence the official opening quotation at the *corbeille*. Universals had closed the day before at three thousand and thirty francs; and he had given an order to Nathansohn to buy a hundred shares, which another *coulissier* was to offer at three thousand and thirty-five. This would be a rise of five francs.

'All right! the quotation will reach us;' said Mazaud.

And he came back to the groups of brokers, who had now mustered in full force. There were sixty of them all told, and, in spite of the regulations, they were already doing business among themselves, at the mean quotation of the day before, whilst waiting for the ringing of the bell. Orders given at a predetermined fixed rate did not influence the market, since it was necessary to wait until this rate should be quoted; it was the orders to buy or sell on the best terms available, the execution of which was left to the broker's judgment, that provoked the continual oscillations in one or the other sense. A good broker should be possessed of shrewdness and foresight, a quick head, and agile muscles—for rapidity often ensures success—to say nothing of the necessity of having a good connection in the banking world, of securing information from all parts, and particularly of being the first to receive telegrams from the provincial and foreign money markets. And in addition to all this, a strong voice is needed, in order to be able to shout loudly.

One o'clock struck, however; the peal of the bell passed like a gust of wind over the surging sea of heads, and the last vibration had not died away when Jacoby, with both hands resting on the velvet-covered handrail, shouted in a roaring voice, the loudest of the whole corporation of stockbrokers: 'I have Universals! I have Universals!'

He did not name any price, but waited to be interrogated. The sixty brokers had drawn near and formed a circle around the *corbeille*, where a few *fiches*, just thrown away, had already set spots of bright colour. Face to face, the brokers, like duellists at the outset of a fray, scrutinised one another, eager to see the first quotation established.

'I have Universals!' repeated Jacoby in his deep, thundering voice: 'I have Universals!'

'What price Universals?' asked Mazaud, in a voice which, albeit thin, was so shrill that it dominated his colleague's in the same way as the strain of a flute rises above a violoncello accompaniment.

Delarocque proposed the last quotation of the previous day. 'At three thousand and thirty I take Universals!' he bawled.

But another broker at once intervened with a higher bid: 'At three thousand and thirty-five deliver Universals!'

This was the *coulisse* price, just coming in and preventing the deal which Delarocque had doubtless intended to make: a purchase at the *corbeille* and a prompt sale at the *coulisse*, so as to secure the five francs' rise.

Accordingly, Mazaud, feeling certain that Saccard would approve of it, made up his mind to carry matters further. 'At three thousand and forty I take! Deliver Universals at three thousand and forty!'

'How many?' asked Jacoby.

'Three hundred.'

Both wrote a line in their memorandum-books, and the bargain was concluded; the first official quotation was established, with a rise of ten francs over the quotation of the day before. Mazaud stepped aside, to give the figure to the quoter who had the Universal on his register. Then, for twenty minutes, there was a perfect flood-gate opened: the quotations of other stocks were likewise established; all the business which the brokers had in hand was transacted without any great variations in prices. And meanwhile the quoters, perched aloft, between the uproar of the *corbeille* and that of the Cash market, which was also feverishly busy, were scarce able to make entries of all the new figures thrown at them by the brokers and the clerks. In the rear, the Rente market was simply raging. Since the opening of the market there was no longer the mere roar of the crowd, similar to the continuous sound of flowing waters, for above all this formidable rumbling there now rose the discordant cries of offer and demand, a characteristic yelping, which rose, and fell, and paused, to begin again in unequal, grating accents, like the cries of birds of pillage in a tempest.

With a smile on his face, Saccard still stood near his pillar. His court had grown yet larger; the rise of ten francs in Universals had just filled the Bourse with excitement, for it had long been predicted that on settling day there would be a crash. Huret had approached with Sédille and Kolb, pretending to regret his prudence, which had led him to sell his shares at the price of twenty-five hundred francs; while Daigremont, wearing an air of unconcern, as he walked about arm-in-arm with the Marquis de Bohain, gaily explained to him why it was that his stable had been defeated at the autumn races. But, above all, Maugendre triumphed, and sought to overwhelm Captain Chave, who persisted nevertheless in his pessimism, saying it was necessary to await the end, which he still believed would be disaster. A similar scene was enacted by the boastful Pillerault and the melancholy Moser, the former radiant over this insane rise, the latter clenching his fists and talking of this stubborn, foolish rise as of some mad animal which, whatever its efforts might be, was certain to be slaughtered eventually.

An hour went by, the quotations remaining much the same; transactions went on at the *corbeille* in proportion as fresh orders were given or fresh telegrams arrived. Business was less brisk, however, than at the outset. Towards the middle of each day's Bourse there is a similar lull in the transactions, a spell of calmness prior to the decisive struggle over the last quotations. Nevertheless, Jacoby's roar and Mazaud's shrill notes were always to be heard, both brokers being very busy with 'options.'

'I have Universals at three thousand and forty, of which fifteen!' shouted one.

'I take Universals at three thousand and forty, of which ten,' replied the other.

'How many?'

'Twenty-five—deliver!'

Mazaud was doubtless now executing some of the orders received from Fayeux. Many provincial gamblers, with a view to limiting their losses, buy and sell on option before venturing to launch out into obligatory transactions. However, all at once a rumour spread and spasmodic shouts arose. There had just been a fall of five francs in Universals, and then in swift succession came another and another drop, so that the price became three thousand and twenty-five.

Jantrou, who had just come back after a short absence, was just then whispering to Saccard that the Baroness Sandorff was in her brougham in the Rue Brongniart, and desired to know whether she ought to sell. Coming at the very moment of the fall, this question fairly exasperated Saccard. In his mind's eye he could see the coachman perched motionless upon his box, whilst inside the carriage, the windows of which were closed, sat the Baroness, consulting her memorandum-book as though at home.

'Let her go to Jericho!' he answered; 'and if she sells, I'll strangle her!'

He had scarcely spoken when, at the announcement of the fall of fifteen francs, Massias came running up as if in response to an alarm-bell, feeling that his services would certainly be required. And indeed Saccard, who had prepared a skilful move for forcing up the last quotations—a telegram which was to be sent from the Lyons Bourse, where a rise was certain—had begun to feel rather anxious at the telegram's non-arrival, for this precipitate drop of fifteen francs might bring about a disaster.

Like a shrewd fellow, Massias did not stop in front of him, but nudged his elbow as he passed, and, eagerly lending ear, at once received his orders: 'Quick, to Nathansohn; four hundred, five hundred, whatever may be necessary!'

This was all managed so swiftly that Pillerault and Moser were the only ones to notice it. They started after Massias, in order to find out his intentions. Now that he was in the pay of the Universal, the *remisier* had acquired great importance. People tried to 'pump' him, to read over his shoulder the orders which he received. And he himself now made superb profits. This smiling, good-natured, unlucky fellow, whom fortune had previously treated so harshly, was astonished by his present success, and declared that this dog's life at the Bourse was endurable after all. He no longer said that a man must needs be a Jew in order to make his way.

At the *coulisse*, in the freezing air which swept through the peristyle, and which the pale afternoon sun did little to warm, Universals had fallen less rapidly than at the *corbeille*. And Nathansohn, warned by his acolytes, had just executed the deal which Delarocque had been unable to effect at the opening: buying in the hall at three thousand and twenty-five, he had sold again under the colonnade at three thousand and thirty-five. This did not take three minutes, and he made sixty thousand francs by the stroke. The purchase at the *corbeille* had already sent the shares up again to three thousand and thirty, by that balancing effect which the authorized and tolerated markets have one upon another. From the hall to the peristyle there was an incessant gallop of clerks, elbowing their way through the crowd with orders. Nevertheless, prices were about to weaken at the *coulisse*, when the order which Massias brought Nathansohn sustained them at three thousand and thirty-five, and even raised them to three thousand and forty; the consequence being that at the *corbeille* the stock again rose to the opening quotation. However, it was difficult to maintain that figure; for evidently enough the tactics of Jacoby and the other 'bear' brokers were to reserve the large sales until the last half-hour, when, amid the confusion, they hoped to overwhelm the market with them and precipitate a collapse.

Saccard understood the danger so clearly that he made a preconcerted sign to Sabatani, who was standing a few steps away, smoking a cigarette with the unconcerned, languid air of a ladies' man. And on observing his patron's signal he at once slipped through the crowd, with all the suppleness of a snake, and made his way to the 'Guitar,' whence, with his ears on the alert, ever attentive to the quotations, he did not cease sending Mazaud orders inscribed upon green *fiches*, of which he held a large supply. None the less, however, so determined was the attack of the 'bears' that Universals again fell five francs.

The third quarter of the hour struck. Another fifteen minutes and the closing bell would ring out. The throng was now whirling and shrieking as if scourged by some hellish torment. Grating, discordant sounds, as though a quantity of copper-ware was being broken up, rang out from the snarling, howling *corbeille*. And at that moment occurred the incident so anxiously awaited by Saccard.

Little Flory, who ever since the opening of the Bourse had been coming down from the telegraph-office every ten minutes with his hands full of telegrams, once more reappeared, forcing his way through the mob, and this time reading a telegram which seemed to delight him.

'Mazaud! Mazaud!' called a voice; and Flory naturally turned his head, as if answering to his own name. It was Jantrou, who wanted to know the news. The clerk was in too great a hurry, however, and at once pushed him aside, full of delight at the thought that Universals would end with a rise; for the telegram announced that the shares were going up at the Lyons Bourse, where the purchases were so large that the effect would necessarily be felt on the Bourse of Paris. And, indeed, other telegrams were now arriving; a large number of brokers were receiving orders. This produced an immediate and important result.

'At three thousand and forty I take Universals!' repeated Mazaud, in his shrill, angry voice.

Thereupon Delarocque, overwhelmed with orders, made a higher bid. 'At three thousand and forty-five I take!'

'I hold at three thousand and forty-five!' bellowed Jacoby. 'Two hundred at three thousand and forty-five!'

'Deliver!'

Then Mazaud himself made a higher offer: 'I take at three thousand and fifty!'

'How many?'

'Five hundred. Deliver!'

However, the frightful hubbub had reached such a pitch, amidst so much epileptical gesticulation, that the brokers themselves could no longer hear each other. And, since the cavernous bass voices of some of them miscarried, while the fluty notes of others thinned out into nothingness, they continued in their professional fury to do business by gestures. Huge mouths were seen to open, from which no distinct sound apparently came, and hands alone spoke—a gesture from the person implying an offer, another gesture towards the person signifying acceptance; whilst raised fingers indicated the quantities, and yes and no were expressed by a nod or shake of the head. Intelligible only to the initiated, this sign-making seemed like one of those attacks of madness which fall upon crowds. In the gallery of the telegraph-office up above women were leaning over, in astonishment and fear at the extraordinary spectacle. One might have thought that a brawl was in progress at the Rente market, where a central group seemed to be furiously resorting to fisticuffs; while the other groups, ever being displaced by the public traversing this part of the hall in either direction, kept on breaking up and forming again in continual eddies. Between the Cash market and the *corbeille*, above the wild tempestuous sea of heads, one now only saw the three quoters, perched on their high chairs, floating on the billows like waifs, with their great white registers before them, and thrown now to left, now to right, by the rapid fluctuations of the quotations hurled at them. Inside the Cash market, where the scramble was at its height, you beheld a compact mass of hairy heads; no faces were to be seen; there was nothing but a dark swarming, relieved only by the small white leaves of the memorandum-books waved in the air. And at the *corbeille*, around the basin which the crumpled *fiches* now filled with a blossoming of divers colours, men's hair was turning gray, bald pates were glistening, you could distinguish the pallor of shaken faces and of hands feverishly outstretched—all the jerky pantomime of speculators, seemingly ready to devour each other if the balustrade had not restrained them. This rage of the last minutes had, moreover, gained the public; men crushed against each other in the hall; there was an incessant sonorous tramping, all the helter-skelter of a huge mob let loose in too narrow a passage; and above the undefined mass of frock-coats, silk hats were shining in the diffused light that fell from the high windows.

But all at once the peal of a bell pierced through the tumult. Everything became quiet; gestures were arrested, voices hushed at the Cash market, the Rente market, the *corbeille*. There remained only the muffled rumbling of the mob, sounding like the continuous voice of a torrent returning to its bed and again following its course. And amidst this persistent if subdued agitation, the last quotations circulated. Universals had reached three thousand and sixty, a rise of thirty francs above the quotation of the day before. The rout of the 'bears' was complete; once more the settlement would prove a disastrous one for them, for large sums would be required to pay the fortnight's differences.

For a moment, Saccard, before leaving the hall, straightened himself to his full height, as if the better to survey the crowd around him. He had really grown so magnified by his triumph that all his little person expanded, lengthened, became enormous. And the man whom he seemed to be thus seeking over the heads of the crowd was the absent Gundermann—Gundermann, whom he would have liked to have seen struck down, grimacing, asking pardon; and he was determined at least that all the Jew's unknown creatures, all the vile Israelites who were there, morose and spiteful, should see him transfigured in the glory of his success. It was his grand day, the day which people still speak of, as they speak of Austerlitz and Marengo. His customers, his friends, had darted towards him. The Marquis de Bohain, Sédille, Kolb, Huret, shook both his hands; while Daigremont, with the false smile of his worldly amiability, proceeded to compliment him, albeit well aware that one is ofttimes killed by such victories at the Bourse. Maugendre could have kissed him on both cheeks, such was his exultation, an exultation tinged with anger, however, when he saw Captain Chave continue to shrug his shoulders. But the perfect, religious adoration was that of Dejoie, who, coming from the newspaper office on the run, in order to ascertain the last quotation at the earliest moment, was standing a few steps away, motionless, rooted to the spot by affection and admiration, his eyes glittering with tears. Jantrou had disappeared, undoubtedly to carry the news to the Baroness Sandorff. Massias and Sabatani were panting, radiant, as on the triumphal evening of a great battle.

'Well, what did I tell you?' cried Pillerault, delighted.

Pulling a very long face, Moser growled out some sullen threats.

'Yes, yes,' said he; 'don't holloa till you are out of the wood. There's the Mexican bill to pay; there are the affairs of Rome, which have become still more entangled since Mentana; and then one of these fine mornings Germany will fall on us. Yes, yes, and to think that those imbeciles keep going up and up, in order, no doubt, that they may fall from a greater height! Ah! it is all over, you'll soon see!'

Then, as Salmon, who was looking at him, remained grave this time, he added: 'Such is your opinion, too, is it not? When things go too well a crash is generally at hand.'

Meanwhile the hall was emptying; there would soon be nothing left in the air but the cigar-smoke, a bluish cloud, thickened and yellowed by all the flying dust. Mazaud and Jacoby, resuming their prim deportment, had gone back into the brokers' room together, the latter more worried by his secret private losses than by the defeat of his customers; while the former, who did not gamble, was filled with delight at the gallant way in which the last quotation had been carried. They talked for a few minutes with Delarocque in order to exchange engagements, still holding their memorandum-books, full of notes, which their settlement clerks would classify that afternoon, in order to debit or credit the various customers with the transactions that had been effected. Meantime, in the clerks' hall—a low, pillared hall, looking not unlike an ill-kept school-room, with its rows of desks and a cloak-room at the farther end—Flory and Gustave Sédille, who had gone there to get their hats, began noisily rejoicing while waiting to know the mean quotation, which the employees of the syndicate, taking the highest and lowest quotations, were now calculating at one of the desks. Towards half-past three, when the placard had been posted on a pillar, Flory and Gustave neighed, and clucked, and crowed, in their satisfaction with the fine result of their deal in Fayeux' orders to purchase. This meant a pair of solitaires for Chuchu, who was now tyrannising Flory with her demands, and six months' allowance in advance for Gustave's *inamorata*. Meantime the uproar continued in the clerks' hall, what with a succession of silly farces, a massacre of hats, and jostling such as that of school-boys just released from their lessons. And, on the other side, under the peristyle, the *coulisse* completed various transactions; while Nathansohn, delighted with his deal, wended his way down the steps through the ranks of the last speculators, who were still hanging about in spite of the cold, which had become terrible. By six o'clock all these gamblers, brokers, *coulissiers*, and *remisiers*, after calculating their gain or loss, or preparing their brokerage bills, had gone home to dress, in order to wind up the day with relaxation in restaurants, theatres, fashionable drawing-rooms, or cosy boudoirs.

That evening, the one subject of conversation among those Parisians who sit up and amuse themselves was the formidable duel upon which Gundermann and Saccard had entered. The women, whom passion and fashion had entirely given over to gambling, made a show of using such technical terms as settlement, options, carry over, and close—without always understanding them. They talked especially of the critical position of the 'bears,' who, for many months, had been paying larger and larger differences at each settlement in proportion as Universals went up and up beyond all reasonable limits. Certainly, many were gambling without cover, getting their brokers to carry them over, as they were altogether unable to deliver; and they kept on at it, still and ever playing for a fall, in the hope that the collapse of the shares was near at hand; but, in spite of all the carrying over—the charges for which increased as money became more and more scarce—it seemed as if the already exhausted 'bears' would be annihilated if the rise continued much longer. The situation of Gundermann, who was reputed to be their chief, was different, since he had his milliard in his cellars—an inexhaustible supply of money which he could keep on sending to the massacre, however long and murderous the campaign might be. That was the invincible force: the power to keep on selling, with the certainty of being always able to pay his differences, until the day of the inevitable fall came and brought him victory.

People talked and calculated the considerable sums which he must have already parted with, the sacks of gold which he had had to bring to the front on the fifteenth and thirtieth of each month, and which had melted away in the fire of speculation like ranks of soldiers swept away by bullets. Never before had he sustained at the Bourse such a severe attack upon his power, which he wished to be sovereign, indisputable; for if, as he was fond of repeating, he was a simple money merchant, and not a gambler, he was on the other hand fully conscious that, to remain this merchant, the first of the world, disposing of public fortune, he must also be absolute master of the market; and he was fighting, not for immediate profit, but for his royalty itself, for his life. Hence the cold obstinacy, the grim grandeur of the struggle. He was to be met upon the Boulevards and in the Rue Vivienne, walking with the step of an exhausted old man, his face pale and impassive, nothing in him betraying the slightest anxiety. He believed only in logic. Madness had set in when Universals had risen above two thousand francs; to quote them at three thousand was sheer insanity; they were bound to fall, even as the stone thrown into the air inevitably falls to the ground; and so he waited. Would he go on with the game even to the end of his milliard? People trembled with admiration around him, with the desire also to see him devoured at last; while Saccard, who excited a more tumultuous enthusiasm, on his side had the women, the drawing-rooms, the whole fashionable world of gamblers, who had pocketed such handsome sums since they had begun coining money with their faith, trafficking with Mount Carmel and Jerusalem. The approaching ruin of the big Jew bankers was decreed; Catholicism was about to acquire the empire of money, as it had acquired that of souls. Only, although his troops were winning heavily, Saccard himself was getting to the end of his cash, emptying his vaults for his continual purchases. Of the two hundred millions at his disposal nearly two-thirds had thus been tied up, so that his triumph was an asphyxiating one, a triumph which suffocates. Every company that seeks to become mistress at the Bourse, in order to sustain the price of its shares, is doomed. For that reason he had only intervened with prudence in the earlier stages. But he had always been a man of imagination, seeing things on too grand a scale, transforming his shady dealings as an adventurer into poems; and this time, with this really colossal and prosperous enterprise, he had been carried off into extravagant dreams of conquest, to so crazy, so vast an idea, that he did not even clearly formulate it to himself. Ah! if he had only had millions, endless millions, like those dirty Jews! The worst was that he already saw his troops coming to an end; he had but a few more millions for the massacre. Then, if the fall should come, it would be his turn to pay differences; and he would be obliged to get someone to carry him over. Despite his victory, the smallest bit of gravel must upset his vast machine. There was a secret consciousness of this, even among the faithful, those who believed in the rise as in the Divinity. And Paris was impassioned the more by this, by the confusion and doubt amid which it tossed, in this duel between Saccard and Gundermann—this duel in which the conqueror would lose all his blood, this hand-to-hand struggle between two superhuman monsters, who crushed between them the poor devils who risked following their game, and seemed likely to strangle one another at last on the heap of ruins which they were accumulating.

All at once, on January 3, on the very morrow of the day when the accounts of the last settlement had been balanced, there was a drop of fifty francs in Universals. This caused great excitement. In truth, everything had gone down; the market, so long over-taxed, inflated beyond measure, was giving way in every direction; two or three rotten enterprises had collapsed with a bang, and, moreover, people ought to have been accustomed to these violent fluctuations, since prices sometimes varied several hundred francs in the same day's Bourse, shifting wildly like the needle of the compass in the midst of a storm. In the great quiver which passed, however, all felt the beginning of the crash. Universals were going down; the cry rose and spread with a clamour, made up of astonishment, hope, and fear.

The next day Saccard, firm and smiling at his post, sent the price up thirty francs by means of large purchases. But on the 5th, despite his efforts, the fall was forty francs. Universals stood merely at three thousand. And from that time each day brought its battle. On the 6th Universals went up again; on the 7th and 8th they again dropped. An irresistible movement was dragging them, little by little, into a slow fall. The Bank was about to be made the scapegoat, offered up in atonement for the folly of all, for the misdeeds of less prominent ventures, all that swarm of shady enterprises, ripened by puffery, raised like monstrous mushrooms in the fermenting compost of the reign. But Saccard, who no longer slept, who every afternoon took up his post of combat, near his pillar, lived in the hallucination of always possible victory. Like the commander of an army who is convinced of the excellence of his plans, he yielded his ground only step by step, sacrificing his last soldiers, emptying the Bank's coffers of their last sacks of money, to obstruct the progress of the assailants.

On the 9th he again won a signal advantage, and the 'bears' trembled and recoiled. Would the settlement of the 15th, like so many before it, be effected at their expense? And he, already without resources, reduced to launching paper into circulation, now dared, like those starving wretches who, in the delirium of their hunger, see immense feasts spread out before them, dared confess to himself the prodigious and impossible object towards which he was tending, the giant idea of repurchasing all the Bank's shares in order to hold all vendors bound hand and foot at his mercy. This had just been done in the case of a little railway company; the Bank which had issued its stock having cleared the market, so that vendors, being unable to deliver, had been forced to surrender as slaves and humbly offer their fortunes and their persons. Ah! if he could only have hunted down Gundermann to such a point as to hold him powerless, unable to sell since he could not deliver! If he could only have seen the Jew bringing him his milliard one morning, and begging him not to take the whole of it, but to leave him enough to buy the half franc's worth of milk which constituted his daily nourishment. But from seven to eight hundred millions would be necessary for such a feat as that. He had already cast two hundred into the abyss; and if he was to succeed, five or six hundred more must be marshalled in battle array. Yes, with six hundred millions he would sweep away the Jews, become the gold king, the master of the world. What a dream! And it seemed so simple; his fever had reached such a degree of intensity that it all appeared a mere question of moving some pawns on a chess-board. During his sleepless nights he raised this army of six hundred millions, and, after sending it forth to fight and be destroyed for his glory, at last found himself victorious, environed by general disaster, and erect upon the ruins of everything.

Unfortunately, on the 10th, Saccard had a terrible day. He was always superbly gay and calm at the Bourse; and yet never had there been such a war of silent ferocity, of hourly slaughter, of ambuscades upon every side. In these secret, cowardly money battles, in which the weak are ripped up in silence, the combatants are influenced by no ties, whether of relationship or friendship. The atrocious law of might prevails, and men devour those around them for fear lest they should themselves be devoured. And thus Saccard felt that he was absolutely alone, with no other support than that of his insatiable appetite, which still kept him erect and ever ravenous.

He especially dreaded the afternoon of the 14th, when the answers on the options would come in. However, he still found money enough for the three preceding days, and instead of bringing a smash-up the 14th strengthened Universals, so that on the morrow, the 15th, which was settling day, they were quoted at two thousand nine hundred and sixty francs, or only a hundred francs below the quotation of December 31. Saccard had feared a perfect disaster, and he pretended to construe this as a victory. In reality, success for the first time rested with the 'bears,' who now received differences after paying them during several months; and, the situation being reversed, Saccard had to get Mazaud to carry him over. From that time the broker found himself heavily involved. The second fortnight of January threatened to prove decisive.

Since he had been struggling in this way amid these daily ups and downs, now falling into the abyss and again rising from it, Saccard had every evening felt an uncontrollable desire for diversion, something which should enable him to shake off his worries, forget the precarious nature of his position. He could not remain alone, but dined out and showed himself everywhere, making the round of the theatres and swell supper-rooms, and affecting the extravagance of a man who has more money than he can spend. He avoided Madame Caroline, whose remonstrances embarrassed him, and who, besides always speaking of the anxious letters which she received from her brother, was herself in despair at the game he was playing, thinking it frightfully dangerous. And he now more frequently saw the Baroness Sandorff at a little place he had taken in the Rue Caumartin, in this wise obtaining the hour of forgetfulness which was necessary for the relaxation of his tired, overworked brain. Sometimes, also, he took refuge there to examine certain papers and reflect upon certain affairs, happy in the thought that no one would come to disturb him. And then sleep would overtake him there; he would doze off for an hour or two, and then the Baroness would not scruple to search his pockets and read the letters in his pocket-book; for he had become completely dumb, she could no longer extract the smallest piece of useful information from him, and, moreover, even when she did contrive to wring a word or two from him, she felt so convinced that he was lying to her that she did not dare to play in accordance with his indications. And while thus stealing his secrets she discovered the pecuniary embarrassment in which the Universal was now beginning to struggle—a vast system of kite-flying, of raising the wind by means of accommodation paper, which it was cautiously getting discounted abroad. One evening, however, Saccard, waking up too soon, had caught her in the act of searching his pocket-book, and had then and there boxed her ears. And subsequently in his moments of worry he took to beating her, by way of relieving his feelings.

However, after the settlement of January 15, in which she had lost ten thousand francs, the Baroness began to nurse a project of treachery. It grew upon her, and at last she went to consult Jantrou about it.

'Well,' the latter answered, 'I believe that you are right; it is time to pass over to Gundermann. So go and see him, and tell him of the matter, since he promised that, on the day when you should bring him some good counsel, he would give you some in exchange.'

On the morning when the Baroness presented herself in the Rue de Provence, Gundermann was as surly as a bear. Only the day before Universals had gone up again. Would he never end, then, with that voracious beast, which had devoured so much of his gold and so obstinately clung to life? That wretched Bank was capable of recovering its position, and its shares would perhaps be on the rise again at the end of the month. He growled at himself for having entered upon this disastrous rivalry, when perhaps he would have done better to have taken a share in the new establishment at the start. Shaken in his ordinary tactics, losing his faith in the inevitable triumph of logic, he would at that moment have resigned himself to a retreat, if he could have effected it without loss. These moments of discouragement, which even the greatest captains at times experience on the very eve of victory, when men and things are really plotting their success, were very rare with Gundermann. If his powerful perceptive powers, usually so clear, were thus disturbed, it was due to the fog that at times envelopes the mysterious operations of the Bourse, which one can never with absolute certainty ascribe to any particular person. Certainly Saccard was buying, gambling; but was he acting for serious customers or for the Bank itself? Upon this point Gundermann could not make up his mind amid all the contradictory gossip which was brought to him. So he was in a rage, and that morning the doors of his spacious office kept slamming, all his employees trembled, and he received the *remisiers* so brutally that their customary procession was turned into a galloping rout.

'Ah! it is you!' he said to the Baroness, without any pretence at politeness. 'I have no time to lose with women to-day.'

She was so disconcerted that she dropped all the preliminaries which she had devised, and then and there blurted out the news she had to impart. 'And if I could prove to you,' said she, 'that the Universal is at the end of its cash, after all the large purchases which it has made, and that it is reduced to the point of getting accommodation paper discounted abroad in order to continue the campaign?'

The Jew had suppressed a start of joy. His eyes remained lifeless, and he answered in the same grumbling voice: 'It isn't true.'

'What! not true? Why, I have heard it with my own ears, seen it with my own eyes.'

And she sought to convince him by explaining that she had held in her hands the notes signed by men of straw. She named the latter, and also gave the names of the bankers who had discounted the paper at Vienna, Frankfort, and Berlin. His correspondents could enlighten him; he would see that it was no mere gossip which she was retailing. And she further asserted that the Bank had been buying and buying on its own account, for the sole purpose of keeping up the rise, and that two hundred millions of francs had already been swallowed up.

Whilst he listened to her with his dismal air Gundermann was already planning his campaign of the morrow, so quick at all mental work that in a few seconds he had distributed his orders and determined upon the amounts. He was now certain of victory, for he well knew from what miry depths this information had come to him, and felt full of contempt for that pleasure-loving Saccard, who was so stupid as to trust a woman and allow himself to be sold.

When she had finished, he raised his head, and, looking at her out of his large dim eyes, exclaimed: 'Well, why should I be interested in what you say? How does it concern me?'

She was profoundly astonished, so unconcerned and calm did he appear. 'But,' said she, 'it seems to me that your position as a "bear"——'

'I! Who told you that I was a "bear"? I never go to the Bourse; I never speculate. All this is a matter of indifference to me.'

And there was such an innocent ring in his voice that the Baroness, doubting and frightened, would in the end have believed him but for certain inflections of too bantering a *naïveté*. He was evidently laughing at her, in his absolute disdain for woman, now that his blood was old and cold.

'So, my good friend,' he added, 'as I am very busy, if you have nothing more interesting to say to me——'

He was evidently about to dismiss her; and she in her fury sought to rebel. 'I have had confidence in you,' she said. 'I spoke first. It is a real trap. You promised me that, if I should be useful to you, you in your turn would be useful to me, and give me some good advice——'

Rising from his chair, he interrupted her. He, who never laughed, gave a slight chuckle, so amusing did he find it to dupe a young and pretty woman in this brutal way. 'Good advice! Why, I do not refuse it, my good friend; listen to me. Don't gamble, don't ever gamble. It will spoil your face; a woman who gambles is not at all nice.'

However, when she had gone off quite beside herself, he shut himself up with his two sons and his son-in-law and distributed the *rôles*, sending at once for Jacoby and other brokers to prepare the grand stroke of the morrow. His plan was simple: to do that which, in his ignorance of the real situation of the Universal, prudence had hitherto prevented him from risking—that is, to crush the market under the weight of enormous sales now that he knew the Universal to be at the end of its resources and incapable of sustaining the quotations. Like a general who wishes to end matters, and whose spies have fully acquainted him with the enemy's weak point, he was going to bring the formidable reserves of his milliard into line. Logic would triumph; all securities which rise above the real value which they represent are doomed.

That very same day, towards five o'clock, Saccard, warned of the danger by his keen scent, called upon Daigremont. He was feverish; he felt that the hour had come to strike a blow at the 'bears,' if he did not wish to be definitively beaten by them. And his giant idea tormented him, that idea of the colossal army of six hundred millions, which must yet be raised in order to conquer the world. Daigremont received him with his usual amiability, in his princely mansion, amid his costly pictures and all the dazzling luxury which his fortnightly profits at the Bourse provided for; no one really knowing whether there was anything solid behind all this show, which seemed ever liable to be swept away by some caprice of chance. So far Daigremont had not betrayed the Universal, but had refused to sell, affecting absolute confidence, happy in thus comporting himself like a good gambler playing for a rise, from which by the way he reaped large profits; and it had even pleased him not to flinch after the unfavourable settlement of the 16th, feeling convinced, as he said everywhere, that the rise would begin afresh. Still he was constantly on the watch, and quite ready to pass over to the enemy at the first grave symptom.

Saccard's visit, the extraordinary energy of which the little man gave proof, the vast idea which he unfolded of buying up every share in the market, struck Daigremont with real admiration. It was madness, but are not the great men of war and finance often only madmen who succeed? At all events, Daigremont formally promised to come to Saccard's aid at the Bourse the next day; he had already taken up strong positions, he said, but he would go to Delarocque, his broker, and extend them; to say nothing of his friends, whom he would also go to see—a complete syndicate, as it were, which he would bring up as reinforcements. In his opinion, they could estimate this new army corps at a hundred millions, for immediate use. That would suffice. Thereupon Saccard, radiant, feeling certain of conquering, decided on his plan of battle—a flank movement of rare boldness, borrowed from the tactics of the most illustrious captains: in the first place, at the opening of the Bourse, a simple skirmish to attract the 'bears' and give them confidence; then, when the 'bears' should have obtained a first success and prices should be falling, Daigremont and his friends would arrive with their heavy artillery, all those unexpected millions, emerging from ambush, assailing the 'bears' in the rear and overwhelming them; they would be crushed to pieces—massacred. Such was the plan, and when it had been agreed upon Saccard and Daigremont separated, shaking hands and laughing triumphantly.

An hour later, just as Daigremont, who was dining out that evening, was about to dress, he received another visit, from the Baroness Sandorff. In her bewilderment she had been seized with the idea of consulting him. She told her fears, and whilst lying as to the feverish spirit of treachery that had prompted her, narrated her visit to Gundermann and repeated the latter's reply. Daigremont, becoming very merry, amused himself by frightening her still more, assuming an air of doubt, as though almost believing that Gundermann had told the truth in swearing that he was not a 'bear.' And, indeed, can one ever tell? 'The Bourse is a real forest, a forest on a dark night through which one has to grope one's way. In such darkness, if you are so ill-advised as to listen to all the silly contradictory stories that are invented, you are certain to come to grief.'

'Then I ought not to sell?' she asked anxiously.

'Sell, why? It would be madness! To-morrow we shall be the masters; Universals will go up again to three thousand one hundred. So stand firm, whatever happens: you will be pleased with the last quotation. I cannot tell you more.'

The Baroness had gone, and Daigremont had at last begun to dress, when a ring at the bell announced a third visit. Ah! this time, no; he would not see the person, whoever it might be. However, when Delarocque's card had been handed to him, he at once exclaimed that the broker was to be shown up. Delarocque came in looking unusually agitated, and Daigremont, seeing that he was unwilling to speak in presence of the valet, sent the latter away, and tied his white cravat himself in front of a high mirror.

'My dear fellow,' said Delarocque with the familiarity of a man belonging to the same club as the person he was addressing, 'this is what brings me. I trust to your friendship, because it is rather a delicate matter. The fact is, Jacoby, my brother-in-law, has just had the kindness to warn me of an assault that is being prepared. Gundermann and the others have decided to give the finishing stroke to the Universal at to-morrow's Bourse. They are going to throw the whole pile upon the market. Jacoby already has orders. Gundermann sent for him.'

'The devil!' ejaculated Daigremont, turning pale.

'You understand, I have customers of mine who are playing for a rise to a very big tune indeed. Yes! I hold orders to the amount of fifteen millions, enough to knock a man into a cocked hat in the case of disaster. So, you see, I jumped into a cab, and am making the round of my leading clients. It is not correct, but the intention is good.'

'The devil!' repeated the other.

'In short, my good friend, as you are playing uncovered, I have come to ask you either to secure me or to abandon your position.'

'Abandon, abandon it, my dear fellow,' cried Daigremont. 'Oh! I don't remain in falling houses; that is useless heroism. Don't buy; sell! My orders with you are for nearly three millions; sell, sell everything!' Then, as Delarocque turned to go, saying that he had other customers to see, Daigremont took his hands and shook them energetically. 'Thank you; I shall never forget. Sell, sell everything!'

As soon as he was alone he recalled his valet, in order to have his hair and beard arranged. Ah, what a blunder! He had this time almost let himself be robbed like a child. That was what came of associating with a madman!

The panic began that same evening, at the Petite Bourse of eight o'clock, which was then held upon the footway of the Boulevard des Italiens, at the entrance of the Passage de l'Opéra; and here only the *coulissiers* operated amid an unprepossessing crowd of brokers, *remisiers*, and shady speculators. Street hawkers moved up and down and gatherers of cigar-stumps crawled on all fours through the tramping groups. The Boulevard was quite obstructed by this obstinate mob, for, although the stream of promenaders occasionally carried it away and dispersed it, it always formed again. That evening nearly two thousand persons remained collected there, thanks to the mildness of the weather, which, with the misty, lowering sky, betokened rain after the terrible cold. The market was very active; Universals were offered on all sides, and the quotations fell rapidly. Rumours soon became current, and anxiety set in. What had happened, then? In an undertone, folks named the probable vendors, according to the *remisier* who gave the order or the *coulissier* who executed it. If the big-wigs were selling in this way, something serious was preparing, surely. And so from eight o'clock until ten there was no end of jostling and scrambling; all the keen-scented gamblers abandoned their positions; there were even some who had time to change sides and become 'bears' instead of 'bulls.' And all went to bed in a fever of uneasiness, as on the eve of great battles.

The weather was execrable on the following day. It had rained all night; a fine, cold rain drenched the city, which the thaw changed into a cloaca of yellow liquid mud. Already, at half-past twelve o'clock, the Bourse began clamouring in this downpour. Everyone having taken refuge under the peristyle and in the hall, the crowd was enormous; and by the dripping from the wet umbrellas the hall itself was soon changed into an immense puddle of muddy, water. Dampness oozed from the black filth of the walls, whilst from the glass roof there fell but a dim, ruddy light, desperately melancholy.

Amid the many evil reports in circulation, the extraordinary stories which were turning people's heads, one and all, on entering, began to look for Saccard and scrutinize him. He was at his post, erect, near the accustomed pillar; and he had the air of other days, the days of triumph, an air of brave gaiety and absolute confidence. He was not ignorant of the fact that Universals had fallen three hundred francs at the Petite Bourse the night before; he scented immense danger. He expected a furious assault on the part of the 'bears;' but his plan of battle seemed to him invincible; Daigremont's flank movement, the unexpected arrival of an army of fresh millions, would sweep everything before it, and once more assure him the victory. Henceforth he himself was without resources; the coffers of the Universal were empty, he had scraped even the centimes out of them; yet he did not despair, Mazaud was carrying him over, and he had so completely won the broker's confidence by acquainting him with the promised support of Daigremont's syndicate, that he had accepted without security further orders for purchase to the amount of several millions. The tactics agreed upon between them were not to let the quotations fall too low at the opening of the Bourse, but to sustain them and wage war pending the arrival of the reinforcements. The excitement was so great that Massias and Sabatani, abandoning useless strategy now that the real situation was the subject of all gossip, came and spoke openly with Saccard, and then ran to carry his last orders, the one to Nathansohn under the peristyle, and the other to Mazaud, who was still in the brokers' room.

It was ten minutes to one o'clock, and Moser, who arrived looking quite pale from the effects of one of his liver attacks, the pain of which had kept him from closing his eyes all the night, remarked to Pillerault that everybody appeared yellow and ill that afternoon. Pillerault, who in the approach of disaster straightened himself up in the swaggering attitude of a knight-errant, burst out laughing. 'Why, it is you, my dear fellow, who have the colic,' said he. 'Everybody else is very gay. We are going to give you one of those thrashings which folks remember as long as they live.'

The truth was, however, that in the general anxiety the hall remained very gloomy under the reddish light, and this was particularly evident from the subdued rumble of the conversation. You no longer heard the feverish outbursts of the days when everything was rising, the agitation, the roar of a tide, streaming from all sides like a conqueror. The Boursiers no longer ran, they no longer shouted; they glided, they talked in low tones, as in a sick room. Although the crowd was very great, and one could not circulate without stifling, only a distressful murmur arose, the whispering of the current fears, of all the deplorable news which folks exchanged in one another's ears. Many remained silent, with livid, contracted faces and dilated eyes, which questioned other faces despairingly.

'And have you nothing to say, Salmon?' asked Pillerault, full of aggressive irony.

'Of course not,' muttered Moser; 'he's like the rest: he has nothing to say; he is frightened.'

Indeed, that day Salmon's silence disturbed no one, such was the deep, mute expectancy of one and all.

It was around Saccard, however, that a stream of customers especially crowded, trembling with uncertainty and eager for an encouraging word. It was afterwards remembered that Daigremont did not show himself that day any more than Deputy Huret, who had doubtless been warned, and was once more Rougon's faithful dog. Kolb, amid a group of bankers, pretended to be absorbed in a big arbitrage affair. The Marquis de Bohain, above the vicissitudes of fortune, quietly promenaded his little pale aristocratic head, certain of winning whatever happened, since he had given Jacoby orders to sell as many Universals as he had charged Mazaud to buy. And Saccard, besieged by the multitude of the others, the believers and the simpletons, displayed a particularly amiable and tranquillizing manner towards Sédille and Maugendre, who, with trembling lips and moist, supplicating eyes, came in search of the hope of triumph. He vigorously pressed their hands, putting into his grasp the absolute promise of victory, and then, like a man who is ever happy, beyond the reach of all danger, he began lamenting over a trifle.

'I am very worried,' said he. 'A camellia was forgotten in my yard during the very cold weather, and it has died.'

The remark ran through the hall, and everybody began deploring the fate of the camellia. What a man that Saccard was, with his impassable assurance, his ever-smiling face! for one could never tell if it were not some mask, concealing frightful anxieties which would have tortured any other.

'The brute! how fine he is!' murmured Jantrou, in the ear of Massias, who was coming back.

Just then Saccard called Jantrou, a sudden recollection coming to him at this supreme moment—a recollection of the afternoon when, in Jantrou's company, he had seen the Baroness Sandorff's brougham drawn up in the Rue Brongniart. Was it again there on this day of crisis? Was the high-perched coachman maintaining his stony immobility in that pelting rain, while the Baroness, behind the closed windows, awaited the quotations?

'Certainly, she is there,' answered Jantrou, in an undertone, 'and heartily with you, thoroughly determined not to retreat a step. We are all here, solid, at our posts.'

Saccard felt happy at this proof of fidelity, although he doubted the disinterestedness of the lady and the others. However, in the blindness of his fever, he believed that he was still marching on to conquest, with his whole nation of shareholders behind him—that infatuated, fanaticised people of the humble and the fashionable worlds, in which pretty women of good position mingled with servant girls in the same impulse of faith.

At last the bell sounded, passing like the wail of a tocsin over the wild sea of heads. And Mazaud, who was giving orders to Flory, hurried back to the *corbeille*, while the young clerk rushed to the telegraph office, greatly agitated on his own account; for, having been losing for some time, through his obstinacy in following the fortunes of the Universal, he had that day risked a decisive stroke, on the strength of the story of Daigremont's intervention, which he had overheard in the office, behind a door. The *corbeille* was quite as anxious as the hall; ever since the last settlement the brokers had plainly felt the ground trembling beneath them, amidst such serious symptoms that their experience took alarm. There had already been some partial collapses; the market, too heavily burdened, exhausted, was cracking in every direction. Was there going to be, then, one of those great cataclysms, such as occur every ten or fifteen years, one of those crises which supervene when gambling has reached an acutely feverish stage, and which decimate the Bourse and sweep it clean like a wind of death? The shouts in the Rente and Cash markets drowned one another, the jostling was rougher than ever, while on high were the tall black silhouettes of the quoters, who were waiting, pen in hand. And Mazaud, standing at his post, with his hands grasping the red-velvet balustrade of the *corbeille*, at once heard Jacoby, on the other side of the circular basin, shouting in his deep bass voice: 'I have Universals! At two thousand eight hundred, I have Universals!'

This was the last quotation of the Petite Bourse of the night before; and, in order to put a stop to the fall at once, Mazaud thought it prudent to take at this price. His shrill voice arose above all the others: 'At two thousand eight hundred I take! Three hundred Universals, deliver!'

Thus was the first quotation fixed. But it was impossible to maintain it. Offers flowed in from all sides. Mazaud struggled desperately for half an hour, but with no other result than that of slackening the rapidity of the fall. What surprised him was that he was no longer sustained by the *coulisse*. What game was being played by Nathansohn, whose orders to purchase he was expecting? And not until afterwards did he learn the shrewd tactics of the *coulissier* who, whilst buying for Saccard, was selling on his own account, having been warned of the real situation by his keen Jew scent. Massias, heavily involved himself as a buyer, ran up, out of breath, to report the rout of the *coulisse* to Mazaud, who lost his head and burned his last cartridges, at once letting fly the orders which he had hitherto been keeping back, in view of executing them by degrees pending the arrival of the reinforcements. This sent the price up a little; from twenty-five hundred it rose to twenty-six hundred and fifty, with the sudden leaps peculiar to tempestuous days; and again for a moment did boundless hope buoy up the hearts of Mazaud, Saccard, all who were in the secret of the plan of battle. Since the quotations were so soon going up again, the day was won, and the victory would be overwhelming when the reserves should fall upon the 'bears' flank, changing their defeat into a frightful rout. There was a movement of profound joy; Sédille and Maugendre could have kissed Saccard's hand, Kolb drew nearer, while Jantrou disappeared, running off to carry the good news to the Baroness Sandorff. And at this moment little Flory, quite radiant, was seen hunting everywhere for Sabatani, now his intermediary, to give him a fresh order to buy.

But it had just struck two, and Mazaud, who bore the brunt of the attack, again weakened, his surprise now increasing at the delay of the reinforcements in taking the field. It was high time for them to turn up; what were they waiting for? Why did they not relieve him from the untenable position in which he was exhausting himself?

Although, through professional pride, he displayed an impassive countenance, a keen chill was rising to his cheeks, and he feared that he was turning pale. Jacoby, in a thundering voice, continued hurling his offers at him, in methodical instalments, but Mazaud ceased accepting them. And it was no longer at Jacoby that he was looking; his eyes were turned towards Delarocque, Daigremont's broker, whose silence he could not understand. Stout and thickset, with a reddish beard, and the smiling beatific air of a man who has amused himself the night before, Delarocque retained a very quiet, peaceable air whilst waiting in this inexplicable fashion. Was he not going to catch at all these offers, however, and save everything, by means of the orders to buy, which must cover the *fiches* in his hand?

Suddenly in his guttural, slightly hoarse voice, he threw himself into the struggle: 'I have Universals! I have Universals!' he called.

And in a few minutes he had offered several millions' worth. Voices answered him, and the quotations collapsed.

'I have at two thousand four hundred!' 'I have at two thousand three hundred!'

'How many?'

'Five hundred, six hundred!'

'Deliver!'

What was he saying? What was taking place? Instead of the expected succour, was this a fresh hostile army emerging from the neighbouring woods? As at Waterloo, Grouchy failed to come up, and it was treason that completed the rout. Under the onslaught of those deep, fresh masses of offers hastening to the attack at the double quick, a frightful panic set in.

Mazaud at that moment felt death pass over his face. He had carried Saccard over for far too large a sum, and he was fully conscious that the Universal was breaking his back in its fall. But his handsome dark face, with small moustaches, remained impenetrable and brave. Exhausting the orders which he had received, he still went on buying in his piercing cockerel-like voice, as shrill as in the hours of success. And opposite him, his counterparts, the roaring Jacoby and the apoplectic Delarocque, despite their efforts at indifference, showed more anxiety than he, for they realised that he was now in great danger, and would he pay them should he fail? Their hands grasped the velvet balustrade, their voices continued shouting as though mechanically, from mere habit, while their fixed glances expressed all the frightful anguish of this tragedy of money.

Then, during the last half-hour, came the smash-up, the rout growing worse and worse, carrying the mob away in a disorderly gallop. After extreme confidence, blind infatuation, came the reaction of fear, and one and all rushed forward to sell, if there was still time. A perfect hail of orders to sell fell upon the *corbeille*: there was nothing to be seen but a rain of *fiches*; and the enormous parcels of shares, thus imprudently thrown upon the market, accelerated the decline, turned it into a veritable collapse. The quotations, from fall to fall, dropped to one thousand five hundred, one thousand two hundred, nine hundred francs. There were no more buyers; none were left standing; the ground was strewn with corpses. Above the dark swarming of frock-coats, the three quoters looked like clerks registering deaths. By a singular effect of the blast of disaster which swept through the hall, the agitation congealed there as it were, the uproar died away as in the stupor of a great catastrophe. A frightful silence prevailed when, after the stroke of the closing bell, the final quotation of eight hundred and thirty francs became known. And meantime the obstinate rain still streamed upon the windows, through which only a doubtful twilight filtered. What with the dripping of the umbrellas and the tramping of the crowd, the hall had become a cloaca, muddy like an ill-kept stable, and littered with all sorts of torn papers; while in the *corbeille* shone the variegated *fiches*, green, red, and blue, scattered there by the handful, and so abundant that afternoon that the vast basin overflowed.

Mazaud had re-entered the brokers' room at the same time as Jacoby and Delarocque. Consumed by an ardent thirst, he approached the buffet, and drank a glass of beer. Then he looked at the immense room, with its long central table, around which were ranged the arm-chairs of the sixty brokers, its red velvet hangings, all its commonplace faded luxury, which lent it the appearance of a first-class waiting-room in a large railway station; he looked at it with the astonished air of a man who had never had a good view of it before. Then, as he was going off, he silently shook hands with Jacoby and Delarocque, exchanging the accustomed grasp with them; and although they all three preserved their every-day correct deportment, they could not help turning pale. Mazaud had told Flory to wait for him at the door; and there he found him, in company with Gustave, who had definitively left the office the week before, and had come there simply as a spectator, always smiling and leading a gay life, without ever asking himself whether his father would, on the morrow, still be able to pay his debts; while Flory, with pale cheeks and an idiotic sneer on his lips, endeavoured to talk, though crushed by the frightful loss of a hundred thousand francs which had just fallen upon him, and the first sou of which he did not know where to get. However, Mazaud and his clerk disappeared in the rain.

In the hall the panic had especially raged around Saccard; it was there that the war had made its ravages. At the first moment he had not understood what was happening; then, bravely facing the peril, he had beheld the rout. What was that noise? Was it not Daigremont's troops arriving? Then, when he had heard the quotations collapse, though he failed to comprehend the cause of the disaster, he stiffened himself up, in order to die standing. An icy chill rose from the ground to his skull; he had a feeling that the irreparable was taking place—this was his defeat for ever; but base regret for money, wrath for lost enjoyment, did not enter into his grief; his heart simply bled with humiliation at the thought that he was conquered, and that this was the splendid, absolute victory of Gundermann, the victory which once more consolidated the omnipotence of that king of gold. At that moment Saccard was really superb, with his slight figure erect as though braving destiny, his eyes never blinking, his face stubbornly set as he stood there alone with the flood of despair and resentment, which he already felt rising against him. The entire hall seethed and surged towards his pillar; fists were clenched, mouths stammered evil words, yet he retained upon his lips an unconscious smile, which might have been taken for a challenge.

At first, through a sort of mist, he distinguished Maugendre, looking deadly pale as Captain Chave led him away on his arm, and, with the cruelty of a petty gambler delighted to see big speculators come to grief, repeated to him that he had prophesied it all. Then Sédille, with contracted face and the crazy air of a merchant whose business is collapsing, came like a good-natured fellow to give him an unsteady shake of the hand, as though to say that he bore him no grudge. At the first shock the Marquis de Bohain had drawn aside, passing over to the triumphant army of 'bears,' and telling Kolb, who also prudently held aloof, what disagreeable doubts he had entertained of that man Saccard ever since the last shareholders' meeting. Jantrou, bewildered, had disappeared again, going off on the run to carry the last quotation to the Baroness Sandorff, who would surely have an hysterical attack in her brougham, as was the case on the days when she lost heavily. And facing the ever silent and enigmatical Salmon, stood 'bear' Moser and 'bull' Pillerault, the latter with a provoking, proud mien, despite his ruin; the other, who had made a fortune, marring his victory with remote anxieties. 'You see, we shall have war with Germany in the spring. All this doesn't smell nice, and Bismarck is watching us.'

'Oh, be quiet, do!' replied Pillerault. 'I again made the mistake of reflecting too much. So much the worse! I must begin over again; all will go well.'

So far Saccard had not weakened. But behind him he heard someone mention the name of Fayeux, the dividend-collector of Vendôme, with whom he had dealings on behalf of numerous petty shareholders, and this name brought him a feeling of uneasiness, reminding him as it did of the vast mass of wretched little capitalists who would be crushed beneath the ruins of the Universal. And suddenly the sight of Dejoie, with a livid, distorted face, acutely intensified this uneasiness, for all the humble folks now so lamentably mixed seemed personified in this poor man whom he knew. At the same time, by a sort of hallucination, there rose before him the pale, desolate faces of the Countess de Beauvilliers and her daughter, who gazed at him in despair out of their large tearful eyes. And at that moment, Saccard, the corsair whose heart was tanned by twenty years of brigandage—Saccard, whose pride it was that he had never felt a trembling in his legs, that he had never once sat down upon the bench, against the pillar behind him—Saccard felt a sudden weakness, and had to drop for a moment upon that bench. The crowd still surged, threatening to stifle him. He raised his head, feeling a need of air, and in a moment he was on his feet again; for up above, looking down upon the hall from the telegraph gallery, he recognised La Méchain, her huge fat person dominating the ghastly battle-field. On the stone baluster beside her lay her old black leather bag. Pending the arrival of the time when she might fill it to overflowing with the worthless shares, she was watching the dead, like a voracious raven that follows armies until the day of massacre.

Then, with a firm step, Saccard walked away, bearing himself erect by an extraordinary effort of will. His whole being seemed empty to him, however; his senses were blunted, so to say; he no longer felt the flagstones, but thought he was walking on a soft woollen carpet. Similarly, a mist obscured his eyes, and a buzzing filled his ears. He no longer recognised people as he left the Bourse and descended the steps; it seemed to him that he was surrounded by floating phantoms, vague forms, dying sounds. Did he not see Busch's broad, grimacing face pass him? Had he not stopped for a moment to speak to Nathansohn, who appeared quite at his ease, and whose voice, weakened by much shouting, seemed to come from a long way off? Did not Sabatani and Massias accompany him amidst the general consternation? He fancied he could see himself surrounded by a numerous group, again Sédille and Maugendre perhaps, all sorts of faces which faded away, became transformed. And as he was on the point of going off into the rain and liquid mud which were submerging Paris, he made his freedom of mind his last boast, and repeated in a shrill voice to all that phantom throng: 'Ah, how worried I am about that camellia of mine which was forgotten in the yard and has been killed by the cold!'

CHAPTER XI
RUIN

That same evening Madame Caroline, in her fright, telegraphed to her brother, who was to have remained at Rome another week; and three days later, hastening to the scene of danger, Hamelin arrived in Paris.

There was a violent explanation between Saccard and the engineer in that work-room in the Rue Saint-Lazare, where, in other days, the enterprise had been discussed and decided upon with so much enthusiasm. During the three days which had just elapsed the smash-up at the Bourse had become more and more complete. Fall following fall in rapid succession, Universals had now dropped to four hundred and thirty francs—seventy francs below par; and the decline was continuing; the whole fabric was fast cracking and crumbling away.

Whilst her brother and Saccard talked, Madame Caroline listened in silence, resolved not to intervene. She was full of remorse, for she accused herself of complicity, since it was she who, after promising to watch, had let everything go on. Instead of contenting herself with simply selling her shares in order to combat the rise, ought she not to have taken some other course—warned people, acted energetically? Worshipping her brother as she did, her heart bled at seeing him compromised in this fashion, with all his great enterprises shaken, the whole work of his life again in question; and she suffered the more since she did not feel herself free to judge Saccard; for had she not loved him, was she not his, linked to him by that secret bond, the shame of which she now felt more than ever? Placed between these two men, a combat raged within her and rent her heart. On the evening of the catastrophe, in a fine outburst of frankness, she had heaped her wrath upon Saccard, emptying her heart of all the reproaches and fears which had so long been swelling it. However, on seeing him smile, still tenacious, still unconquered despite everything, she had reflected that, after her own weakness with him, she had no right to finish him off, to strike him now that he was down. She thought, too, of the strength which he would need to set himself erect again, and so, taking refuge in silence, her demeanour alone giving expression to her blame, she resolved that she would henceforward be nothing but a witness.

However, Hamelin this time became angry, he who was usually so conciliatory, without interest in anything that was not part of his work. He attacked gambling with extreme violence; 'the Universal,' said he, 'had succumbed to the mania for gambling— gambling carried to the point of absolute madness.' Undoubtedly he was not one of those who pretended that a bank could allow its stock to fall in price, like a railway company, for instance. The railway company has its immense plant, which brings in its receipts, whereas the real plant of a bank is its credit; so it finds itself at death's door as soon as its credit totters. Only there was a question of moderation in all this. Though it might have been necessary and even wise to maintain the quotation at two thousand francs, it was madness and utter criminality to push it further, to try to raise it to three thousand and more. Immediately on his arrival, Hamelin had demanded the truth, the whole truth. They could no longer lie to him now, and declare to him, as he had allowed them to declare in his presence at the last shareholders' meeting, that the Bank did not possess a single one of its shares. The books were there and he easily penetrated the lies they contained. He knew, for instance, that the Sabatani account concealed operations carried on by the Bank itself; and in this account, month by month, over a period of two years, he could trace the progress of Saccard's fatal fever.

At first things had been done in a timid way, prudence had been displayed in the purchases, but at last these had become larger and larger, till they had finally reached the enormous figure of twenty-seven thousand shares costing nearly forty-eight millions of francs. Was it not madness, impudent, derisive folly, that transactions of such magnitude should be entered to the account of a Sabatani? And this Sabatani was not the only one; there were other men of straw—employees of the Bank, directors even—whose purchases, entered as carried over, exceeded twenty thousand shares, also representing nearly forty-eight millions of francs. And, moreover, all these were only the completed purchases, to which must be added the time bargains, effected during the last fortnight of January; sixty-seven millions of francs expended on more than twenty thousand shares, delivery of which the Universal had to accept; to say nothing of ten thousand other shares bought at the Lyons Bourse, making another twenty-four millions. And, adding everything together, it was seen that the Bank now had in hand nearly one-fourth of the shares which it had issued, and that it had paid for these shares the frightful sum of two hundred millions. There was the abyss in which it had been swallowed up.

Tears of grief and anger had risen to Hamelin's eyes. To think that this should have happened when he had just so auspiciously laid at Rome the foundations of his great Catholic bank, that Treasury of the Holy Sepulchre which, in the approaching days of persecution, would enable the Pope to be regally installed at Jerusalem, amid the legendary glory of the Holy Places—a bank destined to set the new Kingdom of Palestine beyond the reach of political disturbances, by basing its revenue, guaranteed by the resources of the country, on a series of issues which the Christians of the whole world would vie in taking up! And all this collapsed at one stroke through the imbecile madness of gambling! He had gone away leaving an admirable balance-sheet, coffers full of money, a Bank enjoying such great and speedy prosperity that it was the wonder of the world; and, less than a month afterwards, when he came back, the millions had melted away, the Bank was prostrate, reduced to dust, and there was nothing but a black hole, in which a conflagration seemed to have raged. His stupefaction increased; he violently demanded explanations, wished to understand what mysterious force it was that had driven Saccard to wage this relentless warfare upon the colossal edifice which he had built so as to destroy it, stone by stone, on the one hand, while he pretended to finish it upon the other.

Saccard answered very frankly, and without anger. After the first hours of emotion and annihilation, he had recovered his self-possession, and was again erect and firm, buoyed up by his indomitable hopes. Treachery had rendered the catastrophe a terrible one, but nothing was lost; he was going to retrieve everything. And besides, if the Universal had enjoyed such swift and great prosperity, had it not owed it to the very methods with which they now reproached him—to the creation of the syndicate, the successive increases of the capital, the advance balance-sheet of the last shareholders' meeting, the shares which the Bank retained in hand, and those which had been so wildly purchased *en masse* later on? All these things were connected. If they accepted the success, the risks must be accepted also. When a machine is overheated it bursts. For the rest, he would acknowledge no culpability; he had simply done, more intelligently and vigorously than another, that which every bank manager does; and he did not even abandon his idea of genius—his giant idea of repurchasing all the shares and dethroning Gundermann. Money had been lacking, that was all. And now they must begin over again. A special shareholders' meeting had just been summoned for the following Monday; he was absolutely certain of his shareholders, he said; he would obtain from them the sacrifices that were indispensable, for he was convinced that, at a word from him, they would all bring their fortunes. In the meantime they could jog on, thanks to the small sums which the other financial houses, the great banks, advanced every morning for the pressing needs of the day, through fear of too sudden a crash, which would have shaken them also. The crisis over, all would be resumed, and the enterprise would again become as resplendent as ever.

'But,' objected Hamelin, whom this smiling tranquillity already calmed, 'do you not detect in this help supplied by our rivals a design of securing themselves first of all, and then rendering our fall more complete by delaying it? What worries me is to see Gundermann's hand in the business.'

In fact, in order to avert an immediate declaration of bankruptcy, Gundermann had been one of the first to offer help, in this wise displaying the practical sense of a man who, after setting fire to his neighbour's house, hastens to bring buckets of water, so that the entire neighbourhood may not be destroyed. He was above resentment; he had no other glory than that of being the first money-merchant of the world, the richest and the most shrewd, through having succeeded in sacrificing all his passions to the continuous increase of his fortune.

Saccard made a gesture of impatience, exasperated as he was by this proof which the conqueror gave of his sagacity and intelligence. 'Oh, Gundermann,' he said, 'is playing the high-minded man; he thinks that he stabs me with his generosity.'

A silence ensued, and it was Madame Caroline, hitherto dumb, who at last broke it. 'My friend,' said she, addressing Saccard, 'I have allowed my brother to speak to you, as he was bound to speak, in the legitimate grief which he felt on learning of all these deplorable things. But our situation, his and mine, seems to me clear; it seems impossible, does it not, that he should be compromised if the affair altogether turns out disastrously? You know at what price I sold our shares. People cannot say that my brother stimulated the rise in order to get a larger profit from his shares. And besides, if the catastrophe comes, we shall know our duty. I confess that I do not share your stubborn hopes. Nevertheless, you are right in contending that it is necessary to struggle on till the last moment, and it is not my brother who will discourage you, you may be sure of it.

She was agitated, again harbouring a tolerant feeling towards this man who displayed such stubborn determination. However, she was unwilling that others should perceive her weakness, for she could no longer blind herself to the hateful work which he would assuredly do over again should he have the chance, swayed as he was by the thieving passions of an unscrupulous corsair.

'Certainly,' declared Hamelin, in his turn weary and unable to resist any further. 'I am not going to paralyse you, when you are fighting to save us all. Rely on me, if I can be useful to you.'

And once more, at this last hour, when threatened by the most frightful dangers, Saccard reassured them, reconquered them, taking leave of them with these words, full of promise and mystery: 'Sleep easy. I cannot say more, but I am absolutely certain of setting everything afloat again before another week is over.'

This phrase, which he did not explain, he repeated to all the friends of the concern, to all the customers who, frightened, terrified, came to ask him for advice. For three days past there had been a continuous gallop through his office in the Rue de Londres.

The Beauvilliers, the Maugendres, Sédille, Dejoie, all hastened to apply to him. He received them very calmly, with a military air, with ringing words which restored courage to their hearts; and when they talked of selling, of realising at a loss, he became angry, and shouted to them to do nothing so stupid, promising upon his honour that he would again secure the quotation of two thousand and even three thousand francs. In spite of the mistakes that had been made, they all retained a blind faith in him: if he were left to them, free to rob them again, he would clear up everything, and finally enrich them all, as he had sworn to do. If no accident should happen before Monday, if he were given time to hold the special shareholders' meeting, no one doubted that he would bring the Universal safe and sound out of its ruins.

Saccard had thought of his brother Rougon, and this was the omnipotent aid of which he spoke, unwilling to be more explicit. Having met Daigremont, the traitor, face to face, and bitterly reproached him, he had merely obtained from him this reply: 'But, my dear fellow, it is not I who have dropped you; it is your brother!' Evidently this man was in his right; he had gone into the affair solely on condition that Rougon should be in it; they had formally promised him Rougon; so it was not astonishing that he should retire, since the Minister, far from being in it, was at open war with the Universal and its manager. This was at least an excuse to which there was no reply. Greatly struck by it, Saccard realised what a colossal mistake he had made in thus falling out with his brother, who alone could defend him, make him so far sacred that no one, knowing the great man to be behind him, would dare to complete his ruin. And never had his pride been so severely tried as when he had to make up his mind to ask Deputy Huret to intervene in his favour. For the rest, he maintained a threatening attitude, absolutely refused to abscond, and claimed as a right the help of Rougon, who had more interest than he in preventing a scandal. The next day, whilst awaiting Huret's promised visit on the matter, he simply received a note, in which he was told in vague terms not to be impatient, but to rely upon a satisfactory issue, if subsequent circumstances should not make it impossible. He contented himself with these few lines, which he regarded as a promise of neutrality.

The truth was, however, that Rougon had just taken the energetic resolution to get rid of this gangrened member of his family, who for years had been embarrassing him, keeping him in perpetual fear of some unclean misadventure, and whom he now preferred to cut off at a blow. If the catastrophe came, he was determined to let things take their course. Since Saccard would never voluntarily consent to go into exile, was not the simplest plan to force him to expatriate himself by facilitating his flight after some severe sentence? A sudden scandal, a sweep of the broom, and all would be ended. Moreover, the Minister's position was becoming difficult since he had declared to the Corps Législatif, in a memorable outburst of eloquence, that France would never allow Italy to take possession of Rome. Loudly applauded by the Catholics, severely attacked by the Third Estate, which was becoming more and more powerful, Rougon saw the hour approaching when the latter, aided by the Liberal Bonapartists, would drive him from power if he did not give it a guarantee. And the guarantee, if circumstances required it, should be the abandonment of that Universal Bank which, under the patronage of Rome, had become a disturbing force. Finally, what clinched his decision was a secret communication from his colleague, the Minister of Finances, who, on the point of launching a loan, had found Gundermann and all the other Jew bankers very reserved, and disposed to refuse their capital so long as the market

210

should remain uncertain, at the mercy of adventurers. Gundermann triumphed. Better the Jews, with their accepted sovereignty of gold, than the Ultramontane Catholics masters of the world as they would be should they become the kings of the Bourse.

It was subsequently related that, when the Keeper of the Seals, Delcambre, relentless in his rancour against Saccard, had sounded Rougon as to the course to be pursued with regard to his brother should justice be obliged to intervene, he had by way of answer simply received this heartfelt cry: 'Ah! Rid me of him, and I shall owe you a debt of gratitude!'

From that moment, Rougon having abandoned him, Saccard was lost. Delcambre, who had been watching him ever since attaining power, at last held him on the margin of the Code, on the very edge of the judicial net, and had only to find a pretext to set the gendarmes and judges upon him.

One morning, Busch, furious with himself at not having yet acted, repaired to the Palais de Justice. If he did not make haste, he would never get from Saccard the four thousand francs which were still due to La Méchain on little Victor's famous bill of expenses. Busch's plan was simply to raise an abominable scandal by accusing Saccard of sequestrating the child, which would permit him to spread the whole dirty story before the world. Such a prosecution instituted against the manager of the Universal, amid the excitement created by the crisis through which the Bank was passing, would certainly stir all Paris; and Busch still hoped that Saccard would pay at the first threat. But the Deputy Public Prosecutor, who received him, a nephew of Delcambre, listened to his story with an impatient, wearied air. No! no! there was nothing to be accomplished with such gossip as that; it did not come under any clause of the Code. Disconcerted, Busch grew angry, and talked of his long patience, saying that he had even carried his good nature towards Saccard so far as to deposit funds *en report* with the Universal. Thereupon the other at once interrupted him. What! he had funds in that concern, which was certainly insolvent, and he did not act? Nothing was more simple; he had only to prefer a charge of swindling, for justice had been warned of the fraudulent transactions which were about to bring on bankruptcy. The great blow was to be dealt by means of this charge, not of the other story, that melodramatic affair of a girl who had died of alcoholism, and of a child who had grown up in the gutter. Busch listened with an attentive, serious face, turned into this new path, dragged into an act which he had not come to perform, but the decisive consequences of which he could clearly foresee, for Saccard would be arrested, and the Universal would receive its death-blow. The mere fear of losing his money would have at once made him make up his mind. Moreover, a disaster was in his line, for it would give him an opportunity to fish in troubled waters. Nevertheless he hesitated, said that he would reflect and would come back; and the Deputy Public Prosecutor actually had to force the pen into his hand, and then and there make him write down that charge of swindling, which, as soon as he had been dismissed, was carried by the zealous official to his uncle, the Keeper of the Seals. The affair was clinched.

The next day, at the office of the Bank in the Rue de Londres, Saccard had a long interview with the auditors and the judicially appointed manager, in order to draw up the balance-sheet which he desired to present to the shareholders' meeting. In spite of the sums advanced by other financial establishments, they had had to suspend payment, in view of the increasing demands made upon them. This bank, which, a month previously, had possessed nearly two hundred million francs in its coffers, had

211

not been able to pay its distracted customers more than a few hundred thousand francs. Bankruptcy had been officially declared by a judgment of the Tribunal of Commerce, after a summary report rendered by an expert who had been charged with an examination of the books. In spite of everything, however, Saccard, seemingly unconscious, still promised to save the situation, evincing an extraordinary amount of blind hopefulness and obstinate bravery. And on that very day he was awaiting a reply from the stockbrokers' association, with regard to the fixing of a rate of compensation, when his usher entered to tell him that three gentlemen wished to see him in an adjoining room. Perhaps this was salvation; he rushed out gaily, and found a commissary of police awaiting him, accompanied by two officers, by whom he was immediately arrested. The warrant had just been issued, partly on the strength of the expert's report, which pointed to irregularities in the accounts, but more particularly owing to the charge of abuse of confidence preferred by Busch, who pretended that the funds which he had entrusted to the Universal to be carried forward had been otherwise disposed of.

At the same hour, moreover, Hamelin also was arrested at his residence in the Rue Saint-Lazare. Every hatred and every mischance seemed to have combined, as though implacably bent upon securing the Bank's destruction, and at last the end had come. The specially convened meeting of shareholders could no longer be held; the Universal Bank had lived.

Madame Caroline was not at home at the time of the arrest of her brother, who could only leave a few hastily written lines for her. When she returned and learnt what had happened she was stupefied. She had never believed that they would for a moment even think of prosecuting him, for in her mind his long periods of absence showed that he could have taken no part in Saccard's shady transactions. On the day after the bankruptcy, both he and she had stripped themselves of all that they possessed, in order to swell the assets, and to emerge from this adventure as naked as they had entered it. And the amount of money which they thus surrendered was a large one, nearly eight millions of francs, in which were swallowed up the three hundred thousand francs which they had inherited. Her brother arrested, Madame Caroline at once gave herself up to applications and solicitations, living only to soften the lot and prepare the defence of her poor George, and bursting into tears, in spite of her courage, whenever she thought of him, innocent, behind the prison bars, bespattered by this frightful scandal, his life wrecked and soiled for ever. To think of it! He so gentle and so weak, full of childlike piety, a 'perfect simpleton,' as she said, outside his technical work! And, at first, she became wroth with Saccard, the sole cause of the disaster, the artisan of their misfortune, whose hateful work she traced and clearly judged, from the days of the beginning, when he had gaily derided her for reading the Code, to these days of the end, when, paying the severe penalty of failure, he was about to be called to account for all the irregular practices which she had foreseen and allowed to be committed. Then, tortured by this haunting remorse of complicity, she became silent, and tried not to openly concern herself with him, resolving to act indeed as if he were not in existence. Whenever she had to mention his name, it seemed as if she were speaking of a stranger, of an opponent whose interests were different from her own. She, who visited her brother at the Conciergerie almost every day, had not even asked for a permit to see Saccard. And she was very brave; she still occupied her apartments in the Rue Saint-Lazare, receiving all who presented themselves, even those who came with insults on their lips, thus transformed into a woman of business, determined to save what little she could of their honesty and happiness.

During the long days which she passed in this way, upstairs, in that work-room where she had spent such delightful hours of toil and hope, there was one spectacle which particularly distressed her. Whenever she approached one of the windows, and cast a glance at the neighbouring mansion, she could not behold without a pang at the heart the pale profiles of the Countess de Beauvilliers and her slaughter Alice behind the window-panes of the little room in which they lived. Those February days were very mild; so that she also often noticed them walking, slowly and with drooping heads, along the paths of the moss-grown garden which the winter had ravaged. The results of the crash had been frightful for those poor creatures. They who a fortnight previously could have commanded eighteen hundred thousand francs with their six hundred shares could now only get an offer of eighteen thousand for them, since the price had fallen from three thousand to thirty francs. And their entire fortune had at one stroke melted away. All had vanished—the twenty thousand francs of the dowry, so painfully and thriftily saved by the Countess; the seventy thousand francs borrowed upon Les Aublets, and the two hundred and forty thousand francs which the farm had eventually fetched when it was in reality worth four hundred thousand. What was to become of them, since the mortgage upon their house in Paris alone consumed eight thousand francs a year, and they had never been able to reduce their style of living below seven thousand, in spite of all their niggardly practices, all the miracles of sordid economy which they accomplished, in order to save appearances and keep their station? Even if they were to sell their shares, how could they henceforth live, provide for their wants out of that paltry sum of eighteen thousand francs, the last waif of the shipwreck? The Countess had not yet been willing to look the imperious necessity in the face. The only course was to leave the mansion, and abandon it to the mortgagees, since it was impossible for her to continue paying the interest. Rather than wait for its sale to be advertised, she had better at once withdraw to some small apartments, there in concealment to eke out a straitened existence, down to the last morsel of bread. However, she resisted, because this meant severance from all that she had clung to, the annihilation of all that she had dreamt, the crumbling of the edifice of her race which for years her trembling hands had sustained with heroic obstinacy. The Beauvilliers, tenants, no longer living under the ancestral roof, dwelling in the houses of others, in the confessed misery of the conquered: really, would that not be the crowning degradation? And so she struggled on.

One morning Madame Caroline saw the mother and daughter washing their linen under the little shed in the garden. The old cook, now almost powerless, was no longer of much help to them; during the late cold weather they had had to nurse her; and it was the same with the husband, at once porter, coachman, and valet, who had great difficulty in sweeping the house and in keeping the old horse upon his legs, for both man and beast were fast growing halt, worn out. So the ladies had set resolutely about their housework, the daughter sometimes dropping her water-colours to prepare the meagre slops upon which all four scantily lived, the mother dusting the furniture and mending the garments and shoes, so enwrapped in her ideas of petty economy that she imagined they were effecting savings in dusters, needles, and thread now that she handled these herself. Only, as soon as a visitor called, it was a sight to see both of them run away, throw off their aprons, wash themselves, and reappear as mistresses with white and idle hands. On the side of the street their style of living had not changed, their honour was safe: the brougham still went out with the horse properly harnessed, taking the Countess and her daughter to make their calls; the guests of every winter still assembled at the fortnightly dinners; there was not a dish less upon the table, not a candle less in the candelabra. And it was necessary to command a view of the garden, as Madame Caroline did, to know what terrible to-morrows of fasting paid for all that show, the lying façade of a vanished fortune. When she saw them promenading their mortal melancholy, under the greenish skeletons of the centenarian trees, in the depths of that damp pit, closely hemmed in by the neighbouring houses, she was filled with immense pity, and withdrew from the window, her heart rent by remorse, as if she felt that she had been Saccard's accomplice in bringing about this misery.

Then, another morning, Madame Caroline experienced a yet more direct and grievous sorrow. She was informed that Dejoie had called, and she bravely resolved to see him.

'Well, my poor Dejoie,' she began, but on noticing the pallor of the old fellow's face she stopped short quite frightened. His eyes seemed lifeless, his features were distorted, and his very tall figure had become both shrunken and bowed.

'Come,' she added, 'you must not let the idea that all this money is lost prostrate you.'

'Oh, madame, it isn't that,' he answered in a low voice. 'At the first moment, no doubt, it was a hard blow, because I had accustomed myself to believe that we were rich. When a man's winning the fever flies to his head, he feels as though he were drunk. But, *mon Dieu*! I was ready to go to work once more; I would have worked so hard that I should have succeeded in getting the sum together again. But you do not know——' He paused; big tears were rolling down his cheeks. 'You do not know,' he added. 'She is gone!'

'Gone! Who?' asked Madame Caroline in surprise.

'Nathalie, my daughter. Her marriage had fallen through; she was furious when Theodore's father came to tell us that his son had already waited too long, and that he was going to marry the daughter of a haberdasher, who would bring him nearly eight thousand francs. Oh, I can understand her anger at the thought of no longer having a copper, and remaining single! But I who loved her so well! Only last winter I used to get up at night to see if she were well covered. And I deprived myself of tobacco in order that she might have prettier hats, and I was her real mother; I had brought her up; I lived only for the pleasure of seeing her in our little rooms.'

His tears choked him; he began to sob.

'You see, it was the fault of my ambition,' he continued. 'If I had sold out as soon as my eight shares had given me the dowry of six thousand francs, she would now have been married. But, you know, they were still going up, and I thought of myself; I wanted first an income of six hundred francs, then one of eight hundred, then one of a thousand; especially as the little one would have inherited this money later on. To think that at one time, when the shares were worth three thousand francs apiece, I had twenty-four thousand francs before me, enough to give her a dowry of six thousand and retire, myself, on an income of nine hundred! But no! I wanted a thousand; how stupid! And now my shares don't represent as much as two hundred francs even. Oh! it was my fault; I should have done better to have thrown myself into the water!'

Greatly distressed by his grief, Madame Caroline allowed him to relieve himself. Still she was desirous of knowing what had happened. 'Gone, my poor Dejoie!' she said, 'how gone?'

Then embarrassment came over him, and a slight flush rose to his pale face. 'Yes, gone, disappeared, three days ago. She had made the acquaintance of a gentleman who lived opposite us—oh! a very good-looking man, about forty years old. In short, she has run away.'

And while he gave details, seeking for fitting words in his embarrassment, Madame Caroline in her mind's eye again beheld Nathalie, slender and blonde, with the frail grace of a pretty girl of the Parisian pavements. She again saw her large eyes, with their tranquil, cold expression reflecting egotism with such extraordinary clearness. She had suffered her father to adore her like an idol, conducting herself with all propriety so long as it was her interest to do so, so long as there remained any hope of a dowry, a marriage, a counter in some little shop where she would be enthroned. But to continue leading a penniless life, to live in rags with her good old father, to have to work again, oh! no, she had had enough of that kind of life, which henceforth had no prospect to offer. And so she had taken herself off, had coldly put on her hat and boots to go elsewhere.

'*Mon Dieu!*' Dejoie continued, stammering, 'there was little to amuse her at home, it's true; and when a girl is pretty, it is provoking for her to waste her youth in weary waiting. But all the same she has been very hard. Just fancy, she did not even bid me good-bye, did not even leave a word of a letter, not the smallest promise to come to see me again from time to time. She shut the door behind her and it was all over. You see, my hands tremble, I have been like an idiot ever since. It is more than I can bear; I am always looking for her at home. After so many years, *mon Dieu!* is it possible that I have her no more, that I shall never have her any more, my poor little child?'

He had ceased weeping, and his wild grief was so distressing that Madame Caroline caught hold of both his hands, unable to find any other words of consolation than: 'My poor Dejoie, my poor Dejoie.'

At last, to divert his attention, she again spoke of the downfall of the Universal. She expressed her regret at having allowed him to take any shares; she judged Saccard severely without naming him. But the old fellow at once became animated again. The passion for gambling which had seized upon him was still alive in his heart. 'Monsieur Saccard?' he said, 'oh! he did quite right to keep me from selling. It was a superb affair; we should have conquered them all, but for the traitors who abandoned us. Ah! madame, if Monsieur Saccard were here, things would go on differently. It was our death-blow when they threw him into prison. And only he can save us. I told the judge so: "Restore him to us, monsieur," I said, "and I'll confide my fortune to him again. I'll confide my life to him because you see he's like Providence itself. He does whatever he likes."'

Madame Caroline looked at Dejoie in stupefaction. What! not a word of anger, not a reproach? This was the ardent faith of a believer. What powerful influence, then, could Saccard have had upon the flock, in order to place it under such a yoke of credulity?

'In fact, madame, that was the only thing I came to tell you,' Dejoie resumed; 'and you must excuse me for having spoken to you of my own sorrow. I only did so because

I couldn't control myself. However, when you see Monsieur Saccard, be sure to tell him that we are still on his side.'

He then went off with his faltering step, and she, left to herself, for a moment felt horrified with existence. That poor man had broken her heart; against the other, the man whom she did not name, she felt increased anger, and had to put forth a great effort in order to restrain an outburst. However, other visitors had arrived, and it was necessary she should see them. She had not a moment to herself that morning.

Among the number the Jordans particularly distressed her. They came together, Paul and Marcelle, like a loving husband and wife who act conjointly in all serious matters, to ask her if there were really no hope of their parents the Maugendres, getting something more from their Universal shares. In this direction, too, there had been an irreparable disaster. Prior to the great battles of the last two settlements, the old awning manufacturer had already possessed seventy-five shares, which had cost him about eighty thousand francs; a superb affair, since these shares at one time, when quoted at the price of three thousand francs apiece, had represented two hundred and twenty-five thousand francs. But the terrible part was that, in the passion of the struggle, Maugendre had played without depositing any cover, believing in Saccard's genius and buying incessantly, so that the frightful differences which now had to be paid—more than two hundred thousand francs—had just swallowed up the rest of his fortune, that income of fifteen thousand francs accumulated by thirty years of hard work. He had nothing left; in fact, he would be barely freed from debt, after selling that little residence in the Rue Legendre of which he was so proud. And in this disaster Madame Maugendre was certainly guiltier than he.

'Ah! madame,' explained Marcelle, whose charming face remained fresh and gay even in the midst of catastrophes, 'you cannot imagine how mamma had changed! She, so prudent, so economical, the terror of her servants, always at their heels, always checking their accounts, had reached such a point that she talked of nothing but hundreds of thousands of francs. She urged on papa—oh! he was not nearly so brave as she was, but would willingly have listened to Uncle Chave if she had not made him crazy with her dream of gaining the big prize, the million. They caught the fever through reading those horrid, lying financial papers; and papa was the first to get it, and tried to hide it in the beginning; however, when mamma caught it, she who had so long professed a hatred of all gambling, everything blazed up and it wasn't long before they were ruined. To think that the rage for gain can so change honest folks!'

Jordan thereupon intervened, amused by a recollection of Uncle Chave which his wife's words had just brought to his mind. 'And if you had seen Uncle Chave's calmness amid these catastrophes!' said he. 'He had prophesied it all and was quite triumphant. He had not once failed to attend the Bourse, he had not once ceased to play his petty cash game, content with carrying his fifteen or twenty francs away every evening, like a good employee who has faithfully done his day's work. Millions were falling around him on all sides, giant fortunes were being made and unmade in a couple of hours, gold was raining down by the bucketful amid the thunderclaps; and all the while he calmly continued making his little living.'

Then Madame Caroline replied to their questions. 'Alas, no!' she said. 'I do not think that your parents can hope to get anything from their shares. All seems to me ended. The shares are now at thirty francs, they will fall to twenty francs, to a hundred sous apiece. Ah, *mon Dieu*! what will become of those poor people, at their age, accustomed to comforts as they are?'

216

'Why,' answered Jordan, simply, 'we shall have to look after them. We are not very rich yet, but things are taking a better turn, and we shan't leave them in the street.'

He had just had a piece of luck. After so many years of thankless toil, his first novel, issued at first as a newspaper serial, and then in book form by a publisher, had suddenly proved a big success; and he now found himself in possession of several thousand francs with all doors henceforth open before him. And he was all eagerness to set to work again, certain of attaining to fortune and glory.

'If we cannot take them to live with us,' he resumed, 'we will secure a little lodging for them. We shall arrange matters in some way.'

A slight trembling came over Marcelle, who was looking at him with bewildered tenderness. 'Oh! Paul, Paul, how good you are!'

And she began to sob.

'Come, my child, calm yourself, I beg of you,' Madame Caroline repeated in bewilderment; 'you must not grieve like this.'

'Oh! let me be; it is not grief. But really, it is all so stupid! When I married Paul, ought not mamma and papa to have given me the dowry which they had always spoken about? Under the pretext, however, that Paul no longer had a copper, and that I was acting foolishly in keeping my promise to him, they did not give us a centime. Ah! they are well punished! If they had given me my dowry they could have had it back now. That would always have been something saved from the Bourse!'

Madame Caroline and Jordan could not help laughing; however, that did not console Marcelle, who only cried the more.

'And then, it is not only that,' she stammered. 'But when Paul was poor, I had a dream. Yes! as in the fairy tales, I dreamed that I was a princess, and that some day I should bring my ruined prince ever so much money, to help him to become a great poet. And now he has no need of me, I have become nothing but a burden, I and my family! It is he who is to have all the trouble, who is to make all the presents. Ah! I stifle at the thought!'

Paul, however, had caught her in his arms. 'What are you talking about, you big silly? Does the wife need to bring anything? Why, you brought yourself, your youth, your love, your good-humour, and there is not a princess in the world that can give more.'

These words at once pacified her. She felt happy at finding that she was loved so well, and realised indeed that it was very stupid of her to cry.

'If your father and your mother are willing,' continued Jordan, 'we will get them a place at Clichy, where I have seen some ground floors, with gardens, at a very reasonable figure. Our little nest is very nice, but it is too small, and, besides, we shall be needing every inch of room.' Then smiling again, and turning towards Madame Caroline, who was greatly touched by this family scene, he added: 'Yes, there will soon be three of us; we may as well confess it, now that I am earning a living! So you see, madame, here she is about to make me a present—she who weeps at having brought me nothing!'

Madame Caroline, who to her incurable despair was condemned to remain childless, looked at Marcelle, who was blushing slightly. Her eyes filled with tears. 'Ah! my dear children, love each other well,' she said; 'you alone are reasonable, you alone are happy!'

Then, before they took their leave, Jordan gave some particulars concerning the newspaper 'L'Espérance.' With his instinctive horror of business matters, he spoke of the office as a most singular cavern, where, himself alone excepted, the entire staff, from the director to the door porter, had engaged in speculation; and he, because he had not gambled, had been looked upon with intense disfavour and treated with contempt by all. Moreover, the fall of the Universal, and especially the arrest of Saccard, had virtually killed the journal. There had been a general scattering of the contributors, and Jantrou alone obstinately clung to the waif, beggared but hoping to derive a livelihood from the remnants of the wreck. He was now quite done for; those three years of prosperity during which he had to a monstrous degree enjoyed everything that could be bought, had finished him off. It was a case similar to that of those starving people who die of indigestion on the day when they sit down to table. And the curious feature, though logical for that matter, was the final downfall of the Baroness Sandorff, who, driven to desperation, longing to recover her money, had, amid all the confusion of the catastrophe, become this scoundrel's mistress.

Madame Caroline turned slightly pale on hearing the Baroness's name; but Jordan, who did not know that the two women had been rivals, went on telling his story. It appeared that on returning to the newspaper office one day to endeavour to obtain some money due to him, he had actually caught Jantrou boxing the Baroness's ears. Yet she had suffered it, clinging to him, perhaps, because she thought that he could give her 'tips,' thanks to his position as an advertising agent. And so she was now rolling lower and lower, carried along that downward course by her passion for gambling, that passion which corrodes and rots everything, which turns one of even the highest and proudest race into a human rag, a waste scrap swept into the gutter. To think of that drunkard, a prey to every vice, belabouring that lady of the aristocracy with all the brutality of a professional bully!

With a gesture of grievous pain, Madame Caroline made Jordan stop. It seemed to her as though she herself were bespattered by this excess of degradation. At the moment of leaving, Marcelle took hold of her hand in a caressing way. 'Pray don't think, dear madame,' said she, 'that we came here to annoy you. Paul, on the contrary, stoutly defends Monsieur Saccard.'

'Why, certainly!' the young man exclaimed. 'He has always been very kind to me. I shall never forget the way in which he relieved us of that terrible Busch. And then, too, he is wonderfully clever and energetic. When you see him, madame, be sure to tell him that we are still deeply grateful to him.'

When the Jordans had gone, Madame Caroline made a gesture of silent wrath. Grateful? Why? For the ruin of the Maugendres? Those Jordans were like Dejoie; they went away repeating the same words of excuse, the same good wishes. And yet they knew; that writer who had passed through the world of finance, with such a fine contempt for money, was certainly not an ignorant man. However, her own revolt continued and grew. No, there was no pardon possible, there was too much mud. Jantrou might have boxed the Baroness's ears, but that did not avenge her. It was Saccard who had rotted everything.

That same day Madame Caroline was to go to Mazaud's with reference to certain documents which she desired to ladd to the brief of her brother's case. She also wished to know what would be the broker's attitude in case the defence should summon him as a witness. Her appointment with him was for four o'clock, after the Bourse; and, on finding herself alone, she spent more than an hour and a half in classifying the information which she had already obtained. She was beginning to see more clearly through the heap of ruins. She had first asked herself where the money could have gone. In this catastrophe, in which two hundred millions had been swallowed up, if some pockets had been emptied, others must have been filled. Moreover, it seemed certain that the bears' rakes had not gathered in the whole sum; a frightful leakage had carried away a good third. On days of disaster at the Bourse, it is as though the soil absorbs some of the money—it wanders away, a little sticks to all fingers.

However, Gundermann alone must have pocketed fifty millions; and Daigremont, from twelve to fifteen. The Marquis de Bohain was also mentioned as a big winner. His classic stroke had once more succeeded: playing through Mazaud for a rise, he refused to pay his differences, though he was receiving nearly two millions from Jacoby, through whom he had played for a fall. This time, however, although well aware that the Marquis had transferred his property to his wife, like a vulgar sharper, Mazaud, quite bewildered by his heavy losses, talked of taking legal proceedings against him.

Almost all the directors of the Universal, moreover, had carved themselves large slices—some, like Huret and Kolb, realising at a high figure before the collapse; others, like the Marquis and Daigremont, adopting treacherous tactics and going over to the 'bears;' to say nothing of the fact that at one of the last meetings, when the Bank was already in difficulties, the board had credited each of its members with a bonus of a hundred and odd thousand francs. Finally, at the *corbeille*, Delarocque and Jacoby were reputed to have won large sums, while Nathansohn was said to have become one of the kings of the *coulisse*, thanks to a profit of three millions which he had realised by playing on his own account for a fall, while playing for Saccard for a rise. The extraordinary feature of his luck was that, having made very large purchases on behalf of the Universal which could no longer pay, he would certainly have failed, and have been 'posted,' if it had not been found necessary to pass the sponge over all the transactions of the *coulisse*, making it a present of the sums which it owed since it was undoubtedly insolvent. So little Nathansohn earned the reputation of being both very lucky and very adroit. And what a pretty and amusing adventure it was to be able to pocket one's winnings without being called upon to pay what one has lost!

However, all the figures remained vague; Madame Caroline could not form an exact estimate of the gains, for the operations of the Bourse are carried on with great mystery, and professional secrecy is strictly observed by the brokers. Even their memorandum-books would have told her nothing, no names being inscribed on them. Thus she in vain tried to ascertain what amount Sabatani had carried off with him on disappearing after the last settlement. That was another ruin, and a hard blow for Mazaud. It was the old story: the shady client, at first received with distrust, depositing a small security of two or three thousand francs, playing cautiously until he had established friendly relations with the broker, and the insignificance of his cover had been forgotten; then launching out, and taking to flight after perpetrating some brigand's trick. Mazaud talked of posting Sabatani, just as he had formerly posted Schlosser, a sharper of the same band, the eternal band which 'works' the market, in the same way as the robbers of olden time 'worked' a forest. And the Levantine, that half-Oriental, half-Italian, with velvet eyes, over whom all the women had grown crazy, had now gone to infest the Bourse of some foreign capital—Berlin, so it was said—pending the time when he should be forgotten at the Bourse of Paris, and could come back again, ready to repeat his stroke, amid general toleration.

Besides her list of the gains, Madame Caroline had drawn up one of the disasters. The catastrophe of the Universal had been one of those terrible shocks that make a whole city totter. Nothing had remained firmly standing. Other establishments had begun to give way; every day there were fresh collapses. One after another the banks went down, with the sudden crash of bits of walls left standing after a fire. In silent dismay folks listened to these repeated falls, and asked where the ruin would stop. But what struck Madame Caroline to the heart was not so much the downfall of the bankers, the companies, the men and things of finance, all destroyed and swept away in the tempest, as the ruin of the many poor people, shareholders, and even speculators, whom she had known and loved, and who were among the victims. After the defeat she counted her dead. And these were not only her poor Dejoie, the imbecile, wretched Maugendres, the sad Beauvilliers ladies, whose misfortune was so touching. Another tragedy had upset her, the failure of the silk manufacturer, Sédille, announced on the previous day. Having seen him at work as a director, the only one of the board, she said, to whom she would have entrusted ten sous, she declared him to be the most honest man in the world. What a frightful thing, then, was this passion for gambling! Here was a man who had spent thirty years in establishing, by dint of labour and honesty, one of the firmest houses in Paris, and who, in less than three years, had so cut and eaten into it that at one stroke, it had fallen into dust! How bitterly he must now regret the laborious days of former times, when he had still believed in the acquirement of fortune by prolonged effort, before a first chance gain had filled him with contempt for work, consumed him with the dream of gaining in an hour, at the Bourse, the million which requires the whole lifetime of an honest merchant! And the Bourse had swept everything away—the unfortunate man remained overwhelmed, fallen from his brilliant position, incapable of resuming business and disqualified from doing so, with a son, too, whom poverty might perhaps turn into a swindler—that Gustave, the soul of joy and festivity, who was living on a footing of from forty to fifty thousand francs worth of debts and was already compromised in an ugly story of some promissory notes signed in favour of a woman.

Then there was another poor devil who distressed Madame Caroline, the *remisier* Massias, and yet God knew that she was not usually tender towards those go-betweens of falsehood and theft! Only she had known Massias also, known him with his large, laughing eyes and the air of a good dog who has been whipped, at the time when he was scouring Paris seeking to obtain a few small orders. If, for a moment, in his turn, he had at last believed himself to be one of the masters of the market, having conquered luck in Saccard's wake, how frightful had been the fall which had awakened him from his dream! He had found himself owing seventy thousand francs, which he had paid, when, as so many others did, he might have pleaded that the matter was one of gambling, and that payment therefore could not be legally enforced. However, by borrowing from friends, and pledging his entire life, he had committed that sublime and useless stupidity of paying—useless, since no one felt the better of him for it; indeed, folks even shrugged their shoulders behind his back. His resentment, however, was only directed against the Bourse, for he had relapsed into his disgust for the dirty calling which he plied, and again shouted that one must be a Jew to succeed in it. Nevertheless, as he was in it, he resigned himself, still hoping that he might yet win the big prize provided he had a keen eye and good legs.

It was the thought, however, of the unknown dead, the victims without a name, without a history, that especially filled Madame Caroline's heart with pity. They were legion, strewn in the thickets, in the ditches full of weeds, and in this wise there were lost ones, wounded ones, with the death rattle in their throats, behind each tree-trunk.

What frightful silent tragedies were here!—the whole throng of petty capitalists, petty shareholders, who had invested all their savings in the same securities, the retired door-porters, the pale old maids living with their cats, the provincial pensioners who had regulated their lives with maniacal rigidity, the country priests stripped bare by almsgiving—all those humble beings whose budgets consist of a few sous, so much for milk, so much for bread, such precise and scanty budgets that a deficiency of two sous brings on a cataclysm! And suddenly nothing was left, the threads of life were severed, swept away, and old trembling hands incapable of working groped in the darkness in bewilderment; scores and scores of humble, peaceful existences being at one blow thrown into frightful want. A hundred desperate letters had arrived from Vendôme, where Fayeux, the dividend collector, had aggravated the disaster by flight. Holding the money and shares of the customers for whom he operated at the Bourse, he had begun to gamble on his own account at a terrible rate; and, having lost, and being unwilling to pay, he had vanished with the few hundred thousand francs which were still in his hands. All round Vendôme, even in the remotest farms, he left poverty and tears. And thus the crash had reached even the humble homesteads. As after great epidemics, were not the really pitiable victims to be found among these people of the lower middle class whose little savings their sons alone could hope to reaccumulate after long years of hard toil?

At last Madame Caroline went out to go to Mazaud's; and as she walked towards the Rue de la Banque she thought of the repeated blows which had fallen upon the broker during the last fortnight. There was Fayeux, who had robbed him of three hundred thousand francs; Sabatani, who had left an unpaid account of nearly double that amount; the Marquis de Bohain and the Baroness Sandorff, both of whom refused to pay differences of more than a million; Sédille, whose bankruptcy had swept about the same amount away; to say nothing of the eight millions which the Universal owed him, those eight millions for which he had carried Saccard over, that frightful loss, the abyss into which from hour to hour, the anxious Bourse expected to see him tumble. Twice already had a catastrophe been reported. And, in this unrelenting fury of fate, a last misfortune had just befallen him, which was to prove the drop of water that would make the vase overflow. Two days previously his clerk Flory had been arrested, convicted of having embezzled a hundred and eighty thousand francs. The demands made upon the young man by Mademoiselle Chuchu, the little *ex-figurante*, the grasshopper from the Parisian pavements, had gradually increased: first, pleasure parties representing no great expense, then apartments in the Rue Condorcet, then jewels and laces; and that which had ruined the unfortunate, soft-hearted fellow had been his first profit of ten thousand francs, after Sadowa, that pleasure-money so quickly gained, so quickly spent, which had made him long for more and still more in his feverish passion for the woman who cost him so dear. But the extraordinary feature of the story was that Flory had robbed his employer simply to pay his gambling debt to another broker; a singular misconception of honesty due to the bewilderment that had come over him in his fear lest he should be immediately posted. And no doubt he had hoped he would be able to conceal the robbery, and replace the money by some miraculous operation. He had wept a great deal in prison, in a frightful awakening of shame and despair; and it was related that his mother, who had arrived that very morning from Saintes to see him, had been obliged to take to her bed at the house of the friends with whom she was stopping.

What a strange thing is luck! thought Madame Caroline, as she slowly crossed the Place de la Bourse. The extraordinary success of the Universal Bank, its ascent to triumph, conquest, and domination, in less than four years, and then its sudden collapse, a month sufficing to reduce the colossal edifice to dust—all this stupefied her. And was not this also Mazaud's story? Never had a man seen destiny smile upon him in such an engaging way. A broker at the age of thirty-two, already very rich through the death of his uncle, and the happy husband of a woman who adored him and who had presented him with two beautiful children, he was further a handsome man, and daily acquired increased importance at the *corbeille* by his connections, his activity, his really surprising scent, and even his shrill voice—that fife-like voice which had become as famous as Jacoby's thunder. But suddenly the ground began cracking around him, and he found himself on the edge of the abyss, into which a mere puff of air would now suffice to blow him. And yet he had not gambled on his own account, being still protected from that passion by his zeal for work, by his youthful anxiety. This blow had fallen on him through his inexperience and passion, through his trust in others. Moreover, people keenly sympathised with him; it was even pretended, with a deal of confidence, that he would come out of it all right.

When Madame Caroline had gone up to the office, she plainly detected an odour of ruin, a quiver of secret anguish in the gloomy rooms. On passing through the cashier's office, she noticed a score of persons, quite a little crowd, waiting, while the cashiers still met the engagements of the house, though with slackening hands like men who are emptying the last drawers. The 'account' office, the door of which was partially open, seemed to her asleep, for its seven employees were all reading their newspapers, having but few transactions to attend to, now that everything was at a standstill at the Bourse. The cash office alone showed some signs of life. And it was Berthier, the authorised clerk, who received her, greatly agitated himself, his face pale, through the misfortune which had fallen on his employer.

'I don't know whether Monsieur Mazaud will be able to receive you, madame,' said he. 'He is not well, for he caught cold through obstinately working without a fire all last night, and he has just gone down to his rooms on the first floor to get a little rest.'

Madame Caroline insisted, however. 'Oh, pray, monsieur, try to induce him to see me just for a moment,' she said. 'The salvation of my brother perhaps depends upon it. Monsieur Mazaud knows very well that my brother was never concerned in the transactions at the Bourse, and his testimony would be of great importance. Moreover, I want to get some figures from him; he alone can give me information about certain documents.'

At last, in a hesitating way, Berthier asked her to step into the broker's private office. 'Wait there a moment, madame,' he said. 'I will go and see.'

On entering this room Madame Caroline felt a keen sensation of cold. The fire must have gone out during the previous day, and no one had thought of lighting it again. But what struck her even more was the perfect order that prevailed here, as if the whole night and morning had been spent in emptying the drawers, destroying the useless papers, and classifying those which ought to be kept. Nothing was lying about, not a paper, not a letter. On the writing table there were only the inkstand, the pen-rack, and a large blotting-pad, on which there had merely remained a package of the *fiches* which Mazaud used—green *fiches*, the colour of hope. And with the room thus bare, an infinite sadness fell with the heavy silence.

In a few minutes Berthier reappeared. 'I have rung twice, madame,' he said, 'but here was no answer, and I do not dare to insist. Perhaps you will ring yourself on your way down. But I advise you to come again.'

Madame Caroline was obliged to retire; nevertheless, on reaching the first-floor landing, she again hesitated, and even extended her arm in order to ring the bell. But she had finally decided to go away, when loud cries and sobs, a muffled uproar, coming from the apartments, rooted her to the spot. And all at once the door opened, and a servant rushed out, with a scared look, and vanished down the stairs, stammering: 'My God! my God! Monsieur——'

Madame Caroline stood motionless before that open doorway, by which a wail of frightful grief now distinctly reached her. And she became very cold, divining the truth, a clear vision of what had happened arising before her. At first she wanted to flee; then she could not, overcome as she was by pity, attracted by the calamity she pictured, experiencing a need to see and contribute her own tears also. So she entered, found every door wide open, and went as far as the *salon*. Two servants, doubtless the cook and the chambermaid, stood at the doorway with terrified faces, stretching their necks into the room and stammering: 'Oh, monsieur! O God! O God!'

The dying light of that grey winter day entered faintly between the heavy silk curtains of the room. However, it was very warm there; the remnants of some huge logs lay in glowing embers in the fire-place, illumining the walls with a red reflection. On a table a bunch of roses, a royal bouquet for the season, which the broker had brought his wife on the previous day, was blooming in this greenhouse temperature, scenting the whole room. It was like the perfume of all the refined luxury which the apartment displayed, like the pleasant odour of luck, of wealth, of happiness in love, which for four years had flourished there. And, lighted by the ruddy glow from the fire, Mazaud lay on the edge of the sofa, his head pierced by a bullet, his clenched hand upon the stock of a revolver; while, standing before him, his young wife, who had hastened to the spot, was giving vent to that wail, that continuous wild cry which could be heard upon the stairs. At the moment of the report she had been holding in her arms her little boy, now four years and a half old; she had brought him with her, and his little hands were clasped around her neck in fright; while her little girl, already six, had followed her, hanging to her skirt and pressing against her. And hearing their mother cry the two children were crying also, crying desperately.

Madame Caroline at once tried to lead them away. 'Madame, I beg of you—— Madame, do not stay here.'

She was trembling herself, however, and felt as if she would faint. She could see the blood still flowing from the hole in Mazaud's head, falling drop by drop upon the velvet of the sofa, whence it trickled on to the carpet. On the floor there was a large stain, which was growing yet larger. And it seemed to her as if this blood reached her, and bespattered both her feet and hands. 'Madame, I beg of you, follow me,' she said.

But, with her son hanging from her neck and her daughter clinging to her waist, the poor woman did not hear, did not stir, stiffened, planted there so firmly that no power in the world could have uprooted her. All three of them were fair, with complexions of milky freshness, the mother seemingly as delicate and as artless as the children. And in the stupor of their dead felicity, in this sudden annihilation of the happiness which was to have lasted for ever, they continued raising their loud cry, the shriek which expressed all the frightful suffering of the human race.

Then Madame Caroline fell down upon her knees, sobbing and stammering, 'Oh, madame, you rend my heart! For mercy's sake, madame, take yourself away from this spectacle; come with me into the next room; let me try to spare you a little of the evil that has been done you.'

And still the group remained there, motionless, wild and woeful, the mother and her two little ones, all three with long light loose hair. And still the frightful shrieking went on, that cry of the blood-tie which rises from the forest when the hunters have killed the sire.

Madame Caroline had risen, her head whirling. There were sounds of steps and voices; a doctor, no doubt, had come to verify the death. And she could remain no longer, but ran away, pursued by that abominable and endless wail, which she fancied she still heard, amid the rolling of the passing vehicles, when she had reached the street.

It was growing dark; the night was cold, and she walked slowly, fearing that people might arrest her, taking her for a murderess, with her haggard look. Everything rose up before her—the whole story of that monstrous crash, which had piled up so many ruins and crushed so many victims. What mysterious force was it then which, after building that golden tower so quickly, had just destroyed it? The same hands that had constructed it seemed to have become infuriated with it, seized with a fit of madness, determined not to leave one stone of it standing on another. Cries of sorrow arose on all sides; fortunes crumbled with a sound akin to that which is heard when the refuse of demolished houses is emptied into a public 'shoot.' The last domains of the Beauvilliers, the savings of Dejoie scraped together sou by sou, the profits which Sédille had realised from his silk-works, the bonds of the Maugendres, who had lately retired from business, were all flung pell-mell, with a crash, into the depths of the same cloaca, which nothing seemed to fill up. There were also Jantrou, drowned in alcohol; La Sandorff, drowned in mire; Massias, again forced to lead the wretched life of a dog, chained for ever to the Bourse by debt; Flory, a thief, in prison, expiating the weaknesses of his soft heart; and Sabatani and Fayeux, fugitives, galloping off in fear of the gendarmes. And there were the unknown victims, still more distressing and pitiable, the great flock of all the poor that the catastrophe had made—the poor, shivering in abandonment, crying with hunger. Then, too, there was death—the pistol-shots that re-echoed from the four corners of Paris; there was Mazaud's smashed head and Mazaud's blood, which, drop by drop, amid the luxury of a drawing-room and the perfume of roses, bespattered his wife and his little ones, shrieking with grief.

And then all that she had beheld, all that she had heard during the last few weeks poured forth from Madame Caroline's wounded heart—found vent in a cry of execration for Saccard. She could no longer keep silent, no longer put him aside as if he did not exist, so as to avoid judging and condemning him. He alone was guilty; it was shown by each of these accumulated disasters, the frightful pile of which terrified her. She cursed him; her wrath and her indignation, so long repressed, overflowed in a revengeful hatred, the hatred of evil itself. Did she no longer love her brother, then, that she had waited until now to hate the terrible man who was the sole cause of their misfortune? Her poor brother, that great innocent, that great toiler, so just and so honest, now soiled with the indelible stain of imprisonment, the victim whom she had forgotten, though he was dearer than all the others! Ah, that Saccard might find no pardon! that no one might dare to plead his cause any further, not even those who continued to believe in him, not even those who had only known his kindness!—that he might some day die alone, spurned and despised!

Madame Caroline raised her eyes. She had reached the Place de la Bourse, and saw the Temple of Money in front of her. The twilight was falling. Behind the building a ruddy cloud hung in the fog-laden wintry sky—a cloud like the smoke of a conflagration, charged with the flames and the dust of a stormed city. And against this cloud the Bourse stood out grey and gloomy in the melancholiness born of the catastrophe which, for a month past, had left it deserted, open to the four winds of heaven, like some market which famine has emptied. Once again had the inevitable, periodical epidemic come—the epidemic which sweeps through it every ten or fifteen years—the Black Fridays, as the speculators say, which strew the soil with ruins. Years are needed for confidence to be restored, for the great financial houses to be built up anew, and time goes slowly by until the passion for gambling, gradually reviving, flames up once more and repeats the adventure, when there comes another crisis, and the downfall of everything in a fresh disaster. This time, however, beyond the ruddy smoke on the horizon, in the hidden distant parts of the city, it seemed as though one could hear a vague sound of splitting and rending, betokening the end of a world—the world of the Second Empire.

CHAPTER XII
FROM HORROR TO HOPE

The investigation of the case progressed so slowly that seven months had gone by since the arrest of Saccard and Hamelin, and the case had not yet been entered on the roll. It was now the middle of September, and that Monday Madame Caroline, who went to see her brother twice a week, was to call at the Conciergerie at about three o'clock. She now never mentioned Saccard's name, and had a dozen times replied to his pressing requests to come and see him by formal refusal. For her, rigidly resolved on justice, he was no more. But she still hoped to save her brother, and became quite gay on visiting days, happy at being able to tell him of the last steps that she had taken, and to bring him a bouquet of his favourite flowers.

So that Monday morning she was preparing a large bunch of red carnations when old Sophie, the Princess d'Orviedo's servant, came down to tell her that her mistress wished to speak to her at once. Astonished and vaguely anxious, Madame Caroline hurried up the stairs. For several months she had not seen the Princess, for she had resigned her position as secretary of the Institute of Work immediately after the catastrophe of the Universal. She now only went to the Boulevard Bineau from time to time, and then merely to see Victor, who at present seemed to have been mastered by the rigid discipline, though he still retained an artful expression, with his left cheek larger than the right one, and his mouth twisted into a ferocious grimace. A presentiment at once came to Madame Caroline that she had been sent for by the Princess on his account.

The Princess d'Orviedo was at last ruined. Less than ten years had sufficed her to restore to the poor the three hundred millions of her husband's estate stolen from the pockets of over-credulous shareholders. Although she had required five years to spend the first hundred millions on extravagant works of charity, she had managed in four years and a half to sink the other two hundred in founding establishments of still greater luxury. To the Institute of Work, the St. Mary's Infant Asylum, the St. Joseph's

Orphan Asylum, the Châtillon Asylum for the Aged, and the St. Marceau Hospital, she had added a model farm near Évreux, two convalescent homes for children on the banks of the Marne, another Asylum for the Aged at Nice, hospitals, model dwellings, libraries, and schools in the four corners of France, to say nothing of large donations to charities already in existence. She was still swayed, moreover, by the same desire of princely restitution; it was no question of flinging a crust to the wretched out of compassion or fear; she was bent upon giving all that is nice and beautiful, the enjoyments and superfluities of life, to humble folks possessed of nothing, to weak ones whom the strong had despoiled of their share of delight—in a word, it was as though the palaces of the wealthy had been flung wide open to the beggars of the high roads, so that they also might sleep in silk and feast off golden plate.

During ten years there had been no pause in the rain of millions which, amid endless complications with contractors and architects, had provided marble dining-halls, dormitories enlivened with bright paintings, façades as monumental as Louvres, gardens blooming with rare plants, indeed superb works of every kind; and the Princess now felt very happy, carried away by intense joy at finding her hands to be at last clean, unsoiled by the possession of even a centime. Indeed, she had actually managed to run into debt, and was being sued for a balance of accounts amounting to several hundred thousand francs, which her lawyers were unable to get together, so utterly had her vast fortune been frittered away, flung to the four winds of charity. And now a board nailed over the carriage entrance in the Rue Saint-Lazare announced the approaching sale of the mansion, the final sweep which would carry away the last vestiges of that accursed money, picked up in the mire and blood of financial brigandage.

Old Sophie was waiting for Madame Caroline on the landing in order to usher her in. Quite furious with the turn things had taken, the good creature scolded all day long. Ah! she had prophesied that her mistress would end by dying a beggar! Ought she not rather to have married again, so as to have children by another husband, since the one secret desire of her heart was to become a mother? Sophie herself had no reason for complaint or anxiety, as she had long since been provided with an annuity of two thousand francs, on which she was now going to live in her native village near Angoulême. Nevertheless, it made her angry to think that her mistress had not even kept back for herself the few sous that were needed every morning to pay for the bread and milk upon which she now subsisted. Incessant quarrels broke out between them. The Princess smiled, with her divine smile of hope, answering that she would need nothing but a winding-sheet when at the end of the month she should have entered the convent where her place had long been marked out for her, a convent of Carmelites walled off from the entire world. Rest, eternal rest! that was her goal.

Madame Caroline found the Princess as she had seen her for the last four years, clad in her everlasting black dress, her hair concealed by a lace fichu, still looking pretty at the age of thirty-nine, with her round face and pearly teeth, but having a yellow complexion, as after ten years of cloister life. And the small room, like the office of a provincial process-server, was littered with countless papers all jumbled together—plans, accounts, portfolios, all the waste paper connected with the squandering of three hundred millions of francs.

'Madame,' said the Princess, in her slow, gentle voice, which no emotion now could cause to tremble, 'I desired to acquaint you with some news that was brought to me this morning. It relates to Victor, the boy whom you placed at the Institute of Work.'

Madame Caroline's heart began to beat violently. Ah! the wretched child, whom his father, in spite of his formal promises, had not even gone to see, during the few months that he had known of his existence, prior to being imprisoned in the Conciergerie. What would become of the lad henceforth, she wondered. And she, who forbade herself all thought of Saccard, was continually compelled to think of him through the disturbing influence of her adoptive motherhood.

'A terrible thing happened yesterday,' continued the Princess—'a crime which nothing can repair.'

And thereupon, in her frigid way, she began to relate a frightful story. Three days previously, it seemed, Victor had obtained admission into the infirmary by complaining of insupportable headaches. The doctor of the Institute had suspected this to be the feigned illness of an idler, but in point of fact the lad was really a prey to frequent neuralgic attacks. Now on the afternoon in question it appeared that Alice de Beauvilliers had come to the Institute without her mother, in order to help the sister on duty with the quarterly inventory of the medicine closet. Victor happened to be alone in the adjoining infirmary, and the sister, having been obliged to absent herself for a short time, was amazed on her return to find Alice missing. She had begun to search for her, and at last, to her horror and amazement, had found her lying in the infirmary most severely injured—in fact, more dead than alive. Beside her, significantly enough, lay her empty purse. She had been attacked by Victor, and, brief as had been the sister's absence, the young miscreant had already contrived to flee. The astonishing part of the affair was that no sound of struggle, no call for help, had been heard by anyone. In less than ten minutes the crime had been planned and perpetrated, and its author had taken to flight. How could Victor have thus managed to escape, vanish, as it were, without leaving any trace behind him? A minute search had been made throughout the establishment, but it had become evident that he was no longer there. He must have gone off by way of the bathroom, which was entered from the infirmary corridor, and have jumped out of a window overlooking a series of roofs which gradually became lower and lower as they approached the Boulevard. However, this route seemed such a perilous one that many refused to believe that a human being could have traversed it; and thus the mode of Victor's escape remained somewhat doubtful. As for Alice, his unfortunate victim, she had been taken home to her mother, and was now confined to her bed, delirious, in a high fever.

Madame Caroline was so profoundly astounded by this awful story that it seemed to her as if all the blood in her heart were freezing. She thought of the young miscreant's parentage, and shuddered at the remembrance that Saccard was his father.

'I do not wish to reproach you, madame,' concluded the Princess, 'for it would be unjust to hold you in the least degree responsible. Only, you really had in this boy a very terrible *protégé*.' And, as if a connection of ideas had arisen in her mind, she added: 'One cannot live with impunity amid certain surroundings. I myself had the greatest qualms of conscience, and felt myself an accomplice when that Bank lately went to pieces, heaping up so many ruins and so many iniquities. Yes, I ought never to have allowed my house to become the cradle of such abomination. But the evil is done, the house will be purified, and I—oh! I am no more—God will forgive me.'

Her pale smile, of hope at last realised, had reappeared on her features, and with a gesture she foreshadowed her departure from the world, the end of the part which she had played as a good invisible fairy—her disappearance for evermore.

Madame Caroline had caught hold of her hands and was pressing and kissing them, so upset by remorse and pity that she stammered out disjointed words. 'You do wrong to excuse me,' she said; 'I am guilty—that poor girl, I must see her, I will go to see her at once.'

And thereupon she went off, leaving the Princess and her old servant to begin their packing for the great departure, which was to separate them after forty years of life together.

Two days previously, on the Saturday, the Countess de Beauvilliers had resigned herself to the course of abandoning her mansion to her creditors. For six months past she had not been able to pay the interest on the mortgage, and, what with costs of all sorts and the ever-present threat of foreclosure and enforced sale, the situation had become intolerable. Accordingly, her lawyer had advised her to let everything go, and to retire to some small lodging, where she might live on next to nothing, whilst he endeavoured to liquidate her affairs. She would not have yielded; even to the very annihilation of her race, the downfall of the ceilings upon her head she would have persisted, perhaps, in her efforts to keep up her station, and to make it appear that she was still possessed of means, had not a fresh misfortune all at once prostrated her. Her son Ferdinand, the last of the Beauvilliers—that useless young fellow, who, kept apart from all employment in France, had become a Pontifical Zouave in order to escape from his nullity and idleness—had died ingloriously at Rome, his blood so impoverished, his system so severely tried by the oppressive sun, that, already ill, suffering from a complaint of the chest, he had not been able to fight at Mentana.[28]

When the tidings of his death reached the Countess she felt a void within her, a collapse of all her ideas, all her plans—all the laboriously raised scaffolding which for so many years had so proudly upheld the honour of her name. Four and twenty hours sufficed; the walls cracked, and a spectacle of distressing misery stood revealed among the ruins. The old horse was sold; the cook alone remained, doing her shopping in a dirty apron, buying two sous' worth of butter and a quart of dry beans; whilst the Countess was perceived on the footway wearing a muddy skirt and boots which let in the water. It was the advent of pauperism in a single night; and such was the force of the disaster that it swept away even the pride of this woman, who believed so firmly in the good old times, and who had so long warred with the century in which she lived. She and her daughter had taken refuge in the Rue de la Tour-des-Dames, in the house of an old wardrobe dealer who had become a devotee and let out furnished rooms to priests. In this house the two women secured a large, bare room of dignified, mournful aspect. At the further end of it was an alcove, in which stood a couple of small beds; and when one had shut the folding doors with which this alcove was provided—doors covered with paper similar to that on the walls—the room became transformed into a parlour. This circumstance had somewhat consoled the poor creatures.

On the Saturday, however, the Countess had not been installed in the place for a couple of hours when an unexpected and extraordinary visit again plunged her into anguish. Alice fortunately had just gone out. The visitor was Busch, with his flat dirty face, greasy frock-coat, and white cravat twisted like a cord. Warned by his scent that the favourable moment had come, he had finally decided to push forward that old affair of the acknowledgment of ten thousand francs which the Count de Beauvilliers had signed in favour of Léonie Cron.

With a glance at the apartment, he took in the widow's situation. Had he waited too long? he wondered. However, like a man capable, on occasion, of urbanity and patience, he explained the case at length to the frightened Countess. This was really her husband's handwriting, was it not? It clearly told the story, upon which, by the way, he did not insist. Nor did he even conceal the fact that, fifteen years having elapsed, he did not believe that she was legally obliged to pay. However that might be, he was simply his client's representative, and knew that she was resolved to test the question in the law courts, and raise the most frightful scandal, unless the matter were compromised. When the Countess, ghastly pale, struck to the heart by the revival of the frightful past, expressed astonishment that they had waited so long before applying to her, he invented a story, saying that the acknowledgment had been lost, and found again at the bottom of a trunk; and, as she definitively refused to look into the matter, he went off, still evincing great politeness and saying that he would return with his client, though not on the morrow, as she would not then be at liberty, but either on the following Monday or Tuesday.

When the Monday came the Countess de Beauvilliers had quite forgotten that ill-dressed man and his cruel story, distracted as she was by the awful calamity which had befallen her daughter, who had been brought home to her delirious, and whom she had put to bed and nursed with tear-dimmed eyes. At last Alice had fallen asleep, and the mother had just sat down, exhausted, crushed by the unrelenting fury of fate, when Busch again presented himself, accompanied this time by Léonie.

'Madame, here is my client, and this matter must now be settled,' said the Jew.

At sight of Léonie, Madame de Beauvilliers shuddered. She looked at her, and saw her clad in crude colours, with coarse black hair falling over her eyebrows, her face broad and flabby, her whole person sordid and vile; and the Countess's heart was tortured, her woman's pride bled afresh after so many years of forgiveness and forgetfulness. O God of Heaven, to think it was for such creatures as this woman that her husband, the Count, had betrayed her!

The interview began. Neither Busch nor Léonie sought to mince matters, but spoke out plumply, crudely, with brazen faces. The woman was already telling her ignoble tale in a hoarse voice, spoilt by dram-drinking, whilst Busch unfolded and displayed the Count's promise to pay her ten thousand francs, when a moan came from the alcove, and Alice began stirring under her coverlet. Only one of the folding-doors was closed, and the Countess, with a gesture of anguish, hastened to shut the other one. Ah, that only her daughter might get to sleep again, see nothing, hear nothing, of all this abomination!

Léonie, however, was fairly launched, and went on with her narrative, speaking at last so impudently, so coarsely, that Madame de Beauvilliers, in furious exasperation, raised her hand to strike her.

'Be quiet! be quiet!' cried the Countess; whilst Léonie, in a fright, instinctively raised her elbow to shield her face, like one accustomed to be beaten.

And then a fearful silence fell, soon broken, however, by a fresh plaint from the alcove, a low sound like that of stifled sobbing. The Countess heard it. 'Well, what do you want?' she asked, trembling and lowering her voice.

Busch thereupon intervened: 'Why, madame, this girl wants to be paid, and she is right. Your husband signed that paper, and it ought to be honoured.'

'Never will I pay such a debt.'

229

'Then we shall take a cab on leaving here and go to the Palais de Justice, where I shall lodge the complaint which I have already drafted, and which you can see here. In it are related all the facts which Mademoiselle has just told you.'

'But this is abominable blackmailing; you will not do such a thing.'

'I beg your pardon, madame, I shall do it at once. Business is business.'

Intense weariness, utter discouragement, took possession of the Countess. The last flash of pride, which had kept her up, had just given way, and all her violence, all her strength, fell with it. She clasped her hands and stammered: 'But you see to what we are reduced. Look at this room. We have nothing left; to-morrow, perhaps, we shall even lack bread to eat. Where do you expect me to get the money? Ten thousand francs, my God!'

Busch smiled, like a man accustomed to fish in such ruins. 'Oh, ladies like you always have resources! You will find the needful if you look carefully.'

For a moment he had been watching an old jewel-casket, which the Countess had left on the mantel-shelf that morning after emptying a trunk, and he scented the precious stones within it with unfailing instinct. His eyes shone indeed with such a flame that Madame de Beauvilliers followed the direction of his glance, and understood. 'No, no!' she cried: 'the jewels, never!'

She seized hold of the casket as if to defend it. Those last jewels which had so long been in the family, those few jewels which she had kept through periods of the greatest embarrassment as her daughter's only dowry, and which now were her final resource! Part with them? 'Never! I would rather give my flesh,' she cried.

But just then there was a diversion; Madame Caroline knocked and entered. She arrived in a distracted state, and stopped short in astonishment at the scene upon which she had fallen. In a few words she asked the Countess not to disturb herself, and would have gone away but for a supplicating gesture from the poor woman, which she thought she could understand. So she remained there, motionless, apart from the others, at the further end of the room.

Busch had just put on his hat again, while Léonie, more and more ill at ease, went towards the door.

'Then, madame, there is nothing left for us but to retire,' said the Jew.

Yet he did not retire, but on the contrary repeated the whole story, in terms more shameful still, as if to further humiliate the Countess in presence of the new-comer— this lady whom he pretended not to recognise, according to his custom when he was engaged in business.

'Good-bye, madame,' he said at last, 'we are going to the office of the Public Prosecutor at once. The whole story will be in the newspapers within three days from now. And for that you will only have to thank yourself.'

In the newspapers! This horrible scandal upon the very ruins of her house! It was not enough, then, that the ancient fortune should have crumbled to dust; everything must roll in the mud as well. Ah! might not the honour of the name at least be saved? And with a mechanical movement she opened the casket. The ear-rings, the bracelet, three rings appeared, brilliants and rubies, in old-fashioned settings.

Busch had eagerly drawn near. His eyes softened with a caressing gentleness. 'Oh!' said he, 'these are not worth ten thousand francs. Let me look at them.'

His sensual passion for precious stones had burst forth, and he was already taking the jewels up one by one, turning them over, holding them in the air, with his fat, trembling, loving fingers. The purity of the rubies especially seemed to throw him into

230

an ecstasy; and those old brilliants, although their cutting was sometimes unskilful, of what a marvellous water they were!

'Six thousand francs!' said he, in the hard voice of an auctioneer, hiding his emotion under this estimate. 'I only count the stones; the settings are merely fit for the melting pot. Well, we will be satisfied with six thousand francs.'

But it was too severe a sacrifice for the Countess. Her violence revived; she took the jewels away from him and held them tight in her convulsed hands. No, no! it was too much to require that she should also throw into the gulf those few stones, which her mother had worn, and which her daughter was to have worn on her wedding day. Burning tears started from her eyes, and streamed down her cheeks, in such tragic grief that Léonie, her heart touched, distracted with pity, began tugging at Busch's coat to force him to go off. She herself wished to leave, feeling that it was not right to give so much pain to that poor old lady, who seemed so good. Busch, however, watched the scene very coldly, now confident that he would carry the jewels off with him, knowing, as he did, by long experience that fits of crying, with women, betoken the collapse of the will; and so he waited.

Perhaps the frightful scene would have been prolonged if at that moment a distant, stifled voice had not burst into sobs. It was Alice, calling from the alcove: 'Oh! mamma, they are killing me! Give them everything, let them take everything away! Oh! mamma, let them go away! They are killing me, they are killing me!'

Then the Countess made a gesture of desperate abandonment, the gesture of one who would have given her very life. Her daughter had heard; her daughter was dying of shame. That sufficed, and she flung the jewels at Busch, and hardly gave him time to lay the Count's acknowledgment upon the table in exchange, but pushed him out of the room, after Léonie, who had already disappeared. Then the unhappy woman again opened the alcove, and let her head fall upon Alice's pillow; and there they remained, both exhausted, overwhelmed, mingling their tears.

Swayed by a feeling of revolt, Madame Caroline had been for a moment on the point of intervening. Could she allow that wretch to strip those two poor women in that fashion? But she had just heard the shameful story, and what could be done to avoid the scandal? For she knew him to be a man to carry out his threats. She herself felt ashamed in his presence, in the complicity of the secrets which they shared. Ah! what suffering, what filth! A feeling of embarrassment came over her; why had she hastened to this room, since she could find neither words to say nor help to offer? All the phrases that came to her lips, questions, mere allusions with regard to the terrible event of the day before, seemed to her out of place, cruel in presence of the suffering victim. And what help could she have offered which would not have seemed like derisive charity, she who was also ruined, already embarrassed as to how she might contrive to live pending the issue of the trial? At last she advanced, with eyes full of tears and arms open, overcome by infinite compassion, wild emotion which made her whole being tremble.

Those two miserable, fallen, hopeless creatures in that vulgar lodging-house alcove were all that remained of the ancient race of the Beauvilliers, formerly so powerful, exercising sovereign sway. That race had owned estates as large as a kingdom; twenty leagues along the Loire had belonged to it—castles, meadows, arable land, forests. But this immense landed fortune had gradually dwindled with the progress of the centuries, and the Countess had just engulfed the last shreds of it in one of those tempests of modern speculation of which she had no comprehension: at first the twenty thousand francs which she had saved, accumulated for her daughter sou by sou, then the sixty thousand francs borrowed on Les Aublets, and then the farm itself. The mansion in the Rue Saint-Lazare would not pay her creditors. Her son had died far from her and ingloriously. Her daughter had been brought home to her in a pitiable condition, perhaps also destined soon to die. And the Countess, formerly so noble, tall, and slender, perfectly white, with her grand past-century air; was now nothing but a poor old woman, destroyed, shattered by all this devastation; while Alice, without beauty or youth, displaying her elongated scarecrow neck, had a gleam of madness in her eyes—madness mingled with mortal grief as she mourned over the irreparable. And they both sobbed, sobbed on, without a pause.

Then Madame Caroline did not say a word, but simply took hold of them and pressed them tightly to her heart. It was the only thing that she could do; she wept with them. And the two unfortunates understood her; their tears began to course more gently. Though no consolation was possible, would it not still be necessary to live, to live on in spite of everything?

When Madame Caroline was again in the street she caught sight of Busch conferring with La Méchain. He hailed a cab, pushed Léonie into it, and then disappeared. But, as Madame Caroline was hurrying away, La Méchain marched straight up to her. She had no doubt been waiting for her, for she immediately began to talk of Victor, like one who already knew what had happened on the previous day at the Institute of Work. Since Saccard's refusal to pay the four thousand francs she had been living in a perfect rage, ever exerting her ingenuity in search of some means by which she might further exploit the affair; and thus she had just learnt the story at the Boulevard Bineau, where she frequently went, in the hope of hearing something to her advantage. Her plan must have been settled upon, for she declared to Madame Caroline that she should immediately begin searching for Victor. The poor child! she said, it was too terrible to abandon him in this way to his evil instincts; he must be found again, if they did not wish to see him some fine morning in the dock. And as she spoke, her little eyes, peeping out of her fat face, searchingly scrutinised the good lady, whom she was happy to find in such distress, for she reflected that, after she had found the boy, she would be able to get some more five-franc pieces out of her.

'So it is agreed, madame,' she said. 'I am going to look after the matter. In case you should desire any news, don't take the trouble to go all the way to the Rue Marcadet, but call at Monsieur Busch's office, in the Rue Feydeau, where you are certain to find me every day at about four o'clock.'

Madame Caroline returned to the Rue Saint-Lazare, tormented by a new anxiety. There was that young monster free, roaming the world; and who could tell what evil hereditary instincts he might not seek to satisfy, like some devouring wolf? She made a hasty meal, and then took a cab, consumed by her desire to obtain some information at once, and having time, she found, to go to the Boulevard Bineau before her visit to the Conciergerie. On the way, amidst the agitation of her fever, an idea seized hold of her and mastered her: to call on Maxime first of all, take him to the Institute, and force him to concern himself about Victor, who was his brother after all. He, Maxime, alone remained rich; he alone could intervene and deal with the matter to some purpose.

But Madame Caroline had no sooner entered the hall of the luxurious little residence in the Avenue de l'Impératrice than she felt a chill. Upholsterers were removing the hangings and carpets, servants were covering the chairs and chandeliers; while from all the pretty trifles which were being moved about came a dying perfume, like that of a bouquet thrown away on the morrow of a ball. And in the bedroom she found Maxime between two huge trunks in which his valet was packing a marvellous outfit, as rich and delicate as a bride's.

As soon as he perceived her the young man spoke, in a dry, frigid voice. 'Ah! is it you? Your visit is well timed. It will save me from writing to you. I have had enough of it all, and I am going away.'

'What! You are going away?'

'Yes, I start this evening; I am going to spend the winter at Naples.'

And when, with a wave of the hand, he had sent his valet away, he continued: 'You are mistaken if you imagine that I have been at all amused at having my father in the Conciergerie during the last six months! I am certainly not going to stay here to see him in the dock, though I utterly detest travelling. But then they have fine weather in the South; I am taking what I am most likely to require, and perhaps after all I shan't feel so much bored.'

She looked at him as he stood there so correctly groomed; she looked at the overflowing trunks, in which lay nothing belonging to wife or mistress, nothing but what served for the worship of himself; and all the same she made the venture.

'I had come to ask a service of you,' she said; and forthwith she told the story—Victor a bandit, Victor a fugitive, capable of every crime. 'We cannot abandon him,' she added. 'Come with me; let us unite our efforts.'

He did not allow her to finish, however, but, turning livid, trembling from fear, as if he had felt some dirty murderous hand upon his shoulder, exclaimed: 'Well, that was the only thing wanting! A thief for a father, an assassin for a brother! I have remained here too long; I wanted to start last week. Why, it is abominable, abominable, to put a man like me in such a position!'

Then, as she insisted, he became insolent. 'Let me alone, I tell you. Since this life of worry amuses you, stay in it. I warned you, remember; it serves you right if you weep to-day. But, for my own part, rather than put myself out for them in the slightest degree, I would sweep the whole villainous crew into the gutter.'

She had risen to her feet. 'Good-bye, then.'

'Good-bye.'

And, as she withdrew, she saw him summoning his valet again, and superintending the careful packing of a *nécessaire de toilette*, the silver-gilt pieces of which were chased in the most gallant fashion, especially the basin, on which was engraved a round of Cupids. While she pictured him going away to live in forgetfulness and idleness, under the bright sun of Naples, she suddenly had a vision of the other one, hungry, prowling, on a dark, muggy night, with a knife in his hands, in some lonely alley of La Villette or Charonne. Was not this the answer to the question whether money is not education, health, and intelligence? Since the same human mire remains beneath, does not all civilisation reduce itself to the superiority of smelling nice and living well?

On reaching the Institute of Work Madame Caroline experienced a keen feeling of revolt at sight of all the vast luxury of the establishment. Of what use were those two majestic wings, one for the boys and the other for the girls, connected by the monumental pavilion reserved for the offices? Of what use were those yards as large as parks, those faïence walls in the kitchens, those marbles in the dining-halls, those staircases and corridors broad enough for a palace? Of what use was all that grandiose charity if they could not, in such spacious and salubrious surroundings, straighten an ill-bred creature, turn a perverted child into a well-behaved man, with the upright reason of health?

She went straight to the director, and pressed him with questions, wishing to know the slightest details. But the drama was veiled in obscurity; he could only repeat what she had already learnt from the Princess. Since the previous day the investigations had continued, both in the Institute and in the neighbourhood, but without yielding the slightest result. Victor was already far away, galloping through the city, in the depths of the frightful unknown. He could not have any money left, for Alice's purse, which he had emptied, had only contained three francs and four sous. The director, moreover, had avoided informing the police, in order to spare the poor Beauvilliers ladies from public scandal; and Madame Caroline thanked him, promising that she herself would take no steps at the Prefecture, in spite of her ardent desire to know what had become of the lad. Then, in despair at going away as ignorant as she had come, it occurred to her to repair to the infirmary to question the sisters. But even there she could get no precise information, though she enjoyed a few minutes of profound appeasement in the quiet little room which separated the girls' dormitory from that of the boys A joyous tumult was now rising from the yards; it was playtime, and she felt that she had not done justice to the happy cures effected by open air, comfort, and work. Lads were growing up here who would certainly prove strong and healthy men. Four or five men of average honesty to one bandit, surely that would still be a fine result, in the chances that aggravate or diminish hereditary vices!

Left alone for a moment by the sister on duty, Madame Caroline had just approached a window to watch the children playing below, when the crystalline voices of some little girls in the adjoining infirmary attracted her. The door was half open; she could witness the scene without being noticed. This infirmary was a very cheerful room, with its white walls and its four beds draped with white curtains. A broad sheet of sunlight was gilding all the whiteness, a blooming of lilies, as it were, in the warm atmosphere. In the first bed on the left she clearly recognised Madeleine, the little convalescent whom she had seen there, eating bread and jam, on the day when she had brought Victor to the Institute. The child was always falling ill, consumed by the alcoholism of her race, so poor in blood, too, that, with her large womanly eyes, she was as slender and pale as the saints that one sees in stained-glass windows. She was now thirteen years old, and quite alone in the world, her mother having died from violence during a drunken orgy. And Madeleine it was who, kneeling in the middle of her bed in her long white nightdress, with her fair hair streaming over her shoulders, was teaching a prayer to three little girls occupying the three other beds.

'Join your hands like this, open your hearts very wide.'

The three little girls were also kneeling amid their bed-clothes. Two of them were between eight and ten years old, the third was not yet five. In their long white nightdresses, with their frail hands clasped and their serious and ecstatic faces, one would have taken them for little angels.

'And you must repeat after me what I am going to say. Listen! "O God, please reward Monsieur Saccard for all his kindness; let him live long and be happy!"'

Then, in their cherubs' voices, the adorably faulty lisping of childhood, the four girls, in an impulse of faith in which all their pure little beings were offered up, repeated simultaneously:

'O God, please reward Monsieur Saccard for all his kindness; let him live long and be happy!'

Madame Caroline experienced a sudden impulse to enter the room and hush those children, and forbid what she regarded as a blasphemous and cruel game. No, no! Saccard had no right to be loved; it was pollution to allow infancy to pray for his happiness. Then a great shudder stopped her; tears rose to her eyes. Why should she force those innocent beings, who as yet knew nothing of life, to espouse her quarrel, the wrath of her experience? Had not Saccard been good to them, he who was to some extent the creator of this establishment, and who sent them playthings every month? She was profoundly agitated, again finding in all this a proof that there is no man utterly blameworthy, no man who, amid all the evil which he may have done, has not also done much good. And while the little girls again took up their prayer, she went off, carrying away with her the sound of those angelic voices calling down the blessings of heaven upon the conscienceless man, the artisan of catastrophes, whose mad hands had just ruined a world.

As she at last alighted from her cab on the Boulevard du Palais, outside the Conciergerie, she discovered that in her emotion she had forgotten to bring the carnations which she had prepared that morning for her brother. There was a flower-girl near by, selling little bouquets of roses at two sous apiece; and she purchased one, and made Hamelin, who was very fond of flowers, smile when she told him of her thoughtlessness. That afternoon, however, she found him unusually sad. At first, during the earlier weeks of his imprisonment, he had been unable to believe that the charges against him were serious. His defence seemed to him a simple matter: he had been elected chairman against his will; he had had nothing to do with the financial operations, having been almost always absent from Paris and unable to exercise any control. But his conversations with his lawyer and the steps that Madame Caroline had taken, with no other result than weariness and vexation of spirit, had finally made him realise the frightful responsibilities that rested on him. He would be held partially responsible for the slightest illegalities that had been perpetrated; it would never be admitted that he had been ignorant of a single one of them; he would be regarded as Saccard's accomplice. And it was then that in his somewhat simple faith as a fervent Catholic he found a resignation and tranquillity of soul that astonished his sister. When she arrived from the outer world, from her anxious errands, from the midst of the harsh, turbid humanity which enjoyed freedom, it astonished her to find him peaceful and smiling in his bare cell, to the walls of which, like the pious child he was, he had nailed around a small black wooden crucifix four crudely coloured religious prints. However, as soon as one puts oneself in the hand of God there is no more rebellion; all undeserved suffering becomes a guarantee of salvation. Thus Hamelin's only sadness arose from the disastrous stoppage of his enterprises. Who would take up his work? Who would continue the resurrection of the East, so felicitously commenced by the United Steam Navigation Company and the Carmel Silver Mining Company? Who would construct the network of railways, from Broussa to Beyrout and Damascus, from Smyrna to Trebizond, which was to set young blood flowing through the veins of the Old World? For, despite everything, he still believed in it all; he said that the work begun could not die; he only felt grieved at no longer being the hand chosen by Heaven for its execution. And especially did his voice break when he sought to know in punishment of what fault God had not permitted him to found that great Catholic bank, which was destined to transform modern society, that treasury of the Holy Sepulchre which would restore a kingdom to the Pope and finally make a single nation of all the peoples, by taking from the Jews the sovereign power of money.

And this also he predicted, this inevitable, invincible bank; he prophesied the coming of the just man with pure hands who would some day found it. And if on that Monday afternoon he seemed anxious, it must have simply been because, amidst all the serenity of a man accused and about to be convicted, he had reflected that on emerging from prison his hands would never be sufficiently clean to resume the great work.

He listened absent-mindedly while his sister explained to him that newspaper opinion seemed to be growing a little more favourable to him. And then, without any transition, looking at her with his dreamy eyes, he inquired, 'Why do you refuse to see him?'

She trembled; she clearly understood that he referred to Saccard. Shaking her head she answered No, and No again. Then, with considerable embarrassment, in a very low voice, he said:

'After what he has been to you, you cannot refuse; go and see him!'

O God! he knew. An ardent flush suffused her countenance; she threw herself into his arms to hide her face, and she stammered, and asked who could have told him, how he could know that thing which she had thought known to none, especially himself.

'My poor Caroline,' he answered, 'I learnt it long ago by anonymous letters from wicked people who were jealous of us. I have never spoken to you about it; you are free, we no longer think alike. I know that you are the best woman on earth. Go and see him.'

And then gaily, his smile reappearing on his face, he took down the little bouquet of roses, which he had already slipped behind the crucifix, and placed it in her hand, adding, 'Take him this, and tell him that I am no longer angry with him.'

Upset by her brother's compassionate tenderness, experiencing at the same time frightful shame and delightful relief, Madame Caroline did not resist any further. Moreover, ever since morning, the necessity of seeing Saccard had been growing upon her. Could she abstain from warning him of Victor's flight, of that atrocious affair which still made her tremble? At the outset of his imprisonment he had set down her name among those of the persons whom he desired to see; and she had only to say who she was and a warder at once led her to the prisoner's cell.

When she entered, Saccard, with his back to the door, was sitting at a little table, covering a sheet of paper with figures. He rose quickly, with a shout of joy. 'You! Oh, how kind you are, and how happy I am!'

He had taken one of her hands in both his own. She was smiling with an embarrassed air, deeply moved, unable to find the right word to say. Then, with her free hand, she laid her little bouquet among the sheets of paper, covered with figures, that littered the table.

'You are an angel!' he murmured, delighted, and kissing her fingers.

At last she spoke. 'It is true, it was all over, I had condemned you in my heart. But my brother wished me to come.'

'No, no, do not say that! Say that you are too intelligent, that you are too good, and that you have understood, and forgive me.'

With a gesture she interrupted him. 'Do not ask so much, I implore you. I do not know myself. Is it not enough that I have come? And, besides, I have something very sad to tell you.'

Then, in an undertone, she swiftly told him of the awakening of Victor's savage instincts, his attack upon Mademoiselle de Beauvilliers, his extraordinary, inexplicable flight, the fruitlessness thus far of all search, the little hope there was of ever finding him. He listened to her, astonished, without asking a question or making a gesture; and, when she had finished, two big tears dilated his eyes and rolled down his cheeks, while he stammered: 'The wretched fellow! the wretched fellow!'

She had never seen him weep before. She was deeply agitated and astonished, so singular did these tears of Saccard seem to her, gray and heavy, coming from afar, from a heart hardened and debased by years of brigandage. Immediately afterwards, moreover, he burst into noisy despair. 'But it is frightful; I have never embraced this boy. For you know that I had not seen him. *Mon Dieu*! yes, I had sworn to go and see him, and I did not have the time, not a free hour, with all those cursed business matters which were devouring me. Ah! that is always the way; when you don't do a thing immediately, you are certain never to do it at all. And so now you are sure that I cannot see him? They might bring him to me here.'

She shook her head. 'Who knows,' she answered, 'in what unknown depths of this terrible Paris he may now be?'

For another moment he continued striding up and down, dropping scraps of phrases as he walked. 'The child is found for me, and here I lose him. I shall never see him now. The fact is, I have no luck; no! no luck at all. Oh! *mon Dieu*! it is just the same as in the matter of the Universal.'

He had just sat down again at the table, and Madame Caroline took a chair opposite him. With his hands wandering among his papers, the whole voluminous brief which he had been preparing for months past, he at once went into the history of his case and explained his methods of defence, as if he felt the need of showing her that he was innocent. The prosecution relied, first, on the repeated increases of capital devised both to bring about a feverish rise in the quotations, and to make people believe that all the shares of the Bank had been taken up; secondly, on the simulation of subscriptions and payments, by means of the accounts opened with Sabatani and other men of straw; thirdly, on the distribution of fictitious dividends under the form of a release of the old shares; and, finally, on the purchase by the Bank of its own stock, all that wild speculation which had brought about the extraordinary, fictitious rise, by which the Bank's coffers had been drained, and the Bank itself killed. These charges he answered with copious and passionate explanations: he had done what every bank manager does, only he had done it on a large scale, with the vigour of a strong man. There was not one of the heads of the firmest houses in Paris but ought to share his cell, if logic were to count for anything. They made him the scapegoat, however, answerable for the illegalities of all. What a strange way of apportioning the responsibilities! Why did they not prosecute the directors also—the Daigremonts, the Hurets, the Bohains—who, in addition to their fifty thousand francs of attendance fees, had received ten per cent. of the profits, and had dabbled in all the jobs? Why also was complete impunity granted to the auditors, Lavignière among others, who were allowed to plead their incapacity and their good faith? This trial was evidently going to be a monstrous piece of iniquity, for they had had to set aside Busch's charge of swindling, as alleging unsubstantiated facts; and the report made by the expert, after a first examination of the Bank's books, had just been found to be full of errors. Then, why the bankruptcy, officially declared on the strength of that report and Busch's charge, when not a sou of the deposits had been embezzled, and all the customers would re-enter into possession of their funds? Had they simply wished to ruin the shareholders? In that case they had succeeded; the disaster was becoming greater and greater, immeasurable. And he did not charge himself with this; he charged the magistracy, the government, all those who had conspired to suppress him and kill the Universal.

'Ah, the rascals! if they had left me free, you would have seen—you would have seen!'

Madame Caroline looked at him, impressed by his lack of conscience, which was becoming really grand. She remembered his theories of former days, the necessity of speculation in great enterprises, in which all just reward is impossible; gambling regarded as human excess, the necessary manure, the dung-heap from which progress grows. Was it not he who, with his unscrupulous hands, had madly heated the enormous machine, until it had burst to atoms and wounded all those whom it carried along with it? Was it not he who had desired that senseless, idiotic, exaggerated quotation of three thousand francs per share?

He had risen from his seat, however, and was walking up and down the little room with the spasmodic step of a caged conqueror.

'Ah! the rascals, they well knew what they were doing when they chained me up here,' he said. 'I was on the point of triumphing and crushing them all.'

She gave a start of surprise and protest. 'What! triumph? Why, you hadn't a sou left; you were conquered.'

'Evidently,' he rejoined, bitterly, 'I was conquered and so I am a blackguard. Honesty, glory, are simply other names for success. A man must not let himself be beaten, for otherwise he will find himself a fool and a fraud on the morrow. Oh, I can guess very well what they are saying; you need not repeat their words to me! They talk of me as a robber; they accuse me of having put all those millions in my pocket; they would strangle me, if they held me in their clutches; and, what is worse, they shrug their shoulders with pity, look upon me as a mere madman, a man of no intelligence. That is it, eh? But, if I had succeeded! Yes, if I had struck down Gundermann, conquered the market, if I were at this hour the undisputed king of gold, what a triumph would there then have been! I should now be a hero, I should have Paris at my feet.'

She openly opposed him, however. 'You had neither justice nor logic on your side,' said she; 'you could not succeed.'

He had stopped short in front of her, and became angry. 'Not succeed, nonsense! Money was lacking, that was all. If Napoleon, on the day of Waterloo, had had another hundred thousand men to send to the butchery, he would have triumphed, and the face of the world would have been changed. And if I had had the necessary few hundred millions to throw into the gulf, I should now be the master of the world.'

'But it is frightful!' she cried, revolting. 'What! Do you think there have not been ruins enough, not tears enough, not blood enough as it is? You would have more disasters still, more families stripped, more unfortunates reduced to begging in the streets!'

He began tramping to and fro again, and with a gesture of supreme indifference shouted: 'Does life concern itself about that? At every step we take we stamp out thousands of existences.'

Silence fell; she watched him with a freezing heart as he marched up and down. Was he a knave? Was he a hero? She trembled as she asked herself what thoughts he could have revolved, like a great captain, conquered and reduced to powerlessness, during the six months that he had been confined in that cell; and then only did she

238

glance about her and espy the four bare walls, the little iron bedstead, the deal table, and the two straw-bottomed chairs. To think of it! He who had lived amid lavish, dazzling luxury!

But suddenly he sat down again, as if his legs were weary; and then he began talking at length in an undertone, as though making a kind of involuntary confession.

'Gundermann was right,' he said; 'fever is worth nothing at the Bourse. Ah, the rascal, how happy he is in having no blood or nerves left him! I believe, however, that he has always been like that, his veins flowing with ice instead of blood. I am too passionate, that is evident. There is no other reason for my defeat; that is why my back has been so often broken. And it must be added that, if my passion kills me, it is also my passion that gives me life. Yes, it bears me on, it lifts me up on high, and then strikes me down and suddenly destroys all its work. Enjoyment is, after all, perhaps only the devouring of self.'

Then he was stirred by a fit of anger against his conqueror. 'Ah! that Gundermann, that dirty Jew, who triumphs because he has no desires! The whole race is summed up in him, frigid, stubborn conqueror that he is, on the march towards sovereign sway over the whole world, amid the nations whom he buys up one by one by means of his omnipotent gold. For centuries past his race has been invading us and triumphing over us, no matter how much it may have been cuffed and kicked. He already has one milliard: he will have two, he will have ten, he will eventually have a hundred, he will some day be the master of the earth. I have been shouting this from the housetops for years past, but no one seems to listen to me. Everybody thinks it the mere spite of a jealous speculator, when it is the very cry of my blood. Yes, hatred of the Jew, I have it in me—oh! very deep, in the very roots of my being!'

'What a singular thing!' quietly murmured Madame Caroline, who, with her vast knowledge, practised universal toleration. 'To me the Jews are men like any others. If they are apart, it is because they have been put apart.'

But Saccard, who had not even heard her, continued with increasing violence: 'And what exasperates me is that I see governments the accomplices of these rascals, governments at their very feet! Thus the Empire has sold itself to Gundermann! As if it were impossible to reign without Gundermann's money! Certainly, Rougon, that great man my brother, has behaved in a very disgusting manner towards me; for I have not told you of it before, but I was cowardly enough to seek a reconciliation before the catastrophe, and, if I am here, it is because it pleased him. But no matter; since I embarrass him, let him get rid of me; I shall feel no anger against him, except with regard to his alliance with those dirty Jews. Have you thought of that? the Universal strangled in order that Gundermann may continue his commerce; every Catholic bank that grows too powerful crushed, as a social danger, in order to ensure the definitive triumph of the children of Israel, who will devour us, and that soon. Ah, Rougon should be careful! He will be the first to be eaten, swept away from the post of power to which he clings, and for which he betrays everything. His game of see-saw is very cunning, with its guarantees given one day to the Liberals and the next day to the Reactionaries; but it is a game at which one always ends by breaking one's neck. And, since everything is cracking and falling, let Gundermann's desires be accomplished, he who predicted that France would be beaten, if we should ever have a war with Germany! We are ready; the Prussians have only to cross the frontier, and take our provinces!'

With a terrified, supplicating gesture, she begged him not to talk like that. It was as though he were calling down the thunder of heaven. 'No, no! do not say such things. You have no right to say them. Moreover, your brother had nothing to do with your arrest. I know from a certain source that it was Delcambre, the Keeper of the Seals, who did it all.'

On hearing this Saccard's wrath fell, and he smiled. 'Oh, the fellow is taking his revenge!' he said. She gave him a questioning look, and he added: 'Yes, an old affair between us—I know in advance that I shall be condemned.'

She doubtless suspected the truth, for she did not insist. A brief silence prevailed, during which he again took up the papers on the table, absorbed in his fixed idea.

'It is very kind of you to have come,' he said at last, 'and you must promise me you will come again, because you are a good counsellor, and I wish to submit my projects to you. Ah, if I only had some money!'

She quickly interrupted him, seizing this opportunity to enlighten herself upon a question which had haunted and tormented her for months. What had he done with the millions which he must possess for his own share? Had he sent them abroad, buried them under some tree known to himself alone? 'But you have plenty of money!' she exclaimed. I The two millions you made after Sadowa and the nine millions which your three thousand shares represented, if you sold them at the rate of three thousand francs apiece!'

'I, my dear,' he cried, 'I haven't a copper!'

And he spoke these words in so frank and despairing a voice, he looked at her with such an air of surprise, that she was convinced he said the truth. 'Never have I had a sou when my enterprises have turned out badly,' he continued. 'Don't you understand that I ruin myself with the rest? Certainly, yes, I sold my shares, but I bought others also; and where my nine millions, together with two other millions, have gone, I should be greatly embarrassed to explain to you. I really believe that my account with poor Mazaud left me thirty or forty thousand francs in his debt. No, I haven't a sou left; it has been the clean sweep, as usual.'

She was so relieved, so elated, by this answer that she began to jest about the ruin of herself and her brother. 'We too, shall have nothing left when all is over,' she said, 'I do not know even whether we shall have enough to feed us for a month. Ah, that money, those nine millions you promised us, you remember how they frightened me! Never had I lived in such a state of uneasiness, and what a relief it was on the evening of the day when I had surrendered everything in favour of the assets! Even the three hundred thousand francs which we had inherited from our aunt went with the rest. That is not very just. But, as I once told you, one sets little store by money found, money that one has not earned. And you can see for yourself that, despite everything, I am now gay and can laugh.'

He stopped her with a feverish gesture; he had taken the papers from the table, and was waving them in the air. 'Nonsense!' he said, 'we shall be very rich.'

'How?'

'What! do you suppose that I abandon my ideas? Why, for six months past I have been working here, sitting up at nights and reconstructing everything. The imbeciles look upon that advance balance-sheet as a crime, pretending that, of the three great enterprises, the United Steam Navigation Company, the Carmel mine, and the Turkish National Bank, only the first has yielded the expected profits! But if the two others are

240

in peril, it is because I have not been there to see to things. When they let me out, however—yes, when I have become the master again, you will see, you will see——'

With supplicating gestures she tried to keep him from continuing. But he had risen, and straightening himself up on his short legs, cried out in his shrill voice: 'The calculations are made; there are the figures, look! The Carmel mine and the Turkish National Bank are mere playthings! We must have the vast network of the Oriental railways; we must have all the rest, Jerusalem, Bagdad, the whole of Asia Minor conquered. What Napoleon was unable to do with his sword, we shall do with our pickaxes and our gold! How could you believe that I had thrown up the game? Napoleon came back from Elba, remember. I, also, shall only have to show myself, and all the money of Paris will rise to follow me: and this time there will be no Waterloo, I assure you, because my plan is a rigorously mathematical one, foreseen to the very last centime. So at last, then, we shall strike down that wretched Gundermann! I only ask four hundred millions, perhaps five hundred millions of francs, and the world will be mine!'

She had succeeded in taking his hands, and pressed herself against him. 'No, no!' she exclaimed. 'Be silent, you frighten me.'

And yet, in spite of herself and of her fright, a feeling of admiration rose within her. In this bare, wretched cell, bolted in, separated from the living, she had suddenly become conscious of an overflowing force, a resplendency of life: the eternal illusion of hope, the stubborn obstinacy of the man who does not wish to perish. She sought for her anger, her execration, and could no longer find them within her. Had she not condemned him, however, after the irreparable misfortunes which he had caused? Had she not called down chastisement upon him, solitary death amidst universal contempt? But of all that she now only retained her hatred of evil and her pity for sorrow. Again did she succumb to that conscienceless, active power, as to some violence of nature, necessary no doubt. And although this was but a woman's weakness, she yielded to it with delight, swayed by her maternal nature, that infinite need of affection which had made her love him even while not esteeming him.

'It is finished,' she repeated several times, without ceasing to press his hands in hers; 'can you not calm yourself and rest at last?'

Then, as he raised himself to press his lips on her white hair, the locks of which fell over her temples with the tenacious abundance of youth, she held him back, and added, with an air of absolute resolution and profound sadness, giving the words their full significance: 'No, no! it is finished—finished for ever. I am glad to have seen you a last time, that there may remain no anger between us. Farewell!'

As she started off, she saw him standing by the table, really moved by the separation, but already instinctively rearranging the papers which he had mingled in his fever; and the little bouquet of roses having shed its petals among the pages, he shook these one by one, and, with a touch of the fingers, swept the remnants of the flowers away.

Not until three months later, towards the middle of December, did the affair of the Universal Bank at last come into court. It occupied five sittings of the Tribunal of Correctional Police,[29] and excited lively curiosity. The Press had made an enormous sensation of the catastrophe, and most extraordinary stories had been circulated with regard to the delay in the trial. The indictment drawn up by the officials of the Public Prosecution Office was much remarked. It was a masterpiece of ferocious logic, the smallest details being grouped, utilised, and interpreted with pitiless clearness.

241

Moreover, it was said on all sides that condemnation had been predetermined on. And, in fact, the evident good faith of Hamelin, the heroic demeanour of Saccard, who fought his accusers step by step throughout the five days, the magnificent and sensational speeches for the defence, did not prevent the judges from sentencing both defendants to five years' imprisonment and three thousand francs fine. However, having been temporarily set at liberty on bail, a month before the trial, and having thus appeared before the court as defendants still at liberty, they were able to lodge an appeal and to leave France in twenty-four hours. It was Rougon who had insisted on this *dénouement*, not wishing to be burdened with a brother in prison. The police themselves watched over the departure of Saccard, who fled to Belgium by a night train. The same day Hamelin had started for Rome.

And then three more months rolled away, and in the early days of April Madame Caroline still found herself in Paris, where she had been detained by the settlement of their intricate affairs. She still occupied the little suite of rooms at the Orviedo mansion, which posters still advertised for sale. However, she had just overcome the last difficulties, and was in a position to depart, certainly without a sou in her pockets, but without leaving any debts behind her, and so she was to start the next day for Rome, in order to join her brother, who had been fortunate enough to secure an insignificant situation as an engineer there. He had written to her saying that pupils awaited her. It was a re-beginning of their lives.

On rising on the morning of this the last day which she would spend in Paris, she was seized with a desire not to quit the city without making some attempt to obtain news of Victor. So far all search had been vain. But, remembering the promises of La Méchain, she said to herself that perhaps this woman might now know something; and that it would be easy to question her by going to Busch's office at about four o'clock. At first she rejected the idea; for what was the use of taking this step? Was not all this the dead past? Then she really suffered, her heart overflowed with grief, as for a child whom she had lost and whose grave she had failed to strew with flowers on going away. So at four o'clock she made her appearance in the Rue Feydeau.

Both doors on the landing were open, some water was boiling violently in the dark kitchen, while, on the other side, in the little office, La Méchain, who occupied Busch's arm-chair, seemed submerged by a heap of papers, which she was taking in enormous packages from her old black leather bag.

'Ah, it is you, my good madame!' she said. 'You come at a very bad moment. Monsieur Sigismond is dying. And poor Monsieur Busch is positively losing his head over it, so much does he love his brother. He does nothing but run about like a crazy man; he has just gone out again to get a doctor. I am obliged to attend to his business, you see, for he has not bought a share or even looked into a claim for a week past. Fortunately, I made a good stroke just now—oh! a real stroke, which will console him a little for his sorrow, the dear man, when he recovers his senses.'

Such was Madame Caroline's astonishment that she forgot she had called about Victor. She had recognised the papers which La Méchain was taking by the handful from her bag. They were some of the shares of the Universal Bank. The old leather was fairly cracking, such a number of them had been packed into the bag; and the woman went on pulling out more and more, very talkative in her delight. 'I got all these for two hundred and fifty francs,' she said; 'there are certainly five thousand, which puts them at a sou apiece. A sou for shares that were quoted at three thousand francs! They have fallen almost to the price of waste-paper. But they are worth more than that; we shall sell them again for at least ten sous apiece, because they are wanted by bankrupts. You understand, they have had such a good reputation that they look very well in a list of assets. It is a great distinction to have been a victim of a catastrophe. In short, I had extraordinary luck; ever since the battle, I had scented the ditch where all this merchandise was sleeping, a whole lot of dead 'uns, which an imbecile who didn't know his business has let me have for nothing. And you can imagine whether I pounced upon them! Ah, it did not take long; I cleaned him out of them very speedily!'

Thus chattering, she displayed the glee of a bird of prey on some field of financial massacre. The unclean nutriment upon which she had fattened oozed forth in perspiration from her huge person; while, with her short, hooked hands, she stirred up the dead—those all but worthless shares, which were already yellow and emitted a rank smell.

But a low, ardent voice arose from the adjoining room, the door of which stood wide open, like the doors opening upon the landing. 'Ah!' she said, 'there is Monsieur Sigismond beginning to talk again. He has been doing nothing but that ever since this morning. *Mon Dieu*! and the boiling water! I was forgetting it. It is for some *tisane*. My good madame, since you are here, will you just see if he wants anything?'

La Méchain hurried into the kitchen, while Madame Caroline, whom suffering attracted, entered Sigismond's room. Its nudity was enlivened by a bright April sun, whose rays fell upon the little deal table, covered with memoranda, bulky portfolios, whence overflowed the labour of ten years; and there was nothing else except the two straw-bottomed chairs, the few volumes heaped upon the shelves, and the narrow bed in which Sigismond, propped up by three pillows, and clad to his waist in a short red flannel blouse, was talking, talking incessantly, under the influence of that singular cerebral excitement which sometimes precedes the death of consumptives. He was delirious, but had moments of extraordinary lucidity; and in his thin face, framed with long, curling hair, his dilated eyes seemed to be questioning the void.

When Madame Caroline appeared, he seemed to know her at once, although they had never met. 'Ah! it is you, madame,' he said; 'I had seen you, I was calling you with all my strength. Come, come nearer, that I may speak to you in a low voice.'

In spite of the little shudder of fear which had seized upon her, she approached, and sat down on a chair close to the bed.

'I did not know it, but I know it now,' continued Sigismond. 'My brother sells papers, and I have heard people weeping there, in his office. My brother, ah! it pierced my heart like a red-hot iron. Yes, it is that which has remained in my chest, it is always burning there because it is abominable, that money—the poor people who suffer. And by-and-by, when I am dead, my brother will sell my papers, and I do not wish it—no, I do not wish it!'

His voice gradually rose, assumed a tone of supplication. 'There, madame, there are my papers, on the table. Give them to me; we will make a parcel of them, and you shall carry them away, all of them. Oh, I was calling you, I was waiting for you! Think of it! My papers lost! all my life of study and effort annihilated!' And as she hesitated to give him what he asked, he clasped his hands: 'For pity's sake,' he said, 'give them to me, so that I may be sure that they are all there, before dying. My brother isn't here, so he won't say that I am killing myself. Come, I beg you.'

Upset by the ardour of his prayer, she yielded. 'But I do wrong,' said she, 'since your brother says that it does you harm.'

'Harm! Oh, no. And besides, what does it matter? Ah! I have at last succeeded in setting the society of the future on its feet, after so many nights of toil! Everything is foreseen, solved; there will be the utmost possible justice and happiness. How I regret not having had the time to write the work itself, with all the necessary developments! But here are my notes, complete and classified. And you will save them, won't you? so that another may some day give them the definitive form of a book, and launch it through the world.'

He had taken the papers in his long thin hands, and was turning them over amorously, while a flame once more kindled in his large, fading eyes. He spoke very rapidly, in a curt monotonous tone, with the tic-tac of a clock-chain which the weight unwinds; and 'twas indeed the sound of the cerebral mechanism working without a pause whilst the death agony progressed.

'Ah! how I see it, how clearly it rises before me, the city of justice and happiness! There one and all labour, with a personal labour, obligatory, yet free. The nation is simply an immense co-operative society, the appliances become the property of all, the products are centralised in vast general warehouses. You have performed so much useful work; you have a right to so much social consumption. The hour's work is the common measure; an article is worth what it has cost in hours; there is nothing but exchange between all producers, by the aid of labour notes, and that under the management of the community, without any other deduction than the one tax to support the children and the aged, to renew the appliances and to defray the cost of gratuitous public services. No more money, and therefore no more speculation, no more robbery, no more abominable trafficking, no more of those crimes which cupidity prompts, girls married for their dowry's sake, aged parents strangled for their property, passers-by assassinated for their purses! No more hostile classes, employers and wage-workers, proletarians and *bourgeois*, and therefore no more restrictive laws or courts, no armed force protecting the iniquitous monopolies of the few against the mad hunger of the many! No more idlers of any sort, and therefore no more landlords living on rents, no more bondholders kept in sloth—in short, no more luxury and no more poverty! Ah! is not that the ideal equity, the sovereign wisdom, none privileged, none wretched, each by his own effort securing happiness, the average human happiness!'

He was becoming excited, and his voice grew soft and distant, as if travelling far away, ascending to a great height, into the very future whose coming he announced.

'Ah! if I entered into details. You see this separate sheet, with all these marginal notes: this is the organisation of the family, free contract, the education and support of children provided by the community. Yet this is not anarchy. Look at this other note; I desire that there should be a managing committee for each branch of production, so that by ascertaining the real wants of the community the output may be proportionate to the consumption. And here is another detail of the organisation: in the cities and the fields industrial and agricultural armies will manœuvre under the leadership of chiefs whom they will have elected, and obey regulations which they will have voted. Stay! I have also indicated here, by approximate calculations, how far the day's labour may be reduced twenty years hence. Thanks to the great number of new hands, thanks especially to machinery, men will work only four hours a day, perhaps only three; so you see how much time they will have left them to enjoy life! For this will not be a barracks, but a city of liberty and gaiety, in which each will be free to take his own pleasure, with plenty of time to satisfy his legitimate appetites, to taste the delights of love, strength, beauty and intelligence, and to take his share of inexhaustible nature.'

By the gesture he made, a gesture which swept round the miserable room, it seemed as though he possessed the whole world. In this nudity in which he had lived, in this poverty exempt from want in which he was dying, he made a fraternal distribution of the earth's goods. It was universal happiness, all that is good and that he had not enjoyed, which he thus distributed, knowing that he would never enjoy it. He had hastened his death that he might make this supreme gift to suffering humanity. And indeed his hands wandered, groping among the scattered notes, while his eyes, which could no longer see earthly things, filled as they were by the dazzling of death, seemed to espy infinite perfection, beyond life, in an ecstatic rapture which illumined his entire face.

'Ah! how much more activity there will be, entire humanity at work, the hands of all the living improving the world! No more moors, no more marshes, no more waste lands of any kind! Arms of the sea are filled up, obstructive mountains disappear, deserts change into fertile valleys, with waters flowing from every direction. No prodigy is unrealisable; the great works of the ancients cause a smile, so timid and childish do they seem. The earth is at last inhabitable. And man is completely developed, full-grown, in the enjoyment of his true appetites, the real master at last. Schools and workshops are open; the child freely chooses his trade, which his aptitude determines. Years go by, and the selection is made after severe examinations. It no longer suffices that one should be able to pay for education, it is necessary to profit by it. Each one thus finds himself classed, utilised according to his degree of intelligence, by which means public functions are equitably distributed, in accordance with the indications of Nature herself. Each for all, according to his powers! Ah! active and joyous city, ideal city of healthy human work, in which the old prejudice against manual labour no longer exists, in which one sees great poets who are carpenters, locksmiths who are great *savants*! Ah! city of the blest, triumphal city towards which mankind has been marching for so many centuries, city whose white walls I see shining yonder—yonder, in the realm of happiness, in the blinding sunlight.'

His eyes paled: his last words came indistinctly, in a faint breath; and his head fell back, an ecstatic smile still playing about his lips. He was dead.

Overcome with pity and emotion, Madame Caroline was looking at him, when a whirlwind, as it were, suddenly swept into the room. It was Busch, coming back without a doctor, panting and worn out with anguish; while La Méchain, at his heels, explained that she had not yet been able to prepare the *tisane*, as the water had boiled over. But he had perceived his brother—his little child, as he called him—lying on his back, motionless, with his mouth open and his eyes fixed; and he understood, and gave vent to a shriek like that of a slaughtered animal. With a bound he threw himself upon the body and raised it in his two big arms, as if to infuse life into it again. That terrible devourer of gold, who would have killed a man for ten sous, who had so long preyed upon the filth of Paris, now shrieked aloud with abominable suffering. His little child, O God! he whom he put to bed, whom he fondled like a mother! He would never have his little child with him any more! And, in a fit of mad despair, he seized upon the papers scattered over the bed, tore them up and crushed them, as if wishing to annihilate all that imbecile labour which he had ever been jealous of, and which had killed his brother.

Then Madame Caroline felt her heart melt. The poor man! he now filled her with divine pity. But where, then, had she heard that shriek before? Once only had the cry of human grief brought her such a shudder. And she suddenly remembered, it was at Mazaud's—the shriek of the mother and her little ones at sight of the father's corpse. As if incapable of withdrawing from this scene of suffering, she remained a few minutes longer, and rendered some services. Then, at the moment of starting off, finding herself alone again with La Méchain in the little office, she remembered that she had come to inquire about Victor. And so she questioned her. Oh, Victor—well, he was far away by this time, if he were still running! She, La Méchain, had scoured Paris for three months, without discovering the slightest trace of him. So she had given it up; the bandit would be found, sure enough, some day, on the scaffold. Madame Caroline listened, frozen and dumb. Yes, it was finished; the monster had been let loose upon the world, had gone forth to the future, to the unknown, like a beast frothing with hereditary virus, and fated to spread the evil with every bite.

Outside, on the footway of the Rue Vivienne, Madame Caroline was surprised by the mildness of the air. It was five o'clock; the sun, setting in a soft, clear sky, was gilding the signboards of the distant boulevard houses. This springtide, so charming with its renewal of youth, seemed like a caress to her whole physical being—a caress which penetrated even to her heart. She took a deep breath and felt relieved, happier already, with a sensation of invincible hope returning and growing within her. It was doubtless the beautiful death of that dreamer, giving his last breath to his chimera of justice and love, which thus moved her, for she herself had dreamt of a humanity purged of the execrable evil of money; and it was also the shriek of that other one, the exasperated bleeding tenderness of that terrible lynx, whom she had supposed to be heartless, incapable of tears. Yet no, she had not gone away under the consoling impression of so much human kindness and so much sorrow; on the contrary, she had carried despair away with her—despair at the escape of that little monster, who was galloping along the roads and sowing the ferment of rottenness from which the earth could never be freed. Why, then, should she now feel renascent gaiety filling her whole being?

On reaching the boulevard she turned to the left and slackened her pace, amid the animation of the crowd. For a moment she stopped before a little hand-cart, full of bunches of lilac and gilliflowers, whose strong perfume enveloped her with a whiff of springtide. And within her, as she resumed her walk, she felt a flood of joy arising, as from a bubbling source, which she was fain to restrain, to press back with her hands. For she had understood, and did not wish it. No, no, the frightful catastrophes were too recent; she could not be gay, she could not surrender to that flow of eternal life which uplifted her. And she tried to continue mourning; she recalled herself to despair by recapitulating all the cruel memories. What! she would laugh again, after the downfall of everything, after such a frightful mass of miseries! Did she forget that she was an accomplice? And she recalled the facts, this one, that one, that other one, in weeping over which she ought to spend all her remaining days. But between her fingers pressed upon her heart the bubbling sap was growing more impetuous, the source of life was overflowing, thrusting obstacles aside in order to course more freely, throwing the flotsam against either bank, so that it might flow along clear and triumphant in the sunlight.

From that moment Madame Caroline was conquered, and had to surrender to the irresistible force of Nature's rejuvenescence. As she sometimes said with a laugh, she could not remain sad. The trial was over; she had just touched the very depths of despair, and here was hope reviving again—broken, bleeding, but as tenacious as ever, growing and spreading from minute to minute. Certainly she retained no illusions; life, like Nature, was undoubtedly unjust and ignoble. Why, then, should one be so irrational as to love it, desire it, relying—like a child to whom is promised a pleasure ever deferred—on the far-off unknown goal towards which it is ever leading us? However, when she turned into the Rue de la Chaussée-d'Antin, she no longer even reasoned; the philosopher, the *savante*, the woman of letters that she was, had abdicated, weary of the vain inquiry into causes; and she remained a mere human creature, whom the beautiful sky and balmy atmosphere filled with happiness, who savoured the simple enjoyment of health, of listening to the firm tread of her little feet upon the pavement. Ah! the joy of being, is there really any other? Life! Give us life—life such as it is, however abominable it may be—life with its strength and its eternal hope!

On returning to her apartments in the Rue Saint-Lazare, which she was to leave the next day, Madame Caroline finished packing her trunks; and, on making the circuit of the workroom, which was already empty, she saw upon the walls the plans and water-colours, which she had resolved to tie up in a single roll, at the last moment. But as she stopped in turn before each sheet to remove the tacks at the corners, a dreamy mood came over her. She was once more living those far-off days which she had spent in the East, in that country which she had so dearly loved, and whose dazzling light she seemed to have retained within her; she was again living, too, those five years which she had just spent in Paris, those five years of daily crisis and mad activity, full of the monstrous hurricane of millions which had traversed and ravaged her existence; and from all the ruins, still warm, she already felt a complete florescence germinating, budding in the sunlight. Although the Turkish National Bank had fallen after the collapse of the Universal, the Steam Navigation Company remained erect and prosperous. Again she beheld the enchanted coast of Beyrout, where, in the midst of huge warehouses, stood the managerial buildings, the plan of which she was just dusting. Marseilles had been brought close to Asia Minor, the Mediterranean was being conquered, nations were being drawn together, and possibly pacified. And in the Carmel gorge, that water-colour which she was taking down from the wall, did she not know, from a recent letter, that a whole people had grown up there? The village of five hundred inhabitants, at first nestling round the mine, had now become a city of several thousand souls, with roads, factories, schools, a complete civilisation, fertilising the wild, dead nook. Then there were the sketches and plans for the railway from Broussa to Beyrout, by way of Angora and Aleppo, a series of large sheets, which she rolled up one by one. Years would go by no doubt before the Taurus passes would be traversed by the iron horse; but life was already flowing in from every direction, the soil of the ancient cradle of humanity had just been sown with a new crop of men, the progress of to-morrow would sprout up there, with an extraordinary vigour of vegetation, in that marvellous climate, under the dazzling sun. And was not this the reawakening of a world, humanity enlarged and happier?

Madame Caroline tied up the bundle of plans with some strong twine. Her brother, who was waiting for her at Rome, where both were going to begin their lives anew, had earnestly urged her to pack them carefully; and, as she tied the knots, she thought of Saccard, whom she knew to be now in Holland, again busy with a colossal enterprise—the draining of some immense marshes, the conquest of a little kingdom from the sea, by means of a complicated system of canals. He was right: money has hitherto been the dung-heap in which the humanity of the morrow has grown; money, albeit the poisoner and destroyer, becomes the ferment of all social vegetation, the compost necessary for the great works which make life easier. Did she at last see clearly? Did her invincible hope come from her belief in the usefulness of effort? Above all the mud stirred up, above all the victims crushed to death, above all the abominable suffering which each forward step costs humanity, is there not an obscure, far-off goal, something superior, good, just, and final, whither we are going without knowing it, and which ever inflates our hearts with a stubborn need of life and hope?

And Madame Caroline, with her face still and ever young under its crown of snowy hair, remained gay in spite of everything, gay as though rejuvenescence came to her with each returning April of the world's old age. And at the shame-fraught recollection of her *liaison* with Saccard she began to think of the frightful filth with which love also has been soiled. Why then should money be blamed for all the dirt and crimes it causes? For is love less filthy—love which creates life?

NOTES

[1]The authorised stockbrokers, who stand in a railed-off space in the centre of the Bourse. This space is called the *Corbeille*, or basket.—*Trans.*

[2]The outside brokers, jobbers, keepers of bucket-shops, &c.—*Trans.*

[3]An individual who brings business to a broker, and receives a *remise* or commission on the transaction.—*Trans.*

[4]1864.

[5]The father of the present President.—*Trans.*

[6]Schleswig-Holstein.

[7]Little cards upon which stockbrokers note the orders of their customers.—*Trans.*

[8]The late Baron James de R.—*Trans.*

[9]'The living wage.'—*Trans.*

[10]Twelve millions sterling.

[11]'L'Œuvre du Travail.'

[12]Paris stockbrokers usually have separate staffs for their 'cash' and their 'account' transactions.—*Trans.*

[13]Forty millions sterling.

[14]Saccard should have visited Whitechapel. It should be remembered that M. Zola is not himself attacking the Jews. He is merely sketching, the portrait of a Jew-hater. As a matter of fact, M. Zola has many personal friends among members of the Hebrew race.—*Trans.*

[15]The French Jack Sheppard,—*Trans.*

[16]The great Paris auction-mart.—*Trans.*

[17]The large vestibule gallery of the Palais Bourbon.—*Trans.*

[18]This picture of the Cité de Naples is by no means overdrawn. Some years ago (1880-85) I well remember visiting the Cités tenanted by rag-pickers and street hawkers round about the Rue Marcadet and the Route de la Révolte, and their condition fully corresponded with the description given by M. Zola above. When M. Zola visited England last autumn, and I accompanied him round the East-end of London, he remarked to me that even the worst dens shown to him contrasted favourably with the abodes of many of the Parisian poor. And such undoubtedly is the case. But, on the other hand, there is quite as much depravity among the poor of London as among the poor of Paris.—*Trans.*

[19]The date of Louis Napoleon's *coup d'état.*—*Trans.*

[20]As witness Mirès and the Caisse des Chemins de Fer, Pereire and the Crédit Mobilier, Bontoux and the Union Générale, Lesseps and Panama, &c., &c.—*Trans.*

[21]This reminds one of a reverend gentleman who in a similar way extolled the blessings and benefits of the Liberator Society.—*Trans.*

[22]Five o'clock tea was not then, as now, an institution in Parisian society. Tea, when drunk at all, made its appearance in the drawing-room some hours after dinner.—*Trans.*

[23]One can imagine these words in the mouth of a certain eminent financier whose victims are at the present time (January 1894) supplicating their countrymen for a trust to relieve their need.—*Trans.*

[24]Pius IX.

[25]'It is the will of God.' The cry of the old Crusaders.—*Trans.*

[26]Between France and the new kingdom of Italy with regard to the independence of the Papal States.—*Trans.*

[27]See *ante*, p. 241.

[28]The battle in which the Garibaldians were defeated by the French and Papal forces commanded by the notorious General de Failly. This was the first engagement in which the Chassepôt rifle was ever used, and De Failly telegraphed to the Emperor Napoleon III. that the new arm 'had done wonders.'—*Trans.*

[29]Prisoners brought before the tribunals of Correctional Police are not tried by jury, but by three judges. The Ministers of Napoleon III. were very fond of bringing political offenders before these courts in order to ensure condemnation, which would have been uncertain at the Assizes.—*Trans.*

Made in the USA
Monee, IL
22 August 2022

12162476R00138